THE CHILDREN'S HOUR

Stories of Long Ago

A BOOK TO GROW ON

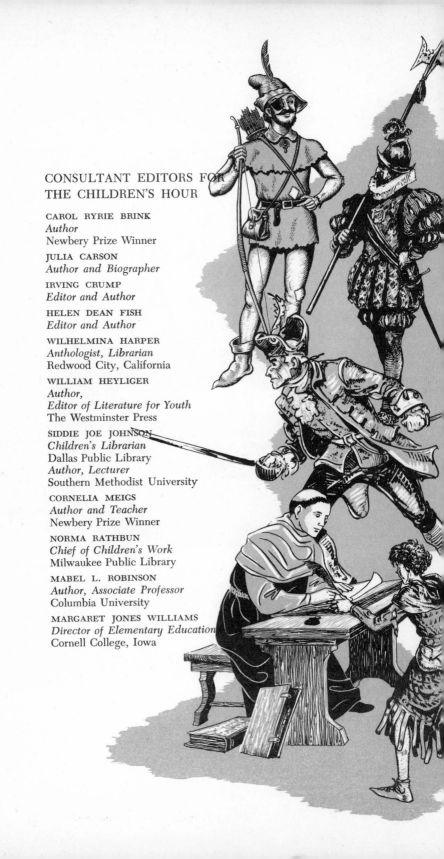

CONSULTANT EDITORS FOR
THE CHILDREN'S HOUR

CAROL RYRIE BRINK
Author
Newbery Prize Winner

JULIA CARSON
Author and Biographer

IRVING CRUMP
Editor and Author

HELEN DEAN FISH
Editor and Author

WILHELMINA HARPER
Anthologist, Librarian
Redwood City, California

WILLIAM HEYLIGER
Author,
Editor of Literature for Youth
The Westminster Press

SIDDIE JOE JOHNSON
Children's Librarian
Dallas Public Library
Author, Lecturer
Southern Methodist University

CORNELIA MEIGS
Author and Teacher
Newbery Prize Winner

NORMA RATHBUN
Chief of Children's Work
Milwaukee Public Library

MABEL L. ROBINSON
Author, Associate Professor
Columbia University

MARGARET JONES WILLIAMS
Director of Elementary Education
Cornell College, Iowa

THE CHILDREN'S HOUR

MARJORIE BARROWS, *Editor*

Stories
of Long Ago

MATHILDA SCHIRMER
Associate Editor

DOROTHY SHORT
Art Editor

THE SPENCER PRESS, INC. • *Chicago*

Acknowledgments

The editor and publishers wish to thank the following publishers, authors, and artists for permission to reprint the following stories and illustrations included in this book:

APPLETON-CENTURY-CROFTS, INC., for "The Golden Cup of Kasimir" by Eric Kelly from *St. Nicholas Magazine*, copyright, 1923, The Century Company.

THE BOBBS-MERRILL COMPANY, INC., for "Dungeon Deep" from *The Book of Ralf* by Phillis Garrard, copyright, 1952, by The Bobbs-Merrill Company, Inc.

COLLINS YOUNG ELIZABETHAN for "The Cuckoo in the Nest" by Patricia Brougham.

DOUBLEDAY AND COMPANY, INC., for story and illustrations for "Robin Finds a Way" from *The Door in the Wall* by Marguerite de Angeli, copyright, 1949, by Marguerite de Angeli.

HOUGHTON MIFFLIN COMPANY for "On Kublai Khan's Service" from *He Went with Marco Polo* by Louise Andrews Kent, copyright, 1935, by Louise Andrews Kent.

LONGMANS, GREEN AND COMPANY, INC., for "Adventure in Candle Street" from *Moonshine in Candle Street* by Constance Savery.

THE MACMILLAN COMPANY for "Hitty's Shipwreck" from *Hitty: Her First Hundred Years* by Rachel Field; and "At the Fall of Pompeii" from *Buried Cities* by Jennie Hall.

SCOTT, FORESMAN AND COMPANY, *Boys' Life*, and the estate of Constance Lindsay Skinner for condensed version of "Out of Defeat" by Constance Lindsay Skinner from *Paths and Pathfinders* by William S. Gray, Robert C. Pooley, and Fred G. Walcott. Copyright, 1946, by Scott, Foresman and Company.

CHARLES SCRIBNER'S SONS for full color illustration by N. C. Wyeth for "Robin Hood and the Shooting Match" from *The Merry Adventures of Robin Hood* by Howard Pyle, copyright, 1933, by Charles Scribner's Sons.

THE VIKING PRESS, INC., for "Adam to the Rescue" from *Adam of the Road* by Elizabeth Janet Gray, copyright, 1942, by Elizabeth Janet Gray and Robert Lawson, and pictures by Robert Lawson from the book.

EDNA BECKER for "At the Boar Hunt."

LAURA BENÉT for "The Box a Bee Crept In."

IVY BOLTON for "The King's Cygnet."

FLORENCE CHOATE for story and pictures for "Adventure in a Chimney."

KARL KNIPE for "Six Bells" from *Lucky Sixpence* by Emilie Benson Knipe and Alden Arthur Knipe, first published by The Century Company.

MARGARET LEIGHTON for "Fisherman's Luck," first published by *The Portal;* and "The Parchment Door," first published in *Child Life Magazine*.

ELOISE LOWNSBERY for "The Might of a Song."

MARGERY BLAIR PERKINS for "The Stranger in the Wood," first published in *Child Life Magazine*.

DOROTHY LATHROP for illustrations for Ivy Bolton's "The King's Cygnet."

MARIE LAWSON for illustrations for Laura Benet's "The Box A Bee Crept In."

KEITH WARD for illustrations for Edna Becker's "At the Boar Hunt."

Great pains have been taken to obtain permission from the owners of copyright material. Any errors that may possibly have been made are unintentional and will gladly be corrected in future printings if notice is sent to the Spencer Press, Inc.

Contents

Part I: FOR YOUNGER READERS

Patricia Brougham

THE CUCKOO IN THE NEST

ILLUSTRATED BY *Clarence Biers*

NATHANIEL CLARKE lifted up his long and heavy skirts and clambered clumsily over the piles of stage furniture and clothesbaskets that barred his way to the back of the stage.

"Graceful," said a mocking voice, "mighty graceful for a young Queen, if a gentleman may say so."

"Good evening, James." Nat sat down on an upturned box and grinned at his cousin. "Were you in the theater tonight?"

"I was. And now I've come to wait for you. Will you be long?"

"No." Nat pulled off his wig of curls with a sigh of relief and standing up, began to wriggle out of his dress. "Oh, but these things are hot! I'm glad I'm a girl only some of the time."

"And you won't be able to be that for very long," said James, looking at his cousin consideringly, "for you're growing over-tall."

"You say that just to frighten me." Nat took off a satin slipper and threw it at James. "I'll be a boy player for a long time yet."

James pressed the slipper against his heart. "Oh, that I might keep this little shoe to remind me of you!"

Nat threw the other one. James, grinning wickedly, waited till his cousin was struggling helplessly with a petticoat tape and then rammed both slippers down Nat's neck. Nat ducked and butted James into an empty clothesbasket, lost his own footing and fell in on top of him. Helpless with laughter they

1

struggled with each other, jammed into the basket together.

"Enough!" said a deep voice above them, and a massive arm hoisted Nat from his undignified position. "Master Clarke, this is not a nursery."

"No, Master Burbage." Nat shook himself and looked up apologetically. "You see, sir, this is my cousin and . . ."

". . . And he mocked you," said Richard Burbage, regarding James, who was still sitting in the basket. "A likely looking young man. Can *you* act, sirrah?"

"No, *sir!*" James struggled hastily to his feet, looking quite alarmed. "I'm to be a goldsmith, sir."

"A very dignified trade," said Burbage gravely. "Remember, sirrah, dignified."

He strode away, leaving the two boys looking after him; Nat with admiration, James with astonishment.

"Are all players touched in the head? Your man Will Kempe, that half-awake Shakespeare, and now this! I fear for your safety, cousin!"

"Sirrah, you insult my friends."

"Friends! So now, Master High and Mighty Actor, these great ones are your friends? Your masters rather, I think. And *one* you have displeased."

Nat shook his head. "I don't think Master Burbage is really displeased. He pretends to be a great bear, but he rarely bites. Come, James, I'm ready now."

James was an incurable tease, and it was not often that Nat had a chance to get his own back. Tonight it was different. As he sat with his cousins and his aunt round the supper table he told them gravely what the great Richard Burbage had said.

"A dignified trade—*very* dignified. He could see, of course, that although James's feet were sticking far above his head he was, nevertheless, a *very* dignified gentleman. Anyone who looks at James, especially when his feet are above his head and his hair is in his eyes, can *see* he is dignified."

To the younger members of the family this was delightful, and they crowed with mocking laughter.

"He also said," went on Nat, enjoying his appreciative au-

2

dience, "that he should be an actor. He thought him the right type of young man to be an actor."

"What?" Dorothy's blue eyes opened wide. "*James* a boy player! With his satanic looks?"

"Oh, no, cousin." Nat was very serious. "Not a *boy* player but a real actor. At least"—he looked at James speculatively— "I think he meant that. But perhaps I am wrong, and he was thinking of James for the young girl's part in our next play."

James spluttered into his soup. "Strutting play actors," he said. "I would not be an actor for all the world."

"No," agreed Nat gravely, "you would never be an actor, James. It takes brains you see. But Master Burbage, seeing you only in the half-light and with your heels higher than your head, might have thought you had brains."

A wooden spoon came down hard on Nat's head, and it was only by Aunt Sarah's intervention that peace was restored.

"All the same," said Dorothy, "I do not really see that James is so much more unsuitable for a boy player than you are, Nat. I cannot see why they use boys for the women's parts. Why don't they have girl players?"

"Girls!"

"On the stage!"

"Women in the theater!"

Aunt Sarah, Nat, and James stared at Dorothy in horror. She calmly went on with her supper.

"Why not? Are they not just"—she looked at Nat boldly— "just as *pretty* as boys? And would they not look better in women's clothes than boys? And have they not *just* as many brains?"

"No," said James with decision.

"They would be a great nuisance," said Nat.

" 'Twould not be respectable," said Aunt Sarah.

"I do not agree with any of you," said Dorothy calmly.

"But ——"

"Enough," said Aunt Sarah, firmly. "We'll talk of it another time. Tonight I want to tell you all how you are to manage while I am away these next few days. Elizabeth, you are to

3

stay with our neighbor, Mistress Cook. Johnny and Mary will come with me. Lucy is to go to her godmother, and you, James, and you, Nat, are to stay here and take care of Charles and Dorothy."

Charles looked up. "I need no care taken of me."

"You will have it nevertheless," said his mother.

"Such care," said Nat, loftily, "as I am able to spare from my profession as a rogue and a vagabond and as James is able to spare from his *very* dignified trade."

The next morning Nat and James got up early to carry Aunt Sarah's bundle down to the ferryboats. She and the two youngest children were going to visit relations on the Surrey side, and they had arranged with a carter to take them from Southwark. All the way to the river she kept up a stream of admonitions, advice, and instructions, until at length James thrust the bundle into her hand, kissed her cheek and said firmly: "Now, Mam, you must be off. We shall all live without you, I promise you." He lifted Johnny into the boat, and Nat stowed Mary in beside him, and as the ferryman rowed off they stood on the river's edge and waved.

"Well, I must to work." James turned to his cousin. "And you, my vagabond?"

"To the theater. There's a rehearsal this morning, and I've much to do before it can start."

James crowed with laughter as he went on his way. "Assuredly! For you must, of course, first write the play and then cast the parts and then paint the furniture . . ." his voice died away as he disappeared.

When Nat got to the theater it was still almost empty. He loved this first hour or so in the morning when he had the theater almost to himself and could pretend that he was already a great actor. He began his work—dusting the stage furniture, brushing and attending to the stage clothes which his master, the great comedian Will Kempe, would need that day, helping to collect the necessary stage properties.

He staggered on to the stage with a heavy throne and set it down.

"Dickon," he called to another boy. "From where you stand does that throne seem to be positioned aright?"

Dickon looked critically at the stage. "Yes, it looks right. And you look as if you are playing the King."

"Oh, but I am!" Nat grinned, and striking an attitude he began to recite one of Richard Burbage's most famous parts.

Unfortunately for Nat, he was, almost without knowing it, a fine mimic. He did not *mean* to imitate the great Burbage, but the moment he started on the familiar speech he fell automatically into an imitation of Burbage's voice, delivery, and gestures, and Dickon, seating himself, was a fascinated audience.

Nat came to the end of his speech, and Dickon began to

clap when a voice, too familiar, rang out alarmingly. "A fine performance, Master Clarke, but I am looking for a scullion, not a king."

Nat turned, horror-stricken, as Burbage strode on to the stage and grasped him firmly by the shoulder.

"My wife's maidservant is sick abed, and there are dishes to wash. Go to my house and stay there till I give you leave to come away."

"But sir . . ."

"Well, sir?" The actor's voice was full of hostility, and Nat cringed despite himself.

"I am not—" he began, and stopped, abashed. He had been going to say he was not Burbage's boy but Will Kempe's, but he decided it would be wiser to hold his tongue.

"You are not an *actor*, sirrah. Go!"

Nat crept off the stage, too ashamed and unhappy even to speak to Will Kempe, who passed him as he slunk away.

Kempe watched Nat go and turned to Burbage with raised eyebrows. "That's my boy, Dick."

"I know it. But he deserves punishment!"

"He is a good boy. What has he done?"

"He—" said Burbage, and stopped. "It is between him and me," he said loftily.

Kempe was silent. He knew his friend and employer to be a man of quick, short-lived temper, and he thought it might be kinder to Nat not to take the matter further until Burbage had calmed down. Later he buttonholed Dickon, who had escaped as quickly as possible from the scene.

"Dickon, you were in the theater early this morning with Nat?"

"Yes, sir."

"Do you know what's amiss between him and Master Burbage?"

Dickon looked at him with dancing eyes. "I do, sir, but if I were to tell—"

"Come now!" Will, too, could be firm when it was necessary. "Is Nat not my boy?"

6

It was too good a joke to keep to oneself anyway, and Dickon told the story with a wealth of actorish detail. Kempe listened gravely. " 'Twas rude of him."

" 'Twas indeed, sir," said Dickon, solemnly.

"And fiendish funny," said Kempe with a sudden howl of laughter, and went off to tell the other comedians, swearing them to secrecy beforehand.

So while Nat washed dishes for Mistress Burbage, a kindly soul, who couldn't understand why Dick had sent her a boy player instead of a maidservant, the story of his misdemeanor was passed from actor to actor and laugh after laugh echoed round the theater whenever Burbage was out of earshot. But not even Kempe, or the playwright, Shakespeare, dared to mention the subject to the great man himself.

After two days of punishment, Nat, released early by the sympathetic Mistress Burbage, ran down to the theater, and waited outside the entrance until Kempe came out.

Seeing him, the comedian stopped and looked down at him in silence. "Well, sirrah?" he said at length.

"Sir, when may I come back to you?"

"Are you to be allowed back at all?"

"Oh, sir!"

"You were mighty rude, Nat."

"Oh—you know?"

"Oh, Nat, Nat, why was it not me that you imitated? Or Barnes or any of the others, but why Master Burbage?"

"Sir," said Nat, his face scarlet with sincerity. "I did not *mean* to do it, I really did not. I started to speak the speech, and in a trice there I was—Burbage! Can you not understand?"

Could he not? Kempe knew only too well how easy it was to fall into another man's mannerisms. He smiled. "You're a true actor, Nat. Or you *were*!"

"And I must be again. Master Kempe, it is about the new play that I am worried, for you told me Master Burbage was considering me for the young girl—the best part I have ever had."

"The best part you *would* ever have had. Master Burbage

7

is hearing some new boys read the part tomorrow. He does not want to hear you."

"Oh!" Nat clutched at his master's cloak. "Oh, sir, can you not help me please!"

"I've tried, Nat, but he's in a rare temper with you. This time, boy, you must be patient and let the part go. In a week he will have calmed down, and next time you may stand a chance. I'm sorry, boy, but you have courted trouble and got it. Next time you're moving furniture, Nat, move it, and do not waste the company's time. When Master Burbage's temper seems more even, I will ask him to let you return."

The next day Nat was more unhappy than ever. He went about his task without so much as a smile, and resented even Mistress Burbage's kindly efforts to cheer him.

Late in the afternoon she came into the kitchen where he was cleaning boots and asked him to bear a message to her husband.

"But he has forbidden me the theater."

8

"Not if you come from me. He is not so unreasonable."

Nat was doubtful. Knowing how quick Burbage always was to jump on any defaulter, he wondered if he would be able to explain his mission before he was turned out again. However, he took the message Mistress Burbage gave him and made his way reluctantly to the theater.

Master Burbage was on stage with the rest of the company, and Nat was able to creep up to the wings unobserved. What he saw on the stage made his blood boil. His temples throbbed and he felt himself go scarlet with rage and disappointment. For there, in front of him, was a line of small boys, and it was obvious that Burbage was hearing them read the part that was to have been Nat's.

His depression vanished in anger. He would *not* deliver his message and go back to the kitchen. *This* was his place, the theater, and he would stay here and watch the black-hearted villain who had robbed him of his great chance, while he selected some niminy piminy boy to play *his* part. He slid behind a pile of heavy curtains and watched.

The boy who was reading was not good, but Nat, running his eye along the line of children waiting to be heard, felt his heart sink. There was one there whom any actor-manager would take almost on sight. He had a heart-shaped, oddly familiar face, surmounted by short auburn curls. His eyes were wide, and he was slim and graceful. All Nat could hope for now was that the boy read badly.

He was doomed not only to disappointment but to one of the biggest surprises of his life. The auburn-haired boy stepped forward at a word from Burbage and began to read the part in a voice that Nat recognized only too clearly. No wonder the heart-shaped face was familiar. It belonged, without a doubt, to his cousin Dorothy.

Nat forgot everything else in his horror at the discovery. If Aunt Sarah should come home from Surrey and find her daughter turned boy player she would never get over it. He leapt up from his hiding place and sprang on to the stage, shouting: "No! You can't do this!"

Burbage swung round, and his handsome face whitened with temper. "Sirrah, I told you not to come here."

"But sir—I—"

Burbage did not move. "Will," he said, in the suddenly quiet voice that always silenced the most unruly audience, "remove this boy and tell him I will brook neither disobedience nor interference in my company."

"But Master Burbage—"

"Come, Nat." Kempe took Nat's arm, but the boy shook him off and darted towards Dorothy. He had forgotten his own private troubles, he was careless of Burbage's anger; he only thought now that Dorothy was in his and James's charge and that he must save her from disgrace and ridicule. He gripped her by the shoulders and shook her gently.

"Go home! Go home at once! You cannot stay here."

Burbage thrust himself between the two, almost knocking Nat down in his fury. "So you would hit a younger boy, would you?"

Breathless, Nat turned on him and spat out: "No, I would not hit h—" —he caught himself in time—"a child. But I will thank you, sir, to leave this to me."

There was a breathless silence in the theater. The rest of the company, amazed, but fascinated as actors must be by real-life drama, stood motionless, watching the three figures in the center of the stage, and waiting.

This time there was no roar of anger from Burbage. He was past that now. The irritations of the last few days had come to a climax, and he spoke coldly, every word a sharp point with which he deliberately hurt the boy in front of him.

"I have had all that I can bear. Two months ago I went to some trouble to persuade your aunt and your employer to let you join my company, and in return you have been noisy when I would have quiet; have turned my theater into a school-room, rollicking with your cousin; have mocked me vilely. All these things I might have forgiven, but jealousy of another actor I will not overlook. No boy player shall bully a smaller boy in this company because he fears to lose a part. This time

10

you will go forever, though you *are* Will Kempe's boy. Waste no time. Go now!"

There was a moment's silence. Then Nat, trembling and defeated, turned and walked silently towards the exit. Kempe made a move to follow him, but Burbage said sharply: "Will!" and the comedian hesitated.

It was all too much for Dorothy. She had at last begun to realize the magnitude of what she had done. What had started as a gay adventure had turned, for Nat at least, into tragedy. She started forward: "Nat!"

He turned and looked at her, and she realized that he was not going to give her away. She ran towards him and threw her arms around him. "You shall not go."

Kempe was upon her like a bullet from a gun. "So you know this boy, Nat?"

"Of course he knows me," burst out Dorothy. "He is my cousin."

Burbage sank on to a chair. "Another of them!"

"Is this true, Nat?" asked Kempe, and Nat nodded.

"Brother to the black-haired goldsmith?" asked Burbage, and she laughed suddenly.

"Not brother—"

"Cousin!" cried Nat warningly, but Dorothy shook her head. " 'Tis no use, Nat." She went across to Burbage and stood in front of him, her hands clasped in front of her. "Not brother to James. Sister."

"What?"

The breath that everyone had been holding came out in a hiss. Burbage looked at her with dilated eyes, and the company's two playwrights leaned forward, fascinated by the odd little play being enacted.

"I am a girl, sir," said Dorothy simply. "I have cut off my hair and put on my brother's clothes."

Burbage put a hand to his head. "And what, miss, is your mother about to let you get into such an escapade?"

"She is in Surrey, sir. I am in my brother's charge and Nat's. That is why he would have me go home."

Burbage covered his eyes. "Angels and ministers of grace, defend us!"

Kempe had his hand on Nat's shoulder. "Why did you not tell us, boy?"

It was Dorothy who answered him. "For my sake, sir. He knew I would be disgraced before you all."

Burbage looked up. His voice shook slightly. "If any member of this company ever discloses what has happened here this afternoon he will be instantly dismissed." He looked across at his playwright. "Will, is there not a story for you here in this—this comedy of errors?" Suddenly he was laughing, throwing back his head in that fine abandonment to amusement that so endeared him to his company when his mood was good. "We will remember this among ourselves; but for the sake of Mistress . . .?"

"Dorothy."

". . . Dorothy—we will forget it elsewhere." Still laughing, he took Dorothy's hand. "As for you, sweetheart, if ever we have women in the theater you may come to me and I will take you to be heroine to my hero and we will set the town talking with our performance. But now, go home and grow your hair again."

Dorothy smiled. "And Nat? For though I can't be an actor, he *must* be, for he cares for nothing else."

"He is a villain."

"But to save himself he could have betrayed me."

"And to save yourself, you could have kept silent."

"We are both very noble characters," said Dorothy, smugly.

This time everybody laughed, and she grinned round at the company, sure of herself, as she always would be.

"My noble character, Nat," said Burbage. "Get ale for us all, for this has been a thirsty business. And when you return you must read the part, for if I cannot have your cousin in it, I will have you."

Will Kempe drew a trembling hand across his forehead. "Deo gratias," he murmured to Will Shakespeare, "another storm weathered."

13

Florence Choate

ADVENTURE
IN A CHIMNEY

ILLUSTRATED BY THE AUTHOR

SWEEP, sweep, chimney sweep!"

The cry echoed down the narrow street. Miss Sally Bacon opened the door of her little shop and peered out. Her chimney needed a sweeping. A man and boy stood outside, and Miss Sally called them in.

The man was a rough looking fellow. He dragged one foot. "'Urt in the war, ma'am, fighting for me country. The father o' this 'ere lad was kilt in the same. Me neph'w, ma'am."

Miss Sally turned to the boy. He looked eleven or twelve years of age, was thin, covered with soot. His wide blue eyes shone like light spots in the black little face. He was dressed in a man's coat and pantaloons and a pair of rough boots. Miss Sally had seen many a sweep, but never as shabby a one as this.

She watched with disfavor the dirty marks their boots made on her floor she had mopped up only this morning. They followed her into the kitchen. It was back of the shop, the chimney in the center. The house was old, like Miss Sally herself, only older still. Her grandsir' had built it, years ago, in the early days of Salem.

She had lived there all her life. There'd been a big family once; now only she was left. She could remember as a tiny child the sweeps climbing up that chimney. The little Sally had always been fearful that they'd fall, but many a sweep had gone up since, and none had ever fallen. The chimney had been built to give a foothold, her grandsir' had once explained.

14

Miss Sally hung a canvas over it now, and spread others on her chairs. It was a dirty job, having one's chimney cleaned. The boy helped in a sullen, dispirited way, while the man sprawled himself on the settle and lit a pipe. Tina, Miss Sally's cat, retreated under the table; she considered the chimney-corner her own property and hated to be disturbed.

Miss Sally looked around. "Everything is ready now, if you wish to start."

"Yes, ma'am," said the boy. He dived in under the canvas and went up the chimney. They could hear him faintly, way up at the top, *sweep, sweep,* then a step down, *sweep* again. Once in a while they'd hear him cough, then the broom would stop. It was a dirty chimney.

"Has the boy a cold?" asked Miss Sally, looking with disfavor at his master.

"Nay, ma'am, 'tis the soot in his nose," he answered. "It's soft I am with this lad. H'is the only one I 'ave left. Me neph'w, ma'am. Richard's 'is name. Simeon's mine, an' 'e's none but me to care for 'em, ma'am. We're no o' these parts, an' tied to no place, for that matter. We 'as an itchin' in our bones, that keeps us movin', ma'am."

The bell tinkled in the shop. It was some children on their way to school. They bought some lollypops and slate pencils. "That lad's cough," Miss Sally thought, as she dropped some lozenges into her pocket, then went back toward the kitchen, for she mustn't leave that man alone; she didn't like his looks.

She was just crossing the little hall that went between the rooms, when she heard a scream and then a thud. They came from the chimney. She ran in. The sweep had fallen; it was what she had expected all her life.

The man, Simeon, had torn aside the canvas; the lad lay there, perfectly still. "Get up!" Simeon snarled and gave him a kick. Miss Sally got a sight of his cruel face; the man was taken off his guard.

"How dare you?" She pushed past, giving him a shove. "Can't you see the lad is badly hurt?" She picked the child up and carried him to the settle. He was a light weight, only

15

skin and bones. "I think ye've starved him. Now go for a doctor."

"Where shall I find a doctor?" he muttered sullenly, but even he could see that the lad was terribly hurt.

"Doctor Burnham on Federal Street. If he can't come, get his son, young Doctor Samuel. Go quickly!"

When young Doctor Samuel came, he carried the boy upstairs and put him in Miss Sally's clean spare-room bed. They got off the dirty clothes. His leg was broken.

Simeon had followed them upstairs. "His leg is broke, ye say? When'll he work again?"

The doctor turned and looked at him grimly. "There are old bruises on this lad. What right have you to the child?"

"Every right in the world," said Simeon. "He's me dead brother's lad, an' I've give 'im care an' victuals since he was a wee babe. An' now, what I wants to know is, when he'll work again?"

"It will be two months at least," said Doctor Samuel, "and I don't know what we'll do with him."

He looked at Miss Sally, but she had made up her mind already. "He'll best rest here with me," she said. "When he's fed up and the leg's knit, well, that's another matter. But, Doctor, can we wash him a bit after you bind the splints on?"

Simeon blustered and threatened, but he had no real wish to take a sick, disabled child, so finally left. "I'll be back in two months time to claim me lawful property," he declared, "an' it'll mean 'arm to any that comes 'tween him an' me."

Through all this the boy had not spoken a word, but his eyes were fixed on Simeon. Occasionally he would give a rasping little cough. "He's starved to begin with," said the doctor. "I'm sure it was sheer weakness that made him fall."

The bell of the shop rang unheeded many times that morning. Miss Sally Bacon was busy somewhere else. It was a different looking boy that lay in that dainty bed after the doctor set his leg, and they fed and washed him. He was white as the sheet, but clean. "A comely lad, after all," Miss Sally declared.

Doctor Samuel came often during the next few days, and he brought a bundle of outgrown clothes that had belonged to his sister's boys, and she sent jelly and custard and fresh cream, to put flesh on the little sweep's bones. The boy couldn't be brought to speak of Simeon or say from where they had come.

He mended slowly. The doctor made a little crutch from the forked branch of a tree, when with his one good leg, he could hobble about the room. It was almost three weeks before

17

he tried to go downstairs. They were steep, so he went down sitting.

"And we'll not talk or worry now about the going up," Miss Sally told him, "but I think it will be the same."

Richard laughed. It was the first time, and did Miss Sally's heart good.

"That man shall not have him," she thought, as she fixed him on the settle and watched the firelight flicker over his fine features. "There must be a way to keep a little lad from harm."

The gossip had been disturbing. Simeon was still about Salem. He had been seen looking in Miss Sally's window the night before. It made her creep. That morning the doctor came for his usual visit, and Miss Sally told him. He was very concerned. There had been thieving in the town. If Simeon was about, it seemed to point to him.

That afternoon the doctor brought the constable. Richard would have to tell about his master.

Richard looked at them. His eyes were round with terror. "I dare not, sir," he whispered. "He's uncommon strong—and if I tell he'll—"

Doctor Samuel went over to the settle, and sat beside the lad. He thrust out his arm. "Look at that," he said. "I am strong, too, and the law is stronger than us both, and iron bars are stronger still. That's where Simeon will be if he's a thief. You can help us prove this. Richard, you must speak."

Richard looked about fearfully. The two men bent their heads to listen. "Yes, sir, he is a thief, and worse. 'Tis two years agone since he took me, and I know it well. He picks and steals all he can lay his hands upon. I would be up the chimney, and Simeon always said that if I told—"

"Is Simeon his real name?" asked the constable. "From where does he come, and what is he to you?"

"Simeon was what he called hi'self; I knew no other name. He was no kin o' mine, sir."

"Where did he get hold of you, Richard? Try and tell us all you know."

18

The boy told his story, diffidently, hesitating. He had come from a little town in Connecticut. His father, mother, and two sisters had died, all at the same time, of the dreaded throat distemper. Then he had been put on the town. Simeon had come through and taken him from the workhouse. The rascal had evidently put on a good face before the authorities and promised to teach him a trade.

"And so he did," said the boy bitterly. "He taught me to sweep, but he kicked me and starved me and—"

Miss Sally wouldn't stand it any longer. "You've badgered the child enough," she said. "Look at him, he's shaking from head to foot. You've got what you want, so leave him alone."

"You're right," said Doctor Samuel. "And we have gotten what we want; we shall make short work of that rascal. He's even bolder now since he's lost the lad's wages."

After they went, Richard lay back; he was exhausted. Miss Sally pulled over a low chair and sat beside him. She patted his shoulder.

"Oh, ma'am, I hated to have ye know about the thievin'. Mayhap ye think I'm just the same, not tellin' like, or a poor coward, to be so feard o' Simeon."

Kind Miss Sally gave him another pat. "I don't blame you a mite," she said, "and you're going to make a new start and forget all that. You'll bide here with me till your leg's well. We'll write to your town to find if you've kith or kin, but anyway, do something to get you placed decent."

Richard looked at her with adoring eyes. "Ye've been so good to me, ma'am, it'll be like heaven to bide."

The doctor wrote to Connecticut, and the answer came back. The boy had no kin. It was suggested that they put him in the workhouse.

"I'll keep him for the present, if you'll look out for some honest tradesman who'll give him a chance," said Miss Sally.

There was one bad thing. Simeon hadn't been caught yet. It might be that he had seen the constable come to interview Richard; from that day he disappeared.

"But he'll not come back," the constable assured them.

19

"Valuable as the boy was to him, he wouldn't be worth a term in jail, and that's where the knave will find himself, if he comes anywhere near Salem."

They told Richard that he need no longer fear Simeon, that he had gone, never to return. When the doctor told him he chirped up like a little robin, and hopped about like a robin, too. He got very deft with his crutch, and was here, there, and everywhere.

"Never saw such a change in a child!" Everyone said it, and Miss Sally said it more than anybody. She was proud enough when she looked at his round, happy face. There's no denying it, Miss Sally Bacon was getting a great attachment for her little chimney-sweep.

Soon he would hop in the shop to wait on customers. He saved Miss Sally many a step. It was a cent shop, as they called it—a package of tea, or a pound of raisins, a bobbin of tape, or a candle, marbles and muslin, sweets for the children, a little bit of everything.

Children were the best customers. They all loved Miss Sally, and they loved her shop. They swarmed there whenever they had a copper or two to spend.

They liked Richard, too. Miss Sally would sometimes hear them talking and laughing together. His laugh was just as merry as any of them.

"Bless his heart," she'd say to herself. "I hope he's making the right change and keeping strict account, but anyway, it will do him good to get with young folks."

The lad had been with her for over two months now. After the splint had come off the break had still ached. "He'd best stay a bit longer; meanwhile we can look about for a permanent place."

They had both put Simeon out of their minds, Miss Sally especially. She said that of course he wouldn't dare to come now. She didn't know Simeon.

One night it was Thursday and prayer meeting, for a good church member like Miss Sally. It was raining, a bad night, but she finally put on her oldest bonnet and went.

FLORENCE CHOATE

Richard sat by a low fire; it was very quiet in the house. He was nodding, almost asleep. Suddenly the bell of the shop rang out sharply; perhaps some neighbor was caught without tea for breakfast. Miss Sally never refused to do the favor of selling after hours.

The lad woke himself, took the candle, and went in. The door stuck with the dampness, so he gave a pull. There was a push from without. The door burst open. Richard fell back and dropped the candle. It went out; the shop was in total darkness, but he had seen. It was Simeon!

He could hear him too, tramping in and shutting the door. "Where are ye, brat? 'Tis like ye to drop the light. Where are ye, I say?"

Simeon stumbled, then grasped the boy by the shoulder. "I've come for ye, get up." He pulled Richard to his feet. By now their eyes were accustomed to the darkness, and they could see a faint light coming from the kitchen.

The man dragged the boy in. He threw him onto the settle, then went to the fire and lit another candle. It was half-past eight; Richard could see the hands of the clock. Simeon looked about. "Where does the old woman keep her victuals?"

"Over there." There was corned beef in the cupboard, bread, half a pie. Simeon ate it all, then wiped his mouth with his greasy sleeve. He came over to Richard. "Ye don't seem to be over glad to see me!"

Richard didn't answer.

"Well," said Simeon, "glad or not, you go. You don't get out o' me sight again." He took the boy by the shoulder, held the light with the other hand, and went back into the shop.

With sure instinct he found the till. Business had been brisk that day and Simeon emptied out a pile of silver and copper coins. He looked about for some way to carry it, and saw a leather fire bucket hanging behind the door. He poured the money in, together with some tobacco and snuff. He marched back to the kitchen, put the candle on the table and held Richard by both shoulders.

He stared steadily into the boy's eyes, and spoke slowly. "Now

22

where does the old woman keep her silver? I'm going to have it even if I have to wait till she gives it to me. But it will save time an' trouble if ye tell me where it is."

"There's a box o' it in the chest yonder."

Simeon threw the boy from him. Richard half tumbled into a chair. He watched the thief take out Miss Sally's prized silver spoons and stuff them into the bucket. The fire was almost out and the kitchen dark; it was lit only by the one flickering candle. "Now what else?"

"There's more money in the Dutch oven. Miss Sally doesn't use it, only as a hiding place."

Simeon laughed. "Ah," he said, "that's even better."

There was her box of savings, mostly gold. Richard had seen her counting it once; she had trusted him even as much as that.

The man laughed again as he dumped it into the bucket. "Anything more?" he asked.

"I—I—don't want to tell ye." The boy staggered over and fell on his knees. "Simeon, don't make me tell ye."

"Tell me," the man raised his arm. "Tell me, quick."

"In the very back o' the oven, ye'll find something. In the very back."

The oven was deep, the opening small. In his cupidity the thief thrust himself in, even his head. He reached, and reached again. He had let the bucket drop to the ground, so he could reach with both hands.

Richard was right there, kneeling. The chimney was over his head as he looked up. Then he grabbed the bucket.

It was not for nothing that Simeon had taught the chimney sweep his trade. In the chimney he was a monarch, sure of his ground. He felt by instinct for the rough stones that gave him a foothold. He could hear Simeon snarling with rage. Richard was out of his reach now, and he stopped to swing the heavy bucket over his shoulder.

"Ye varment, ye dirty brat, come down, or I'll climb an' fetch ye down."

The boy threw his head back and laughed. Simeon and his

23

stupid threats! It was harder to climb now; he must go cautiously.

"I'll smoke ye out." Simeon was piling logs on the fire, but Richard was almost at the top. His hands were stinging from the hot stones, but he didn't notice. What should he do with the bucket? Smoke wouldn't harm that, it would be safer here. He felt about, and his fingers touched a ledge of stone— one of the other flues. He balanced the bucket on it, then drew himself out of the chimney; now he was on the roof.

The fresh air was good. The boy crouched, drawing it in, but his work was not over. It was a long sloping roof, as was the fashion when Grandsir' built the house. It was a help now. The kitchen was in the back; he had to go that way, but he must be quiet.

The shingles were wet and slippery, but the patter of the

24

rain helped him. It was not so far from the ground. Could he jump; would his leg stand it?

Then he saw a tree; one of its branches almost touched the roof. Richard was light and as agile as a monkey. He jumped at it, pushed himself along, then shinnied down the trunk. He was in Miss Sally's garden.

The church was near and, leg or not, he was going to get there in time. He ran up the steps and in. They were singing a hymn and he stood for a second, abashed. Then he saw Miss Sally, and everyone saw him. Even the melodeon stopped playing, for Richard was a strange sight in a prayer meeting. Black with soot, wet, bedraggled, he ran up the aisle.

"Miss Sally," he shouted. "Simeon be here, an' if they go quick, they'll bag him."

The prayer meeting broke up. Fortunately the constable was there, and he took several others with him. They all had stout sticks, and they got Simeon, for he was still thinking he'd bring Richard down. The rascal was locked in Salem jail that night, tried and sentenced later. That was really the end of him.

And Richard? Well, Richard climbed the chimney once again. It was to bring down the fire bucket, the contents safe, though a little smoky. He gave it to Miss Sally. "Miss Sally, ma'am, the chimney's terrible sooty. I'm set on sweeping it for ye before I go away."

"Go away?" Miss Sally looked at Richard over her spectacles. "Richard, how would you like to be my boy, my real boy this time, to go to school and grow up a gentleman like Doctor Samuel?"

A slow grin lit up the sooty little face; the eyes and teeth made spots of light. "Oh, ma'am, do ye really mean it?"

Miss Sally smiled back. "Yes," she said, "I really do."

Robin, son of Sir John de Bureford, was crippled by an unknown disease while waiting to travel to the castle of Lindsay, where he was to serve as page while his parents were away in the service of the King. His father's servants desert him when the plague strikes London, and Brother Luke of a near-by monastery rescues the child and cares for him in the cloister. When at last Robin is carried by Brother Luke and John-go-in-the-wynd, a friendly minstrel, to Lindsay, he is welcomed and pitied. Soon the castle is besieged by the Welsh, and though still lame, Robin finds a way to serve his lord.

Marguerite de Angeli

ROBIN FINDS A WAY

ILLUSTRATED BY THE AUTHOR

THE fog held for days. The Welsh could not get beyond the outer wall of the castle, and the English inside could not tell what strength the enemy possessed. They might be encamped on the surrounding hills, or they might be only a small company. Several of the guards on the wall had been injured, and sometimes the yeomen could tell that an arrow had struck home in the enemy's camp. Most of the time there was only watchful waiting on both sides. The Welsh had a machine for catapulting stones, most of which thudded harmlessly into the courtyard. Sometimes one struck the inner wall, but most of them fell short, dropping into the moat.

Inside the keep women occupied themselves with spinning,

weaving, and embroidery. It helped the time to pass more quickly. The children played with toy soldiers and blocks, with hobbyhorses and with dolls. Sometimes Robin told them tales or sang songs, but he spent most of the time in the chamber where he slept, working on the Saxon harp.

William Wise had set up a workbench for him and had finished the tool of hardened iron. There was a small lathe for turning the keys and a vise all arranged so that Robin could sit on a stool to reach them. The tool for making the holes was sharp, so that part was not difficult.

Just as John-go-in-the-Wynd had said, it was harder to turn the keys on the lathe so they would fit exactly. They were either too large and would not go in, or, when they had been turned smaller, they were too small and would not hold the strings in tune.

But Robin was learning patience. He had found out that the harder it was to do something, the more comfortable he felt after he had done it.

Sir Peter had stood all of one night on the bastion, directing and encouraging the men. They had managed to drive off a raiding party that was trying to scale the wall. Now he was in bed with a chill, and Lady Constance waited upon him.

The food in the larder dwindled, and there were many people to be fed. Besides the garrison and the household there were the yeomen from the town and those who had sought refuge when the portcullis was raised.

Usually there was a good supply of salt fish kept in barrels, but fish had not been plentiful the past summer, so now the supply was meager. There was mutton, to be sure, but it was all on four legs and scattered over the downs beyond the castle and town. The winter kill had not taken place because they waited for freezing weather. There was flour to last for a short time, but the yearly portion from the peasants' holdings was to have been brought to the castle the following week. Besides, there had been a small crop of grain because of the summer's drought.

Then the water began to fail. As Robin came into the Hall

at suppertime he passed the table where the retainers sat. Denis leaned to whisper in the ear of Adam the Yeoman.

"There is scarce a foot of water in the well," he whispered. "Just now as I drew it to fill this ewer the cook told me."

"How came this?" asked Adam. " 'Tis known that this is a good well. Tell not her ladyship, and send the word around that the water must be used sparingly or 'twill not last the week out, even for drinking." He thought a moment, then said,—

"Someone must go for help, or we shall be forced to surrender the castle. It might be that Sir Hugh Fitzhugh would come to our aid, for he, too, is in danger from the Welsh if they break our defense. But whom shall we spare? All are needed at their posts."

"Let me go," said Robin. "I can go out the small door at the north whilst it is early morning. No one will suspect me. They think me a poor shepherd. I shall borrow a smock from William the Farrier's son, and if I am seen, I shall appear stupid. We shall keep it secret, for if Sir Peter were to find out my plan he would forbid me to go, not knowing how strong I am."

"But thou'rt only a lad!" Adam objected, "and art cumbered with crutches as well. And how wilt thou cross the river? The bridge is well guarded at both ends."

"I shall go well, never fear," Robin assured them confidently. "I have it all in my head how it shall be done. I shall find John-go-in-the-Wynd at his mother's cottage in Tripheath village. John shall set forth from there for Sir Hugh and his men. Now, let us plan. First, I want you, Denis, to bring me the smock, and some rags to wrap about my legs. Then, see you, find me a hood that is worn and faded. Besides, I shall need long leather thongs to tie the crutches to my back, for I shall swim the river."

"Fear you not the soldiery?" queried Denis anxiously. "Will you not fall down the steep bank? 'Tis a far distance to the bottom of the ravine, and—" He stopped suddenly, because one of the maids appeared.

"See to it," said Robin with a quick nod.

That evening there was no gathering about the fire. Every-

28

one was restless. The hounds were still uneasy, walking about, cocking their ears at the least sound.

Lady Constance went to examine the stores. Robin was afraid she would discover how low the water was in the well. Instead, she seemed confident that there was sufficient.

"How fortunate we are that there is plenty of water," she said. "Sir Peter says that our well has never failed."

Denis looked at Robin, knowing that he shared the secret.

Denis, knowing Robin's plan, was in a fidget to be through with his duties and find William the Farrier's son and borrow his clothes. He would probably be with his father at the forge, repairing pikes and lances and heating oil for pouring onto the enemy in case they should pierce the outer castle wall.

Robin put on his warmest under tunic and carefully put away the little harp and all the parts and tools so that they would be safe. He looked at it regretfully, hating to leave it.

Then, when all was ready except changing his clothes, he sought out Brother Luke, for he knew that the friar would give him help and encouragement.

Dressed in the patched and ragged smock, his legs wound about with bits of rag to hold the ill-fitting hosen, Robin tried to sleep away the early part of the night, but excitement kept him wakeful. Even when he dozed, he was aware of what he was about to do. He counted over all the things he must remember. He must go softly with the crutches. He must remember the leather thongs. As Brother Luke had told him, he mustn't forget oil for the rusty lock of the door in the wall. He must keep D'Ath quiet.

Just before dawn Brother Luke touched him.

"Come, my son," he whispered. "We shall say the office before it is time to set forth on thy mission."

When the prayers were finished, Robin pulled on the faded hood, tucked the leather thong inside it, and followed the friar. D'Ath rose from sleep to follow after, but Robin touched his head and whispered a command for him to stop.

"D'Ath, stay you here," he said, wishing very much that the dog could go with him.

29

They went down a half flight of steps and across the hall of the keep to the winding stair, making their way quietly among the sleeping servants. They went very slowly, for Robin's crutches tapped an alarm when he made haste, and the least misstep would have sent him clattering down.

There was still fog when they came into the open, but it had begun to drift and there was a gray dawn just beginning to break.

"Who goes there?" demanded the sentry at the door, but seeing Robin and the friar, he allowed them to pass, thinking they were bent on some holy errand.

Robin shuddered.

"Art fearful, my son?" asked the friar.

"Not truly," answered Robin, "though 'tis weird in the fog."

"Aye, 'tis an eerie feeling to be out in the cheerless dawn, not knowing at what moment an enemy may appear out of the fog," agreed Brother Luke. And at that moment a face did appear, but it was only one of the guards, who thought the two were on their way to the chapel.

They reached the sally port in the north wall without meeting anyone else. Brother Luke dripped oil into the lock before trying to open the door.

Robin listened.

"Hark!" he whispered. "I hear the Welsh sentry outside. We can count the paces and can tell how far away he is. One, two, three, four—" They counted forty paces. "Now!" Slowly the door opened and Robin slipped outside.

"Benedicite," whispered the friar in blessing, and closed the door.

Quickly Robin moved away from the door and the wall. In a moment he was at the edge of the deep ravine. He could hear the river far below but could not see it for the fog.

Now began the dangerous descent. Carefully Robin tested each clod of earth, each bit of stone, before trusting his weight to the crutches, praying the while that the fog would hold. Sometimes he slid on his haunches, sometimes seedling trees held him till he was able to find sure footing.

"If I should start a stone rolling," he thought, "the whole Welsh army will be upon my neck."

It seemed hours to Robin that he was sliding, groping, laboring down the treacherous cliff, but it was only a few moments, for the light of morning had scarcely changed when he reached the bottom and found himself at the edge of the river.

He stopped only long enough to fasten the crutches onto his back with the leathern thong and to wind his hood into a kind of hat that perched on top of his head. Then he plunged into the icy water, not allowing himself to consider whether he had the courage to do it.

When first the water closed over him Robin thought he could not bear it. The crutches were awkward. His chest felt tightly squeezed and as if sharp knives pierced him. He seemed unable to breathe, and his head felt ready to burst. But he struck out fiercely, and after a few strokes began to breathe more easily. Warmth crept through his body and a feeling of power, as if nothing could be too difficult for him. He swam strongly across the swift current toward the path he had seen from the top of the tower.

What if the enemy should be camped on the other side? Suppose they wouldn't believe he was the poor shepherd he pretended to be? Suppose he found it impossible to get up the bank on the other side?

"Anyone could *not* do it," he said to himself stubbornly, and thrashed his arms more fiercely.

At last he felt the stones of shallower water under his feet, the bank appeared mistily green, and he was able to hold himself steady with one hand while he untied the crutches and set them under his armpits. The bank was not very steep after all, and in a moment he was at the top, ready to go on. His teeth chattered in the rising wind.

His feet felt as if they had been frozen. His hands were so numb with cold he could hardly hold the crutches to steady them as he walked. He paused long enough to let down the hood into its proper shape. The warm wool felt good, although it was wet along the edges. Then he looked about for signs of

31

the path. It had shown so clearly from the top of the tower. He moved along the bank a few paces where generations of peasants had worn a "highway," and soon came to the path. The fog was lifting somewhat with the wind, and Robin, looking back once, caught sight of the castle he had left behind. He even caught a glimpse of the sentry along the narrow ridge just where he had so lately escaped by the door in the wall.

After passing through a patch of brush and willows, Robin came out into a field. He still could not see very far ahead, but the path was straight before him, so he began to swing along as fast as he could, his crutches making great sweeping circles, his feet covering the ground in tremendous strides. There seemed to be no one about, so he made haste without regard to noise, and gradually the numbness in his hands and feet began to ease. Across the field he went, swing-step, swing-step, swing-step.

The fog wavered and lifted, swirled about in sudden drafts, floated across the path in thin layers, showed a patch of blue sky for an instant and glimpses of trees ahead.

Suddenly a voice rang out.

"*Who goes there?*"

" 'Tis but I, Robin," he answered in a meek voice, and the chill that ran down his spine was not all from the dampness of his clothing.

"Robin who?" the voice went on.

"Robin—Crookshank, some call me," answered Robin.

The fog parted, showing the fierce and scowling head of a man.

The guard drew near where he could see the boy.

"Aah," he said. "Art tha' but a shepherd boy, then?" he asked, seeing Robin's poor clothes. "And hast fallen into the river? Come, then, lad, and warm tha'self by the fire. Be not frighted. We'll not hurt thee." He took Robin's arm and tried to draw him toward the camp, which now Robin could see just at the side of the field, for now the fog was fast disappearing. But Robin held back and shook his head, trying to think what he must say and how he must speak.

32

"Nay," he began, trying to appear stupid, " 'tis na far to the cottage." He edged away, bobbing his thanks, and went on as fast as he dared up the other side of the field and through the hedgerow. He did not stop until he was well beyond earshot of the men in the camp, then stood only for a moment to draw long, steadying breaths.

He chuckled at the way he had fooled the Welshman.

From that point on the path led through a wood and downward toward the valley of a stream which joined the one surrounding the castle. There were no cottages near at hand, but across the stream and beyond a low-lying field and a rising slope Robin could see the wood that extended to the edge of the village where the church tower stood. The sky now was filled with fast-flying clouds, and the fog was gone. The stream was shallow enough for Robin to go across on foot, and the little wetting he got was nothing after swimming the river.

The wood behind him hid Robin from the camp in the field, for which he was thankful, because the rising ground slowed his going, and he felt as if he were a fair target for arrows. It seemed as if he would never come to the top of the field and the hedgerow separating it from the forest beyond. When he reached the shelter of the great trees, Robin sank down into a bed of bracken to rest. He was very tired.

When breathing was easier and the pain of effort but a dull ache, Robin rose to go on. How much farther had he to go? Would John be there when he arrived? Would he be able to get help in time?

Even through the forest the path was well marked, because it was one that had been used for centuries. The peasants went over it to and from the villages to gather wood or to pasture the sheep.

In about an hour the forest began to thin, and Robin could see the blue smoke coming from the cotters' chimney pots. Which cottage belonged to John's mother? Robin remembered that John had said it was on the heath and near the church. He could see such a cottage from where he stood, so he made his way toward it hopefully. It was so exciting to be within sight of help that Robin forgot that he was tired and hungry, he forgot that he was still cold from his dousing in the river and the fright he'd had. He began to cut across the heath toward the cottage but had not gone far when John himself came out of the door.

Robin stopped. "John!" he called at the top of his voice. *"John! Oh, John-go-in-the-Wy-y-y-nd."*

John heard him and looked his way, then came running.

"Master Robin!" he exclaimed. "What's amiss? How came thou here?"

Without waiting for an answer he grasped Robin's crutches and swept him up into his arms, because he could see that Robin had come as far as he was able. It had been Robin's plan to issue orders as his father might have done; to have been lordly and commanding. But it was such a relief to be cared for and to have the weight of his body taken from his aching armpits that he allowed John to carry him and said not a word until he was laid upon the straw pallet.

An old woman stood by the fire stirring something in a pot. She looked at Robin but didn't speak. A cat mewed and coaxed her, rubbing against her skirts.

"The castle is in danger!" said Robin at once. "The Welsh have taken the town and are at the gates of the outer bailey. The food is giving out. The water low in the well. You must get help. You must get it soon."

"But how came thou here?" said John, amazed. "How didst escape the sentry?" John was already putting on his hood and fastening his leather jerkin.

He went on without waiting.

"Knowest what force the Welsh have?"

"No," said Robin, "the fog has kept us from seeing. But whenever we tried to make a sally into the town, we were forced back."

"I shall be gone straight away. Stay thou here for safety and to rest."

John-go-in-the-Wynd was well named, for go he did, closing the door behind him almost before he had finished speaking.

Robin sighed. It was good to be able to rest.

"Come, now," said the woman, as she took off Robin's clothes to dry them. "Thou'lt be famished with hunger. I'll bake thee a bannock." As tired as he was, Robin grinned. She went to the cupboard and took out a flat cake which she put on a hot stone to bake.

Robin slept after the woman fed him and didn't wake until the sun was low in the west. The sound of the door opening was what really woke him. It was John.

Robin was up on his elbow in a second.

"Did you not go then?" he asked in bewilderment. Then he realized he had slept and that it was late in the day. "Did you find help then?"

"Yes, already they are well on their way from my lord Hugh Fitzhugh's castle," said John. "A large force of foot soldiers and a company of lancers go by the drovers' road, one company by the way through wood and field and another going around to attack from the other side of the town by way of Letham Bridge. It hath been agreed that we shall give the signal from the bell tower of the church. There are no better bowmen in England. The siege will be lifted. Thou'lt see!"

35

"I want to see it," declared Robin. "I want to see it all!"

"See it thou shalt," promised John. "Now, Mother, serve forth yon porridge, for I have not broken my fast this day."

The mother bustled about, putting the porridge into a bowl for all to dip into and drawing a bench up to the table.

John laid out the little harp, put bread into his pouch, and stuck a knife in his belt. "I am no warrior," he said to Robin. "I am but a messenger and minstrel. But who knows? I might find myself close to the enemy. Closer than I would like," he added with a shrug.

The meal was soon over, and they made ready to start.

"Think you I can go so far again this day?" asked Robin anxiously.

"Thou hast no need to think of that," John assured him. "I can carry thee right well, as the good friar did. The harp and the crutches we shall strap on so they will not cumber us." He fastened the crutches to his side and the harp around Robin's neck, so it hung down his back. "Soon thou'lt be carrying thine own harp, God willing."

"Fare thee well, old Mother," said John, embracing her. "Up, now, young master," he said to Robin, and with that they left the cottage and went on their way.

"How shall we go?" asked Robin, as John strode down the path on the way out of the village. "Shall we go by the way I came here? Or by way of Letham Bridge?"

"Neither," answered John-go-in-the-Wynd. "I know still another way. I know a path leading through the forest to the southeast. It goeth past the priory where we shall ford the river. We can come at the town easily from there. Then we can wait for nightfall, and indeed it will be nightfall ere we arrive, but there will be a moon.

"We shall creep along the river, under cover of the reeds and willows, and enter the town through the shoemaker's house, which is on the wall. He is known to me, and we have a signal between us. He knoweth the sound of my harp, and the certain tune I play will tell him we have need of him. From there it is quite simple to get into the graveyard of the church, thence into the church itself, and into the tower. There we shall see all and hear all if we are not deafened by the bells."

"What an adventure to tell my father!" cried Robin.

Although he carried Robin, John trotted along at a good speed, for he knew every curve in the path. It was only a short way to the ford of the river, near the priory, and from there across fields covered with grazing sheep to the forest. There they rested. When they reached the top of the hill beyond, John pointed out the drovers' road far below. There, glints of light on lance and pennant, helmet, and moving figures showed Robin the fast-moving company of soldiers. Because it was nearly dusk and suppertime, blue smoke rose from every chimney pot in the village they had left, and in the low places mist began to rise.

"We must make haste," said John, lifting Robin again to his back, "or we shall be too late."

When they had to cross open country again, John kept to the hedgerows so they would not be seen, and as they came nearer to Lindsay, he kept well away from every barn and outbuilding.

"For aught we know the Welsh may be encamped out here on this side of the castle as well as on the other," he explained. "They might question even a minstrel such as I. 'Tis safer for our skins to go softly."

By the time they reached the place where the drovers' road led, John halted before crossing the road to observe the sentry. They waited for the sound of his footsteps to die away around the town. The moon was high, and by keeping well in the shadow of a tree they were able to cross the road without being seen.

"Ah," said John with a sigh of relief. "So far we have come safely. Soon Sir Hugh's men will encircle the town. By then we shall be in the church tower to give the signal for attack."

"We have not seen the enemy on this side of the town," whispered Robin hopefully.

"No," agreed John. "Because they have taken the town, and will be inside the walls. There is more need of outposts to the

37

south and west, where the two bridges are, and where the roads leading from them are well traveled. The Welsh will reason that there is little likelihood of danger from this road because it is well known that Sir Peter and his cousin Sir Hugh are not on friendly terms. Sir Peter is for the King and for England. Sir Hugh is not. But they are of one family, and were once like brothers. I had little difficulty in persuading him. Sir Hugh."

"Perhaps they will be friends from now on," said Robin. "Perhaps Sir Hugh will be won for the King."

"It may be." John nodded. "Most of the lords in this part of the country are for keeping their lands to themselves. But times are changing, and we have a good king."

"Hark!" whispered Robin again. "All is still. The sentry is at the far end of his walk. Shall we go then?"

"Aye, 'tis time," said John. "Hast the little harp safe?"

"'Tis safe," said Robin, grasping John about the neck and getting himself settled on his back.

They crept forward again, shielded by the darkness, and made their way along a narrow path that followed the wall until the rising ground told John they were near to the shoemaker's cottage. There again they halted, to make sure no sentry was about. John, letting Robin slip to the ground, fitted the crutches under his arms and took the harp from about his neck.

The tune he played was mournful and slow, but it must have reached the ears of the shoemaker. John was just beginning to play it for the third time when there was an answer to it in the form of a bagpipe jig. Robin could see John bobbing his head up and down happily because his playing had brought forth the right response. There followed another period of waiting while the sentry passed again on the wall. They scarcely breathed until he had turned again and was going the other way. By counting his steps they knew when he was far enough away for them to act.

Then, without warning, a sort of chair was let down from a window high in the wall. John fastened Robin into it and gave

38

Robin found his mother's arms around him

the rope a jerk. Robin was hauled aloft so quickly that he had no time to think what he should do or what he should say. He found himself being lifted inside the upper room of a small house and the window drawn to. He faced a little man, who cautioned him to silence while again they waited for the sentry to come and to go.

There was no light in the room except the moonlight that came in through the window.

"This is really exciting," thought Robin.

He wished that John had been able to come into the house with him.

He heard the "tramp, tramp" of the sentry and the thudding of the pikestaff as it struck the stone when the sentry turned at the wall of the house. The sound lessened, and once more the rope was lowered.

This time it was for John. Robin could see the iron wheel under the window which turned like a windlass to let out the rope.

In a moment John stood in the room with him. The rope and iron wheel were stored in an innocent-looking chest. The shoemaker quickly lifted the wheel out of the strong wooden block which held it, covered with a flat board and cloth. The shoemaker motioned for Robin and John to follow him down the steep stair leading to the house below.

They did not linger in the house, but with a few words to the shoemaker, left by way of the garden. There was a door in the wall leading into the graveyard of the church, where John and Robin slipped quietly from one great tombstone to another. They entered the church by the sanctuary door, startling the sacristan who slept and ate in a small room off the entrance porch.

"Who art thou?" he called, hearing the creak of the door. "Art friend or foe?"

"Hist!" warned John, stepping quickly toward the light of the lantern held by the sacristan. "We are friends. I am John-go-in-the-Wynd, minstrel. This lad is young Master Robin, friend and ward of Sir Peter. He hath this day saved us all."

39

The sacristan held the lantern up in order to see John's face.

"Now I mind thee," he said, nodding his head. "I knew thy father."

John told the sacristan how Robin had come to warn him and to get help, and described the plan he had made with Sir Hugh to sound the bells giving the signal for attack.

"Come with me, then," said the sacristan, leading the way.

They went down the long, dark aisle of the church to the door of the tower.

"Give me thy crutches here, young master," said John. "Canst thou climb the ladder or wilt go pickaback? 'Tis a great height, but there are resting places."

"I can do it," said Robin shortly. Had he not climbed to the towers and turrets of the castle many times?

They had just reached the belfry when it was time for curfew to ring. The bells began an ear-splitting clamor.

"Down flat, and cover thy ears—quick!" shouted John.

They flattened themselves on the platform and endured the deafening sound.

"We shall go to the top first," said John, "for it is yet too soon to give the signal, and from there we shall see somewhat."

From the belfry to the top of the tower it was another thirty feet of climbing. When they reached the top Robin fell in a heap onto the platform with every bit of strength gone from his legs and arms. It slowly returned. In a little while he was able to rise and stand beside John, looking out over the town.

"We agreed that I should wait an hour after curfew, when the moon will be nearly overhead," said John. "That allows time for all companies to be in place, and with the sounding of the bell to move in about the town and castle wall at once."

"How can you tell when it has been an hour?" asked Robin.

"By the feel of it," said John. "Besides, I shall play 'Love a Garland Is' and 'Lament of a Lass.' That will be half of the hour." He unslung the harp from Robin's back and began the music.

While they waited for the rest of the hour to pass, John pointed out the familiar turrets of the castle, the north tower where they had stood that day, and the tower of the keep where the household waited for deliverance. He strummed on the harp between times.

They tried to see into the hills about the town, but saw only the quiet countryside bathed in moonlight. In the town, supper fires sent up blue smoke, and here and there was the red glare of torchlight and campfire. Glints of moonlight on helmet or shield shone from the walls where sentries walked, but very little sound could be heard at that height.

The hour was up.

"Now," said John, "it is time for the alarm. Stay thou here, and I shall return. Cover thy ears well, but watch to see what happens." He was gone through the hatch into the darkness below. Robin waited, his skin prickling with excitement. Would the signal be at the right time? Would the arrows find their mark and lift the siege?

Bong! BONGGG! BONGGG! BONGGG! BONG! BONGGG!!!!

The great bell rang, sending waves of sound that went out over the hills and came echoing back into the stone of the bell tower, which trembled with the vibration.

At first Robin could see nothing different from what he had seen before. Then, it was as if a part of the landscape itself moved off there toward the south, just below the edge of the town. Gathering from the slopes were tiny moving figures, now in the open, now lost in shadow. Robin searched for another sign, this time in the direction of Letham Bridge. The sign was there where he could see more clearly.

John came up, breathing hard.

"What's to be seen?" he asked. "Are they moving? Hast seen any arrows fly?" He looked to the Letham Bridge.

Then it came.

A hail of arrows that were like dark rain sped from on-coming yeomen, dropping the sentries on the bridge and picking off men of the guard manning the wall of the town. From where they stood Robin could see it all as plainly as if it had been a toy village set in a toy landscape, and the soldiers, toy

41

soldiers. He saw pikemen strike down sentries of the enemy at the town gate and take prisoner the Welsh guards. He saw the company of Sir Hugh's men enter and take the town.

It had been a complete surprise.

When John-go-in-the-Wynd saw what was happening and realized that the plan had been successful, he tossed his hat into the air and clasped Robin in his arms.

"We've won!" he shouted. "The Welsh are routed! Lindsay is saved once more!"

Then, setting Robin on his feet again, he said,

"Stay thou here, and watch how the Welsh are marched out of the town whilst I go below. Thou'lt hear such a peal of bells as shall nigh wake the dead lying below." Down he went again through the hatch to the belfry.

With the pealing of the bells, flares went up from castle and town, windows and doors opened. The peal of bells stopped. John came back and together they watched the lifting of the siege. They could see people running about through the streets embracing one another, tossing caps and hats into the air, and in other ways showing their joy at being freed of the Welsh invaders. In a short while they saw the enemy marched out of town.

Tears streamed down Robin's cheeks.

"I must not cry," he thought, wiping them away. "Not even for joy."

"Now," said John, lifting Robin aloft, "thou'lt be carried on my shoulder—so. For thou'rt the hero of this victory," and together they went down the long stretches of ladder and stair to the ground.

"Make haste," said Robin. "Let us go to the keep at once, so Sir Peter and Lady Constance shall know that I am safe and well. Brother Luke will be sure of it, for his prayers have followed me this day. That I know."

All the way through the town square John made his way with Robin on his shoulder high above the villagers dancing in the dawn of returning day.

They were greeted with cheers at the castle gate and fol-

lowed across the courtyard to the inner gate and to the keep by the cheering crowd.

Alan-at-Gate-saw them from the gatehouse. The drawbridge was lowered and the portcullis raised, and just inside the whole company of the household stood to receive them. Sir Peter was in the center with his sons and the two pages. Near him was Lady Constance with her women and little Alison. D'Ath whimpered joyfully beside Brother Luke.

Sir Peter held out his arms and helped Robin to the ground, placing the crutches to support him. Then, placing his hand upon Robin's head, he spoke solemnly.

"Now, before God and this company," he said, "I do hail thee Conqueror and true son of thy noble father."

Lady Constance embraced Robin and the women made much of him. D'Ath was too well bred a dog to push himself forward, but his eager prancing and wriggling finally brought him to Robin's side, where he thrust his long, cold nose into Robin's hands.

John-go-in-the-Wynd was called forward. He was given a holding of land for his own and a portion of sheep. With it went certain rights for hunting and fishing to be his and his heirs forever.

Brother Luke gave Robin his blessing and went with him to his chamber.

"It seems long since I left here," said Robin, looking around as if he expected things to be changed. But there was the cross over his bed, and there on the workbench the little harp just as he had left it, waiting for the strings to be fastened to the keys.

"Much hath happened in this one day," said Brother Luke. "I should like to hear how thy journey went. By thy look, thou hast fared well, except for needing a good wash and a sleep. Off with thy borrowed clothes and once more I shall care for thee."

Sleep overtook Robin even before Brother Luke had finished.

The days grew short and very cold. Everyone went about with a red nose and a cloud of frozen breath. Robin was glad of the woolen gloves made for him by Lady Constance. They were snug and warm and decorated with needlework on the back.

The river ran more slowly now, and ice began to form along the edges. Robin stopped swimming and took his exercise in other ways. He spent a great deal of time with Adam Bowyer shooting at a mark and was already at work again in the carpentry shop making a viol such as Piers Nitingale used.

The harp was finished. Robin had learned how to tune it by tightening the strings and could play it a little. Brother Luke was teaching him to sing a carol, because it was near to the Feast of Christmas. There would be singing and caroling in the Hall and Robin remembered his father's letter and hoped that Christmas would bring his father and mother to the castle.

One day before the Feast of Thomas the Apostle, and after the Feast of St. Lucy (the thirteenth of December), Robin was with Sir Peter in the armory. The coats of mail, the helmets, the lances, pikes, bows and arrows were being put in order, and the great two-handed sword hung on the wall.

"See you here," said Sir Peter. "This is where the blow struck my helmet. There is a dent as large as a basin." He rubbed his head where the helmet had been thrust in.

Robin ran his fingers around the ugly cavity, imagining how it would feel to be struck with a mace. He was thinking of his father and wondering whether he, too, had been wounded.

"Will the Scottish wars have ended, think you?" he asked.

"I have had no word directly," answered Sir Peter. "There have been rumors about that troops of returning soldiers have been seen. Some were going southward along the highroad. John-go-in-the-Wynd might tell us if he were here, but he has not been nigh the castle for weeks. I dare say he is busy building shelter for his new flocks and gathering wood for the winter that his old mother may be warm."

Robin said no more, but after that he went often to the top of the keep to scan the countryside for signs of horsemen. Sometimes he could see nothing for fog or rain. Sometimes the air was crisp and clear, and he could see far beyond the hills. Once a cloud of dust on the road moving toward the town kept him excited for an hour, but it proved to be only a flock of sheep being driven to market. Once a company of lancers appeared, but they turned southward.

On the afternoon of the Eve of Christmas Robin was at his post on top of the keep with Adam Bowyer, who was on watch. It began to snow. Robin watched while the silent whiteness covered the hills and the roofs of the town. Far, far below he could see a hawking party. He could see the pages coming from the forest, dragging the yule log and branches of holly to decorate the Hall.

Suddenly Adam Bowyer cried, "Look! Look yonder!" He pointed east, where the road led into the highroad and to the town gate. Robin left the north side of the tower and joined Adam, looking toward where he pointed. The snow dimmed what he saw, but it was clear enough. A company of knights and men at arms rode towards the castle. At the head rode the King, for only he wore the royal colors and the royal quarterings of the banners. At his side rode one who sat his horse as only Robin's father did. In the midst of the great company were ladies, pikemen, men at arms, and yeomen. That must be the Queen. Was it the Lady Maud there beside her in the center? It must be!

Robin burst into a cheer.

"It is true!" he shouted. "It is true! The Scottish wars are over, and my father is alive!" He must say nothing about his mother, for fear Adam would think him babyish. He dashed down the winding stair as fast as he dared, crossed the inner ward to the Hall, thump, slip, thump, slip, and then to the solar to find Sir Peter. Thump, slip, thump, slip, thump, slip, thump, slip!

Sir Peter roared with laughter at Robin's attempt to tell him about the approaching company, for he knew from the moment he had seen Robin's shining face the good news.

"Shall I go to the gate to be there when they enter, think you?" asked Robin anxiously.

"Do what seems best, my boy," said Sir Peter. "Go stand

beside Alan-at-Gate or stay you here by my side. I know what a fever of excitement is in thy bones, but do what you most want to do." Robin felt as if he must run to meet the company, must see his father, and feel the comfort of his mother's arms about him. Yet he felt timid about facing either of them. They would find him so changed.

"If I stand beside you, my lord, they will surely know it is I. If they see me in the courtyard, they may think I am but one of the stableboys. I shall stay here."

"Come, lad," said Sir Peter. "Let us go to the window of the tower. There we can see the company cross the drawbridge, and before they have dismounted we can be back ready to welcome them in the Hall at the head of the stair."

Before leaving the Hall, Sir Peter called Denis, the page, and sent word to Lady Constance to be ready to greet the noble visitors. He and Robin went quickly up the winding stair to the turret overlooking the drawbridge. They reached it in time to hear the pounding of the hoofs on the timbers of the bridge and to see the waving banners. The handsome erect figure of Sir John de Bureford was fitting company for the noble-looking King. And there, there was Robin's lovely mother, the veil of her coif floating and mingling with that of the Queen whom she attended.

There was no time for greeting or waving. The tumult of horse and weapon made too much noise for voices to have been heard. Sir Peter grasped Robin and swung him across his back. They went swiftly back the way they had come and were standing in welcome at the head of the great staircase as the company entered.

Who spoke first or what was first said it would be hard to tell. Robin found himself bowing to kiss his mother's hand, then felt her soft arms about him.

"Robin, my Robin," she whispered, and for a moment said no more, but only held him close, as if she could not let him go. The crutches fell to the stone floor with a great clatter. Robin's father bent to pick them up, laughing to keep from showing how deeply he was moved by the sight of them.

"He is my son, too," he said, gently tugging at the mother's close-enfolding arms and holding Robin at arm's length to look into his face.

"You are grown," he said. "Your eyes no longer outrace your chin as do a child's. You've now the look of a youth!" Sir John embraced his son warmly. Nothing was said of crutches or of misshapen legs, or of ill fortune or of good.

Sir Peter spoke. "Shall we not allow our guests to retire?"

"Yes," agreed the King. "Later we shall hear news of the war's ending and how all have fared this long year. Let us go our several ways and meet again in the Hall, for we are spent with weariness and soiled with travel."

With another touch of his mother's hand, Robin left the company and went to find Brother Luke and to make himself ready for the audience.

There never was such merrymaking as took place in the Hall that Christmas Eve. Such ballads sung! Such tales told!

Branches of holly and spruce decked the Hall and filled the air with fragrance. The yule log burned on the hearth, and flaming torches filled the sconces.

The King and Queen sat enthroned in the great chairs on the dais. A tapestry was draped on the screen behind them and rich Eastern carpets beneath.

Sir Peter and Lady Constance sat at one side of the King and Queen and Sir John and Lady Maud at the other.

Robin entered the Hall with Brother Luke as he had been commanded, and at a signal came forward to stand before the dais. He wore a black velvet doublet and carried the Saxon harp on his back. As usual, D'Ath followed at his heels.

Robin felt as though the Hall were as long as London Bridge, for when he entered all was quiet, and his crutches seemed to make a great sound on the stone floor. Servants and courtiers bowed as he passed.

What was going to happen?

What had the King to say to him? Would his parents leave him and go back to London?

At last he reached the dais. The King rose and stood over

Robin, lifting from his own shoulders a chain of gold set with medallions of fine workmanship; then he spoke.

"Can you kneel, my son?" he asked.

"I can for a little time, Sire," answered Robin, "long enough to say 'Our Father'." He dropped to the cushion, supporting himself with one crutch. The friar took the other.

"Robin, son of Sir John de Bureford," the King said solemnly, "it hath been told to us what service you have done for the lord of this castle and me, King of the whole realm of England and France. You are a true son of a noble father. Though but a youth, you have shown courage a man might be proud to call his own."

The King spread out the jeweled collar and dropped it onto Robin's shoulders, saying, "This shall be a token of our high regard and with it go our grateful thanks.

"Rise, young Robin," he commanded, and himself raised Robin to his feet.

Robin was filled with gratitude to the King, because now his father could be proud of him. He could not speak for a moment, and indeed knew nothing to say. But cheers and hand clapping began to make such a noise and clatter that no speech could have been heard.

When the noise had quieted a little, Robin was quieter, too. He remembered the carol he had been learning for this very night, and words came to him.

"Sire," Robin began, "I do thank you for this great honor, and I beg you to accept my song of Christmas." He brought forward the little harp he had grown to love and sang this carol:

> Come to Bethlehem and see
> Him whose birth the angels sing;
> Come, adore on bended knee,
> Christ the Lord, the new-born King.
> Gloria in excelsis Deo
> Gloria in excelsis Deo.

When the song was ended, once more the Hall rang with

shouts and cheers. "Sir Robin! Sir Robin!" Robin found himself standing between his mother and his father. Sir Robin. Was it *he?*

"Sir," he addressed his father, "mind you not that I must go thus, bent over, and with these crutches to help me walk?" For he must know the worst at once.

Gravely Sir John answered, "The courage you have shown, the craftsmanship proven by the harp, and the spirit in your singing, all make so bright a light that I cannot see whether or no your legs are misshapen."

"As for me," said Lady Maud, slipping her arm about Robin, "what a comfort it will be to know that wars will never claim you. And you can come home, for there is now no need for you to stay here at Lindsay. Nor is there further need for me to be with the Queen. She is now in good health. When the Feast of Christmas is over, we shall all go home to London. Brother Luke shall come with us to be your tutor, if he will."

When the midnight office was said in the church, the whole household trooped back to the Hall, where tables were spread for the feast. Platters were heaped with food and carried in by pages and esquires. A giant boar's head came first in order, then pasties and whole suckling pigs, pigeons and geese roasted with feathers on. The meats were followed by flaming puddings and bowls of wassail, chestnuts, and apples.

D'Ath and the other hounds feasted, too, for all the scraps were thrown into the rushes on the floor.

It was nearly dawn when Robin felt himself lifted onto Brother Luke's back, for he had fallen asleep.

"Where am I?" he asked in bewilderment. "What has happened?"

"Thou'rt here, Sir Robin," said the friar. "Safe with all thy loved ones. 'Tis the Feast of Christmas, and thou hast found the door in thy wall."

51

Laura Benét

THE BOX A BEE CREPT IN

ILLUSTRATED BY *Marie Lawson*

JOANNA'S eyes opened suddenly and sharply. It was time; there was plenty for her to do. She was her father's son, the only messenger boy he had, and bent on an important errand. Jumping out of bed she poured cold water from a pitcher and bathed, pulled on stockings and skirts and plaited her hair. It was October and the air was nipping; but in and about the little town of Eynesburg in Germany the trees were turning crimson and gold.

In her hurry to get down the wooden stairs to help her mother dish out porridge she stumbled and fell. "Joanna," her father was calling. "Joan." He was already in his workshop. She ran there swiftly. In the center of the room, surrounded by scraps of wood, carving tools and pots of color, sat her father wrapping up something that he held carefully upon his knees and bent over as if he could barely see it.

"Father, I am ready."

Still he did not answer but took off his spectacles, wiped them, set them on his nose again, and, finally with a long sigh, gave the thing he had been holding into her hands. It was an oblong chest carved from walnut and covered with delicate tracery and figures. The little girl wondered as she looked at it, thinking that of all her father's work it was the most choice and lovely. The colors in it were rich and deep and it was big enough to hold a heavy bunch of keys.

"Oh Father, Father, it is the prettiest of all your boxes."

"And probably the last I shall ever make," said her father sadly. "Go eat your breakfast, child! The way is long."

Joanna bobbed up and down like an excited manikin.

"And what shall I do when I reach Düsseldorf?" she asked.

52

"Master Füger will go with you and show you the way. If he cannot go, Carl will. Once in the town you will stay at your uncle's house for the night. But first deliver box and scroll at the Guild Hall in my name before you sleep."

"Shall you get the prize, my Father?"

"That is as the good God wills."

"Yes, Father, and now come to breakfast."

Joanna's heart beat fast, not only because of her important errand. Was she not going to deliver her father's work at the Guild Hall where the Count himself was to give a prize for carving? But she was taking with her something as dear. All the time she swallowed her porridge her thoughts were racing.

As far back as Joanna Lindner could remember at all, she remembered her father's workshop. The smell of the fragrant woods that took life and shape under his carving, the oil with which he rubbed them, the wonderfully fashioned pieces, the color that poured out of pots when her eager fingers knocked them over—all this beauty was far more fascinating than dolls or pets. So, instead of playing dolls, she had begged for the scraps of wood that fell under his bench and whittled them with a knife into rude doll furniture. In time she was noted in their neighborhood for the things that she could make.

Her father first taught her, and her skill grew until he was proud of it. The fingers, with which she plucked geese, thumped pillows or helped her mother stir pots, became wonderfully deft when she touched wood. This summer there had been a great red flower unfolding its petals in their little garden. The curve of the petals and their color so bewitched her that she copied it in wood. With such tools as she had and others begged from her father, she worked on a little oval box until it took on the likeness of an unfolding bud. Colored red, it held all the joy of the woods. When the light caught it, it gleamed like the flower. She had lost much sleep from her box bed with its gay quilt to finish her work.

"All my secrets are in you," she whispered at night when she shut it tight into the wall cupboard.

Carl helped. Carl Muller was her friend, and they played

53

and squabbled together in and out of school. "Carl, wilt not make me a key for my box?" she asked one day.

"How do you not know, Joan, that I'll not set a mouse to gnaw a hole out of your precious box? That will make the key fit all the easier," he teased.

She boxed his ears and ran away down the street. But in spite of his red ears he ran after her and overtook her. "Joan, wait, just wait!" he called good-naturedly. "As sure as my father is the best silversmith hereabouts, I'll make you the finest key in Eynesburg!"

Carl's father had stronger eyes than Joanna's, though he did do such fine work on watches and bracelets and rings, and Carl had been taught by him. The thought that her father's eyes were dimming made Joanna very sad. He needed so much to win the Count's prize and receive a badge naming him as the best woodcarver and painter in the countryside. Many carvings he had made of late were good enough; but the color was put on unevenly and uncertainly. On the chest she had seen this morning, however, the color was clear and strong like a last flare of sunset.

And Carl had made the key for her box! When he brought it back, she had dragged him up to her room. "Hide it, hide it! Oh, Carl, where didst think of a *bee*?"

Carl flushed with pleasure. "See, Joan, he nibbles at the flower," he said, setting the box on the table. Into the center of a petal he had fitted an ingenious little lock, the scutcheon of which was shaped exactly like a bee—and the key that went into it was like the sharp sting.

Taking his hand, she said, "I'll tell you another secret, Carl," and she talked softly into the very ear she had boxed so hard a few days before. "I shall carry my box to the shop that the pretty girl keeps on the Street of the Lindens in Düsseldorf. She will sell it for me. Then I can buy Father a new pair of spectacles."

"Spectacles? To see colors as well as you see them? Pff!" said Carl, scoffing. "Your father's eyes are too old. He will never see better than he does now."

54

"But he is master carver in Eynesburg and all the neighbors know it," flashed his daughter.

"Now did I say that he was not?" answered Carl. "Be not such a pepper pot, Joan."

And so the box was made, ready to go with Master Lindner's chest to Düsseldorf.

Master Füger had rheumatism in his feet. It was Carl after all who was to go with her, and the two plodded along the road in the autumn sunlight, swinging between them a covered basket holding the walnut chest. Nestled beside it under covering was the red box—the flower box with the bee sleeping in it. Joan had smuggled it in at the last minute beside their lunch of bread and cheese, cakes and milk.

The forest paths were lonely and the children had been told to keep to the road. "Maybe, Joan," said Carl with the caution of eleven years, "some wagon going to town for the festival will pick us up. 'Tis only five miles."

But either the travelers were too intent on their own business or thought that two children and a heavy basket would be a needless load, for men on horseback clattered past, carts rattled by, and nags in cart shafts snorted, yet none thought of saving two pairs of short and weary legs. Tired and hungry, Carl and Joanna began to nibble at the luncheon as they sat by the roadside and watched the birds.

A galloping sound came along the highway. A red-faced farmer driving a pair of strong horses was almost upon them before they could scramble aside to avoid being kicked. Over went the basket as a large dog smelt sausage.

"Oh, Father's chest will have its vines knocked off and my box will be broken in two," shrieked Joanna. But the cart's owner stopped the horses.

"Wilt ride to Düsseldorf with the grain sacks, if there it be that you are going?" he said with a broad smile. "But be quick."

The chest of the master carver was put back into the basket and handed to the driver; then he and Carl swung Joanna up between them to a snug, empty corner between the huge sacks. Carl took a flying leap and landed beside her. In their bustle

and hurry they did not notice that Joanna's cherished box lay
unseen on the grass, having rolled out of its nesting place.
The man cracked his whip, the horses trotted, Carl put his
arm about his friend to steady her, and her head nodded to the
tune he whistled. As she dozed and woke and dozed again, she
heard the farmer say,

"Art going to the Guild Hall, boy? I hear tell of much
bidding for a box, a fine box to hold the keys of the city
when the Count comes tomorrow."

The keys of the city! What did that mean?

"Wake up, Joan! Here we are!" said Carl's excited voice. The
cart stood in front of a great building and dark was falling.

As they climbed down awkwardly and thanked the farmer, a porter at the door laid a large, firm hand on Carl's shoulder.

"Only those may enter who submit their work as craftsmen," he said, puffing.

Carl spoke up, stoutly. "We be the son and daughter of craftsmen. My father is Master Muller, the silversmith, and she is the daughter of Master Lindner of Eynesburg whose work we bring."

And Joanna took from her blouse her father's scroll. The clouds cleared from the porter's face. "Go forward to the hall— in front there." He pointed.

The crowd was thick as flies on a hot, rainy day. Clinging to each other and to the big, much jostled basket, Carl and Joanna at last reached the end of the hall. Here a sharp-faced man in a robe trimmed with fur stood on guard by a table where were heaped carved articles of every kind and color. In spite of their beauty he looked sour and cross. Carl again made his little speech. Drawing the basket toward him, the official, saying nothing, lifted out the walnut chest, took the scroll that Joan, even in her fright, did not forget to give him, and slammed back the empty basket.

"Come, let us be quick. I'm so hungry. Aren't you?" cried Carl, boylike and ready to dash out of a side door. But at that minute, Joan remembered her box. She opened and peered into the basket, her spirits sinking. In a flutter she ran back to the great table where the gruff guard stood.

"My own box, my little box! Good sir, let me look inside my father's chest for it."

"Canst not," said the guard sternly. "All work once given is under the seal of the city's protection."

"Oh, but I must. What can have happened to it? Oh, Carl, what shall we do?"

A group of three or four competitors came crowding up to the table, pushed Joanna to one side, and drowned out her cry completely. Carl sensibly led her away, and they took the street that led to her uncle's. She said not a word but cried all the way, big salt, silent tears. "Oh, my box, my box that I loved so much with its key and lock like the bee," every one of her sobs said.

"Tell your uncle. He will think of something to do."

"No, no."

Joanna's aunt and uncle thought the two children looked tired and set them down to a fine supper.

"Tomorrow you shall see the great procession, Joan," said her kind aunt, wondering at her tear-stained face. "The Count will ride in it and before the prize is given, the Burgomaster and men of the town will welcome him at the city gate and ride back with him. At the Guild Hall they will give him the keys of the city on a satin cushion."

"But wherefore?" faltered the little girl.

"To show him that Düsseldorf and all that is in it are his to take," answered her uncle shortly, stroking his beard.

But Carl was so excited in hearing about the trappings that the horses would wear that she said no more about the lost box. But that night she cried herself to sleep. Next morning she whispered of it to her aunt and was told, "Your uncle will help you, Joan; only wait until today is over."

"If it is lost, lost, I cannot sell it in the Street of the Lindens."

"Dear child, it is gone, no doubt—picked up by some passing peddler. Thou must have left it by the roadside."

In a flash it came to Joanna that this was what had happened. The whole gorgeous pageant of the day was spoiled for her. But her uncle's household and all the city were gay and bustling. Since her uncle was a merchant he secured a window in one of his warehouses, looking out on the square in front of the Guild Hall. Speeches were to be made there when the Count and his train rode in. Clomp-clomp went the feet of the horses, clatter, clatter over the cobblestones. To and fro in the morning sun and wind waved the banners. The plumes and brocade in the costumes of the Count's men shone like mirrors, almost throwing sparks, as they came on in stately fashion from the great gate, with a guard of honor of the first citizens riding beside them. On to the square where the Burgomaster and aldermen waited for their prince.

58

In spite of his splendor Joanna thought the Count looked very tired, more tired than her father. Seated in the canopied chair that had been placed for him, he listened to the fine words of the Burgomaster's speech without any interest. At last a horn blew and a page boy came bearing something on a cushion. Kneeling before the Count he spoke. Joanna peeped to see what it was that he held and listened to the words that dropped slowly from his lips.

"May it please your Highness to accept the keys of your fair city of Düsseldorf and the box in which we offer them—the work of Master Lindner of Eynesburg."

Joanna's heart came up in her throat. As the Count bowed and took the chest in his hands, she knew it indeed to be her father's. Would it win the prize? Her beating heart nearly choked her. Then she saw the Count as he held it gently, turn it over and examine it from every side. "It is beautiful," he said aloud. "Beautiful and cunningly made and by a master hand. But I would, good friends, that I knew who fashioned this tiny box? One of my men picked it up, caught in a bush it was, and shaped like a flower in which the bee nestles. It hath greatly taken my fancy!"

59

He put his hand to the wallet at his side and drew out—none other than her red box. "Who can have dropped such a dainty thing?" he asked, when a voice rang out from the warehouse:

"That box is *mine!* I made it, please your Grace," added poor Joanna hastily, seeing scandalized looks on the faces of her aunt and uncle and the nobles and the Burgomaster. "And my friend Carl, here, made the key."

"So." The Count looked up to the window sill of the warehouse, found her shining truthful face and seemed delighted. "So, this key, beelike, supped honey from thy box. What is thy name, small one?"

"Joanna, your Grace, daughter of Master Lindner of Eynesburg."

"Like father, like daughter," said the Count. "Lift her down, my men, and bring her to me and the boy likewise."

Soon both children knelt before the Count and, seeing his eyes twinkle, were not one bit afraid. He held up the box.

"It is this little bee in the flower of wood that flew to me for safety when none saw it," he said kindly. "I like it well. Wilt give it to me, Joanna for a five mark piece?"

"Oh, my lord, of course," she stammered, "with no pay."

"Couldst do naught to thy liking with five marks?"

"Yes, your Grace. Buy my father a pair of spectacles that he may work the better."

The Count laughed. "Carl, what wilt *thou* do with the money?" he said, thrusting his hand into his wallet.

"Be apprenticed, straightway, your Grace."

The Count handed each of them a heavy gold piece of five marks. As she took it wonderingly, Joanna stammered, "But—is not—should not my father receive this for the prize, your Grace?" and her words were sad.

A great guffaw rose from the crowd and much muttering, but the Count put up his hand and answered simply, "There is honey of goodness in your heart, my Joanna. Have no fear, for your father shall be rewarded. But this little box that a bee has slept in shall be close to *my* heart while I live!"

60

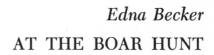

Edna Becker

AT THE BOAR HUNT

ILLUSTRATED BY *Keith Ward*

HUGH and Denis were hunting frogs in the moat which ran along in front of the castle. Hugh thought frog hunting almost too childish a sport for him, but Denis, six years his junior, had begged so hard that finally Hugh had yielded and gone with him. It really wasn't such bad sport after all, Hugh thought, if one pretended one was a knight hurling spears at a foe.

All Hugh's dreams were centered on the time when he should be a knight. He pictured himself mounted on a fiery war horse—Tencendur he would call him after Charlemagne's great charger—dressed in shining mail, and carrying a shield with some symbol blazoned on it—a red lion, probably.

In a few years, he would be sent to the castle of some nobleman—probably the Count of Perseigne's—to receive his knightly training. The Count of Perseigne and Hugh's father were old friends; they had been companions in arms years ago. Each of them kept several nobly-born lads to be their squires, as was the custom, training them for knighthood.

Long ago, when Hugh was still a little boy, this count had spoken to Hugh's father, Sire Francois, Count of St. Bernon, about having Hugh come to be his squire when he reached the proper age—from fourteen to sixteen years. He would be fourteen in a short time, and he was eager to begin his training, for the sooner he started, the sooner he would be knighted, and that was what he lived for. Although he was a stalwart lad,

61

tall and strong for his age, his father said he must wait another year or two.

Hugh chafed under the thought—a great boy like him waiting that long. It was ridiculous! If only he could do something to prove to his father that he should go now. He felt sure he could perform his duties; he knew quite well what they would be.

At first he would carry his master's shield, lance, and sword to learn how to handle them. Later when he had arms and a suit of mail of his own, his training in the tiltyard would begin. There he would learn to hold his lance steady while his horse was going at full gallop and to strike the point fairly at the shield of the quintain, the quintain being a manikin dressed in armor and mounted on a post. When he had mastered quintain, he would meet an actual opponent. Then he would try to strike his lance so hard against his opponent's shield that either the lance splintered or the opponent was thrown from the saddle. At the same time he must keep his own body covered with his shield to avoid a fatal blow himself.

Further than this, he must constantly attend his master, assist him to dress, wait on him at table, care for his horse, and stand on the edge of the lists at tournaments, ready to rush in and drag him from under the trampling hoofs, should he be unhorsed.

Hugh knew that it would be hard work, but he felt sure he would be repaid when on that glad day he could say to his master, "Fair Sire, I demand of you knighthood!" He hurled his spear at a frog. If only he could prove himself in some way, so that his father would let him go as soon as he was fourteen.

When the two boys had hunted up and down the moat several times they found the frogs had grown wary, and decided to go out to the lists to see if the knights were tilting. On the way they stopped at the falconry to see their hawks. Hugh had a goshawk and Denis a smaller sparrow hawk. Denis had ridden in several hawk hunts with his sparrow hawk sitting hooded on his wrist. He knew just how to hold it so that the motion

KEITH WARD

of the horse did not bother it and how to remove the hood at the proper time to allow the hawk to fly up after the game.

After watching the head falconer for a time teaching a bird to strike at a dummy, they wandered on toward the lists. Hearing the clash of arms every little while, they decided that the knights must be tilting and were disappointed when

they found it was only the squires playing at quintain. But their father, Sire Francois, was instructing them, and it would be fun to watch, they thought.

The squires were still deep in the game when a horseman came galloping down the road. He pulled up his horse at the lists and hailed Sire Francois. Hugh and Denis pressed closer to hear what he was saying and were as excited as anyone when they learned that a wild boar, the largest and fiercest heard of for a long time, had been seen in the forest beyond the river, and that a hunt was being organized for the morrow. Would St. Bernon join the chase?

Would they join? Sire Francois was overjoyed at the prospect of a good hunt. An air of excitement hung over the castle that evening. Weapons were sharpened and hunting horns taken down. Sire Francois was so excited himself that he could scarcely settle down to his customary game of chess. He was trying to concentrate on his next move when Denis came and stood beside him.

After a bit, he said, "May I ride in the hunt tomorrow, Father?"

Sire Francois eyed him gravely. "Another year before you ride after the hounds. Such a hunt is too fast for a seven-year-old boy."

Denis had ridden ever since he was a wee fellow and was an excellent little horseman. He wanted to ride in the hunt so badly that he stammered, "I rode well in the last hunt with the hawks. I—I think I could follow the hounds."

"You rode well, it is true, little Denis, but a hunt with the hounds is a much faster hunt than one with the hawks. Another year or two and you shall go."

Denis' eyes filled with tears, but he bit his lip manfully. He knew if he said more it might anger his father, and he might not allow him to ride in the next hawk hunt. Hugh, who was playing chess with his father, knew how badly Denis wanted to go. It had not been very many years since he himself had entreated vainly. He saw Denis' trembling lip and wished suddenly that he could make it possible for his brother to ride along.

After a moment's thought he said, "May my brother go if I ride beside him and drop behind with him when the hunt becomes too fast?"

After a little consideration, his father said, "You have always been trustworthy, my son, and if you promise to look out for your brother and drop behind with him, he may go."

The bright sun of a May morning never beamed more brightly than did Denis' face when he heard his father's words. To be allowed to ride in a real hunt after the hounds!

The next morning the castle was astir long before day-break. Horses were saddled; weapons which escaped the eye the night before were found. The horses were brought to the courtyard just as the sun was rising. After the hunters were mounted there was much riding about before they were finally ready to start.

Each hunter was armed with knife, spear, and bow and arrows. The more important members of the party had horns. Sire Francois' horn was a beautiful thing, made of ivory and chased with gold. It swung from his neck on a cord of bright red silk. Neither Hugh nor Denis had horns, but Hugh had a boar-spear and a knife, and Denis clutched his frog-spear.

Horses neighed and stamped in their eagerness to be off; dogs strained at their leashes. The hunters were but little less excited than the horses and dogs—that is, all except Denis; he was more so. He looked very small sitting on the back of his big long-legged horse. It was a great day for him—always before he had ridden his small horse—and the fact that the horse on which he sat was so old that the others disdained to use it mattered not at all to him. He felt that he was a real hunter on a real horse.

At last they were off. They swept out of the courtyard, through the bailey, past the lists and exercise grounds, and off across the fields. It took several hours to reach the forest where the boar had been seen—in fact it was almost noon before they were near enough to unleash part of the dogs.

Free at last, the dogs tore away and before long began raising an uproar in the forest. The hunters hurried to the spot and saw that the dogs had found the boar's tracks. Sire Francois unleashed his best bloodhound and set him on the trail. The dog bounded away, nose to the ground, and with him the dogs which had been loosed before. The hunters followed the dogs through thicket and bramble, and in this mad chase many of them became separated. Now and then they met hunters from other houses who were also trying to follow the boar to its lair.

Denis was growing tired. It seemed to him that they had ridden for a long, long time. They had become separated from the main hunt and were riding aimlessly along, eight or nine of them together. Denis wished he had known the hunt was going to be like this and thought he would not have wanted to come so badly if he had. Frog hunting seemed a very desirable sport just then. He ate the food he had brought and felt a little better for a while.

The little party kept together and rode till mid-afternoon without finding any of the others. While they were crossing a big open space, the wind changed suddenly, and they heard, very faintly, the bloodhound's heavy baying. The hunters began riding furiously and kept urging their horses on to greater speed. Hugh and Denis happened to be riding near the head of the party. Hugh noticed that Denis was drooping in the saddle and guessed that he was weary. When the others began

66

digging in their spurs, Hugh motioned for Denis to fall behind, for he knew that from then on the riding would be furious.

Denis, only too glad to do so, pulled on the reins, but the old hunter, hearing the dogs, and seeing the other racing horses, had gone mad with excitement. Fired with the chase, he paid no attention to his little rider; laying back his ears, and stretching out his neck, he ran for all that was in him. Denis sawed on the reins, but the horse took the bit in his teeth and dashed away at a speed that no one would have thought he could attain. Denis yanked desperately. He was pulling with all his strength, when suddenly, with a jerk that almost flung him from the saddle, one of the reins broke. Terrified, he clutched the horse's mane.

When Hugh saw what had happened, a chill swept through him. What could he do? None of the others saw Denis' plight, so engrossed were they in the chase. Shouting was useless, for they would only think he was urging his horse to greater speed; they could not possibly have heard what he said over the thunder of hoofs.

Denis was clinging to his horse's mane with both hands now; one foot was almost out of the stirrup. Hugh saw that if anything was going to be done, he must do it and do it quickly. He jabbed in his spurs, and his horse pressed ahead. Bit by bit he gained, but it was slow progress, for Denis' horse was doing his best.

If Denis fell while going at that pace, he would surely be injured, should he escape being trampled by the horses behind him. Hugh beat his horse with his spear. Speed! Speed! Now he was only a head behind. Denis' foot was out of the stirrup, and he was clinging desperately to the horse's neck.

By this time some of the others had noticed what had happened, but they were not near enough to do anything, and, going at such a mad pace, there was little chance of their overtaking Hugh.

Denis was doing all he could, but he could not hold on much longer. He began slipping. Hugh reached for him, but it was too far. He tried again, and as he did so, the rider behind gave Hugh's horse a stinging cut across the flanks. As he leaped ahead, Hugh leaned far out of the saddle and reached for Denis once more, but how he ever caught the chubby seven-year-old and swung him into his own saddle, nobody knows, but he did it. It seemed like a miracle.

Hugh pulled his panting horse to a walk. Several of the others slowed down also and came to help quiet Denis, who was clinging to his brother and sobbing wildly. Hugh's own face was white and drawn, and his heart was hammering, but . . . he had saved Denis.

When they had recovered a bit, they rode on into the forest which now resounded with shouts and blasts from hunting horns. They had no trouble in finding the others, who greeted them with a great shout. Sire Francois had been much alarmed when the advance party dashed up and with them Denis' horse, riderless, until he was told that the lad was with his brother. He did not wait to hear the details, for he had just slain the boar and was in a fever of excitement.

When the newcomers had heard about the slaying of the boar, one of them told how Hugh had saved Denis, ending, "The lad has strength in his arms; he will make a mighty knight."

In all his life, Hugh had not been as happy as he was when his father laid his arm across his shoulders, and said, "I am proud of you, my son. Ask a favor and it shall be granted."

Hugh knew his father meant something like a new horse, another falcon, or a bow and arrow, but seeing that the moment was propitious, and that his father was in a generous mood, he said, "Let me go to Perseigne and begin my knightly training on my next birthday."

Sire Francois let out a great roar of laughter which was taken up by the crowd. "Granted!" he shouted. "You have proved yourself worthy." And the forest rang with shouts of congratulation.

NICK ATTWOOD was fortunate to have been born in the days of William Shakespeare and Queen Elizabeth, for that was England's Golden Age, and all manner of adventures and exciting experiences were possible then.

Eleven-year-old Nick, a gallant lad with yellow hair and a beautiful singing voice, runs away from home only to be kidnapped by a band of strolling players. He tries to escape many times without success and is finally taken to London. There Nick is placed under the care of Master Nathaniel Gyles, head of the Cathedral schools of acting and music, who trains Nick's beautiful voice. Nick's best friend in this school is Colley Warren, a quiet, dark-eyed lad, with a voice as beautiful as Nick's own. When Queen Elizabeth invites the boys to sing on Christmas day at court they are filled with joy.

John Bennett

A GIFT FROM THE QUEEN

ILLUSTRATED BY *Reginald Birch and Frances Eckart*

CHRISTMAS morning came and went as if on swallow-wings, in a gale of royal merriment. Four hundred sat to dinner that day in Greenwich halls, and all the palace streamed with banners and green garlands.

Within the courtyard two hundred horses neighed and stamped around a water fountain playing in a bowl of ice and evergreen. Grooms and pages, hostlers and dames, went hurry-scurrying to-and-fro; cooks, bakers, and scullions steamed about, leaving hot, mouth-watering streaks of fra-

69

grance in the air; bluff men-at-arms went whistling here and there; and serving-maids with rosy cheeks ran breathlessly up and down the winding stairways.

The palace stirred like a mighty pot that boils to its utmost verge, for the hour of the revelries was come.

Over the beech-wood and far across the black heath, the wind trembled with the boom of the castle bell. Within the walls of the palace its clang was muffled by a sound of voices that rose and fell like the wind upon the sea.

The ambassadors of Venice and France were there, with their courtly trains. The Lord High Constable of England was come to sit below the Queen. The earls, too, of Southampton, Montgomery, Pembroke, and Huntington were there; and William Cecil, Lord Burleigh, the Queen's High Treasurer, to smooth his care-lined forehead with a Yuletide jest.

Up from the entry ports came shouts of "Room! room! room for my Lord Strange! Room for the Duke of Devonshire!" and about the outer gates there was a tumult like the cheering of a great crowd.

The palace corridors were lined with guards, the same guards who had marched the boys in the day before . . . Gentlemen pensioners under arms went flashing to-and-fro. Now and then through the inner throng some handsome page with wind-blown hair and rainbow-colored cloak pushed to the great door, calling: "Way, sirs, way for my Lord—way for my Lady of Alderstone!" and one by one, or in blithe groups, the courtiers, clad in silks and satins, velvets, jewels, and lace of gold, came up through the lofty folding-doors to their places in the hall.

There, where the Usher of the Black Rod stood, and the gentlemen of the chamber came and went with golden chains about their necks, was bowing and scraping without stint, and reverent civility; for men that were wise and noble were passing by, men that were handsome and brave; and ladies sweet as a summer day, and as fair to see as spring, laughed by their sides and chatted behind their fans, or daintily nibbled comfits, lacking anything to say.

70

"Master Skylark, thou shalt have thy wish," said Queen Elizabeth

The windows were all curtained in, making a night-time in midday; and from the walls and galleries flaring links and great bouquets of candles threw an eddying flood of yellow light across the stirring scene. From clump to clump of banner-staves and burnished arms, spiked above the wainscot, garlands of red-berried holly, spruce, and mistletoe were twined across the tapestry, till the room was bound about with a chain of living green.

There were sweet odors floating through the air, and hazy threads of fragrant smoke from perfumes burning in rich braziers; and under foot was the crisp, clean rustle of new rushes.

From time to time, above the hum of voices, came the sound of music from a room beyond—cornets and flutes, fifes, lutes, and harps, with an organ exquisitely played, and voices singing to it; and from behind the players' curtain, swaying slowly on its rings at the back of the stage, came a murmur of whispering childish voices, now high in eager questioning, now low, rehearsing some doubtful fragment of a song.

Behind the curtain it was dark—not total darkness, but twilight; for a dull glow came down overhead from the lights in the hall without, and faint yellow bars went up and down the dusk from crevices in the screen. The boys stood here and there in nervous groups. Now and then a sharp complaint was heard from the tire-woman when an impatient lad would not stand still to be dressed.

Master Gyles went to-and-fro, twisting the manuscript of the Revel in his hands, or pausing kindly to pat some faltering lad upon the back. Nick and Colley were peeping by turns through a hole in the screen at the throng in the audience-chamber.

They could see a confusion of fans, jewels, and faces, and now and again could hear a burst of subdued laughter over the steadily increasing buzz of voices. Then from the gallery above, all at once there came a murmur of instruments tuning together; a voice in the corridor was heard calling, "Way here, way here!" in masterful tones; the tall folding-doors at the

71

side of the hall swung wide, and eight dapper pages in white and gold came in with the Master of Revels. After them came fifty ladies and noblemen clad in white and gold, and a guard of gentlemen pensioners with glittering halberds.

There was a sharp rustle. Every head in the audience-chamber louted low. Nick's heart gave a jump—for the Queen was there!

She came with an air that was at once serious and royal, bearing herself haughtily, yet with a certain grace and sprightliness that became her very well. She was quite tall and well made, and her quickly changing face was long and fair, though wrinkled and no longer young. Her complexion was clear and of an olive hue; her nose was a little hooked; her firm lips were thin; and her small black eyes, though keen and bright, were pleasant and merry withal. Her hair was a coppery, tawny red, and false, moreover. In her ears hung two great pearls; and there was a fine small crown studded with diamonds upon her head, beside a necklace of exceeding fine gold and jewels about her neck. She was attired in a white silk gown bordered with pearls the size of beans, and over it wore a mantle of black silk, cunningly shot with silver threads. Her ruff was vast, her farthingale vaster; and her train, which was very long, was borne by a marchioness who made more ado about it than Elizabeth did of ruling her realm.

"The Queen!" gasped Colley.

"Dost think I did na know it?" answered Nick, his heart beginning to beat tattoo as he stared through the peep-hole in the screen.

He saw the great folk bowing like a garden full of flowers in a storm, and in its midst Elizabeth erect, speaking to those about her in a lively and good-humored way, and addressing all the foreigners according to their tongue—in French, Italian, Spanish, Dutch; but hers was funny Dutch, and while she spoke she smiled and made a joke upon it in Latin, at which they all laughed heartily, whether they understood what it meant or not. Then, with her ladies in waiting, she passed to a dais near the stage and stood a moment, stately, fair, and proud, while all her nobles made obeisance, then sat and gave a signal for the players to begin.

"Rafe Fullerton!" the prompter whispered shrilly; and out from behind the screen slipped Rafe, the smallest of them all, and down the stage to speak the foreword of the piece. He was frightened, and his voice shook as he spoke, but everyone was smiling, so he took new heart.

"It is a masque of Summertime and Spring," said he "wherein both claim to be best-loved, and have their say of wit and humor, and each her part of songs and dances suited to her time, the sprightly galliard and the nimble jig for Spring, the slow pavone, the stately peacock dance, for Summertime. And win who may, fair Summertime or merry Spring, the winner is but that beside our Queen!"—with which he snapped his fingers in the faces of them all—"God save Queen Bess!"

At that the Queen's eyes twinkled, and she nodded, highly pleased, so that everyone clapped mightily.

The play soon ran its course amid great laughter and applause. Spring won. The English ever loved her best, and the quick-paced galliard took their fancy, too. "Up and be doing!" was its tune, and it gave one a chance to cut fine capers with his heels.

Then the stage stood empty, and the music stopped.

At this strange end a whisper of surprise ran through the hall. The Queen tapped with the inner side of her rings upon the broad arm of her chair. From the look on her face she was whetting her tongue. But before she could speak, Nick and Colley, dressed as a farmer boy and girl, with a garland of house-grown flowers about them, came down the stage from the arras, hand in hand, bowing.

The audience-chamber grew very still—*this* was something new. Nick felt a swallowing in his throat, and Colley's hand winced in his grip. There was no sound but a silky rustling in the room.

Then suddenly the boys behind the players' curtain laughed together, not loud, but such a jolly little laugh that all the people smiled to hear it. After the laughter came a hush.

73

Then the pipes overhead made a merry sound as of shepherds piping on oaten straws in new grass where there are daisies; and there was a little elfish laughter of clarionets, and a fluttering among the cool flutes like spring wind blowing through crisp young leaves in April. The harps began to pulse and throb with a soft cadence like raindrops falling into a clear pool where brown leaves lie upon the bottom and bubbles float above green stones and smooth white pebbles. Nick lifted up his head and sang.

It was a happy little song of the coming and the triumph of the spring. The words were all forgotten long ago. They were not much: enough to serve the turn, no more; but the notes to which they went were like barn swallows twittering under the eaves, goldfinches clinking in purple weeds beside old roads, and robins singing in common gardens at dawn. And wherever Nick's voice ran, Colley's followed, the pipes laughing after them a note or two below; while the flutes kept gurgling softly to themselves as a hill brook gurgles through the woods, and the harps ran gently up and down like rain among the daffodils. One voice called, the other answered; there were echolike refrains; and as they sang Nick's heart grew full. He cared not a stiver for the crowd, the golden palace, or the great folk there—the Queen no more—he only listened for Colley's voice coming up lovingly after his own and running away when he followed it down, like a lad and a lass through the bloom of the May. And Colley was singing as if his heart would leap out of his round mouth for joy to follow after the song they sung, till they came to the end and the skylark's song.

There Colley ceased, and Nick went singing on alone, forgetting, caring for, heeding nought but the song that was in his throat.

The Queen's fan dropped from her hand upon the floor. No one saw it or picked it up. The Venetian ambassador scarcely breathed.

Nick came down the stage, his hands before him, lifted as if he saw the very lark he followed with his song, up, up, up

74

into the sun. His cheeks were flushed and his eyes were wet, though his voice was a song and a laugh in one.

Then they were gone behind the curtain, into the shadow and the twilight there, Colley with his arms about Nick's neck, not quite laughing, not quite sobbing. The manuscript of the Revel lay torn in two upon the floor, and Master Gyles had a foot upon each piece.

In the hall beyond the curtain was a silence that was deeper than a hush, a stillness rising from the hearts of men.

Then Elizabeth turned in the chair where she sat. Her eyes

were as bright as a blaze. And out of the sides of her eyes she looked at the Venetian ambassador. He was sitting far out on the edge of his chair, and his lips had fallen apart. She laughed to herself. "It is a good song, signor," said she, and those about her started at the sound of her voice. "*Chi tace confessa*—it is so! There are no songs like English songs—there is no spring like an English spring—there is no land like England, *my* England!" She clapped her hands. "I will speak with those lads," said she.

Straightway certain pages ran through the press and came behind the curtain where Nick and Colley stood together, still trembling with the music not yet gone out of them, and brought them through the hall to where the Queen sat, everyone whispering, "Look!" as they passed.

On the dais they knelt together, bowing, side by side. Elizabeth, with a kindly smile, leaning a little forward, raised them with her slender hand. "Stand, dear lads," said she, heartily. "Be lifted up by thine own singing, as our hearts have been uplifted by thy song. And name me the price of that same song—'twas sweeter than the sweetest song we ever heard before."

"Or ever shall hear again," said the Venetian ambassador, under his breath, rubbing his forehead as if just wakening out of a dream.

"Come," said Elizabeth, tapping Colley's cheek with her fan, "what wilt thou have of me, fair maid?"

Colley turned red, then very pale. "That I may stay in the palace forever and sing for your Majesty," said he. His fingers shivered in Nick's.

"Now that is right prettily asked," she cried, and was well pleased. "Thou shalt indeed stay for a singing page in our household—a voice and a face like thine are merry things upon a rainy Monday. And thou, Master Lark," said she, fanning the hair back from Nick's forehead with her perfumed fan—"thou that comest up out of the field with a song like the angels sing—what wilt thou have: that thou mayst sing in our choir and play on the lute for us?"

Nick looked up at the torches on the wall, drawing a deep, long breath. When he looked down again his eyes were dazzled, and he could not see the Queen.

"What wilt thou have?" he heard her ask.

"Let me go home," said he.

There were red and green spots in the air. He tried to count them, since he could see nothing else, and everything was very still; but they all ran into one purple spot which came and went like a firefly's glow, and in the middle of the purple spot he saw the Queen's face coming and going.

"Surely, boy, that is an ill-considered speech," said she, "or thou dost deem us very poor, or most exceeding stingy!" Nick hung his head, for the walls seemed tapestried with staring eyes. "Or else this home of thine must be a very famous place."

The maids of honour tittered. Further off somebody laughed. Nick looked up, and squared his shoulders.

They rubbed the cat the wrong way.

It is hard to be a stranger in a palace, young, country-bred, and laughed at all at once; but down in Nick Attwood's heart was a stubborn streak that all the flattery on earth could not cajole nor ridicule efface. He might be simple, shy, and slow, but what he loved he loved: that much he knew: and when they laughed at him for loving home they seemed to mock not him, but home—and *that* touched the fighting-spot.

"I would rather be there than here," said he.

The Queen's face flushed. "Thou art more curt than courteous," said she. "Is it not good enough for thee here?"

"I could na live in such a place."

The Queen's eyes snapped. "In such a place? Marry, art thou so choice? These others find no fault with the life."

"Then they be born to it," said Nick, "or they could abide no more than I—they would na fit."

"Haw, haw!" said the Lord High Constable.

The Queen shot one quick glance at him. "Old pegs have been made to fit new holes before today," said she; "and the trick can be done again." The Constable smothered the rest of that laugh in his hand. "But come, boy, speak up; what hath

77

put thee so out of conceit with our best-beloved palace?"

"There is na one thing likes me here. I can na bide in a place so fine, for there's not so much as a corner in it feels like home. I could na sleep in the bed last night."

"What, how? We commanded good beds!" exclaimed Elizabeth, angrily, for the Venetian ambassador was smiling in his beard. "This shall be seen to."

"Oh, it *was* a good bed—a very good bed indeed, your Majesty!" cried Nick. "But the mattress puffed up like a cloud in a bag, and almost smothered me; and it was so soft and so hot that it gave me a fever."

Elizabeth leaned back in her chair and laughed. The Lord High Constable hastily finished the laugh that he had hidden in his hand. Everybody laughed. "Upon my word," said the Queen, "it is an odd skylark cannot sleep in feathers! What didst thou do, forsooth?"

"I slept in the coverlid on the floor," said Nick. "It was na hurt,—I dusted the place well,—and I slept like a top."

"Now verily," laughed Elizabeth, "if it be floors that thou dost desire, we have acres to spare—thou shalt have thy pick of the lot. Come, we are ill used to begging people to be favored—thou'lt stay?"

Nick shook his head.

"*Ma foi!*" exclaimed the Queen, "it is a queer fancy makes a face at such a pleasant dwelling! What is it sticks in thy throat?"

Nick stood silent. What was there to say? If he came here he never would see Stratford town again; and *this* was no abiding-place for him. They would not even let him go to the fountain himself to draw water with which to wash, but fetched it, three at a time, in a silver ewer and a copper basin with towels and a flask of perfume.

Elizabeth was tapping with her fan. "Thou art bedazzled like," she said. "Think twice—preferment does not grow gooseberry on the hedge-row every day; and this is a rare chance which hangs ripening on thy tongue. Consider well. Come, thou wilt accept?"

Nick slowly shook his head.

"Go then, if thou wilt go!" said she; and as she spoke she shrugged her shoulders, illy pleased, and turning toward Colley, took him by the hand and drew him closer to her, smiling at his guise. "Thy comrade hath more wit."

"He hath no mother," Nick said quietly, loosing his hold at last on Colley's hand. "I would rather have my mother than his wit."

Elizabeth turned sharply back. Her keen eyes were sparkling, yet soft.

"Thou art no fool," said she.

A little murmur ran through the room.

She sat a moment, silent, studying his face. "Or if thou art, upon my word I like the breed. It is a stubborn, froward dog; but Hold-fast is his name. Ay, sirs," she said, and sat up very straight, looking into the faces of her court, "Brag is a good dog, but Hold-fast is better. A lad who loves his mother thus makes a man who loveth his native land—and it's no bad streak in the blood. Master Skylark, thou shalt have thy wish; to London thou shalt go this very night."

"I do na live in London," Nick began.

"What matters the place?" said she. "Live wheresoever thine heart doth please. It is enough—so. Thou mayst kiss our hand." She held her hand out, bright with jewels. He knelt and kissed it as if it were all a doing in a dream, or in some unlikely story he had read. But a long while after he could smell the perfume from her slender fingers on his lips.

Then a page standing by him touched his arm as he arose, and bowing backward from the throne, came with him to the curtain and the rest. Old Master Gyles was standing there apart. It was too dark to see his face, but he laid his hand upon Nick's head.

"Thy cake is burned to a coal," said he.

Hitty, a doll made of lucky mountain-ash wood, who sits in the window of an antique shop, here remembers one of her most thrilling adventures. Over a hundred years ago she had sailed aboard the *Diana-Kate* with her owner, Phoebe Preble, and Captain and Mrs. Preble, to search for whales in the South Seas. Captain Preble had decided to take his family on this voyage although his sailors were against it. They felt it was unlucky to have women aboard ship. But no one could have foreseen what dangers actually lay in store for them before the return voyage.

Rachel Field

HITTY'S SHIPWRECK

ILLUSTRATED BY *Esther Friend*

I WENT with Phoebe everywhere and that is how I came to be upon such familiar terms with whales, an advantage such as few dolls can boast. Now as I sit in the antique shop and look up at the whaling print hanging over the desk, it seems strange to me that I can remember just such scenes. First there would be the thrilling cry from the lookout aloft: "There she blows!" or, more often, just "Blo—o—ows!" Then the *Diana-Kate* would become all a-bustle. Our course must be changed to bring us as near as possible to where the pale jet of water, which the whale sent up like a fountain, had been last sighted. Meantime the long-boats would be made ready to swing out at the order from Captain Preble to "lower an' fetch him." Sometimes five boats put out for the chase, more often three, the men bending briskly to their oars, as

81

they sped toward that dark-gray mound that looked as big as Huckleberry Hill at home and yet disappeared as suddenly as it had come, to rise again at an entirely different spot.

Jeremy Folger was the first to "strike" a whale, but no one begrudged him the glory, for he had to drive more than one iron into the great creature and was himself all but swept into the sea when the whale became gallied and nearly upset the long boat. It was a sperm whale of extraordinary size, such as any captain and crew might covet. All the men received shares of the oil, and so they were determined not to let such a prize escape. With Phoebe and Andy I watched the boats lowered and saw them speed away, each leaving a white trail behind. There were five rowers in each of the three and their oar blades moved like one as they pulled away from us in the strong sea sunshine.

"Greasy luck, boys!" called Captain Preble as he watched them go.

How should I, a little wooden doll, be able to tell of such things—of those boats that looked no bigger than pea pods scurrying through the water toward that enormous gray shape that appeared and disappeared so mysteriously, sending its ghostly stream of water high in air? I cannot believe that I did actually see this for myself, and yet I know that it was so. Indeed, as luck would have it, the whale made such a wide circle in its fight that it brought up near enough for us to see much of the chase. Andy pressed close to the low rail, shading his eyes with his hands as he strained to make out the figures in the longboats.

"There 'tis!" he cried, so shrilly Phoebe almost dropped me over the side in her excitement to follow his pointing forefinger. "It's white-waterin' again. See it spout! Jeremy's boat's ahead. I can tell his red 'n' white shirt."

"Where?" Phoebe hopped up and down beside him, holding me close.

"Why, there, in the bow. Watch now, he's goin' to strike in a minute!"

The oars suddenly hung poised in midair and the little slip

of a boat seemed about to vanish under the glistening dark mass above it.

In that second of time I suddenly had a sickening recollection of the picture in the illustrated Bible . . . Somehow I had not before connected that great sea creature with the whales we were to capture. Now I knew that they were one and the same, and I seemed to see poor Jeremy instead of the man in the picture being swallowed up in that awful abyss.

But next thing I knew Andy was screaming out jubilantly that Jeremy had "struck his whale."

"Now they're off for a Nantucket sleigh-ride," he told Phoebe. "That's what they call it," he explained, "when the harpoon's in fast and they can just play out the rope an' follow him round."

"But I don't see the whale anywhere now," protested Phoebe.

"He'll be up again pretty quick," Andy assured her, "he can't get very far the way they've got him hooked."

It was certainly the truth. Presently the dark shape rose from the water again, struggling and plunging this time, trying to shake himself free. His great sides showed sleek and glittering in the sun, more water spouted into the air, and the sea was churned white and swirling by the gigantic lashings of his tail. How long he dragged the boat after him, or how many times he plunged under water to reappear again with more furious wallowings, I do not know. At last, however, there were streaks of red mixed with the white foam. A cry went up from watchers aboard the *Diana-Kate*.

"Whale's gallied. It'll be fin-out soon."

Sure enough, before many more minutes the lashings grew less frequent, then they ceased altogether. The whale's great body rose a little more out of the water, then turned over slowly till a sharp black fin showed plainly. There came another shout from those on deck and still more from those in the boats.

"Well, we got him," said Captain Preble with satisfaction, as he turned to his wife. "Think maybe you could fix up somethin' extra in the grub line to celebrate?"

Next day the cutting-in began and I was to know the whale

83

still more intimately. Even after all these years I can remember how it looked stretched out at full length alongside of the ship. By the time Phoebe brought me on deck the morning after our first chase, the men were lowering a little platform upon which they stood with long hooks, knives, and other implements that looked altogether too sharp to please me. With ropes and various lines they managed to hoist the whale up, meantime having begun cutting it in such a manner that the blubber peeled off in long strips as neatly as if it had been an apple. But apple it was not as we very soon discovered once it was aboard and in the try-works. I began to wonder how there would be any whale-oil left to be stored in the casks, so much of it ran over the decks. The whole ship reeked of it. But no one paid any attention to this except Mrs. Preble, who said she had never in all her days smelled such a smell or seen such a mess of grease. The men only laughed and said this was "greasy luck!" They went their different ways—some to toil at the hoisting and cutting, others to mince the hunks of blubber into pieces for the try-pots, and still others to skim off the scraps that kept the fires going night and day.

Thick black smoke rose and hung over us amidships like a queer umbrella, while at night the light of the fires made a dull red glow. This added to the heat and oiliness aboard. The men worked continuously with only a few hours off for rest.

"Got to push it through so's we can go after another," Captain Preble explained, as he came to eat his supper a few nights later, his hands so stiff from the work of cutting-in that he could scarcely hold his knife and fork.

Even Andy was pressed into service mincing and carrying. He went about very proudly, stripped to the waist like the rest, his trousers rolled to his knees. Sometimes his face was so black from oil and smoke that his blue eyes looked very strange in the midst of it and his red hair topping it even stranger. Phoebe and I were not allowed to venture very near the try-works. Her father had been firm about this.

"Can't have you gettin' underfoot an' maybe scalded," he told her.

84

So it came about that we took our place on an old barrel-head some yards away, but near enough to watch much of the work. I was relieved we were no nearer, for I had no desire to find myself swimming in the boiling try-pots and I might easily have slipped in along with a piece of blubber.

Scarcely was one whale turned into oil before they would be off for another, and, indeed, on one occasion, when a whole school of them was sighted, they took several and towed them back to the ship. It was strange to see these enormous gray bulks anchored near by with small flags fastened to our irons to show they were our property. By this time a couple of other whaling vessels had arrived in the grounds. There was considerable rivalry among them, even though we were several miles from one another. There was talk among the men about going "gamming." One never hears that word nowadays, but then it was common enough among seafaring people. It meant paying social visits from one ship to another while at sea. All the men were anxious to do this, but Captain Preble decided that the cutting-in must be finished first. There was some grumbling over this, and some very black looks on the part of Patch, who evidently began to feel he was first in command instead of second. In his time off duty he was often to be found deep in conversation with some of the men, and from his expression I felt that no good would come of it.

It was unfortunate, therefore, that the ship we had intended signaling should sail away without hailing us before the last whale we had taken was more than a third minced and in the try-works. Words passed between the Captain and his first mate over this and before long the whole ship was divided as to which was in the right. Patch held that the men had a right to ask for leave to go gamming, while those who sided with the Captain maintained that to call a halt in the work would be to lose not only time but also perhaps considerable blubber and so in the end affect their shares of the oil. The Captain went about his duties quietly as if nothing had occurred out of the ordinary, but down in their cabin late at night I heard him talking it over with his wife.

"It's the last trip I take Patch on as mate," he told her. "He come to me so well recommended I thought I was lucky to have him along, especially with his taking on more shares in the vessel than any of the others who applied, but he's been makin' a regular nuisance of himself lately."

"Well, I ain't surprised, Dan'l," Mrs. Preble remarked. "I thought right from the start he had the meanest, shiftiest eye I ever did see. But 'twa'n't my place to pick your men."

"He's able enough," the Captain went on. "I couldn't honestly say he don't know the ropes or steer a straight course, but all I know is I'll feel pretty glad when we've struck our last whale and the casks are filled and we're headin' for the home port."

"Glad is nothin' to what I'll feel," his wife returned with a sigh.

But no one would have guessed from the Captain's manner on deck how he felt about things when he was below in his own cabin.

Mrs. Preble did her best in the galley. She scraped the sugar and molasses barrels clean to keep up a supply of cookies and gingerbread and stood ready and willing to fry up any messes of fresh fish the men might catch. Finally, however, our last and finest sperm whale was taken. All the boats had put out after it and two reached it almost at the identical moment. There was some confusion, and orders from those in command of each boat were not followed. At least this was the story we heard afterward on board the *Diana-Kate*. At all events, there was an argument as to which had struck it first, Jeremy's harpoon, or another's. Since an extra share of the oil was allowed the one whose iron first fastened itself in the whale, the men began to take sides among themselves. They neglected their work to discuss and argue, and when Captain Preble was heard to declare that neither should benefit, their dissatisfaction grew.

Still, unpleasant as this was, none of us dreamed of the danger so shortly to threaten all our lives, least of all I who had come to feel almost as secure upon this world of wood and canvas as I had in the Preble farmhouse.

I think it must have been round midnight; it was still dark, at any rate, when there came a sharp cry on deck and the quick thud of bare feet hurrying above us. Almost immediately after, we heard the call: "All hands on deck." That meant something out of the ordinary was happening, though what it might be on such a calm night in the tropic seas I could not imagine. Phoebe woke up and was all for going above, but her mother said no, they would only get in the men's way. Her father would come down to them when he could. So we three waited breathlessly in the hot, close-pressing darkness.

Then Captain Preble was at the door, his eyes red and watering.

"Dan'l, what's the matter?" cried his wife.

"The ship's afire," he told her as quietly as he could. "Must have got started down in the blubber room, the Lord knows how. I'm afraid it's spreadin', but we're doin' all we can to fight it."

"How is it now?"

" 'Mid-Midships and for'ard. 'Twon't reach here for a good while yet. We're lowerin' wet sails on the flames; sometimes that'll smother 'em, but I'm afraid it's got too much headway."

"And the vessel fairly reekin' with whale oil, too . . ." I saw Mrs. Preble cling to him suddenly as if she were no bigger than Phoebe who sat up in her bunk listening. "Oh, Dan'l, what chance have we got?"

"Well, we won't give up fightin' it 'fore we have to," he answered. "I'm not one to leave my ship till the last, but if the worst comes to the worst and we do have to take to the boats we'll make out. It's better round here than some places we could have selected. So don't you go and get gallied, Kate."

"Who says I'm goin' to?" She was her old self again. "Phoebe 'n' I'll be ready when you need us."

"Better get some things together," he cautioned her, "what you and Phoebe might need, in case—" he broke off abruptly and turned toward the door. Even in the dim light I could see how haggard and pale his face showed under his tan and the smudges of smoke. But he squared his shoulders and went above. Presently we heard his voice bellowing orders and the scurrying of feet obeying them.

Phoebe and her mother began to get into their clothes and were soon busy collecting their belongings. Mrs. Preble moved steadily to and fro from the two chests to the bunk, where she tied and retied her things into tight bundles. Phoebe, following her mother's example, collected all my things, the blue chest, the carved footstool, and my little hammock, and put them into a splint basket. After that she dressed me and laid me in beside them. She kept asking innumerable questions: Did her mother think the ship would burn up soon? Would there be room for them all in the boats? Where would they go if they left the ship? Did her mother think the men had set the blubber room afire on purpose? To all of which Mrs. Preble had to answer that she knew no more than Phoebe.

Presently Andy came down to our cabin. But he had no progress to report. In spite of all they could do, the fire was gaining on them. The wet canvas they lowered on it only made a dense, choking smoke before the flames burst out in new places.

"They all say we ain't got a chance to save her," he announced. "It's just a question of how long we can stay aboard and steer her to the best place for bein' picked up. Old Patch he thinks he knows more 'n the Captain 'bout it, an' some of the men are takin' his side."

Mrs. Preble listened to him in silence. Then she began to gather up her things.

"You take this bundle," she told him, "and come along with me. Here, Phoebe, take your things, too; if there's any trouble I don't aim to stay cooped up down here."

We found most of the crew gathered about Captain Preble and Patch, who stood arguing by the deck house with charts and maps in their hands. We waited at the top of the companionway and listened to them. Phoebe held my basket on her arm, so I had a good view of sea and sky and the familiar figures before us. A faint pink was coming into the sky, but the large tropic stars still showed pale and clear. Some of those nearest the horizon made little trails of brightness on the water, which was so smooth that the *Diana-Kate* scarcely moved at all. There was no wind to speak of, the sails barely stirred above us. We could not actually see the flames, for the smothering canvases were still down, but gray rolls of smoke curled up from between the boards and poured out in the region of the try-works. It was thick, heavy smoke that made people's eyes water and choked in their throats. Once again I found it a decided advantage to be made of wood.

I cannot recall much of what passed between the two men. Indeed, many of their words meant nothing to me, though even I could tell from their looks and tones that they were in violent disagreement. It was evident that the ship must be abandoned sooner or later; the important question had now become how to steer her remaining course so that we would find ourselves in the most likely position to be rescued by the next passing ship. The mate was set upon one direction, and Captain Preble was equally determined on the opposite one.

Nearly all the crew seemed to side with Patch, insisting that since the situation had become so desperate they had a right to take matters in their own hands and save themselves as best they could. Captain Preble was not one to give in easily. Besides, he felt strongly that there were more chances of rescue by remaining aboard the ship as long as possible and then making for some islands he found charted. But Patch claimed his islands were better. He grew more excited every moment and swore the Captain's plan was as good as murder and he would not stand by and be party to it. There were mutterings and ugly looks and it soon became clear that feeling ran too high to be overcome. Several of the men refused to go aloft or take the Captain's orders. Time was passing that should have been used to good advantage, and still the smoke curled up, blacker and heavier each time I looked. Andy complained that the deck scorched his bare feet, and Mrs. Preble kept tight hold of Phoebe's hand, though she never took her eyes away from her husband's face.

Suddenly I saw him fold the chart he had been holding. Very quietly he put it into his breast pocket before he turned to Patch again.

"Steer your own course, then," he said in a voice that was so strange I hardly knew it for his. "Take the long-boats and put off, the whole plagued lot of you. I'd rather go to the bottom, me and mine, than bicker with such a comp'ny of good-for-nothing land-lubbers. Take the longboats and go, I tell you, and it can't be too soon to suit me!"

"Oh, Dan'l," I heard his wife whisper under her breath, "what have you gone an' done?"

But she made no outcry and stood quietly in her place watching Patch and the men hurry off to lower the boats.

"Stay here by me, Kate." I heard the Captain issuing commands as if his family had been some of the crew. "You, too, Andy and Phoebe, an' you're not to move, no matter what."

We stood together in a little group by the deckhouse, as the men ran to and fro. But not all, for Jeremy, Reuben, and Bill Buckle had taken their places by Captain Preble.

91

"We're with you, sir," they had said. "We'll stand by as long's the ship can hold her beams together."

The sun came up out of the sea in a fiery ball and was well up in the heavens by the time the five boats were lowered. But this time there were no cheery calls from those aboard, no answering shouts. We watched them pull away in silence, and I saw Mrs. Preble's lips tremble as Phoebe's might just before she began to cry. They had hoisted small canvas sails in each boat and as they moved off over the water they looked like white triangles of paper against the blue.

I shall never forget that sight, or the steady grimness with which the men pulled away, with hardly a backward look. Such kindly, pleasant friends many of them had been to us, too. I have often wondered what became of them—if they fared any better than we, or if, as the Captain believed, they steered a course to certain disaster.

It would be impossible for any pen, least of all one held in the hand of a doll, to describe our next few hours or tell how we waited under a sort of makeshift canvas tent the men hoisted astern in order that we might be protected from the heat and smoke which rapidly spread to every part of the vessel. Meantime, those three and the Captain put all their strength and skill together in a desperate effort to sail us within sight of the group of islands the Captain knew must lie somewhere to the southwest. To keep a burning ship afloat, not to speak of maneuvering it in the right direction, is not exactly an easy undertaking. Captain Preble and the three kept at it as long as possible, but finally even they gave in.

"Well, Kate, get yourself and Phoebe ready," the Captain said at last, his face streaked with smoke and sweat. "We've got the stern boats yet, and Bill's below gettin' what food an' water they've left us."

A rope ladder had been let down. It swayed giddily as Jeremy clambered up and over the side.

"Mercy!" cried Phoebe's mother in dismay, "I'll never be able to go down that."

It seemed for a minute as if she were more afraid of this

92

than the fire. She looked more hopefully toward the boat that had not yet been lowered. But Jeremy explained that she would be more comfortable in the larger of the two.

"You hold right on to me, ma'am," he told her. "I'll give you a hand over the rail. Hoist your petticoats right up and don't stand on no ceremony."

The Captain now appeared to add his encouragement. So over the side she went, hand over hand, with Jeremy going first in case she should let go.

Andy and Bill Buckle now came up with some kegs of food and water to add to those already on the boats. Captain Preble had his smaller compass, a lantern, some instruments, and the log book. He looked more grave than I had ever seen him. A smear of smoke ran like a dark scar across one cheek, his eyes were red and swollen.

"Bill," he said, giving his last orders, "you 'n' Jeremy take Andy with you an' the extra stuff there in the other boat. Reuben and I'll look out for the women folks." Even in the midst of such danger I could not but be pleased to hear myself and Phoebe put in the same class with Mrs. Preble. "Keep your boat as close to ours as you can," he cautioned. "If I'm right in my reckoning we'd ought to sight one of the group 'fore dark."

During this conversation Phoebe had set me down in the basket on top of one of the large wooden kegs of salt meat, while she went to look for a piece of carved whalebone she had dropped. Her father, evidently fearing she might venture too near the danger line, went after her and, picking her up in his arms, hustled her over the side to Jeremy and hence into the boat. This all happened very quickly, in the twinkling of an eye, as the saying goes, though no eyes were in the mood to do such a thing in those last moments aboard the *Diana-Kate*. I was disappointed not to go along with Phoebe but comforted myself with the knowledge that I was upon one of the provision kegs and therefore sure to be taken on the other boat. So I waited, somewhat anxiously, I must confess, while the last preparations were being made. Once I thought I heard

Phoebe calling from below, but the others were either too busy lowering the second boat or making too much noise to hear her. I knew she must be asking for me, and this did not make me feel any easier.

I heard the Captain issuing more orders. Then Bill Buckle began stowing the things in the second boat. The next minute I expected my turn to come—but it never did. For just as he was about to return for my keg and another even larger, some one shouted to him from below that there was not a moment to spare. Flames, higher than the men were tall, suddenly began to shoot out on both sides of the try-works and to wrap themselves about the nearer mast. They waited for nothing after that. I watched them disappear over the side—boat, men and all—knowing that with them went my last hope of being saved.

It seemed impossible to believe that I had been abandoned to such a fate, and yet I saw the two boats pulling away together. I could even make out the different figures—Andy's blue shirt, Jeremy's checked in red and white, and Mrs. Preble with her best gray beaver bonnet on because she couldn't bear not to save it. Once I was sure I saw Phoebe point back toward the ship. I knew her gesture was meant for me and just for a moment hope stirred in me again. But the boats continued steadily on their way. Soon the smoke that still hung thick about the ship shut them from my sight. Now, indeed, did I feel that destruction was at hand, for what power can save even mountain-ash wood in the midst of a roaring furnace?

Furnace was what the *Diana-Kate* was fast becoming. The heat grew more intense every moment, and now flames were climbing the rigging more swiftly than any sailor had ever been able to ascend it. Terrified as I was, I remember that I could not but note how like those bright fall trees along the Portland road the masts looked, wrapped in fierce, orange flames. The roar and crackle now became almost worse than the heat. I could hear beams crashing in below and a sound that sent answering shivers down to my innermost pegs—the noise of good stout wood being destroyed. I remembered that I,

too, was wood, for all that I had been given form and fashion, so how could I hope to fare better than the rest against this common enemy?

I tried to think of all the cool and pleasant things I could—of snow sparkling on the old pine in the Preble dooryard; of lilacs and apple trees in bloom; of the spire on Meeting House Hill. I thought of the blue and white china on the pantry shelves, and of the crickets chirping through those crisp fall nights. How I envied them now, for surely it must be easier to die by freezing than to be burned to a crisp. It would have been a comfort to turn over on my back so that I need not see the fire eating its way nearer and nearer, but

Phoebe had settled me firmly in the basket. I could not move.

"Only a miracle can save me now," I said to myself.

I had heard someone say that once, but it did not seem likely that one would come to my aid. Why should a doll expect more than a ship? Still, I had been made of mountain-ash wood and the *Diana-Kate* had not. I know of no other way to account for what happened.

Just as it seemed the paint on my face would begin to sizzle, the ship gave a tremendous lurch. I suppose some of the underpinnings must have burned away. At any rate, she pitched over crazily on her side with such force that the keg on which I had been resting rolled completely over. Out of the basket I tumbled; out I flew under the rail and into the water as neatly as a pebble from a slingshot.

"Well," I remember thinking as I took the plunge, "at least I shall not be burned up. Water is kinder to wood than fire and I have heard that salt is a great preservative."

When sailors speak of dying, they say they are going to "join the fishes." I came to understand the meaning of this phrase as few before me can have done. At first, it was not so bad, for I had become entangled with some of the wreckage from the ship. Indeed, I floated about for a long time quite comfortably on a coil of rope till a particularly large wave lifted me off and rolled me over on my face. This was rather less pleasant, but I was still in no mood to be critical when I remembered my narrow escape from the flames.

Here, as I sit at my ease in the antique shop and think of those days and nights that I was tossed from wave to wave, even I find it hard to believe in my own adventures or to think that I could have known those miles of salt sea and tropic sun and stars and felt the touch of those fierce, brightly colored fishes as they came up to nibble at me. They soon gave me up, however, discovering for themselves that I was wood and not to their taste. I was in constant fear that some shark or even a whale might appear and gulp me down with a mouthful of sea water. I could still recall vividly the picture in the Bible at home, and I thought, if a man could be swal-

lowed, how much more easily I might disappear in like manner. But once again a miraculous Providence watched over me.

I think I must have become too water-soaked from days of buffetings to know what went on about me or by what devious and salty ways I came to the Island. But come I did in time along with other bits of wreckage. At any rate, I knew nothing till I found myself in the quiet waters of a rock pool. This was a deep hole worn in the coral and all manner of bright sea-weeds clung to the sides, trailing long, wavering fingers or tresses like green and scarlet hair in the clear water. Small, shelly creatures were moving about on busy missions of their own, and a huge, spiked starfish was twining about my ankle. But I was too spent to struggle. I cared for nothing but to lie still at last after all the batterings I had suffered. The tropic sun blazed down so fiercely that soon those parts of me which were out of water became dried and all crusted over with salt.

And then, impossible though it seems to believe, I heard voices close by. For a moment I thought I must have confused them with the cries of strange birds and the noise of the surf pounding on nearby reefs. But again they came, and this time I knew them for the familiar ones of Andy and Jeremy Folger. Now, even in my joy, a new fear struck me—suppose they should not come to the pool? Suppose I must lie there and hear them go away again without me? "Oh," I thought, "to be able to cry out to them just once. To call out aloud: 'Here, here I am. Take me back to Phoebe.'"

Well, as you have guessed, they found me, else how should I be writing my memoirs today?

Andy bore me back in triumph, and they were all so over-joyed to see me again that no one scolded him for not getting any of the crabs he had been sent to hunt.

"I declare if it ain't a miracle!" Mrs. Preble exclaimed as Phoebe took me to her heart. "Wherever did you find her, Andy?"

"Down in one of those pools 'long shore," he explained with pride, "there was some wood and stuff washed up, too; Jeremy's comin' with what he can find."

"Well, it certainly beats all," Captain Preble remarked, turn-ing me about between his thumb and forefinger. "It takes us the better part of a day to get here, charts and rudder an' four pair of oars, an' she gets here all by herself with no trouble at all."

"Mercy," thought I, "how little he knows about it!"

"I guess she never would have got back to me if she wasn't made of mountain-ash wood," Phoebe reminded them.

This time her mother did not rebuke her.

"I wouldn't have believed how glad I'd be to see that doll again," she said. "It kind of heartens me up some way. Makes me feel maybe this Island's not so far from all creation but what something'll come along to pick us up."

"You keep your courage right with you, ma'am," put in Bill Buckle, who was busy hacking away at some underbrush of rich, damp green. "I always said that doll would bring us luck, and I say so now. I don't care who hears me."

Ivy Bolton

THE KING'S CYGNET

ILLUSTRATED BY *Dorothy Lathrop*

Get you gone, you good for naught varlet!
How many more times am I to tell you not to linger near the
river bed? What are you doing with the swans?" The old
master of the swannery shook the lad he held.

"I be doing no harm, master," Giles Burton pleaded. "I was
but looking at the swans; they be so beautiful."

"A pretty tale! Looking? Stealing, belike, that is what you
are after, rascal. And let me tell you, it will mean the stock
and the pillory for you if you are found touching the swans;
for only the Royal Vintners, the Guild of the Dyers, and the
King's Grace may keep birds on the river Thames. And these
be the King's."

"Leave off shaking the lad, Gilbert. What has he done?"

The voice was that of a lad of twelve and to Giles' astonishment, he was released with a suddenness that sent him sprawling on the ground, while his captor straightened up and saluted.

"He is ever around the swans, your Grace. Thrice within
the last two days have I turned him from the riverside, and
all I get is a lying tale that he was but looking at the swans
because they are so beautiful. He will frighten them."

"I think he will frighten the swans less than you do with
your loud voice," said the boy shrewdly. "They *are* beautiful;
I like to look at them myself."

"Your Grace has the right. You are the seigneur of the
swans. This is a varlet from the scum of the London streets,
and he has no business here."

"He is one of my people," the boy returned. "If I give him
99

permission, he may bide here. I do give it. I am going to talk to him now and you may wait over yonder, Gilbert."

"Your royal mother will not approve of this, your Grace."

"My royal mother is ever willing for me to serve my people, Gilbert. Do as I say."

Unwillingly, the master of the swannery withdrew to the Tower gate. Giles scrambled to his feet and the two lads surveyed each other.

The royal boy was slender and tall for his years. There was promise of muscular strength in the breadth of his shoulders and he carried himself with a boyish dignity. His short hair shone like spun gold under his dark cap and he wore a blue surcoat edged with miniver. The peasant boy was shorter and sturdier, his face a trifle pale from privation, and his homespun well mended but almost threadbare. He spoke shyly.

"It is the King's Grace!"

"Aye, it is Richard," said the royal boy. "What is your name?"

"Giles Burton. I live over by the Cheap. But we used to be in the country, until my father became an artisan of the guilds. I miss the birds and the flowers and I found them here."

"You love the swans?"

"Aye, truly. They be royal birds. See how they gleam in the sunlight!" He pointed.

The river stretched fair in the sunshine and, from the shadowy banks, the swans were swimming out, great snowy birds full of grace. There were old ones on the front, but at the back came the cygnets, some of them almost grown, others still in the ungainly stage of the ugly duckling. Giles leaned forward.

"Does your Grace see that cygnet?" he asked, pointing to a half-grown bird. "Watch and see."

He drew from his wallet a piece of black bread and broke a small portion off in his hand. He gave a low whistle and the cygnet turned and swam towards the bank. It came up close and gobbled the bread which Giles held out, and then put its head against the boy.

"Will your Grace give him some?" Giles held out his bread to the royal lad.

Richard took it and held it out, kneeling by the city lad. The cygnet was shy at first, but the outstretched hand was steady and, at last, he ventured, gobbling the bread with all his might. Then he swam off to a distance and refused to come near again.

Richard sat back on his heels. "How did you get him so tame?" he demanded.

"By throwing bread to him at first," Giles explained. "Then gradually he came within reach of my hand. My lord of Surrey's master of the swans showed me how. You have to keep very still and whistle softly."

"Do you think I could make him come to me?" asked Richard.

Giles nodded. He had forgotten his shyness now.

"Go over a little distance and whistle, your Grace," he said. "Make him come to you."

The cygnet was wary. Richard could not coax him again within reach of his hand, though he watched the royal boy curiously. At last he sailed away in the wake of the others.

Richard stood up. "I mean to tame him," he announced. "Giles, will you come tomorrow? I must go now."

He ran lightly towards the Tower gate and disappeared. The master advanced again.

"You were cozening up to the King," he said sourly. "But I see through you, varlet. Beware how you handle the swans and I give you fair warning that when the regent comes back from Scotland, I shall see to it that there is no more of this nonsense! The King is a spoiled lad, but he will find a working man has rights."

He turned on his heel and stalked back to his post and Giles went soberly away. The tall master was an ill foe, perhaps, but still he had a friend in The King's Grace.

"I have tamed him, Giles." The young King came running to meet the boy a few days later. "He followed me yester afternoon. He came right into the waters of the Tower, unafraid of the state barge or anything else. I brought my royal mother down to see him, but he would not come to see her. He ate from my hand and thrust his head up my sleeve just as they say the old cross swan used to do to Bishop Hugh of Lincoln. See, I shall call him now."

He knelt down and whistled and the cygnet came out at once. Giles smiled as he saw the bird come close to the royal lad.

"Now, do you call him, Giles," Richard urged. "See, he will come from one to another. Do you think we could tame the rest?"

"If we had enough bread, your Grace. My nooning is not enough for all."

"Your nooning? Was it your own meal that you gave the swans?"

"I love them, your Grace."

"After this, I shall bring the food," the young King said, decidedly. "I shall always love this one best, but if I be seigneur of the swans, I must make the others happy, too. Is something wrong with you, Giles? You look troubled."

"I shall not be able to come here much more, your Grace. My father is going to bind me 'prentice to Master Weddon, the cobbler."

"And you like not making shoes?"

"I love not a shop, your Grace. I would rather be with the birds and flowers. But there be many mouths to feed at home and I must take this chance. It would not have come for two years yet, but there is shortage of lads because of the pestilence last year."

"Come whenever you can," said the King regretfully. "I shall miss you, Giles."

They parted and Giles went on his way. The roads seemed very crowded and sounds of discordant voices arose in the distance. The boy slipped into the shadow of a doorway as a rabble poured into the streets. They dashed at one of the gates and the guard fled. Giles stepped out and stopped a lad.

"What is amiss?" he asked.

The boy clutched his arm. "It is the revolt of the peasants," he gasped. "They have taken the City, and the army is in Scotland. Wat Tyler is the leader, and they are burning the Lombard

102

shops and killing anyone who cannot say bread and cheese to suit them."

He scuttled away like a frightened hare and Giles stood pondering. He had heard something of peasant discontent in his old home. Wat Tyler was a malcontent—he had belonged to their own village and was hand in glove with John Ball and Jack Straw, the two men who were stirring up the serfs of England to bitter conflict. If these, as leaders, held the city, there was like to be tragedy, indeed. Suddenly his face grew white. Suppose the news had not reached the Tower—suppose the King— He turned and ran swiftly back. There was the royal lad.

"Into the Tower, quickly, your Grace," Giles called. "The peasants be holding London."

Richard sprang to his feet. "The swans!" he cried. "Will they not hurt them?"

"Get in, your Grace, and bid them open the water gate. I will drive in the swans."

Giles sprang in the boat. The master of the swannery rushed at him. "Leave my boat be," he ordered.

"The peasants are in revolt," the boy called. "I am after the swans."

With his call and his whistle, he brought the birds together, and, paddling gently, drove them through the opened water gate and into the Tower itself. Just as the gate closed, he saw that the King's cygnet was missing. Far up the reaches of the river, he could see the bird swimming slowly and regally. But the howl of the mob was near. If he tried to bring it in now, all would be lost. He brought the boat to land, hid it, and concealed himself in the sedge near the bank.

It was a weary vigil. He heard howls of disappointment from the mob when they found the Tower closed against them. Every now and then flames would come up from the captured city and wild screams would be heard. And still the cygnet stayed up the river, evidently frightened by the noise. At last, the sun set and Giles saw with relief the shadows darkening the river. The mob began to seek elsewhere for amusement. The boy stole out. If he could get the cygnet, perhaps he could attract the attention of the guard and get the bird to the King. He started as he heard a light footstep and turned to face a newcomer.

"Is that you, Giles?" asked Richard.

"What is your Grace doing here?"

"I am looking for the cygnet. I climbed down the wall when the guard was not looking. The cygnet is not with the rest."

"No, he is up the river. But your Grace is mad to be out here unguarded. Get you back."

The King shook his head obstinately. "I want my cygnet, Giles."

A sullen roar sounded down the street. Giles pulled the royal boy into the sedge.

"The mob is coming," he said. "They must not get you."

Startled at the peril, the King crouched beside the other boy. Giles touched his surcoat, embroidered with the royal lions of England. "Take that off," he whispered. "Put on this homespun of mine. I can hide yours under the cloak."

Richard obeyed. Quietly, unobserved by his companion, Giles donned the lions himself. He drew his tattered cloak about them. It would not hide them very well, Giles was sure of that.

"Get back to the Tower, your Grace," he whispered. "Never fear I will look after the cygnet for you."

They rose to their feet and crept out, hugging the shadows, and started to cross the square. The cloudy night was helping them and Giles breathed more freely. If he could only get his royal companion to safety! Then suddenly through a break in the clouds, the full moon sailed into view and in her light the two lads were visible. A group of peasants watched them and caught sight of the broidered lions on Giles' breast.

"The royal lad!" they shouted, and started in pursuit.

Giles shoved Richard toward the Tower. Flinging his cloak from him, he ran in the opposite direction. The peasants saw the surcoat and, as he expected, gave chase. Up and down the narrow streets they ran, twisting and turning. Giles might have outrun the men, but, as he turned by the market place, new ones joined the pursuit. Someone rushed in front of him, tripped him, and he fell. Strong hands dragged him to his feet.

"The royal lad!" a stern voice said. "Here, fools, harm him not. With him in our hands, we can get our terms. Where is Wat Tyler?"

105

"Down Blackheath way, gathering the men there. No use to take the boy to him. Where shall we lodge him?"

"You have the keys of the gaoler, taken when we raided the prison, Simon. Put the boy in the pillory. 'Twill keep him safe and teach him a lesson as well."

The other shouted approval. There was a rush for the keys and in a few moments, Giles found himself helpless, his hands and head locked fast in the wooden frame. Wild shouts rose from the crowd. An egg smashed in his face, and soon heavier missiles were coming. Sticks and stones rained on him. Giles set his lips resolutely. If only Richard got free! Would he be mad enough to come back?

"What have we here, my masters?" The voice was a stern one, and the rabble turned.

"John Ball, John Ball!" they shouted. "We have the King! We have the King!"

"Here in the pillory?" He flashed the torch he held in Giles' face. "Fools all! This is no King. Can you not tell a peasant lad when you see him?"

"He has the lions."

"Get him down. He must know where the King is. I shall question him."

Giles was released. He leaned unsteadily against the wood of the pillory. John Ball spoke. "Where got you the surcoat?"

Giles shook his head. "I will not tell," he answered stubbornly.

"I know," a surly voice interrupted. " 'Faith but he has tricked us. The lad with him was the King and he led us astray." A knife gleamed. "Shall I slit his throat?"

"Nay. A dead peasant lad would do us harm," John Ball said shrewdly. "Carry him to the river and pitch him in. Let him sink or swim. We care not. He will not swim far in this plight."

He was obeyed. Strong hands seized the boy. He was rushed to the river bank and flung in. The cold waters went over his head. Weary and spent as he was, Giles kept his courage. He managed to keep himself afloat, then at last came to the sedges and lay back wearily against the bank. He knew no more.

A soft head was nuzzling at his pocket as he recovered, and he looked up in the dawn to see the King's cygnet close at his side. He put out weary arms and caught the bird. He dared not try to cross the square, but kept to the sedges, sometimes wading, sometimes swimming, but keeping hold of the bird and whistling from time to time. His head felt strangely light; he wondered if he could keep on. Then he found himself at the water gate. A challenge rang from the wall.

"I have the King's cygnet." He held up the bird, felt it taken from him, then fell back into the cold waters again.

There were long days and nights that passed before Giles thought clearly again. He was aware of a woman's hands about him, as he babbled of the King and the cygnet and the pillory and John Ball. But at last there came a day when he woke to his surroundings, to stare at the richly hung walls, at the soft coverlets under which he lay.

"He is better, Richard," a woman's voice said, and Giles tried feebly to rise, for this was Princess Joan, the royal mother herself. It was Richard who pushed him back.

"Lie still," he ordered. "The revolt is over, Giles."

"And your Grace's cygnet?" Giles whispered.

"You saved him. He is swimming near the Tower now. A pretty fright you gave us, Giles, but we heard all you suffered for me. You are going to be no 'prentice. You must bide with me. Gilbert is going to Windsor, and you will be master of the swans. Now sleep and rest. Your father has given consent."

Giles lay back. It was like a fairy dream. And yet it was true. He was to hear the other tale later, of the young King's quelling of the angry rebels on Blackheath, of Wat Tyler's death and the ravage of the city. Now he smiled in utter content—for was not he with royal Richard and master of the King's cygnet?

To WANDER off in the woods was dangerous; Ralf knew this. At the manorhouse with his step-brothers, Gilbert and Harald, and his mother the Lady Elfreda, he would be safe. But Ralf didn't want to listen to the stern warnings of his step-father. Ralf didn't want to go to school either. He preferred drawing on the precious pieces of parchment—not writing Latin verbs. So, on this day, with Harald, Walt, his servant, Bran, his dog, and Sagitta, his hawk, Ralf went to the woods. He didn't know that Udo, a cruel thief, had returned there. And Udo had a special grudge against Sir John. But Ralf, taking a deep breath, was ready for adventure.

Phillis Garrard

DUNGEON DEEP

ILLUSTRATED BY *Matilda Breuer*

RALF sniffed the air, fresh after rain in the night. "I feel like going off somewhere to get cool," he said. "Want to come, Harald?"

His stepbrother's eyes brightened. "Where are you going? Have you permission to miss school?"

"I'll go first and ask afterward." Ralf grinned. "Farewell, my school and books today."

"What about dinner?" asked Harald, who was usually hungry.

"Hob or Joan will give us something to take with us. Where's my mother?"

"She has a headache and is lying down, Marian said."

"I'll leave a message for her with Joan."

"Boo-hoo!" mocked Harald. "You'll catch it, Rafe."

"Who cares? I'll take Sagitta with me, and we'll have a swim in the river. I'll teach you, Harald. My father taught me to swim when I was very small."

"Father has taught Gilbert," Harald said quickly. "But I— I wasn't so good at learning."

"Water-coward!" Ralf teased.

His stepbrother flushed. "I'm not! But I don't like water in my nose and eyes."

"Well, I'll go find Joan. Ho, Walt, what do you want?"

"I heard you say you are going into the forest, young master. May I come with you?"

"Oh, I don't know," Ralf said. "We won't ride—we'll go on foot."

"Yes, young sir. But I can walk easily now. And I'm so tired of being caged up in the house and yard."

"Well, you can come, then. You can carry our food and Sagitta too, if I get tired of her."

A quarter hour later the truants, with the dog Bran and the hawk Sagitta, set out. Walt had a leather pouch slung on his back. It held bread, meat, salt, and raisin cakes. When they entered a grassy track through the forest, Ralf ran ahead, the goshawk on his wrist, exulting in his freedom. He shouted mockingly the Latin verbs he was to have learned this afternoon.

"I wonder if we'll start any rabbits or hares? Bran isn't much good, though," said Harald.

"I don't care if we don't catch anything. I just brought Sagitta to fly her for exercise and to keep her used to me. All I want to do is go wild for a day."

"Me, too," said Harald, admiring his daring stepbrother.

The track of turf and moss was like a green carpet underfoot. Branches met overhead in vaulted arches more beautiful even than the cloister roof in the monastery. The forest was mainly beech trees, with birches and oaks scattered among them. The trunks of the beeches rose like smooth gray columns from the bracken and flowering grasses at their roots. Bright spots of sunlight, shaken through moving leaves, shifted and danced on the path.

The boys trotted along gaily. Now and then one would pause to examine a bird's nest or anything at the roots of a big tree that looked like the burrow of a fox, rabbit, or badger. Red-brown squirrels frisked and chattered overhead. Birds sang and

chirped. "Coo! Coo!" murmured wood pigeons, far away in the dim green forest. Bran ran ahead, sniffing. He was quivering with eagerness and delight as he bounded with huge leaps through the glades where the sun fell on banks of ferns.

Soon they came to a little stream. A ribbon of crystal, it tinkled over pebbles between ferns and mossy stones. After leading them an hour's scramble among the thinning trees, this brook meandered into the river. It grew broader and more sluggish as it threaded the reeds and bulrushes of the low bogland.

Barefooted, the boys squelched happily over the spongy bog

110

moss. Mint grew here, enough to perfume a hundred halls. Willow herb made patches of rosy-red; forget-me-nots dotted the banks with blue; wild iris raised yellow flags.

So at last they came to the river this long way around. Broad and smooth it flowed between its banks. The boys flung themselves down under a willow tree, panting. Ralf whistled for Sagitta, who had been flying above, her bright golden eyes searching for waterfowl.

"Sa-geeta! Sa-geeta!" His call shrilled up into the blue spaces of air. The forest trees sent it echoing back faintly.

"I hope she'll come to me," he added. "I haven't a lure for her. There's a good hawk! Come now!"

With a swoop and whir of wings, the goshawk alighted on a stick he held for her. She cocked her head sideways and edged along the stick toward his hand.

"You shall have a piece of meat. Good Sagitta!" praised Ralf.

She was fed and turned over to Walt to keep. They decided to rest and eat dinner before swimming. The meat and bread tasted good here in the shade. They drank river water from their cupped hands and thought it was as fine as the cider in the hall at home. Bran snapped up the scraps thrown to him. But both Ralf and Harald had to talk hard to persuade Walt to eat the raisin cake. He thought it was a dainty not suitable for those who always ate at the lower tables.

Afterward, they stretched out at their ease, flat on their backs. As they stared up into the leaves and sky, the boys talked lazily. Ralf began to chuckle. "Old Joanie didn't want us to go off this morning. Said it was too far and there were robbers about. Old folks always try to frighten boys about something. Dangerous. Naughty. Will give you a stomach-ache. Pert to your elders."

"Yes, I know," Harald grunted. "Just their dull way."

"Joan gave me a charm and made me learn it," Ralf went on. "It's three flowers of red pimpernel in a little leather bag. I have it around my neck on a string. Now, what was the charm? Oh, yes—

111

"Herb pimpernel, I have thee found
  growing upon Christ Jesus' ground.
The same gift the Lord Jesus
  gave unto thee
When He shed His blood upon the tree.
  "Arise up, pimpernel, and go with me.
    And God bless me,
  And all that shall wear thee. Amen."

Walt was listening eagerly. "That's a very good charm, Master
Ralf," he said, nodding approval.

"Huh! I don't believe much in charms," scoffed Ralf.

Walt looked shocked. "My brother's wife, Margery, can
charm warts away or stop a nosebleed, just as *easy.*"

"Rafe, you'd better get her to put a charm on Master Theo
for you tomorrow, in case he beats you," Harald suggested.

Ralf yawned. "Let's swim now. Or I'll go to sleep. And
what a waste of time *that* would be."

Through the whole long hot summer afternoon they splashed
and played in and out of the water. Ralf paddled like a puppy,
slid under the cool ripples, blew and snorted. Then he floated
on his back. He flipped his hands lazily like fins, as he blinked
up at the blue sky laced over with wispy white clouds. Harald
stayed near the bank, yelling when the water touched his
shoulders. He only pretended to swim, for one foot never left
the river bottom. Walt contented himself with dabbling his
feet. Bran was the best swimmer of all. He surged ahead after
sticks, his paws working smoothly, tail streaming ripples behind him.

Sometimes Ralf and Harald would climb out and lie all bare
and dripping on the bank until the sun warmed and dried
them. Then with a shout Ralf would run back to jump into
the water, sending up showers of spray, ducking his head until
his tawny hair was as sleek as a seal's. He taunted Harald until
his timid stepbrother actually took three strokes with both feet
off bottom.

"The shadows are growing long, young masters," Walt reminded them at last. "We'd better be going."

They let the sun dry them once more. Then they pulled on their shirts, short breeches, and tunics. They were buckling their belts when they saw five rough-looking peasants round a bend of the riverbank and come toward them. To his disgust Ralf recognized the red-bearded Udo among them. Why, he was supposed to be far away!

Ralf pretended not to know Udo, when the boys wished the men good day. "Good day to ye, young sirs. Ye be far afield," said one. His gap teeth made his grin unpleasant.

"A couple of hours' walk will bring us home," Ralf answered carelessly. "Where are you from?"

"We're working our way to hire ourselves out as laborers at Saint Bartholomew's Fair." The man's hair and beard were matted, his eyes shifty as he glanced about sharply.

Ralf didn't like his looks or manner. "Well, we're starting home. Come, Harald and Walt."

113

But as the boys stepped forward, the five men barred their path. They waved their sticks and clubs threateningly. "Not so fast, my young lord!" said Udo. "Suppose ye come with us— we'll show ye the way."

"We know it. Let us pass, fellow!" ordered Ralf, his temper rising. "Here, Walt, give me Sagitta."

"Keep your tongue civil—we're not your serfs to kneel and obey. Seize him!" Udo growled.

Taken absolutely by surprise, Ralf found his arms roughly grasped on either side. The three other men advanced on Harald and Walt. Bran, growling and snapping, sprang at the men's throats. But he fell back, helpless, as a blow from a club caught his ribs.

In another moment the three boys were prisoners. Struggle as they might against the men's grasp, Harald and Walt soon had their hands bound behind their backs with leather thongs. Ralf, with Sagitta on his wrist, cried in fear for her safety, "Watch my hawk! If she gets away she'll tear your eyes out!" Sagitta was indeed snapping her beak savagely and fluttering on her loosely tied leash.

"I'll wring her neck!" Udo grunted through his tangled beard. He stretched out his hand to seize her, but thought better of it. Sagitta's strong beak, fiercely glinting eyes, and curved talons were frightening.

"She'll be quiet if I soothe her. But you must leave my left arm free so I can carry her. Now, what does all this mean?" stormed Ralf. "Sir John Goodwin, my stepfather, will put you all in jail for this!"

"Indeed he will," piped up Harald. "He'll have you whipped and put in the stocks."

"He's already done that once too often," spat the red-bearded leader. "This time we'll get even! By all the foul fiends in creation, he'll do *our* will now. And he'll do it humbly, or else your slit throats shall pay the penalty, my fine young sprigs."

His four companions were all dirty and unkempt, in torn, greasy leather tunics and rabbit-skin caps. They growled approval, and their eyes were crafty as they leered at the boys.

114

They're robbers or outlaws! thought Ralf. A sick misgiving crept into his stomach. Udo has joined a robber band! Ralf looked at Walt, whose face was white, and then remembered. This Udo was also the coward who had struck the lame groom.

"If you want money," Ralf said, eyeing Udo steadily, "we don't have any. And when you're caught, you'll probably be hanged."

A sharp blow from a grimy open hand caught him upon his mouth and cheek. "We want money, sure enough," said Udo. "But not your pennies, brat! Silver and gold to the tune of a hundred pounds will perhaps keep your throats whole— and perhaps 'twill not. Now, march!"

One of the men twisted Ralf's right arm behind his back and held it, so that he could apply a painful pressure if his victim struggled or lagged. Another prodded Walt and Harald with his staff.

The boys, frightened and angry, had to stumble along. One of the men went ahead as a sort of scout, while another kept the rear guard. Bran, whining in pain, was left lying beside the river.

In this wretched fashion the robbers drove the boys to a dark thicket of interlaced branches and creepers. They came into it by a low tunnel through blackberry brambles and hazel bushes. Ralf had been trying to keep his bearings. They must have come a mile or so down the river, and then inland to this spot.

With an oath of relief the leader turned to the boys. "Here's where we stay till nightfall, my young coxcombs. Then we've a finer prison for ye. Now, you—serf, vassal, slave, whatever you are—come here!"

One of the men shoved Walt forward. Udo glared at him. "We've met before this, I think. Want another taste of my club?"

Walt couldn't help flinching, but he managed to say quietly, "I'm no slave. I'm proud to be a servant to my lord, Sir John Goodwin. What do you want of me?"

The man sneered. "You're *my* slave now and will do my

115

bidding. Go back to your proud master and tell him if he values the lives of these two brats here, he'll pay a ransom of a hundred pounds for 'em. Silver coins, foreign coins, gold, jewels, silver chains, rings, dishes—we don't care how he pays it if the value is enough."

"I've never seen that much money. I doubt if my master has half so much in his strongbox," said Walt, bewildered. Silver pennies were the only coins he knew and he had seen very few of those.

"Then let him send to the moneylenders in the town. He has rich lands he could mortgage. But listen, slave! Tell him to send quickly for the money. And advise him not to order out search parties. If he does, his dear boys'll be found with their necks wrung or their throats slit. By all fiends and furies, I swear that!"

"Send him on his way," urged one of the robbers, a big, surly fellow. "Enough of this talk."

"Cut his thongs, then, and kick him along. One more word to you, slave! Tell your master to put the bags of money in the cleft of the big oak in the forest glade called Robin's Dell by the third midnight from this day. And tell him to take care! No spying to see what happens—or never again will he see these pretty boys alive." Udo made a horrible face as he flourished a sharp knife and pretended to draw it across his throat.

Walt looked despairingly at Ralf, who nodded and tried to smile encouragement. Then the groom, limping and unwilling, was kicked and prodded back along the tunnel. He would have to find his way home as best he could through the lonely dark forest.

The robbers squatted down and talked together in hoarse whispers. Ralf signed to Harald to sit down too, for both boys were weary. His two arms were free now, and he began to soothe and caress Sagitta. The goshawk grew quiet in this dark hiding place. Harald, whose wrists were still bound, sat miserable and silent close to Ralf. A little hiccuppy sob shook him now and then. Ralf felt much older than his stepbrother. His mother had told him that Harald was not very strong.

116

He whispered as cheerfully as he could to the younger boy, "They're only bragging windbags. They can't do what they threaten. Don't believe half they say, Harald. Sir John will soon rescue us—see if he doesn't."

"Bub-but they'll kill us if they think he's searching!" said Harald chokily. He tugged vainly at his thongs.

"Keep your courage up. Remember Richard Coeur-de-Lion? The one you call 'the Lionhearted'? He also was a prisoner and held for ransom," Ralf whispered, but his own heart was heavy.

"Poor Bran is dead, I guess," Harald whimpered. "And they'll kill your hawk too, Rafe."

"No, they're afraid of her. She'd claw at anybody who tried to take her."

After what seemed hours, the men drove them on again. In spite of his words to Harald, Ralf was in constant fear the robbers would take Sagitta from him. But they seemed to have forgotten the hawk, quiet in the darkness. They did not seem to think it necessary to bind his hands. They even cut Harald's thongs, for the boy stumbled awkwardly so many times as they blundered along that they lost patience with his slowness.

Through thickets and undergrowth, by narrow paths or none at all, over fallen trees and rocky ground—on and on the exhausted boys were forced to march through the dark night.

"Here it is!" grunted the leader at last. "Where's the rope?"

Harald cried out in fear. Ralf, hungry, tired and wretched, felt a sick shudder shake him. Were they to be strangled so soon?

But the rope was tied around his waist. Then he was swung off his feet and lowered into black emptiness—down . . . down. . . . He swayed dizzily, and the rope cut into his flesh.

His feet bumped on ground, the rope slackened and fell in coils around his neck. A harsh voice called, "Look out below there! Your brother is flying down to you. . . ."

Ralf could just make out Harald's form dangling above him. Down it came in uneven jerks. The boy's feet kicked helplessly. Down Harald was lowered until Ralf heard a frightening sound and a terrified shriek from his stepbrother.

118

"The rope is *breaking!*"

Frantically Ralf plucked at Sagitta's leash to free his wrist.
Then he threw the hawk away and rushed underneath Harald.
He caught the falling boy somehow—anyhow—in his arms. They
both collapsed and rolled over together on the ground. A fearful pain shot through Ralf's ankle. He felt as though he were
sinking into a deep ocean—and then all his feelings were blotted
out in swirling blackness.

"Ralf! Ralf!"

Someone was calling his name, loudly, frantically. But it
sounded a long way off, as if across a wide river. He must
answer. But he couldn't make any sound at all. Well, then, he
must go and see what was wanted. But here again he was
helpless—he couldn't move.

If he could grope out of this darkness, he might do something. He would—he *would* get out!

"Rafe! Speak to me! Oh, Rafe, are you dead?"

Dead? What foolishness was this? Now he was floating up
and up, as if through dark water, until of a sudden his head

119

seemed to break the surface. . . . He opened his eyes. Someone was shaking his shoulder. Who was it and where was he?

"What's—what's the matter?" Ralf muttered crossly. All this was terribly bewildering.

Then he plainly heard Harald give a sob of relief. "Oh, Rafe, thank Our Blessed Lady you are alive! It's been so long. You've just been lying here, so cold and still."

"Well, I am cold. And my ankle hurts like fury. Where are we, Harald? I can't see anything but you. And you look like a dancing black bear."

"We're in a big hole in the ground—or maybe it's a well. I don't know. The robbers put us here, and you caught me when the rope broke with me. You fainted, I guess. Are you hurt?"

"Just my ankle. It feels as if it's broken, but maybe it's only a bad sprain. I remember now what happened. Where's Sagitta?"

"I heard her fluttering awhile back."

Ralf whistled feebly, then called, "Sa-geetta! Sa-geetta!"

He sighed with relief as something soft brushed his cheek. The goshawk, uttering uneasy little cries, was walking about close to him. "Harald, can you catch her? There, there, Sagitta! Gently! See if you can find a stone to tie her leash to, Harald. Oh, I don't want her to get away."

"I have her." Harald sounded triumphant. "And I've knotted her leash around a good-sized stone. She seems quiet and sleepy."

"Good! I feel better now, but I don't dare stand up. I'll take my shoe off, for my ankle is so swollen."

"A hurt ankle should be bound up tightly. I had one once, so I know," Harald said importantly. "But we have nothing to bind yours with."

"Never mind. I'll just lie still. I wonder if poor Walt has got home yet. Mercy, the Manor House will be in a to-do about us!" remarked Ralf. He could not help feeling a little satisfaction as he imagined the scene. "But I hope my mother will not worry too much."

"I wonder if Father will pay the ransom," Harald said, with a shiver.

"He won't give in to robbers tamely" was Ralf's opinion. "I've a plan, Harald, that may help us. But we must wait till daybreak for it. Meanwhile," he added grandly, "we'll just have to be noble captives. Just think, someday the minstrels may make a song about our adventures."

"It would be a fine change from their silly old love stories of brave knights and fair ladies." Harald was recovering his spirits somewhat. "They almost never have boys in their stories. And if they do, they call 'em 'sweet helpless babes' or 'fair children.' Pooh!"

"They don't know *us!*" observed Ralf. " 'Sweet babes'! Here, Harald, help me untie this old rope around my waist. Did you untie your own?"

"Yes, I did." Harald tugged nimbly at the knots. "Look, Rafe, we could coil up the two ropes and make a sort of pillow for your foot to rest on."

This was done and Ralf said his ankle felt much better up. "There's nothing to do now but try to sleep," he said. "How dark it is! There's no moon tonight, but I can see some stars. Lie down beside me, Harald, and we'll keep each other warm."

"Say that pimpernel charm, Rafe. It might help us," whispered Harald.

"That old wives' charm! Don't believe it! But I'll say it and I'll turn the little bag over three times. That's what Joanie told me to do."

He repeated the words slowly, finishing:

> "Arise up, pimpernel, and go with me.
> And God bless me,
> And all that shall wear thee. Amen."

The slow night passed somehow. The boys fell into uneasy dozes, woke, talked a little, slept again. Dawn came at last, and let a gray light into their prison. Ralf woke up and stared about him.

They were lying on the weed-grown floor of a big circular hole. Rocky walls rose up smooth and sheer far above their heads. It was too big for a well, too evenly made for a cave.

121

Ralf noticed that the hole was bottle-shaped, narrowing slightly to the opening, and the walls were blackened as if from soot or smoke. Escape would be almost impossible even if he had the full use of his legs.

Harald was still sleeping, his yellow head pillowed on his arm. Ralf thought over his plan. It was a forlorn hope, but anything was worth trying. He waited impatiently for the full daylight.

A chilly dawn wind blew down into their dungeon. Harald groaned and woke. His face puckered as he saw the steep black walls of their prison. "What a frightful place, Rafe!"

"It's not a bower of beauty," Ralf agreed dryly. He looked thoughtfully at the black and purple bruises on his puffy ankle. Then he dragged himself toward Sagitta, who was sitting on the stone to which she was tethered. She looked as haughty and aloof as the noblest falcons.

Her master talked to her, stroked, petted, and praised her. "That's my noble goshawk. And did you sit all night and guard us? I wish I had some meat for you."

"Meat!" echoed Harald. "I'm so hungry I could eat a snail! Do you think they'll starve us, Rafe?"

"We might get some muddy water and a crust of black bread thrown to us. Captives can't be particular about their food. Do you know what this place is, Harald?"

"No. Just an ugly pit, I guess."

"Well, I believe it's an old limekiln. You know—a pit where they burn limestone to make quicklime."

"Are they going to burn *us?*" Harald cried in alarm.

"No, stupid! This is a very old pit, or else there wouldn't be weeds in it. Probably there's a limestone quarry near by."

"School has made you very wise, Rafe." Harald spoke in real admiration.

"Wait a bit and you'll think I'm as wise as Solomon." Ralf grinned. "See what I have here."

He unfastened the small knife sheath attached to his belt and took out a folded piece of parchment and his stick of sharpened lead. "All real scholars carry these," he explained. "But I do it to make little drawings of things I see, not to write Latin verbs."

"What good are they? Parchment won't help us now."

"Won't it? Wait and see. I'm going to write a message to Sir John, telling him where we are. Then I'll tie it to one of Sagitta's jesses and let her fly. And perhaps she may fly home with it. Remember—Faulk says she has that habit, just like an eyas."

"Ralf!" Harald's eyes were shining. "That's a splendid idea! But—but where are we? How can you tell Father when we don't know ourselves?"

"I watched the stars last night. You know the constellation called Ursa Major in Latin—the Great Bear? Two of his stars always point to the northern lodestar. Well, the lodestar was over my right shoulder all the way. So that means we traveled due westward."

"But how far? We walked and walked. My legs still ache."

"I don't know. Have you ever heard of any limestone quarries about ten or twelve miles away from Goodwins?"

Harald rubbed his forehead anxiously. "Yes . . . I think I've heard my father and old Peter the mason speak of some. Peter helped to build the monastery when he was a boy—that was long before I was born—and he often boasts about it. Oh, now I remember—Peter loves to tell how far something had to be brought. . . . They had to bring it eleven or twelve miles and they floated it down the river on a barge—but I never listened hard. Maybe it was lime. Yes, I think it must have been lime, for the stone quarries are in the moorlands."

"Good thing you took even that much notice. Now for my message." Ralf frowned and sucked the point of his lead. Harald found a flat stone to rest his parchment on. Finally with great effort Ralf wrote a few short sentences in Norman-French. They were addressed to *Sir John Goodwin, lord of Goodwins Manor.*

We are held prisoners in old limekiln hole, perhaps near quarry westward twelve miles or so. Five robbers took us, but there may be more in the band. We are well. You must come armed.

Ralf thought a pinch of Latin would give the message a learned flavor, but hesitated before writing *Filii tui*. Of course he wasn't Sir John's son, but it seemed silly to write *Thy stepson Ralf and thy son Harald*. Besides, he didn't know the Latin for stepson. So he wrote *Filii tui*. Next he drew a little picture of the five robbers, complete with clubs, sticks, straggly hair and beards. The figures were driving two defiant-looking boys before them. The boys' heads were thrown back, and both had curly hair and innocent round faces. He signed *Ralf* with a flourish, and Harald painstakingly wrote his own name underneath.

Carefully Ralf made the letter into a small, tight roll. He fastened it to one of Sagitta's jesses and then slipped the leash from her legs.

"Now, Sagitta, you may fly. Up and away with you! Fly home, my pretty, and tell them where we are. Faulk will be sure to see the message you bring. Up, now!"

He tossed her upward. She fluttered but seemed to find it

124

hard to gain height in the narrow pit. She was used to rising in wide lifting circles. Down she dropped and fluttered to her stone perch. The boys, disappointed, scowled at her and at each other. Ralf struggled up and stood balancing on one foot. "Here, let me lean on your shoulder, Harald. Now!"

He coaxed Sagitta to his wrist. Then he cried, "Hoy! Up we go!" and tossed her the full length of his raised arm. She lifted, caught air in her powerful wings and made narrow spirals upward. Another moment and she had gained the mouth of the pit. Then she was beating strongly, higher and higher into the circle of blue sky that was all the boys could see.

"Well, she's gone," Ralf said, with a regretful sigh. "Hubert, saint of huntsmen, knows if I'll ever see her again."

"Of course you will," Harald said cheerfully. "She'll come riding back with my father to peck the eyes of those—those robbers who dared to capture us. Swoosh! Whang! Snick! You'll see my father's sword flash. I hope he comes soon. I'm so thirsty."

Neither boy had ever gone without food or water for twenty-four hours. They felt so weak and exhausted that time dragged even more heavily. Harald prowled about their narrow prison. But all he discovered was a sort of hollow in the wall. It might have been a filled-in entrance. Big boulders, stones and rubble had evidently been piled there. The pit itself had been cut from solid limestone. Rough masonry work, gray and weatherworn, showed only at the top and the rim of the opening. Ralf nodded wisely. "That was probably the old doorway to the limekiln. It must open out on the slope of the hillside. I expect the door's half hidden by bushes. Look how they hang over the top. We can hardly see the sky."

"How do you know about limekilns and stars and things like that?"

"My father used to tell me always to notice, listen, ask questions, and think things over. I was only little, but I remember." Ralf swallowed suddenly. He pretended to examine his swollen foot. It was puffy and black and blue from ankle to toes.

Over their heads came a hoarse, brutal cry. "Here's something a-coming down! 'Twill keep life in your measly carcasses while we need ye, my dainty young lords."

Two small objects thudded to the floor of the pit. Ralf looked up and called, "A carrion crow has dropped his meat."

A string of oaths told him that his shot had gone home. Harald pounced on the things that had fallen. "See, Rafe, a leather bottle of water and a hunk of rye bread. Oh, lovely water!"

He set his dry lips to the bottleneck and drank until Ralf made a face. "Leave me some, please. You act like a thirsty calf."

They felt much better and braver after this plain fare, though they would have turned up their noses at it even on fast days at home. They even got the idea of trying to escape by cutting toe holds in the walls. But they found the limestone hardened by time and weather. The blades of their small knives soon were worn down and broke.

Their efforts were halfhearted, anyway, because they both knew Ralf couldn't climb the overhanging walls with his useless foot. Besides, one of the robbers might be waiting at the top to seize them.

They tried shouting for help. But Ralf felt sure this was a

126

lonely spot. No one might pass for weeks. And again there was the chance that the robbers were spying on them and might take some horrid revenge.

Then they tried to dig through the place that Ralf thought had been a doorway. But they could not move, with only their bare hands, that mass of rock and stone.

During the long afternoon they dozed a little, in spite of Ralf's throbbing foot and Harald's stomach, which was by no means full. When they were both awake they talked in snatches.

"Master Theo will think I'm just playing truant until he hears the news of our capture." Ralf smiled. "School is safe and almost pleasant, but this is a real adventure. We are like brave young knights. They have to suffer fasting and hardship and keep an all-night watch before the altar before they can win their spurs."

"I'd rather keep vigil before the high table in the hall at home. Oh, Rafe, the things we used to have to eat!" Harald sighed wistfully, as though he were thinking of times long past.

"I don't suppose the rest of them'll feel much like eating until we're found," Ralf said. "I wish I hadn't taken you into the forest."

"I'm glad you did. Truly, this will make Gilbert green. Won't he be furious to think he didn't share our adventure? Now I can crow over him about something. Aha, big brother Gilbert!"

The sunshine left their deep dungeon early. They watched it slide up the walls as shadows fell on the pit floor. Soon twilight came, still and lonely. All day the boys had heard nothing but birds singing in the forest above. There had not been even the crow of a cock or bark of a dog. Now an owl hooted—a sad, unearthly cry.

Once more the boys huddled together and tried to sleep. At night it was hard to keep one's courage up. My father, Ralf told himself, was a valiant knight. He fought the infidels in the Holy Land, and I'm sure he'd have scorned to feel sorry for himself just because he wanted roast chicken and herring pie. I expect he had nothing to eat for weeks and weeks but a

handful of dates and muddy water. And that's our main trouble, really—we're just so terribly hungry. We're sure to be rescued soon—sure to be.

Ralf shifted uneasily on the hard ground. He ached everywhere, from head to foot. The rope footstool for his ankle wasn't very comfortable.

Harald asked him to say the pimpernel charm again. He did so, and also "Our Father." Then he went on with "Hail, Mary, full of grace" and the Creed—"I believe in God, the Father Almighty . . ." Remembering how he had urged Harald to come with him, he added an Act of Contrition. Surely one of these would help, he thought.

So another long night wore away. Harald awoke early. He sniffled and whimpered a little, like a forlorn puppy. Ralf, also wakeful and still feeling big-brotherly, said, "Listen, Harald, and I'll tell you a story about good Saint Cuthbert. He's the patron saint of our monastery. Master Theodoric told us the story in school.

"The saint was very hungry once, just as we are. He was going about preaching, with only one boy for his servant. They walked all day, until the boy asked where they should stop for food. You see, they hadn't taken any provisions with them. Saint Cuthbert replied, 'My son, God will never allow those who trust in Him to perish with hunger.' Soon afterward they saw an eagle flying over a river. When they came nearer it was standing on the bank with a big fish in its claws.

" 'There is the meal that God has sent us,' said the saint. 'Run and take it.' The boy took the fish from the eagle, but his master scolded him. 'Leave the eagle half the fish as her share.' So the lad cut the head off the fish and gave it to the eagle. And so all three had a good meal, by God's grace."

"That's a cheerful story. I hope God will hurry to send us something good to eat," Harald said. He seemed comforted.

Welcome daylight began to creep into their prison. The boys stared at each other. By this time both looked their worst. They were unwashed and uncombed, of course. Their legs, arms, and even their cheeks were scratched and festering from

129

the brambles and thorns through which the robbers had forced them. And now their hands were covered with the gritty dust of the limestone they had tried to move, and their fingernails were broken.

"Joanie," said Ralf, pretending to speak to the old nurse, "take Master Harald, please, and douse him in your big wash-tub. Bring hot water, soap, brush, towels and scrub him well."

Harald let out a yell. Then he said in a surprised way, "Why, that sounds rather pleasant, after all. Goodness, I never thought I'd like a washing. But don't tell Joan, Rafe."

Toward noon by the sun, down came another bottle of water and a small loaf of moldy bread. "Your time is growing short," cried the rough voice above. "If your father is too purse-proud to pay the ransom, see what is waiting for ye!" A broad-bladed knife flashed in the sun. Harald turned a stricken look on Rafe, and stood white and silent.

But Ralf de Grenville felt only rage rise within him. How dared they do this to boys who had never harmed them? How dared they interfere with other people's lives? Everyone had a right to live and be happy, safe from attacks of cruel, greedy savages like these men.

"Go, you—you scum!" he shouted. "Take your ugly face away! You're cowards and brutes! But you'll have to pay for this soon!"

"Oh, stop, Rafe," begged Harald. "You'll only make him angry. And then he'll treat us worse."

But a jeering laugh from above was the only answer to Ralf's outburst.

"Sagitta hasn't flown home, I'm afraid," Harald said sadly. "I wonder if my father can pay the ransom?"

"She might take her time. She might even fly after game first. She was hungry when she left us," Ralf suggested. Though he tried to sound cheerful, he felt very anxious and uncertain. Of course Sir John would raise the ransom for them, if everything else failed. But would the robbers keep their promise to set the boys free? Somehow Ralf couldn't picture his stepfather meekly paying that great sum of money. A rescue was more

130

likely, if Sir John thought it could succeed without harming the hostages. Hostages? That had rather a noble ring.

That afternoon and evening were the worst times yet for the boys. Harald was plainly terrified, though he tried hard to hide his fear. Again they tried to climb the sheer walls—again they failed. They dug like frantic terriers at the filled-in entrance. But they got only bleeding hands for their pains, and Ralf gave his ankle a fresh wrench which made him feel sick and faint.

When the last daylight faded their hope vanished with it. Their longing for home was worse now than being so hungry. Ralf thought of his mother, in her blue robe, leaning over his bed. "Have you said your prayers, Ralf? Shame on you, my lazy son!" Would he ever hear that again?

Then—out of the darkness, the misery and despair, came a sound. Was it the thudding of horses' hoofs? Ralf seized Harald's arm and both strained their ears. Yes, horses! And now a brief command rang out, and other voices could be heard and the jingle of bits.

"Is it Father?" cried Harald. "Shall we shout?"

"No harm in shouting, whoever they are. And I believe they're from the Manor! Yell, Harald!"

The boys both shouted at the top of their lungs, "Help! Help! We're here—in the pit!"

"That was Humphrey's voice then—it *was!*" Harald, weak with hunger, was almost crying with excitement and relief.

Then plainly they heard Sir John Goodwin order: "Run that scuttling rat to earth and hold him fast! But don't cause him harm—I have some need of him."

"*Father!*" yelled Harald again. "We're here!"

Trampling of horses' hoofs, shouts of men, an oath, a laugh, followed by Sir John Goodwin's voice, distinct and close and more welcome than either boy could ever say. "All right, boys! We'll soon have you out of there. They didn't hurt you?"

The boys peered upward but could see only black shapes of men and horses looming against the moonless sky.

"Ralf's ankle is hurt," cried Harald. "Have you caught the robbers, Father?"

"Only one, but by my faith we'll have the others before long. Now, who's going down to help the boys? You, Luke? Good! Dickon and Faulk, take ropes and lower him."

So it was Walt's brother, calm, steady Luke, who soon stood in the pit beside the tired captives. He helped them fasten ropes under their arms. First Harald and then Ralf was drawn up to freedom and safety. Willing hands pulled Ralf over the edge of the old limekiln, and Faulk threw one arm around him to steady him. "Careful of your ankle, Master Ralf."

"Faulk!" Ralf clutched him. "Sagitta—did she fly home with our message?"

The falconer laughed. "Aye, that she did—Saint Hubert bless her! She's a wise and cunning hawk. This afternoon she came

132

a-fluttering down, calm as you please, on the roof of the mews. I caught sight of the parchment she carried and took it to my lord. My faith, we lost no time then in setting out! My master had been hot for pursuit long before this, but the lady Elfreda feared for your lives if the robbers were to get wind of it. In spite of that, we had been searching quietly day and night— in vain until your goshawk brought the message."

"Oh, my noble Sagitta!" exclaimed Ralf, overjoyed. "Isn't she noble, Faulk?" He knew that in the sport of hawking only *falcons* were called noble.

"Aye, she is—hawk or falcon, 'tis all the same," admitted the falconer, with a smile. "Let me tie this kerchief tight around your ankle. But look, here's the master."

Sir John was reining in his big horse before the cowering robber who had been guarding the boys and throwing down their ration of water and bread. The man cringed and jabbered, whining for mercy. Two of Sir John's brawny followers grasped his arms. A torch, held by a mounted man-at-arms, cast a strange, flaring light on the scene.

"Well, will you talk?" said Sir John sternly. "Or must we slit your throat to find your tongue?"

"I tell you, good master, I know nothing about it, or about any band of robbers. I was only snaring rabbits—"

"Rabbits only? Then tell me where your fellow weasels have their hole," Sir John thundered. "Speak up, if your miserable life means anything to you. Your dagger, Dickon!"

Instantly the big blacksmith whipped out his dagger and touched its sharp point to the man's throat. He gave a loud squeal, then burst out in a frightened stammer: "I'll t-tell any-thing—anything, good master! On the edge of the moors—in a tumble-down hut—there's a hollow full of trees called Mur-derers' Dell—that's where we—they—have their hiding place. 'Tis a good safe place, for it's supposed to be haunted, and no-body comes there."

Sir John nodded curtly. "Just as I thought. Tie him up, men, and bring him along on the spare horse. We'll ride on now to drive the other rats from their hole. Meantime the boys must be taken home. Humphrey, take Harald in front of you on your saddle. Faulk, take Ralf."

Did this mean that after all their trials they were not to see the exciting capture of the robber band? Even Harald forgot his tiredness. He raised an outcry. "Oh, Father, *please!* Please let me come with you. I want to see what happens."

Ralf too forgot all his aches in this disappointment. He urged, "Oh, Father, please let us come!"

Sir John turned his head so quickly to look in Ralf's direction that his stepson wondered what had surprised him. It took Ralf a moment to realize that, for the very first time, he had called Sir John "Father." Well, it had slipped out, and somehow he wasn't sorry.

Sir John laughed. "I thought you two would be longing for home and coddling. You're as bad as Gilbert. I almost had to lock him up to keep him from following us. Well . . . you may come. Humphrey, did you bring any food? The lads have had poor meals lately, I'm sure."

Some white rolls stuffed with butter and meat and some homemade wine soon put fresh strength into the boys. "The lady Elfreda made me bring food in my saddlebags," Humphrey explained. "She knew you would be hungry when you were found."

"Finish eating as you ride. Ready, men?" said Sir John. Swiftly the party mounted. The horses began to force their way along a narrow trail that twisted through undergrowth and trees. Sir John had more than a dozen men with him. Ralf heard familiar voices, though it was hard to make out faces in the darkness. He counted Faulk, Humphrey the house steward, Luke, Dickon the blacksmith, Gregory the stableman, old Robin and young Robin, and half a dozen strong men-at-arms and foresters. All carried lances, swords, spears.

They rode silently and slowly, for the horses could make little speed through the forest. The night was black, but the stars overhead gleamed sharply. Ralf, still munching, perched on the saddle in front of Faulk. He held himself erect with an effort. But not for anything would he have missed this chase of the robber band. And his foot, bound up tightly now, was not so painful.

"What happened to Walt?" he asked the falconer. "Did he get home safely with the message for my stepfather?"

Faulk chuckled. "Poor Walt! He had a night he'll always remember. But it turned out well in the end. You see, Walt got lost in the forest. He wandered half the night and came by chance on the hut in Murderers' Dell. He heard men talking inside the hut and thought it must be the robbers' hiding place, for that hut has been empty for years. Walt dared not get close enough to make sure, but he told my lord of his suspicion. And now this rascal's confession has proved Walt right. Long Piers took another party of our men to surround the hut while we came after you. They are there now, waiting only for word from Sir John to close in. They dared not do it until you were safe, for some of the band might have escaped and revenged themselves on you boys."

On they rode through the night, until a low hail sounded just ahead. Sir John gave the order to halt. "Piers?"

A horseman, half hidden in a thicket, urged his mount forward. He saluted with his sword. "Nobody has left the hut," he said rapidly. "They are feasting and singing. My men are posted all around. What about the young masters?"

"We have them safe, thanks to Our Blessed Lady!" answered Sir John. "Pass the word to your men to close in now. Remember—take the robbers unharmed if possible. They'll get their punishment in a court of law. But don't spare your blows if they show fight. Humphrey and Faulk, keep out of this and guard the boys at a safe distance. All right!"

Hearts pounding, both Ralf and Harald strained their eyes to watch through the darkness. It was hard to make out what was happening. Dim candlelight shone through chinks in the shutters. They could just see the broken thatched roof of the old hut, which was set among thick bushes. Behind it the wooded slope of the dell rose up black as pitch against the sky.

Suddenly the hut door was thrown open violently. Dark

135

figures poured out, shouting. Horses reared and shied, blows were struck, oaths were screamed. In the light from the open doorway Ralf saw struggling men appear, then vanish, in hand-to-hand fighting. His blood tingled. This was a real battle! There were many more men in the robber band than the five the boys had seen, and all were fierce and desperate.

Still, it was over quickly. Ralf saw two wild-looking outlaws leap for Sir John Goodwin's bridle. Both brandished clubs. Black Hector plunged and reared. Sir John's short boar spear struck one man's shoulder and sent him reeling backward. The other received a heavy blow on the brow with the flat of Sir John's sword. Then Long Piers's men threw themselves upon the dazed robbers and dragged them away.

"Torches!" shouted Sir John. "Let's see what we have caught!"

"A pretty sight, sir!" sang out Piers. "Line 'em up, men. Our master wants to look 'em over."

Pine torches were lighted and flared up weirdly. The captives, fifteen of them, stood huddled between the men-at-arms. They were a villainous, brutal-looking crew, Ralf thought, with not one good face among them. The leader Udo, streaked with blood from a deep cut over one eye, glared sullenly.

In the flickering light of the torches Ralf could see that Sir John had evidently scorned to wear armor on this quest. He was bareheaded and wore his hunter's tunic and leather leggings bound with crossed thongs. A light shield on his arm was his only protection. His men-at-arms wore hauberks of banded, woven leather, with helmet-shaped caps of the same, and cloth leggings. A bright pennon fluttered from Piers's lance, as gallant and defiant as tall, handsome Piers himself.

It all made a fine picture, Ralf thought, as he sat high on Faulk's saddlebow. He gazed at the Manor House men with pride and admiration. They had made short work of the robbers. And they had taken and given some hard knocks.

Ralf reached over to nudge Harald. "Look at Udo!" he whispered. "I told you he was a big cowardly windbag! Sagitta was a match for the whole lot of 'em—one little goshawk!"

"Bind their arms and guard them well, men," Sir John com-

136

manded. "We must lodge them in the village dungeon tonight, but tomorrow we'll take them to the town jail to await trial. The countryside for fifty miles around will breathe freer now. These rascals have many more crimes than this one to answer for, I think.

"Piers and Oswald, I'll leave the prisoners with you. You and your men know what to do. I'll ride at once to the Manor House to tell the good news to the lady Elfreda." Sir John wheeled his charger toward the boys. "Well, Harald and Ralf, are you satisfied now?"

"Oh, yes!" they both answered together.

"How bravely you all fought!" Ralf gazed at Sir John with great respect. "I wish I were grown up and a soldier."

"Why, Rafe," piped up Harald, remembering their own ordeal, "you're brave already. Father," he went on excitedly, "what do you think? Rafe caught me when my rope broke as they dropped me into that pit. If he hadn't, all my legs and arms and ribs would be broken—every single one. That's how Rafe's ankle got hurt. I fell on top of him."

Sir John sat very still on his big horse. The torchlight played over his clean-shaven face, set tonight in stern, hard lines. But his glance softened as he looked down at the tired, eager boys. "Ralf, that was well done, lad." He smiled. "Here, Faulk, you old war horse—I've kept you out of the fight, but if you'd like to join the others now, why, I'll take Ralf. Hector has a smoother pace than your horse. It may be easier on the boy's ankle."

Faulk's strong arms swung Ralf from saddle to saddle. Now he was proudly perched on tall Hector. With both hands he grasped the horse's tossing, raven-black mane.

Sir John called two men-at-arms to ride with him. Then, leaving the others to get the prisoners into line and follow more slowly, he and Humphrey turned their horses toward home.

They rode in silence for a while. Ralf, supported by Sir John's arm, was half asleep. Drowsily he heard his stepfather speak to him. "Ralf!"

"Yes, sir," he mumbled.

"I'm pleased with you, my boy. That was a good thought—

138

to send a message by your goshawk. And I think you saved Harald from a bad injury when the rope broke."

Ralf wriggled uncomfortably. "That was nothing," he muttered. "Harald was brave. He hardly cried a bit—all that long time."

"And you?"

"I didn't really cry. But I felt like it." Ralf chuckled, remembering. "That's what I got for playing truant. Oh, what a hard punishment Saint Nicholas gave me!"

Sir John laughed. "You'll think twice before you play truant from school again, I'll wager."

"I'm sorry I took Harald along. That was my fault," Ralf said.

"Don't worry about that, Ralf. It will help make a man of him. Joan has coddled him too much since his mother died. And all's well that ends well." Sir John paused, then went on gravely: "You wished to be grown up and a soldier, my boy. But those who are brave and who protect others are soldiers at any age."

"I thank you, Fath—sir," Ralf said gratefully, for the matter of Harald had been on his mind.

"I'd be glad for you to call me 'Father' whenever the whim takes you," Sir John said, in his half-teasing way.

Ralf had been very sleepy, but Sir John's words had shocked him wide-awake. His stepfather surely couldn't mean that he—Ralf—had acted like a soldier! Why, Sir John and he did not see eye to eye, and Sir John had a way of backing up *his* ideas with a willow switch across a boy's shoulders. Still, he was a very fine man for a stepfather. And after this night's work Ralf felt he could overlook painful things that happened in the past. And what about those bits of parchment Sir John had given him? Perhaps it was not just by chance there had been so many.

He said shyly, "It's not that I don't like you, sir, because I do. It's just, well, you know—"

"Right, son," Sir John interrupted. "I understand."

Margaret Leighton

THE PARCHMENT DOOR

ILLUSTRATED BY *Kay Lovelace*

As THE three riders carefully guided their small sturdy horses, one behind the other, along the overgrown path, from somewhere in the shadowed forest about them came the long-drawn howl of a wolf.

Bernard, leading the way, jerked his rein so sharply that his horse reared upon its haunches. Little Gisela, close behind him, gave a gasp and turned, looking fearfully over her shoulder. Alain, who was the last of the three, could see how white her face had grown, how frightened her blue eyes. Alain's own heart had begun to thump unpleasantly fast, but he urged his horse forward until he was abreast with his small cousin.

"Don't be afraid, Gisela. The three of us, mounted as we are, have nothing to fear from a single wolf."

But even as he spoke an answering howl came from another part of the forest—then more. The horses snorted and jerked theirs ears nervously first in one direction, then in another. Alain could feel his own horse begin to tremble.

Bernard, burly and blond and taller by a head than his cousin, slight dark-haired Alain, turned his horse about and circled back. "Ride on, both of you!" he ordered, his voice sharp and strained. "Alain, you take the lead. It sounds to me

140

like the gathering of a pack. Once we are out of the forest they'll not dare to follow us. But since the rear is the place of greatest danger, *I* had best be the one to guard it."

Alain's face flushed, and his gray eyes sparkled with resentment. "I have my own spear. If there is any wolf bold enough to attack horsemen in broad daylight, I can fight him off as well as you, Bernard!" he said.

"Fine words, master Alain! But who killed the buck I carried home yesterday across my saddlebow? If you hesitate to bring down a deer, better not measure your strength against the wolves of the forest!"

Alain's pride revolted fiercely against taking orders from Bernard, who, after all, was no older than he and had only the advantage of size for his authority.

He knew he had not wanted to kill the animal that Bernard had borne home with such pride. The deer had been so beautiful, and they had not needed food. He could not explain this to Bernard who killed for the love of the sport. A wolf was different—one that menaced his little cousin Gisela, whose terror-stricken face reminded him that this was hardly the time for a quarrel. He set his lips and rode on to take his place at the head of the little procession.

In only a few moments they had reached the edge of the forest. The wolves, still an unseen menace, were left behind. It was only in the dead of winter that wolves became bold enough to leave the forest by daylight. And so the danger was past, but Bernard's words still hurt and rankled.

Before the three riders lay a grassy valley from whose center rose a steep, rocky knoll. On this slight elevation, surrounded by a deep ditch and a stockade of pointed timbers stood the high, square, log-built tower with its outlying buildings, which was their home. The structures were simple and crude, thatched with straw and chinked with stones and clay, but they were the dwelling of the great man of the land. Gerhard, father of Bernard and Gisela, ruled these marshes of Brittany in the name of the king of the Franks, Charlemagne.

The ponies galloped down the smooth pasture slope and

141

across the narrow strips of cultivated fields. On the rim of the hills across the valley the sunset lingered, then suddenly was gone. From many different directions flocks and herds, driven by crop-haired peasant boys, barefooted and dressed in skins or the roughest of woven cloth, came back for the night's shelter in the fenced enclosures. Beasts of prey came forth nightly from the dark, encircling forests to prowl through the village, and only high walls and barred gates and doors could keep them out.

Up the dusty roadway between the peasant huts, over the echoing boards of the drawbridge the horses clattered, home at last! And there the three young riders stopped suddenly and sat motionless with surprise, danger, and quarrels alike forgotten. The whole place hummed with activity. Strange horses—Alain counted a dozen of them—were being groomed by the stable boys. From the wide open doorway of the great hall came the sound of many voices. Cooks and serving men hurried back and forth between the hall and the kitchens, working at a feverish pace.

Gisela slipped down from her saddle. "Strangers!" she cried. "Who can they be!" Together the three hurried into the hall.

As Alain's eyes became used to the dark, smoky interior, he saw that there were many tall strangers seated on the benches about the central fire, talking, laughing, and eating the roasted meat passed to them by the kitchen slaves. Others sat at the high table with Count Gerhard, his countess, and Alain's own mother, the widowed Lady Chlotilde. By the light of the torches Alain saw two whom he recognized. One, stalwart, grizzled, with an air of command, was named Hunold, and the other, with the thin, thoughtful face and shaven head, was a churchman, the Bishop Arno.

Alain remembered well the visit these two had made before. Not only were they great nobles of the land, but more, they were envoys of Charlemagne himself. Their task it was to travel about the king's domain and to make sure that his orders were being carried out by the local rulers. Woe to him of whom they reported that he was oppressing the people or failing to observe Charlemagne's decrees! But Gerhard was a loyal vassal, and the visits of the king's inspectors were always welcome here!

The boy recalled, too, that when they had come before, his uncle Gerhard had presented Alain to them. "This is Alain, who is now my ward, the son of my dead brother," he had said. "But perhaps the name of his mother's brother Roland is better known to you, although he was a Breton and no Frank. For it is said that Charlemagne himself called Roland, Count of Brittany, his friend."

Alain remembered that Hunold had said nothing in reply, but had put his big fingers under Alain's chin and tilted the boy's face to the light. He looked down at him long and intently. "Yes," he had said at last. "It is many a year since that heavy day when Roland was slain, but those gray eyes are not easily forgotten. Charles, our king, will be glad of this news for, indeed, he loved Roland well."

And now the king's envoys had come again, and even as Alain took his place behind his mother's chair, the two men were leaning together talking in low tones with their eyes upon the boy.

The Lady Chlotilde put her arm about her son and drew him forward, looking into his face with pride but with a hint of sadness, too, in the eyes beneath her level, dark brows. "These noble messengers of the king have brought news that concerns you, Alain," she said.

"Concerns *me?*" Alain opened his gray eyes wide.

Hunold answered him. "Yes, my boy. When I reported to our king, it pleased him to learn that you, the nephew of his greatly beloved dead comrade, Roland, were grown to be so likely a lad. He has sent us here to bring you back with us to his palace at Aix."

To Charlemagne, at Aix! Alain's heart gave such a leap that he could hardly get his breath. He looked from Hunold to the bishop and from his uncle to his mother, unable to speak. Suddenly across the table his eye caught that of Bernard. Surprise and envy were plain on Bernard's face. To serve the great king himself in his palace! But the bishop had begun to speak, and Alain turned to hear him.

"Our king has become much concerned about the training of the young people in his land," said the bishop. "He feels that since the future of the kingdom will be in their hands, they must be prepared for it. For this reason he has ordered schools set up for all his subjects, whether nobles, common folk, or even serfs, in the monasteries and in the palaces of the bishops. And now, in his own palace at Aix, he has started a school that will serve as a model for all. There his own sons and daughters are taught together with the rest. And there you shall go, Alain, to learn to read and to write."

"To read and write!" cried Alain, astonishment and dismay releasing his voice at last. A young noble might learn to ride and to hunt, to fight with spear and ax and sword—but to lower himself to learn reading and writing! That was incredible!

Count Gerhard's broad, ruddy face sobered. "Read and write? You had not told me this! Surely the king does not mean to make a clerk of him—Roland's kinsman!"

The whole hall had grown suddenly still. In the silence the fire crackled and a log fell, sending a great tower of sparks up among the rafters overhead. The dogs, gnawing their bones in the rushes strewn upon the hard-packed earthen floor, lifted their heads and looked about, struck by the unusual quiet.

The bishop continued smoothly as if nothing of this stir had come to his notice. "No, not a clerk, or a churchman either. But Charles our king is wise enough to know that the welfare of his realm will be safer in hands that have skill in other things as well as the sword."

Gerhard shook his head, plainly troubled. "It is not for me to question the king's orders. If he has sent for the boy, go he must. And it may be for the best—after all, he's but slight and small for his age."

Alain's face grew hot and tears burned suddenly in his throat. This was his sorest point—the fact that he was so much smaller than his cousin Bernard. He met Bernard's glance again; contempt, almost pity was plain in it. Even Gisela looked at him with compassion in her round blue eyes. With a muttered, hardly audible excuse, Alain turned and fled out into the darkness and confusion that filled the courtyard.

In the small, curtained cubicle off the great hall that held his couch, Alain spent a wakeful, wretched night. Morning brought bright sunshine, but the boy's heart was too heavy to respond to its call. Charlemagne's orders must be obeyed, there was no help for that. But to Alain, freeborn, a noble from a long line of fighting ancestors and in whose veins the blood of Roland ran hotly, the king's plan for him seemed a disgrace. What if he were small and slight? He was far quicker on his feet than Bernard, and he knew that, given time, his muscles would harden and strengthen so that he could take his place in the battle-line as well as any man!

Slowly he dressed himself for the journey. He wore his usual linen undergarments, his short tunic of brightly dyed wool, his cross-gartered hose and leather boots. Because the wind was sharp he added a sleeveless vest of fur and flung his long, blue woolen cloak about his shoulders. His few extra garments would be strapped to the back of one of the packhorses.

As he stepped out into the hall his mother called to him from her own alcove, where stood her high wooden bed hung with gayly woven curtains. "I have something for you, my son," she said. She flung back the cover of the great chest that stood at the foot of her bed and took out a smaller chest, carved and painted. This she unlocked with the key that hung on a cord about her neck. Alain watched eagerly as his mother lifted something from the chest—something long and glittering. It was a gold chain, richly carved, and on the end of it hung a shining piece of amber. That, too, was carved into a strange and lovely design.

Holding the chain in her hand, the Lady Chlotilde looked earnestly into Alain's face. "I have not spoken much to you of your uncle, my brother Roland," she said. "And the reason is that he was many years older than I and left our home here in Brittany to serve the king before I can remember. But once, when I was a little maid, smaller even than Gisela, he returned for a visit before setting forth that last fatal time. I remember well how he picked me up to say good-bye. I saw this chain and this amulet gleaming upon his breast and, as a child will, I caught it in my hands. He took it off and gave it to me. He said, 'Keep it, little sister. It has been in our family for many generations, since when, no man knows. If I were to carry it into so far a country it might be lost. It is said to give good fortune to its wearer if it is worn above a brave, true heart.' Then he kissed me and rode away. And so," said the Lady Chlotilde, holding her chin high and crowding back the tears that brightened her eyes, "I give it to you, my son, because I know your heart well, and it is both brave and true. And remember—there are other uses for courage besides battle! Who knows—there may be much greater uses."

Alain stood very straight while his mother put the chain about his neck. Then together they went out through the great hall, out into the sunshine where the others were already mounted and waiting to be gone. Wearing Roland's chain and amulet, how could his courage fail?

By midday Alain was farther from home than he had ever been, even on his longest day of hunting. The forest stretched about the cavalcade, thick and shadowy, silent except for bird calls, the jingle of harness, the sound of horses' hoofs on the thick carpet of leaves, the creak and rattle of the metal plates and rings that were sewn to the leather jerkins of the knights.

They stopped for a lunch of bread and cheese and wine beside a swift-flowing little river. Alain noted that just where the road dipped down to cross the ford there were many great, mossy stones lying scattered about as if they had once formed a bridge.

"Yes," said the bishop, when Alain spoke of this. "Doubtless there was a bridge here, for this that we are traveling was a Roman road, and the Romans were great bridge-builders as well as road-makers."

"A Roman road?" Alain said. "Do you mean that men from the city of Rome, far in the South came here and built roads and bridges?"

146

The bishop and Hunold exchanged looks. "It is high time indeed that our king gave thought to schooling!" said Arno. "When Imperial Rome is forgotten in the land where Romans lived and worked so long!"

On they rode again. Sometimes the road narrowed, but usually it was broad enough for two to ride abreast. The bishop on his white palfrey led the way. He was a silent man whose eyes seemed always to be looking at something far away. Hunold and Alain rode next.

As Alain absently fingered his amulet, a thought occurred to him. He turned to Hunold. "You knew my Uncle Roland?" he asked shyly. "Could you tell me about him?"

Hunold's heavy brows drew together in concentration as he nodded. "Tell you about him? It was many years ago, but perhaps I can remember." He looked off among the trees as if looking into time long past, and then began his story.

As Alain listened, it seemed to him that the enveloping forest melted away from about him. Instead, on either side rose the bare, wind-scoured peaks of the Pyrenees. He found himself glancing fearfully up at the overhanging trees as if they were the rocks that hid the hordes of dark-skinned foemen.

More clearly than the bishop on his white horse, Alain could see Roland on his charger, in golden armor. An ivory horn hung from its baldric—a horn that he was to blow if attacked. Roland going forth to do service for his friend the great Charlemagne. Roland riding into the mountain pass from which he had not returned.

"Of what happened there in the pass no man has real knowledge," said Hunold, "for Roland was slain. Certainly we know he never blew upon his ivory horn which would have summoned warriors to his rescue. Perhaps he did not wish to endanger other lives in order to save his own. Roland was no burly giant—rather he was slight and dark as seem all you Bretons—but he was a great and good knight. And he was gentle, too, and kind. It is sad that such men must be forgotten."

The boy had been so lost in listening that he had not noticed how the forest had begun to thin about them. Now he saw with surprise that they were looking out across an open plain, smooth and fertile, looped by a shining band of river and darkened by clustered orchards and the varied green of cultivated fields.

"Ahead lies the monastery where we shall have shelter for the night," said Hunold, pointing to a group of buildings whose thatched roofs showed above the fruit trees.

Inside the walls of the monastery they found a warm welcome. Hot soup, good, fresh bread, fish from the river, and fruit from the orchard were served to them on long tables in the whitewashed refectory. The stout abbot, anxious to make a

good impression on his important visitors, showed them through the buildings himself.

Alain, following close at the heels of the three men—the abbot, the bishop, and Hunold—listened and looked with all his ears and eyes. At last, in a small room where a western window let in the last of the afternoon light, they found a group of young novices and older monks bent over high, slanting desks, working busily with feathered quills and ink pots. Bishop Arno paused to pick up the battered yellow parchment from which a young man was copying. "What is this?" he asked.

The abbot peered over his shoulder. "That? That is an old manuscript that we found in the chest of records. It is not from the Scriptures, but our king, as you know, has given orders that all the ancient Latin writings are to be copied as well as the holy words of the saints." He looked anxiously into Arno's face. "I trust it does not displease you that we should preserve this heathen's tale?"

The bishop looked at the manuscript closely for a moment, then replaced it on the desk. "I recognize it now. It is part of the writings of the Roman poet, Virgil—an account of the deeds of the great Aeneas. A heathen, as you say, but a hero nevertheless. And written in words which must not be lost to future generations. Write well, my son!" He laid a hand kindly on the shoulder of the young novice, who flushed with pleasure.

The men moved on, but Alain remained behind, watching the quill in the inkstained fingers moving so surely yet so carefully over the fresh white parchment. "Can you read those words as well as write them?" he asked.

The young man nodded. His eyes, in his thin, brown face glowed. "Writing is toil, but reading—that is the greatest pleasure in life! Standing here with this before me I can travel miles across seas and lands I never saw and look upon men and cities now dust for centuries!" he said.

Alain stared at him blankly for a moment. Then his face lighted up as he began to see what the young man meant. "Why that's the way I felt when Hunold was telling me the story of Roland!" he cried. "Do you mean that all these parchments have stories upon them? That reading is like listening to a tale?"

"Some have stories, some have songs, some have prayers, some have the words of saints or even of Our Lord, some have rules and laws of the land. All different, but each is like a doorway into a new world!"

"Alain!" called Hunold from outside. "Come, we must find beds for the night. We'll have to be up and away by sunrise."

Obediently Alain followed the old warrior into the fading twilight, his mind awhirl with new thoughts. Alone at last in one of the clean, narrow rooms that the monks kept ready for travelers, he lay down upon the pile of straw in the corner, but he could not sleep. Something tremendous had happened inside his mind. The world seemed changed.

There was nothing dismal, nothing dreary now in the thought of learning to read and to write. Rather, he looked forward impatiently to the end of his journey. Soon he would be able to read for himself all these tales of forgotten days.

He turned restlessly, and the chain of the amulet slid as he moved; the smooth, cool amber touched his cheek. And then a new idea came to him, so dazzling that he lay perfectly still on his pallet of sweet-smelling straw, while the rising moon shone through the narrow window and threw leaf-shadows on the whitewashed wall above his head. Perhaps he, Alain, could write out the story of Roland some day, just the way Hunold had told it to him there in the dark forest, his words timed to the steady, measured beat of their horses' hoofs! Then, like the song of Aeneas, it would not be forgotten when those who had taken part in it were dead and gone. The name of Roland would stand forever in men's minds, a symbol of gallantry and courage and unfailing loyalty!

There was a smile on Alain's face as he fell asleep.

Beatrice Travers stood at the bow of the *Good Will* anxiously wondering what would happen to her if the British discovered the secret message she was carrying to the rebels in America. When her family in England was forced to separate, twelve-year-old Beatrice was sent to her cousin John Travers in America. At first she was disguised as a boy because John would not take a girl, but her shipmates soon discovered who she really was. Beatrice began her voyage on an American ship, but it was overtaken by the *Good Will*, a British vessel, on which she continued her journey to America. Beatrice is sure that the suspicious British will not discover the secret message, cleverly hidden in the cover of a book.

Now new difficulties arise. The British notify cousin John; but when he learns that it is a girl on board ship he fears a trick and refuses to come for her.

Emilie Benson Knipe
and Alden Arthur Knipe

SIX BELLS

ILLUSTRATED BY *DeWitt Whistler Jayne*

I CAN scarce describe my wretchedness and misery as I sat on that gun-carriage, weeping my eyes out. Perhaps another girl might have been braver, I know not. The blow had fallen so suddenly that I had no chance to summon fortitude. One moment I had been looking forward eagerly to an end of all my troubles, and the next they were upon me again. Worst of all, Mr. Travers had denied me. I could only cry—and cry—and cry!

Mr. Vernon tried to ease my sorrow, but in vain—

"I cannot stand this!" he said at length, almost roughly. "We must do something. Try to cease your weeping and think if there is not a way out of it!"

He rose to his feet and began pacing the deck, muttering to himself now and then, and as often shaking his head, showing all too plainly that no solution came to him.

At length I managed to stay my tears, though, indeed, I still shook with dry sobs, and Mr. Vernon seated himself beside me once more.

"I can see no help for it," he confessed sadly. "If Travers had not been so impudent, the Admiral might have been prevailed upon to let you try again, but now it is useless to look for aid in that direction."

"Yes, I suppose so," I answered hopelessly; "there is nothing to be done, only—only—"

"Only what?" he asked.

"Nothing—except that I should have liked Mr. Travers to know the truth of it," I answered. "Think you they would send a letter to him if I wrote?"

"Nay, that they would not!" he answered. "But," he went on, lowering his voice, "write your letter, and I will see that it reaches him, only you must let me read it. You can understand my reason."

I went at once to my cabin to write the letter. I had not the slightest hope that anything would come of it; my one desire was that my cousin should know the truth and that, perhaps, at some later date he might send to Europe for me to come again. I knew only too well what sort of welcome awaited me in Amsterdam if ever I got there.

I wrote out fully the reasons for my coming and all that had befallen since that distant day when I boarded the *Bouncing Betsey* in London, and told, as well as I was able, just how everything had happened and something, too, of my own sorrow and disappointment. I wanted to tell him of the paper that had been intrusted to me, but dared not, knowing that Mr. Vernon must read it. This left me in a quandary, for I wanted to let Mr. Travers know of my effort to bring it safe into his hands.

I bit the end of my pen in perplexity, trying to solve this riddle, and then there popped into my head what Captain

153

Timmons had told me to do in case I wished to see Mr. Travers privately on a matter of importance.

"Just whisper to him that tea has gone up thrippence a pound," the captain had said. Writing it might do as well, though what I hoped to gain I know not to this day. Still, once having seized upon the idea, I straightway wished to put it into practice, but here another matter came to plague me. To put the sentence in alone, unconnected with anything else in the letter, would excite suspicion, so I tried to think of some manner in which I could include it naturally. At last, after much puzzling, I wrote the following:

I regret that I have no gossip of London for you, but I was there so short a time that I scarce had a chance to see aught but a few shops. Granny says 'tis a most extravagant place, and that tea has gone up thrippence a pound. I know not whether you will be interested in this, but Captain Timmons told me a story of the Boston Tea Party. Perhaps that is the reason it is so high.

I read this over many times, wondering if the true purport of it would be plain to Mr. Vernon, and then, deciding that he would see only what was written, I copied it into the letter and so finished.

Mr. Vernon was on deck, and together we went back to the gun-carriage. He read the letter through, while I sat looking out across the waters to the land where I had hoped to live. That hope was gone now, and I gazed at the shores sorrowfully.

It took him some time, the letter being long, but at last he finished and folded it for me to place the wafers.

" 'Tis a sad letter," said he, "and your information about the tea was somewhat malapropos. Tea is taboo in America these days. But I will see that it starts on its way at once," and, with a smile, he went off.

There was nothing now for me to do but wait until a troopship bound for England should be ready. The hours passed uneventfully, for I had lost interest in everything, and a sort of numbness had come upon my spirits which, though it eased the pain of my disappointment, left me quite indifferent. Even the men who came aboard the ship with vegetables and fruit had ceased to attract my attention, and for the most part I sat by myself on deck, scarce conscious of what went on about me.

One morning, some four days after I had written my letter, I became aware of a man standing before me, holding out some plums as if for sale. He was a young man, as I could see at once, though the rough sort of cap he wore was pulled down over his forehead, and the collar of his rather torn and soiled coat was turned up. I looked at him for a moment and was about to tell him that I did not wish to buy, when he lifted his head suddenly and looked me full in the face, his eyes meeting mine squarely. There was something in the bright glance that held my attention, and then—he deliberately winked!

"Tea has gone up thrippence a pound," he whispered—and I stared amazed.

"Come, buy my plums," he went on in a loud voice. "They are the best in the Jerseys, and I'll make them cheap for an English maid. Do not look so frighted," he added under his breath. "'Tis all right, and I am your cousin John. Come, Mistress, buy my plums."

For a few moments, he went on in this strain, praising the fruit and urging me between whiles to compose myself, and, indeed, I had need to, for my heart was beating furiously, and I was panting from excitement.

We stood alone on the deck, but there were sailors passing constantly, and at such times Mr. Travers, for it was, indeed he, would raise his voice for me to buy, like any hawker.

"Nay, now, do not look so pale!" he said in an undertone.

"But if you are caught, they will hang you for a spy!" I whispered back.

"Indeed, that's true!" he answered, with a reckless little laugh. "But these British are so cock-sure of themselves, they'd never suspect that anyone would dare brave their mightiness. 'Tis their conceit will be their undoing. But enough of that! I was much distressed when your letter reached me and I found what I had done. How did you manage to get it to me?

155

I had not thought they would be so obliging, after my refusal to come for you."

"Mr. Vernon sent it," I answered.

"Not Guy Vernon?" he asked, with a note of anxiety in his voice.

"The same," I replied; "he is aboard this ship."

"And he would know me in any sort of dress," Mr. Travers went on, more to himself than to me. "Oh, well, it makes the adventure the more diverting, that's all. Now what of the message from Captain Timmons? for he would never have given you that word about the tea, if there had not been something behind it."

"I have a paper," I told him. "'Tis most important, though I know not what it is about; but the English know of it, and it is on that account mainly that they wish to keep me prisoner."

It was some minutes before we could go on, for two officers stopped near us and talked for a while, during which time Mr. Travers kept up the patter about the fruit. But not content with showing his wares to me, he must needs go up to the officers as well, while I looked on in a panic.

"They're good, loyal plums," I heard him say; "grown in the Jerseys, and never a Whig near them. Come, Your Excellencies, buy, and mayhap you'll convert a rebel."

The officers, laughing at his audacity, told him to be off, and themselves walked away.

"Where is the paper?" he asked, coming back to me, and I told him.

"I guess what is in it!" he exclaimed. "Would it were in the General's hands."

"Let me get it for you now!" I urged. "I can pretend to go for my purse."

"But I cannot take *you* now," he said.

"Oh, but never mind me!" I replied. "The paper is ever so much more important."

"Nay," he answered, with a resolute shake of his head, "you have brought it so far, you shall take it all the way. Besides I came not for that alone. Indeed, no! I came to fetch my new cousin."

"But how?" I asked, for I could see no way of his doing that.

"Listen!" he said, glancing about him. "Think you, you can come on deck tonight without being seen?"

"Yes, I can manage that," I answered, for the position of the little cubbyhole in which I slept made it easily possible.

"Good!" he exclaimed. "Come then as the ship's bell strikes six tonight. That will be eleven o'clock, as you no doubt know. I will be waiting at the landing-stage for you. Be ready, and come on the stroke of the bell."

"But there is always a guard on the landing-stage," I returned.

"Yes, one," he answered with a smile. "Do not fear that he will stay you. Put on a dark dress and come with the book. Your other things must be left behind. Will you be there?"

157

"Yes," I answered, and was about to speak further, when a step sounded near us and my cousin raised his voice again in praise of his fruit. This same thing had happened so often before that I thought nothing of it, till a voice spoke to me, and I looked up to see Mr. Vernon standing beside us.

"They are fine-looking plums," he said pleasantly.

"Yes," I answered, "I was thinking of buying some, but my purse is below. I will go and fetch it."

"Why trouble?" returned Mr. Vernon, taking a coin out of his pocket. "Let me have the pleasure of presenting you with the fruit. How much are they, fellow?"

"Nay," I hurried to reply, for I feared the moment when he would discover the identity of the man before us. "Nay, he has pestered me so that I have lost my desire for them. Let him go."

"Pestered you, has he? Then we'll teach him better manners!" Mr. Vernon replied, and reaching out a hand he put it under the other's chin and raised the bowed head. "Look up, fellow, and—and—"

He stopped as their eyes met. Mr. Travers said no word, but gazed back at him with a half-reckless, half-serious smile on his face, as if he cared not what was the issue. Mr. Vernon, on the other hand, was visibly affected, and I trembled with fear, for a word from him meant death to my cousin.

How long they stood thus, I cannot tell, but it seemed to me like hours; then in a harsh and rather husky voice, Mr. Vernon spoke:

"Be off with you! and hereafter sell your plums on some other ship; for, if I find you on the *Good Will* again, you'll not get away so easily!"

Picking up his baskets, Mr. Travers hurried along the deck and, a minute later, I saw him run down the ladder and jump into a small boat.

As for Mr. Vernon, he, too, stood watching for a moment and then turned away.

"Mistress Beatrice," he said in a constrained voice, "you have, I fear, been the cause of one man's losing his honor."

"Nay, say not that!" I cried, for I saw that he felt it deeply. "What are the doings of one small maid in this great war of yours? For your kindness and for your friendship I shall ever say a prayer of thankfulness; but I should be sad indeed if, hereafter, when you think of me it should be with regret. And you know he came not to spy," I ended.

He stood looking gloomily at the deck; then he lifted his head with a slight laugh.

"For a moment I thought that I recognized that fellow with the plums, but I must have been mistaken," he said, and without another word he left me.

I was in a flutter of excitement for the rest of that day, and never had I known the hours pass so slowly. My mind dwelt constantly on the prospect of my escape, and I was impatient for the time to come when the attempt should be made.

How Mr. Travers was to accomplish this I knew not. As I looked out over the broad waters of the Bay, and counted the multitude of British ships lying at anchor near us, the task of going in and out among them, without being discovered, seemed well-nigh impossible. Still, I was little concerned with this, never once thinking of failure, but rather busying myself with the part I was to play in the enterprise.

I made the trip from my cabin, along the alleyway to the steps leading to the deck, up these and across to the place where the ladder led down to the landing-stage, not once but a dozen times, so anxious was I to do my share correctly, though, to be sure, I took care to act indifferently, so that anyone noticing me could have no idea of what was going on in my mind.

I went early to my cabin when the night came down and got into my berth to await the time when I should attempt my escape, but I thought eleven o'clock would never come.

All was prepared as best I knew how. I had ready a gown of linsey-woolsey, and under it hung my pack-pocket filled with those things I could not bear to leave behind. They were trifles mostly, the shoe-buckles, a brooch, and the tiny tea-set carved out of a bone by Jim Tasker, the boatswain of the *Bouncing*

159

Betsey. So, with my precious book of Maxims clutched in my hands, I lay and listened for the ship's bell to sound the half-hours.

Finally, when five bells struck, I rose quietly and put on my dress.

Once more I waited and oh, how long it seemed! Everything about the ship was unusually still and the occasional rapid footfalls of those crossing the deck above my head served to make the quiet more complete. My heart beat furiously and my breath came in little gasps, so great was my anxiety.

And still I waited, till at length I was sure it must be past the time and that the sailor, whose business it was to strike the hours, had forgotten.

At length it began to sound and the first tap of the bell seemed so loud and ominous that it startled me; but, summoning all the courage and fortitude I possessed, I stole forth to traverse, I hoped for the last time, the little passage leading away from my sleeping place. I did not meet anyone and once on deck I saw a clear field to the break in the bulwarks where the gangway ladder led to the landing-stage below. Gaining that, and beginning to feel safe, I looked down and there, whistling a tune to himself, was a sailor standing near a lant-horn that made a narrow circle of light over the waters gently lapping the sides of the ship.

I hesitated at the top not knowing what to do, for surely the sailor would put a halt to my flight and rouse the ship should I make a struggle. I was in despair, for I had not ex-pected to see him there, having relied on my cousin's words of assurance that the guard would be taken care of. All then was lost I supposed; for some reason or other the plan had miscarried; still I had been told to be on the landing-stage at eleven o'clock, and the last stroke of the bell had echoed throughout the ship. I would, of course, be discovered but, for all that, I meant to carry out my part to the end, and so took the first step down.

There was a creak, as the ladder moved slightly under my weight, and the sailor, catching the sound, turned and looked

up at me. I noted the surprised expression of his face as he
opened his mouth to speak, but at the same instant a dark shadow came into the circle of light, and a boat touched gently
against the stage. Out of it leapt Mr. Travers, who immediately
sprang upon the guard and thrust a handkerchief or cloth of
some sort into his half-open mouth, thus preventing any outcry.
Then followed a short, sharp struggle; but the guard, taken
wholly by surprise, was no match for the other and, in a moment, was on his back with my cousin atop of him.

Meanwhile I had run down, well knowing what was going
forward, and stood beside the struggling pair.

"Ah, you are just in time," Mr. Travers whispered, looking
up at me with a smile. "This fellow is tougher than I thought
for, and you will have to help, or he will rouse the ship. Bind his

161

arms with that," he ended, nodding toward a coil of rope which he had, doubtless, brought for the purpose.

As quickly as I was able, for, indeed, my fingers trembled greatly, I put the rope under the guard's shoulders. Then, making a noose, I drew it as tightly as I could about his arms while Mr. Travers held him. Once this much was accomplished the rest was simple enough and, in a few moments, he lay helpless, though little the worse for his handling.

"Now into the boat," Mr. Travers whispered, as he straightened up from binding the man's legs.

I was about to do as he bade me when the sound of oars dipped in the water came to us, and I looked out to see the light of a boat rapidly approaching our landing from the other side of the *Good Will*. In a panic of fear I turned to my cousin, but there was no need to warn him. He, too, had seen and heard. Without the loss of an instant he grasped me firmly around the waist, lifted me into the boat, and, giving a huge push with his foot against the landing-stage leaped in after me, and we were adrift on the, then, quiet waters of New York Bay.

But we were too late to escape discovery and, as Mr. Travers gained the thwart and took up the oars, the others were full upon us, and the light from the lanthorn lit up the whole of our boat.

"Halt! Halt!" came the command, but my cousin only pulled the harder, and the next moment we had passed out of the ring of light and were lost in the darkness.

But Lord Bedford had seen enough to arouse more than suspicion and, almost at the same time that he sighted us, they made the landing-stage and there was the guard, gagged and bound, to tell the tale of our flight.

At once there was a great to-do aboard the *Good Will*. A drum was beaten, lights flashed here and there, the tramp of running men came to us over the water, and it seemed scarce a minute before the whole vessel was in wild confusion. Then shots were fired as signals to the ships near by; followed by shouted orders from one to another and from these, in turn, to those farther on; until the entire fleet was astir; eager to capture an "escaping prisoner" who, of course, was I.

I cowered at the bottom of the boat, fearful of the outcome and certain I should be captured. Whichever way I looked there was a ship full of men keen to take us and ready, if need be, to shoot were they not obeyed. Nor was it only the ships we had to fear. Small boats were being launched from every vessel as fast as the men could man them, and soon the bay was dotted with lights which darted here and there looking for us.

Mr. Travers had ceased pulling rapidly and sat with his head turned looking over his shoulder while he guided our boat into the black patches of water. He made no sound as he rowed for, as I saw later, the oars had been muffled by wrapping cloths about them.

Presently a circle of lights surrounded us and I looked in vain for a space of shadow between them, through which we might escape. My cousin must have had some such thought, too, for he leaned forward and whispered to me:

"Lie flat, cousin. 'Tis like to be hot work before we've finished this game of hide and seek."

I did as he told me, well knowing that the British would not hesitate to shoot, but Mr. Travers seemed not to have any fear, if I could judge from the way he spoke. Rather did he appear to enjoy the prospect of "hot work," as he called it. I confess I was feeling far from cheerful; for to me our plight was desperate indeed, nor could I see any way through that circle of lights gradually closing in upon the dark spot where we lay.

I cannot describe how strange a scene it was. We in darkness so dense that I could not distinguish Mr. Travers, though he was within a few feet of me, and yet, all around us were the lights of the ships throwing broad beams on the water, while each of the small boats carried a lanthorn. Our only hope, of course, was to remain in the shadows, and even this hope was rapidly waning.

I thought it could only be a matter of a few minutes when we would be discovered and taken. Cousin John, however, was far from discouraged; he seemed in the best of spirits, as I could tell from the occasional soft chuckles he gave, and, presently, I had an explanation of it.

" 'Tis like the British to be looking for sparks with a lanthorn," he whispered.

"But soon or late they must find us," I said, under my breath.

"Nay, fear not, cousin," he answered confidently. "We're as safe as if we were on Brooklyn Heights."

For all his confident tone I was far from being assured, and the happenings in the next few minutes brought my heart to my throat more than once.

At first there had been a more or less scattered effort on the part of our pursuers, but now all the small boats had formed a wide circle of which we were, somewhat, the center, and now they began to converge toward the spot where we lay. Nearer and nearer they came, cutting down the darkness in all directions until it seemed certain that a few moments more would leave us at their mercy. Meanwhile, Mr. Travers did nothing, or at least, so it seemed to me. Now and then he would pull at the oars slowly and carefully, shifting our position, first this way and then that, but soon it became plain that the limit of the shadows had been reached and that nothing could be done save surrender. A few strokes more and the British boats would be upon us.

Then, to my great surprise, Mr. Travers began to shout at the top of his lungs:

"Ahoy, there! This way! This way! Here they are!" he yelled, and I thought for certain he had fallen daft, for surely this was a strange method of effecting our escape.

I soon saw, however, that my cousin's hail was the result of no thoughtless plan; for at once a great hubbub arose and, amid shoutings and splashings, the British boats began to make toward the sound of Mr. Travers's voice, each one, seemingly, intent upon arriving first and gaining credit for the capture. In so doing they at once broke the ring of lights about us and several, coming together, left a wide unlighted space between them, which Cousin John was quick to take advantage of. Under

164

the noise of the hastening British he pulled swiftly toward the black water, and in a few minutes we were clear of the circle that hemmed us in. Even I could see that, with a little precaution, we were safe enough.

One after another we passed the huge hulks of the ships of the line until, at length, we were free of them all.

"And now, Cousin Beatrice, we can talk to our heart's content," cried Mr. Travers, and he began plying his oars more vigorously than he had heretofore.

"And are we safe at last?" I asked, taking a long breath and scrambling into the seat in the stern.

"Aye," said he, "for though there are plenty of redcoats about, they're on the other side of the bay at Staten Island. But, tell me, have you the paper safe?"

"Yes," I answered, "and I am most anxious to be rid of it."

"No doubt, no doubt," he agreed; "but you must carry it yet awhile, for we have a good way to go before we reach the town, and I do not mean to stop until we are there."

"Cousin," I said anxiously after a few moments, "can you forgive me for being a girl instead of a boy?"

" 'Tis a great tax on my forbearance," he made answer; and, not being able to see his face, I knew not how to take it.

"Even though I am a girl," I went on, "I shall try not to be a burden to you and hope in a little while, after I have learned the customs of America, to be useful. Granny says I'm a good housewife and —"

"Nay," he interrupted, breaking into a hearty laugh, "housekeepers are easy come by, and I have a most excellent one already. But"—and he dropped his voice, so that he spoke seriously—"*sisters* are a different matter, and now that I have found one, I mean to keep her. Do not trouble your head on that score, Beatrice. I'm right glad you're here, and I hope you will soon love me as, by reason of your steadfast courage, I have already begun to love you."

He was much in earnest, as I could tell by his voice, and I was very, very glad.

"I know I shall love you," I answered, a little huskily; "and

166

No one could have any idea what was going on in my mind

I should like you to call me Bee, as they did at home, if you will."

"Good!" he exclaimed. " 'Bee' it shall be, and I am Brother John. Is that agreed?"

"Yes, Brother John," I said.

"That's right," he laughed; "now we shall be truly brother and sister"; and he said it in so kindly a way that all the heart-aches and disappointments were forgotten, and I felt that, though I had, indeed, lost one home, I should soon find another.

We talked while he rowed and he asked me all manner of questions about Granny and the boys. So, with the feeling of safety and the realization that my troubles were at an end, I must have dropped asleep, for one moment I was listening to Brother John's voice in the darkness, and the next I opened my eyes to find that it was broad daylight, and he laughing at me as he still rowed the boat.

"I've been waiting very patiently for you to wake up," he said, half-banteringly. "I want to see that paper now that there is light to read, but you clutched it so tightly in your sleep that I couldn't take it without disturbing you, and that I had not the heart to do."

"Oh, yes, the paper!" I cried, taking up the book and breaking a thread in the cover with my bodkin. "Here it is!" and I drew it forth and handed it to him.

He opened it eagerly, and I saw his face light up with joy.

" 'Tis splendid!" he cried, "and will put some heart in the doubting ones, besides giving us a place to buy powder for our army. Hold it safe, Bee," he went on excitedly, "for the General must have it before he goes on his daily rounds!" and he picked up the oars and rowed furiously.

"And may I not know what it is now?" I asked, for I confess that the contents of the precious document had greatly aroused my curiosity.

"Aye!" he answered heartily. "Though 'tis a secret, you deserve to know, and I need not fear to trust your discretion. 'Tis a letter, Bee, from our agent at the French court, saying that, although King Louis is not at this time willing to come out before the world as a supporter of the new government of America, for fear of war with England, he, nevertheless, bids us count upon him as a friend, and adds that the ports of France are open to us."

There could be no doubt that he was overjoyed, but somehow it seemed little for both the Americans and British to make such a pother over.

I think he must have seen what was in my mind, for he spoke further.

"You cannot possibly understand all it means to us, who are fighting not only the British army and navy, but many of our own people, who, from fear or hope of gain, stick to the Tory side and do all in their power to discourage and hamper us. For us to be able to say that France is our friend will bring money and men to our colors, and we need both sadly. Then, too, the chance to secure arms and ammunition is most important. You have brought glorious news, Bee, glorious! and His Excellency, General Washington, will be overjoyed when you hand it to him!"

Margery Blair Perkins

THE STRANGER
IN THE WOOD

ILLUSTRATED BY *Clarence Biers*

PEDRO could not find the pig. He had wedged his sturdy brown body in its faded green jerkin into a notch high up in a half-dead oak tree, in order to see if he could catch sight of the wandering animal somewhere on the sunbaked plain. But it was nowhere to be seen. Pedro heaved a sigh.

The pig had strayed from the little whitewashed hut which Pedro called home over two hours ago, and he had been hunting for it ever since. He knew too well how many suppers a missing pig meant. Only last winter a big black one had run away, and he had never been able to find a trace of it. Pedro could still taste the watery, meatless stew which had never seemed to half fill his aching nine-year-old stomach. He poked his curly brown head through the dry, crackling leaves to give a last look.

He could see as far as the gray mountains. He could even see the thick stone walls of Olmedo rising out of the yellow plain. For a moment he forgot about the pig. Somewhere beneath those great towers camped the soldiers of the Archbishop of Toledo and the young Prince Alfonso, waiting to meet the army of the king. He knew that great events were taking shape in Castile and that Olmedo would have its share in them. There would be a great battle, one which Castile would long remember. If the King lost, then the young Prince would be the new king.

169

The sun was going down behind the snow-capped mountains now. A cold wind rustled the brown leaves in the tree and blew through Pedro's thin jacket. He shivered a little. It was growing too dark to see anything. He might as well get down out of the tree and start for home. The pig was nowhere about. Nimbly he scrambled down through the branches.

When he reached the lowest bough, he swung himself into the air and landed lightly on the sandy ground. Shaking the bits of bark from his jerkin, he started to run. The gathering darkness made him choose the shortest way home, which was through the wood. To be sure, the wood was gloomy and full of black shadows, and he had never walked through it after dark alone. But if he skirted around it, he would be at least half an hour longer in reaching home.

There was nothing in the wood of which he should be afraid. Pedro had heard that a long time ago a robber had hidden in its dark shadows, then disappeared. The old women of the neighborhood told stories of how his homeless ghost still wandered in the forest and frightened bad children. Pedro told himself that the old women were full of such stories that people only half believed. But he ran a little faster in the direction of the wood, even though he knew there was no such thing as a ghost.

Still he could not put the thought of the robber ghost out of his mind. Suppose the story *were* true! What would he, Pedro, do if he met the ghost this very evening? He drew his jacket more closely around him, as if to shut out his fears with the wind. What did a person say to a ghost? He could not remember ever having heard of anybody actually meeting one.

A rabbit scurried across his path and disappeared in the darkness. It was so quiet that the patter of its little feet sounded very loud in Pedro's ears. He reached the edge of the wood.

Swallowing a lump in his throat, he plunged in among the black trees. The twigs crackled noisily under his running feet. If there were a ghost it would surely hear him. Perhaps, however, he would be out of the forest before the ghost was awake enough to come after him. Some people said that ghosts

170

must sleep during the day. They had to sleep some of the time certainly. And perhaps they did not wake quickly, any more than Pedro did, when his mother called him in the early morning to feed the pigs and chickens.

He looked back over his shoulder just to make sure that the ghost was not behind him now. What he saw made his heart give an extra little hop and then almost stop beating. Coming toward him very fast was a dark shapeless figure. It was tall and thin and had no head. What should he do? His heart almost bursting inside him, Pedro decided to hide behind a tree and let the ghost get ahead of him.

He plunged into the thickets beside the path and pressed his body against a black tree trunk. If he were only a squirrel he could find a hole and disappear into its safe darkness. He peered around the trunk to see if the ghost were still coming. It was almost upon him. He ducked his head. The sound of the crackling branches seemed loud enough to burst his eardrums. He peered out again. The figure was abreast of his tree. Now he could see it clearly. Why, it was only a man after all, and a frightened man, too, for Pedro could hear him making little groaning noises as he swayed along. Perhaps he knew about the ghost, too, and was afraid. Pedro decided to leave his tree and walk with him. Even if he were a stranger, he was better company than a ghost.

Pedro stepped out from behind the sheltering tree trunk. "Señor."

The man jumped at the sound and turned quickly around in the direction from which it had come. His trembling hand leaped to the dagger hanging from his girdle.

Then Pedro came out into the path. The man, seeing that it was only a young boy, sighed heavily with relief and pushed the dagger back into its sheath. "Oh, I thought one of the enemy might be lurking in the wood. One can never be too quick."

"Oh, no, señor, but some folks say that there is a ghost in this wood. Do you think that a ghost would be afraid of a dagger?"

171

The man did not answer, but started hurrying on again. Pedro ran to keep up with him. Though the stranger did not seem to want any company, Pedro stuck close to his side. The ghost might be afraid of two people walking together.

Soon they reached the edge of the woods. There the man stopped. He had wrapped his cape so closely about his face that Pedro could get no glimpse of it. But he seemed not to know where next to go.

Pedro touched the man gently on the arm and spoke. "Perhaps I could help you, Señor, if you will tell me where you want to go. I was born in the neighborhood and have lived here all my life."

The stranger's answer made Pedro's eyes widen with astonishment. "I don't know where I want to go—anywhere away from that!" He waved his hand in the direction from which they had come.

Pedro repeated the words in slow amazement. "You don't know where you want to go, Señor? But where will you spend the night? It is going to be cold."

"I don't know where I am going to spend this night—or any

of the thousand others." The stranger muttered his words into his cape.

This answer astonished Pedro no less than the other had. If the man had no place to stay that night, however, he had best ask him to come home with him. His mother had said one should always help the sick and the homeless.

"Please, sir, if I may be so bold as to say it, you cannot stay out on the plain all night. You will freeze to death. Mother would be very glad to have you stop with us, Señor. She is always most happy to take in those who have no home. She says it is the way she can give thanks to God for giving us a home."

The man looked down at him. "Where do you live and who is your family?"

"We live scarcely a mile farther, Señor. Our name is Lopez, and Mother says we have lived in these parts since the beginning of man. Anyway it is a very long time."

"What does your father do?" The stranger's voice was hoarse and fearful.

"My father is dead, Señor. God take his soul!" Pedro crossed himself. "Mother says I am the head of the family now." He lifted his head proudly, but the man did not appear to notice. He was gazing in the direction from which they had come. Suddenly, without looking down at Pedro, he spoke. "Take me to your home. I can decide there what it will be best for me to do."

Pedro did not think that the man seemed very grateful for the offer of a night's shelter. Without any more words, however, he took the little path to the right, and the two trudged along in the darkness in silence.

Suddenly they heard a voice calling in the darkness. The man stopped in alarm. The voice called again. This time Pedro turned quickly to his companion. "It is my Mother's voice, Señor. We must hurry."

He began to run, and the man hurried along beside him with long strides. The voice came nearer. Pedro ran faster, calling as he ran. "Mother, Mother, here I am."

173

He could make out the shadowy outlines of his mother's plump figure a little distance away. He ran up to her and threw his arms around her ample waist. "Oh, Mother, I'm sorry if I have made you worry."

"Worry!" His mother gave a little snort of exasperation. "Worry—I have been thinking for the last hour that you had met with some accident. Did you find the pig?"

Pedro had forgotten all about the pig. It seemed ages ago that the pig had run away. He shook his head slowly. "I couldn't find it anywhere. I even climbed up into a tree to see if I could spy it, but it was not anywhere to be seen."

Señora Lopez heaved a sigh. "It is probably in the woods somewhere. I don't know what—" She stopped and gave a little start.

Pedro felt her tremble and turned quickly. The stranger had come up silently and was staring at them. He could feel his eyes, though he could not see them.

"Oh, Mother. I met this gentleman in the woods. He has no place to stay tonight, so I invited him to stop with us."

The stranger bowed stiffly. Señora Lopez stood silent for a moment, fumbling with the hem of her white apron. Then she made a stiff little curtsy. "You are welcome to our home, Señor. You will find it very simple, but full of cheer. Come. It is cold. Let us go in."

She turned and hurried away with quick little steps. Pedro and his silent companion followed her. They crossed a narrow wagon rut, which passed for a road. In front of them squatted a little white hut, scarcely higher than the stranger's head. A stubby white candle burned in the window. Señora Lopez pushed open the door. Pedro and the stranger followed her into the hut and closed the door behind them.

The hut had but one room and almost no furniture. In one shadowy corner a pair of mattresses lay on the mud floor. At the other end of the room two huge logs crackled and sputtered in the simple fireplace. Something was boiling in the great black pot which hung from the iron crane over the flames. Around the table in the center of the room were gathered

174

three children with brown hair and great black eyes, just like Pedro's. They stood now in shy amazement, gazing at the stranger, all except the smallest, who had run and hidden her head in the full skirts of her mother's old faded dress. Señora Lopez patted the brown curls.

"This gentleman has come to spend the night with us, children. Pedro met him in the wood on his way home." She loosened little Maria's clinging hands and hurried over to the steaming kettle.

"Didn't you find the pig, Pedro?" Black-eyed Luisa, the oldest sister, had found her tongue again.

Pedro shook his head and turned to the stranger. "Won't you remove your cape and hat, Señor? It is very warm in here."

The man hesitated for a moment. Then with a jerk he took off his mantle and hat and gave them to the boy. For the first time Pedro could really see what his companion was like. He had shaggy gray hair which fell untidily to his shoulders and a long hooked nose. Strangest of all were his pale blue eyes. They did not seem to really look at anything. By his clothes, Pedro could tell that he was a gentleman born, for his tunic was of dark green velvet, like his hat, and the dagger which he had pulled out in the woods was studded with jewels which sparkled in the candlelight.

Pedro hung the cape and hat on a hook and went over to the table. He pulled out a stool. "Won't you sit down, Señor? Mother will have supper ready in a moment."

The stranger sank down on the wooden seat. The children, except Pedro, huddled together on the far side of the table and continued to stare at the newcomer. He sat there in silence, looking at the wall. Señora Lopez brought the steaming bowl of stew and set it in the middle of the table. The children turned their eyes for a moment from the stranger to the pleasant-smelling food. The tiniest one beat the table with her wooden spoon. Her mother made a clicking sound of disapproval with her tongue as she sat down.

"*Gusta!*" she said and dipped her spoon into the bowl. The

176

stranger's muffled *"Gusta"* was lost in the happy cries of the children. The little room was silent except for the clatter of the spoons against the bowl. The dish was soon empty. Then for the first time, the strange guest spoke.

"The best supper I have had in many moons, Señora Lopez. May God reward you for your goodness to a stranger!" He lifted his pale blue eyes and looked at the mother for a moment. But he let them fall quickly again, as if embarrassed by his own words.

"'Tis no trouble at all, Señor, and it is pleasant for us to have company. It is very lonesome here at times." Señora Lopez gave him a friendly smile. "Have you a long journey ahead of you, Señor?"

A frown crossed the man's face. When he finally spoke, the words were almost lost in his gray beard. "A long journey—" His eyelids fluttered wearily. "Yes, a long journey."

Senora Lopez stood for a moment with her hands on her hips, waiting for him to say something more. The children sat silently in their places. Little Maria looked as if she were about to cry.

Just at that moment there was a loud knock on the door. The guest rose from his stool, his eyes bulging with fear. Before Pedro could jump up from the table, the door swung open, and on the threshold stood the handsomest man he had ever seen. He was clad in a suit of silver armor. At his side hung a long sword of gold. Its hilt gleamed with precious stones. As he caught sight of the stranger, he gave a start of amazement. He looked again to make sure he had seen aright and then made a deep bow.

"We have been searching for you since sundown. Needless to say, the army is fearful for your safety." He looked about the bare little room and raised an eyebrow. "I must say, we did not expect to find you here. We stopped only to inquire the way."

The man fumbled with his dagger. "My army—do you mean to say I still have an army?"

The handsome knight bowed again. "The fighting stopped

at nightfall," he said, "It's a victory for Your Majesty's forces."

At the words, "Your Majesty," Pedro's jaw dropped open with amazement. He walked slowly over to the stranger as if in a dream and looked up into his face.

The man nodded his head slowly. "Yes, Pedro López, you see before you the King of Castile and Leon, a coward who flees from the enemy, the most unfortunate of God's creatures." He gazed around the little hovel. "If this were mine," he added, his voice trembling, "I might find peace."

Then remembering himself, he raised his broad shoulders and turned to the knight. "I am ready, Don Beltran. But I wonder what would have happened if you had never found me. It will be pleasant meat for dreams."

Flinging the mantle about his shoulders, he stood for a moment lost in thought. Then with a deep sigh, he placed his hat on his head and walked over to the table. Unfastening his purse, he poured out its contents. A little pile of gold coins rolled out and glittered in the candlelight.

"This is not enough to give to one of the few people to ever show me a kindness." The king turned to Pedro. "Pedro Lopez, when you pray to God tonight, give thanks that you were not born Henry the Fourth, King of Castile and Leon."

With these words he turned and hurried out into the darkness. The silver knight followed and closed the door behind him. The little room was empty again except for the five bewildered members of the Lopez family, gazing at the gold coins in the middle of the table. Pedro went over to his mother, placed his arms around her waist and looked up into her face. Her eyes were glistening with tears.

"What are you crying for, Mother dear? Now we can buy a great many pigs."

Constance Savery

ADVENTURE IN CANDLE STREET

ILLUSTRATED BY

Decie Merwin

WILLIAM and Elizabeth Godden are frequent visitors at the home of Mr. Ned Fane who lives across the street from them in Candle Street. They think he is a very wonderful person, for he is always kind and understanding with children and he is an artist at making beautiful fans. His eight-year-old brother, Oliver, who lives with him, attends Mrs. Trusty's school with William and Elizabeth and is their best friend. Lady Moonshine, as everyone calls nine-year-old Cynthia Delphine, also is staying with him while her mother and father are in India. Moonshine is very spoiled and used to having her own way and she has absolutely refused to live with wealthy Mrs. Hoddesdon, her godmother, as was originally planned. Though this is not Mr. Ned's fault, Mrs. Hoddesdon, who has always been one of his best friends and customers, now becomes very angry with him. As for mischievous Lady Moonshine, she adores him, as do the other children, and she tries to be good, so long as he is around. But at Mrs. Trusty's school, oh, the trouble she gives! Elizabeth tells here some of the exciting adventures they share.

SHE TYRANNIZED over us all from the beginning; soon we dared not resist the slightest wave of that imperious little hand. At first we had rebelled, but she put down rebellion sternly, with cunning pinches and mocking words. Yet we did not dislike her. She was swift to pity and relent; she was generous also, giving away sweetmeats and playthings freely; nor would she ever stand to see the weak oppressed.

We were afraid of Master Henry Oldham, who was a big boy, older than the rest of us and a great bully. He was particularly fond of tormenting Oliver. Lady Moonshine made a slave of Oliver herself, but she would let no one else treat him un- kindly. Once she flew at Henry in a whirlwind of passion, and the next moment, we saw him howling on the floor.

"There!" said Lady Moonshine, standing over him like a lion. "Don't you ever touch Oliver again!"

She was little and frail, Henry tall and stout; but her courage was dauntless. From that day Henry never struck any one as long as he remained at Mrs. Trusty's school.

Fearless on the playground, she was equally daring in school. After the novelty of school-going had worn off, she would not obey Miss Betsy or Miss Sophia or even Mrs. Trusty herself. She drew ugly pictures of them on her slate; she made wilful stitches an inch long in her hemming; she put blue oranges and purple flowerpots into her samplers; and she stitched her name as *Moonshine* instead of *Cynthia*. Punishment did not trouble her in the least.

"It is rather fun," she said. "It has never happened to me before."

So she tried standing on the form and wearing a tall dunce's cap and staying in at playtime; and at last Mrs. Trusty tied her to the leg of the great four-poster bed and said that she should stay there until she promised to be good.

"I never make foolish promises!" said Lady Moonshine, toss- ing her head.

We were all hushed and silent in the schoolroom because it was such a great disgrace to be tied to the leg of Mrs. Trusty's four-poster bed. If it had happened to us, William and I should have died of mortification.

At first no sounds came from the bedroom overhead except a sound of breathing, accompanied by a little biting, gnawing sound that puzzled us. Mrs. Trusty did not hear it. She went on teaching us with her cap tilted sideways on her head, for Lady Moonshine had wriggled a good deal when the hand- kerchief was tied round her hands.

In half an hour's time the breathing and biting noises ceased. They were followed by gentle little flapping movements as if

some one were dancing lightly in bare feet. Miss Betsy laid down my sampler and stepped upstairs.

We did not like to call Miss Betsy's exclamation a screech, but we knew that there was no other word so suited to describe the cry she gave. She screeched in such a way that Mrs. Trusty and Miss Sophia ran upstairs to see what the trouble might be, and we left our books and hastened after our schoolmistresses.

On the floor was a white handkerchief bitten through by sharp little teeth. In the middle of the great big bed sat Lady Moonshine, with Mrs. Trusty's best violet-ribboned lace nightcap on her head, Mrs. Trusty's spare spectacles on her nose, and the handsome puffed and quilted counterpane drawn up round her knees. Mrs. Trusty's three false curls were pinned to the back of the nightcap.

"You saucy miss!" said Mrs. Trusty, making a snatch at the curls.

In an instant Lady Moonshine had sprung to the farther side of the bed—to the floor—to the door—to the stairs. Before anyone could stop her, she was running barefoot down Candle Street in Mrs. Trusty's nightcap, spectacles, and curls.

"Run, Betsy; run, Sophia! Catch her! Bring her back!" commanded Mrs. Trusty, but Miss Sophia said, "No, no," and Miss Betsy screeched again and laid her hand on her heart. Miss Sophia then took the two tall glass vinaigrettes from the dressing-table and handed one to her mamma and the other to her sister. They sniffed hard and felt better. We were hurried downstairs and well scolded by Mrs. Trusty, while Miss Sophia stood shaking her head and Miss Betsy was peeping over the blinds to see whether anyone had observed Lady Moonshine's flight.

"O sister, sister Sophia," she said, wringing her hands. "Mrs. Hoddesdon saw! Mrs. Hoddesdon was taking the air with her friend, Miss Barbara Hanson, and they must have seen the naughty child!"

Poor Mrs. Trusty nearly wept. She was proud of her little school and had been much affronted by Mrs. Hoddesdon's scornful remarks about it. Now she feared that Mrs. Hoddesdon would have cause to speak more bitterly than ever.

But there was worse to come.

Mrs. Hoddesdon did not return to the Great House after she had seen the shocking sight of Lady Moonshine running like a mad thing up Candle Street in her schoolmistress's clothes. Instead, she and Miss Hanson paced slowly up and down, up and down, in front of the school, as if waiting for someone.

And presently down the street came Mr. Ned and Lady Moonshine hand in hand. Lady Moonshine wore shoes and stockings and her Sunday bonnet over smooth hair, and Mr. Ned carried a parcel in which were Mrs. Trusty's curls, spectacles, and cap. Lady Moonshine told us afterwards that he had laughed outright when he first saw her, and under his grave look his eyes were laughing still all the way down the street. But at sight of Mrs. Hoddesdon the laughter died quickly away, as well it might.

Mrs. Hoddesdon stepped forward just as Mrs. Trusty appeared in the doorway.

"I must compliment you on the management, and order of your school, Mrs. Trusty," she said in high, sarcastic tones.

"Your pupils are models of correct and pretty behaviour. Little did I think that I should see my god-daughter, Lady Cynthia Delphine, comporting herself like a street urchin. Her father's confidence in Edward Fane has been sadly misplaced. He will be surprised to find that in his absence she has turned into a mere Romping Molly. Young man, see to it that you prevent a repetition of such behaviour."

She spoke in such a haughty, contemptuous way that once again Mr. Ned reddened from brow to chin. Then, coldly ignoring Mrs. Trusty's flustered apologies, she swept past the house. Lady Moonshine pulled a dozen grimaces as rapidly as a gutta-percha face.

But she apologized to Mrs. Trusty so charmingly that the kind old lady forgave her at once, and she was able to take her place as if nothing had happened. On the way home from school she was boastful.

"You are cowards, William and Elizabeth; you wouldn't have dared to do what I did! But I was not one bit afraid."

"You had nothing to be afraid of," returned William bluntly. "Mrs. Trusty is not dreadful, and you knew that Mr. Ned would not be angry."

" 'I care for nobody, no, not I,' " sang Lady Moonshine. "I don't care what happens; I will have my way."

"But you hurt other people," said William, rather pompously. "You know you do, Moonshine. When you went into Violetta Addern's papa's shop and made her unscrew the huge red jar so that you could drink a little to find out what it was like, it wasn't you that had your toy cupboard locked up for three days as a punishment."

"I don't care," said Lady Moonshine. "Silly little simpering Violetta—I wish her papa had locked up her toy cupboard for a month! I only wanted to find out whether that story about Rosamond and her purple jar was true."

"And we were sent to bed yesterday because we did not tell tales to Papa that it was you who fished his goldfish out of the bowl with Oliver's net, and then forgot to put it back again."

"I don't care," said Lady Moonshine. "I'm glad you were sent to bed. It's good for your health."

"And I was kept in at playtime," said Oliver, "because you rubbed my sums off my slate."

"I don't care!" said Lady Moonshine. "They were all wrong, anyhow."

"Well, you hurt Mr. Ned today," said William triumphantly. "He didn't like being scolded before everybody as if he were to blame and not you. Mrs. Hoddesdon used to be very kind to him, and now she is horrid—and it's your fault."

"I don't c—" began Lady Moonshine, and then she stopped. A delicate pink blush like the inside of a "baby's thumbnail" sea shell tinted her cheeks, and the hardness died out of her little face. This time she did care, and we knew it. Somewhere in that stony child-heart was a place softened by love for Mr. Ned. She did not wish to think that she had hurt him. Instead of sparkling like a cold moon ray, she was gentle and quiet for a moment.

"Well, a little hurt isn't much," she cried, spinning wildly round and round on her toes. "I'll never be really and indeed wicked to him, and I'm better than I used to be, a very great deal better."

And so the days went by, day after slow day, until the hedges were white with May-blossom. The last of the Exhibition fans had been laid in the linenfold press, and in a few days they were to be put into the box that Mr. Ned had been fitting up for their journey with shallow trays and slender wooden bolts.

There came a morning when a letter lay on Mr. Ned's plate, a letter that brought sad tidings. His sister, Miss Fanny, was ill.

Mr. Ned and Miss Fanny were devoted brother and sister, but for nearly two years she had not left her Boarding School to make holiday in Candle Corner. It was far from St. Barnabas Green, and the fees were high, a heavy drain on poor Mr. Ned's slender purse. So holiday season after holiday season came, leaving Miss Fanny away at the school, helping the

185

head mistress to care for some little boarders whose papas and mammas were in India.

"'Tis the loneliness that has fretted her, poor lamb," said old Cherry Throwhawke, reading the letter with her spectacles perched on the edge of her nose. "Do you go right off, Mr. Ned, and take a look at her. She'll be better for seeing you, I'll warrant."

And Mr. Ned decided to go.

Although nobody but Cherry Throwhawke knew it, he walked most of the way to save the coach fares, only taking the coach for a short distance at the beginning and end of his journey, that no one at St. Barnabas Green or the Boarding School might know. Mr. Ned was proud as well as poor. We would never have known what he had done if Cherry had not told us.

Before he went away, he made Lady Moonshine and Oliver

186

promise that they would try to be good children, giving no trouble to either Mrs. Trusty or Cherry Throwhawke.

It was in the evening, just before the coach started from the Market Place, that they made their promise. Lady Moonshine sat on a low stool beside him, her face raised to his with such sweet seriousness that it looked half flower and half angel. Oliver leaned against his knee, playing with the old signet ring that had belonged to their father. William and I stood by the window.

"I shall be away for a week," said Mr. Ned, "but you won't be alone all that time. Miss Weverill has kindly promised to come and sit with you in the evenings—and sister Meg will look in as often as she can, Noll."

"Oh!" said Oliver, so sadly that Mr. Ned laughed.

Mrs. Meg Meggotty was their married sister, some few years older than Mr. Ned. She had married a farmer and horse-breeder away over the marshes beyond the town. None of us liked her, though she was a personable young woman and a capital horsewoman. We did not like her name and we did not like her ways. A whisper had come to us that handsome, dashing Mrs. Meg and her red-headed husband were continually borrowing money from Mr. Ned. Their demands were said to be the chief cause of his poverty and the banishment of golden-haired Miss Fanny.

Mrs. Meg came into quiet Candle Corner like a boisterous breeze, finding fault with everyone in a rough, good-natured but most unpleasant way. She was forever urging Mr. Ned to deal more roughly and harshly with Oliver, asserting that his unfailing gentleness was bad for the boy. But Mr. Ned only smiled and went his own way.

"She won't try teaching me to swim again, will she?" Oliver asked anxiously. "It's so horrid when she does it, brother Ned."

"No," said Mr. Ned. "It's too early in the year for swimming. Tell her that I have forbidden you to bathe at present."

"And riding?" Oliver asked, with a shudder.

"You needn't ride unless you choose. I have told Sister Meg that it is not to be made a matter of obedience."

187

Oliver sighed with relief.

"I shall be the head one in this house when you are gone, Mr. Ned," said Lady Moonshine. "Oliver is a whole year younger than I am, and often frightened. I shall make him do exactly as he is told. And William and Elizabeth shall obey me, too."

Although we knew that Lady Moonshine spoke the truth, we scowled at her. We disliked being reminded that where she led we followed, willy-nilly.

"But I mean to be very good indeed, Mr. Ned," she said. "On Sunday I shall teach Oliver his collect and catechism as well as learning my own, because he is so slow. Which collect shall we learn?"

Mr. Ned took down the big silver-clasped Prayer Book from the shelf. Turning over the pages, he showed her a prayer.

"That isn't the right Sunday," said Lady Moonshine cleverly, after she had read aloud: "O God, forasmuch as without Thee we are not able to please Thee; Mercifully grant that Thy Holy Spirit may in all things direct and rule our hearts; through Jesus Christ our Lord."

"But it is the right collect, I think," said Mr. Ned. "If you are going to be the head one of the house, leading all the others, it is important that you should lead them in the right way. You cannot find that way alone, Cynthia."

Lady Moonshine wriggled uneasily; notwithstanding her promises to be superlatively good, she had made one or two doubtful plans for amusement during Mr. Ned's absence. And she knew that we knew it.

"Do you pray that prayer always when you are the head one?" she asked, trying to turn aside the edge of Mr. Ned's weapon.

"Not in those words, perhaps," said Mr. Ned, "but with that meaning."

And we knew that he spoke truth, and we wondered why he flushed over the words as though they were hard to say.

So he left us; and for a whole week Lady Moonshine and Oliver reigned supreme at Candle Corner.

Promises or no promises, Lady Moonshine did not behave as a young queen should. Oliver tried to be quiet and obedient, but he was pliable and timid. As for William and me, we sometimes rebelled and sometimes yielded; for she frightened and fascinated us as she frightened and fascinated Oliver. Poor Cherry Throwhawke had no easy time with the pair of them, and little nervous Miss Weverill was helpless. Mrs. Meg Meggotty did not trouble herself to ride over the marshes to Candle Corner. "Without there was suffen to be had from him, she nivver keep her word to Mr. Ned," said Cherry with scorn.

Lady Moonshine would not get up early or go to bed at the proper time. She behaved outrageously in lesson hours, and in play hours she ran off to romp on the beach with strange children who did not go to Mrs. Trusty's school. Once she took Oliver and William and me with her; and we had a terrible fight with the strange children and lost our way home and came in all torn and dripping and late. Our papa was so angry that he went across to Candle Corner and desired Cherry to send Lady Cynthia Delphine to speak with him. But Lady Cynthia locked the door of her room and called through the keyhole that she would speak to nobody.

"I refuse to be scolded by William and Elizabeth's ugly old Papa," she shouted. "Only Mr. Ned has any right to scold me, and he never does it, never, because it only makes me worse."

Then Cherry caught Oliver, washed his face and hands, brushed his dark brown hair smooth and flat, put a clean gray blouse over his head, and sent him into the front parlor to be scolded instead of Lady Moonshine.

And Papa, who like Mrs. Meg Meggotty thought that Mr. Ned was not stern enough with Oliver, took this good opportunity of reading poor Olly a long and severe lecture, ending by a threat to tell sister Meg how naughty he had been. He brought Oliver to the playroom where William and I sat writing punishment copies, and he gave Oliver some copies to write, too. Till long past bedtime we wrote in very neat hands: "Every deviation from rectitude deserves due retribution."

This sounded magnificent enough, but Olly had no idea what

189

it meant until we told him that it was really: "Every time you are naughty you ought to be punished."

"Oh!" said Oliver. "It's so much easier to be naughty when brother Ned isn't here. I daren't say 'No' to Lady Moonshine by myself. And she has made a plan that I don't believe we ought to make. We made it on Sunday, but I'm not to tell you."

Oliver would not tell us what the plan was, but it was clear that he was both interested and frightened.

"You ought to have learned your collect on Sunday," said I. Oliver's eyes grew round.

"Why, I forgot all about it!" he said. "So did Moonshine; we never thought."

"That's why you haven't behaved properly this week," said William.

"Well, you're no better than I am!" retorted Oliver indignantly. He would have said more if Papa had not entered to inspect our copies and send him home to bed.

"I wonder what the plan is," said William. "Let's ask Moonshine."

We asked her the next morning. She chased Oliver to the end of Candle Street and pinched him till he screamed. Then she ran back to tell us what she had planned.

"I want to go to the gypsy fair, but Cherry won't let me. She says that Mr. Ned doesn't approve of gypsy fairs, so neither Oliver nor I must go. And oh, William and Elizabeth, it is so lovely! Drums and bands and colored stalls and a giant and a puppet-show and a fat lady. I know what it is like because my papa took me to this very same fair two years ago when it was held near our house. It is not wrong for me to go to fairs, if my papa approves. Cherry is most unkind to say that I may not go without Mr. Ned's permission and she knows he wouldn't give it. And I have no money at present—it is all spent, every penny."

"Then how can you go to the fair?"

"That is my plan," said Lady Moonshine mysteriously.

Finger on lip, she whispered to us— "On Thursday, the den-

190

tist comes to East Market to draw teeth. Cherry is going over in the carrier's cart to have a tooth drawn, and Madgy Dutton is to look after us while she is away because Miss Weverill can't come that evening. Mr. Ned is coming home at ten in the night, but Cherry will be home at eight. If we went to the fair at six, we could have nearly two hours there quite easily. We will make Madgy Dutton come, too. Nobody will know."

"But you have no money," said William and I.

Lady Moonshine smiled.

"Oliver and I intend to hold an Exhibition of Fans," said she. "We shall invite all the children in Mrs. Trusty's school, and we shall make them pay threepence each. That will give us two and ninepence, which will be enough for all we want. They will all come, because I shall pinch anyone who dares to stay away. And I can make the prettiest Exhibition in the world with fans hanging all around the room in the way Mr. Ned described. Oliver and I will hang up the fans at the school dinner-hour and at four o'clock. At five the Exhibition will be ready. I have planned everything and already I have stuck some little small nails into the wall where Cherry is not likely to see them, for hanging up the fans."

"It's very wicked," said William and I.

"It is not," said Lady Moonshine. "No harm can possibly happen to the fans. I shall take the greatest care of them. Mr. Ned has never forbidden us to go to the gypsy fair, and we shall not be going alone, which would certainly be wrong—we are going with our maidservant, Madgy Dutton."

When Lady Moonshine explained the plan in such a good-sounding way, William and I thought that after all the gypsy fair might be an exciting place to visit. We thought of our money boxes and wondered whether we could come too. Papa and mamma would be away for a night and a day.

"You may help me to arrange the Exhibition if you like," said Lady Moonshine carelessly.

I had felt grieved to think that Lady Moonshine should be the chief person to have the handling of Mr. Ned's precious work. In my secret heart I felt that I could make the Exhibition

191

look prettier if I had the arrangement in my own hands. Often in past times I had wondered why Mr. Ned did not cover his walls with fans like flocks of butterflies instead of keeping them in the press. I knew the exact spot that would suit each radiant beauty best.

William and I thought that Lady Moonshine showed great kindness in inviting us to help; but later we did not feel quite so grateful; for we heard her saying to Oliver,

"I asked them because, if there is a scrape, it is better to have four people in it than only two."

It was then too late to draw back. The walls were already glowing with rich and varied colors and delicate shapes. Plumed fans, lace fans, tiffany fans, silken fans, heart-shaped fans, tuft fans, round fans, flag fans, fans with carved ivory, cherry wood, and bamboo—all were there.

Lady Moonshine and I quarrelled more than once over the arranging of the fans. But at last the business was accomplished, and with great pride she produced three striped paper Japanese lanterns, which she hung in different places on the walls.

We admired the Japanese lanterns vastly, although they were cheap little paper lanterns of red and blue. I fear that we liked them fully as well as the dainty fans. After all, we were used to seeing fans, but none of us—save Lady Moonshine—had ever seen a Japanese lantern before.

"I shall light them when the Exhibition opens," said Lady Moonshine. "They will make a pretty light to throw on the fans."

It was broad daylight in warm Maytime, and lanterns were hardly necessary. However, no one contradicted Lady Moonshine. We closed the door and ran off to school.

The other children knew about the Exhibition; they had been carefully warned about the threepences and the pinches. After school was over, we trooped down Candle Street in Lady Moonshine's wake. She went alone into the workroom, lighted the lanterns, and came back to stand by the door with a red glass tumbler from the mantelpiece in her hand.

"The Exhibition is open," she said in a loud voice.

Then the boys and girls passed in, putting their threepences into the tumbler as they went.

Our Exhibition was a success. Every one enjoyed it except Master Henry Oldham, who muttered discontentedly that he would have preferred to see an exhibition of pistols. "Fans—faugh!" said he. But he took care to say it in a whisper out of reach of Lady Moonshine's hand.

Lady Moonshine stood on a chair, telling how the fans were made and saying now and then, "Don't touch, don't touch, don't touch. If a dirty finger touches them, they will be spoilt."

Madgy Dutton stood in the doorway open-mouthed. Madgy was the little maid who helped Cherry. She was one of a ragged, hungry family of thirteen children, engaged by Mr.

193

Ned because he felt sorry for her. Cherry always said that she was more hindrance than help.

We ran to the gypsy fair as soon as the Exhibition had closed, though Madgy Dutton's conscience pricked her. "Missis Cherry did say I wasn't to leave the house nor to let you two go out of my sight," she said. "Suppose now them gypsy folk come and steal the silvers?"

"Pray don't suppose such silly things," said Lady Moonshine.

Like the rest of the world, Madgy feared Lady Moonshine. When we set off down the street, she walked a few steps behind us, small and scared.

"We'll give her a mutton pie to eat," said Lady Moonshine. "I don't care for mutton pies myself, but Madgy thinks they are very good eating. One will cheer her up."

It did. After we had stopped at a stall with "Mutton Pyes" stuck on a board, Madgy grinned and bobbed and we went on gaily together to see the giant and the cherry-colored cat and the puppet-show. We bought gingerbread dogs and red peppermint sticks and Harlequin trumpets; and then we grew tired of the heat and the laughter and noise about us.

"There is horse-racing on the sea-meadow," said Lady Moonshine. "Let us go down to watch it."

The sea-meadow ran long and flat beside the pebbled ridge, and some races were being run there. The meadow was crowded, but it was fresher and cooler under the sky than in the canvas tents. We made our way to the starting-point, where a black-eyed gypsy man with gold earrings and a red sash was making the last arrangements for a race that was just about to be run.

Suddenly Oliver clutched my arm tight.

"Sister Meg—look! Sister Meg's there!"

He had turned as pale as snow. In front of us stood Mrs. Meg Meggotty in green riding dress and feathered hat, speaking to her husband, who was one of the riders in the race.

"If she finds us, she will be angry," he said. "Let's go home quick."

194

I touched Lady Moonshine.

"How extremely provoking!" she said, with a little stamp.

She knew only too well what would happen. If Mrs. Meg found us alone at the fair she would atone for her past carelessness by being doubly enraged. There would be no hope of concealing the escapade from Mr. Ned, and she would probably take care that our mamma and papa should hear of it as well.

In that moment Oliver realized what he had done, and the realization filled him with terror. Mrs. Meg was totally unlike Mr. Ned. We stood looking at her hard, handsome face under the gay hat; we noted the sharp impatience with which she continually struck her whip on the post close at hand; and we heard her voice raised in harsh and angry tones.

"Come away; do let us go home," pleaded Oliver.

The people pressed in front of us, so that we could not see the horses. There was a pistol shot, a cracking sound, a loud roar—they were off! Their faces were turned well away from us, and Mrs. Meg was leaning over the rail hallooing for her husband's horse, "Go it, Tawny Bess. Go on, lass, go on, go on!" as if she were a wild thing.

Lady Moonshine made a quick sign. Tumbling, scrambling, running, scurrying, we were back among the tents long before the results of the race had been shouted across the sea-meadow. Once there we stood and looked at one another.

"Let us go home, quick, quick," pleaded Oliver.

"Nonsense!" said Lady Moonshine. "We must see the ghost panorama first. I have never seen a ghost panorama in my life. Don't be so silly, Oliver. If we are caught, we shan't get into a bigger scrape because we stopped a little later. You can't go home alone; if you do, some one will ask questions. Catch him, William, and make him come."

William and Lady Moonshine dragged Oliver into the tent, which was large and dirty, with a black curtain at one end of it. A few people had gathered, among whom we saw Mrs. Meg's three sons, big stout boys of Oliver's age and more. We could not withdraw without attracting attention, for they were idly

196

staring about them and filliping nuts at their neighbors.

"Now, Oliver, don't be silly," said Lady Moonshine. "Mrs. Meggotty won't come here. She will stay down at the races; we are quite safe as long as those boys don't see us."

Oliver crouched down on the bench, whimpering. I do not know whether he watched the ghost panorama, but I certainly did not. It frightened me, and after the first glance I looked no more. But William and Lady Moonshine stood clapping their hands and jumping about with delight. They would have shouted aloud but for the remembrance that Mrs. Meggotty's George, Harry, and Sammy were in the front row. Madgy Dutton could not shout or clap, such was her wonder and alarm. She sat with her big mouth wide open, murmuring, "Oooooh!"

At last it was over, and we were in the fresh sweet air again, scampering away in obedience to Lady Moonshine's directions. We ran so fast that we were out of the tent long before George, Harry, and Sammy had blustered and banged their way to the door; and in another five minutes we were walking down High Street, staid and sober. We stopped in front of a shop window to make ourselves look neat and tidy before passing the Great House. Lady Moonshine wrinkled her nose delicately as she pirouetted in front of the glass.

"What a smell of burning!" she said. "Now, Oliver, do stop crying. We have had our fun without being caught, and nobody is a penny the worse."

There was indeed a strange, heavy smell of burning in the air, which grew more marked the nearer we came to Candle Street. The Great House had two doors, one facing the High Street, the other opening into Candle Street; and when we turned the corner we saw Mrs. Hoddesdon's maids standing on the six white steps of the Candle Street entrance. They were craning their necks forward and staring, staring, staring. But they were not looking toward us.

All the upper part of Candle Street was hidden by a black curtain of smoke that hid the houses much as the curtain in the tent had hidden the ghost panorama. Suddenly a great red forked tongue of flame pierced the smoke, and by its light we

saw the street crowded with people. Lady Moonshine said in a
quick, terrified voice, "The Fan Exhibition is on fire!"

The red forked flames were leaping from the windows of
the workroom. A ball of cold clay seemed to be stuck inside
our mouths, and we felt ice-cold all over. One of the maids
called to us, "Lady Cynthia, come you here this minute. Mr.
Fane's house is afire. Don't you go up street, you'll be trampled
underfoot by the folk that's helping to put the fire out. Come
you here, you together."

Thrusting her fingers into her ears to shut out their calls,
Lady Moonshine dashed up the street. We all followed her.

To enter Candle Corner or Paradise House was impossible;
for the street was filled with people carrying buckets and run-

ning and shouting. We were pushed backward and forward until we at last found ourselves squeezed into a dark niche between two houses, where we stood watching the flames and hearing the hiss-s-s-ss of water flung by men and women who had made a chain of buckets from Candle Corner across Sea Walk, along the pebble ridge and down into the sea. Huge Leathery Girling, the blacksmith, stood last in the line; and when the crowd parted, we could see his mighty arms raised high with the buckets, flinging shower after shower of silver sea spray through the broken windows of the workroom.

And then, shuddering in terror, we saw that the crowd, pushing and jostling, had driven Mr. and Mrs. Meggotty to our shadowed niche. Somehow, Mrs. Meggotty knew about the great Fan Exhibition; we supposed that one of our school-fellows had told her. Oh, how angry she was! In her loud, harsh voice she was storming at every one—at Mr. Ned for his absence from home, at Miss Fanny for being ill, at Cherry for having a tooth drawn, and at us, oh, most of all at us! She raved at us each in turn, ending with Oliver. As he was her own brother, she did not mind what she said about him; and her face grew perfectly crimson under her feathered hat as she called him all manner of names, promised him most fearful punishments, and used words that we had never heard before. Even Mr. Sam Meggotty stopped her at last.

"Whoa, there! Steady on, old girl," said he. "Leave something for Ned to say when he comes home!"

The men in the crowd roared with laughter. We could not think that Mr. Sam had said anything that was in the least amusing. Our knees were trembling under us, and we felt chilled and sick. Oliver shivered like an aspen leaf, his teeth were chattering, and his eyes looked as though they could not see.

Now whether Mr. Sam had caught sight of us and wanted to shield us from his wife, I cannot say; but I know that at that moment he ran forward to fill a gap in the chain of buckets, calling out, "Here, Meg, come on—lend a hand, can't you?"

At once Mrs. Meg was beside him and the buckets were

swinging from her strong hands to his. She was working away with a will, her arms powerful almost as Leathery Girling's.

A man in front of us said, "No wonder she ranted! She and old Sam have lost a pretty penny over the races yonder, and they owe money in all quarters. They were looking to Ned to help Sam out of this scrape as well as the rest—and now the poor fellow won't be able to give them a fourpenny piece! They've been a dead weight round his neck for years, but this is the end of it. Old General Hoddesdon is their chief creditor, I believe—him that's brother-in-law to old Madam down at the Great House. He's as hard as the nether millstone. Ned can't help them when he's ruined himself."

"Ruined?" said the other man.

"Aye, ruined," said the first speaker. "Stock in trade gone, and no cash to buy more. I was sorry to hear what she said about the timid little chap, but it's true for all that—young Oliver and that elf of a child have ruined him between them."

Lady Moonshine stepped suddenly forth from the darkness, laid her hand on the man's arm, and said clearly, "What does 'ruined' mean? What will Mr. Ned do?"

The man started. His face, which was ugly and kind, became very red as he and his friend stood together to hide the entrance to the niche from Mrs. Meggotty.

"I didn't know you and Noll were there, little lady," he said politely, "else I shouldn't have spoken. Well, I'm afraid Mr. Fane won't have much money for a long time to come. You two played a sad trick this afternoon, you see. But never you mind. He's young, and he'll work his way up again. Now my advice to you is: keep you quiet and out of the way until he comes home. He won't be nigh so hot about it as Mrs. Sam Meggotty there. It's none of her business, so just you hide yourselves up and don't let her see you. Look, it's not going to be such a bad business after all. The workroom's burnt out, but the rest of the house is all right; they're getting the fire well under now."

Even as he spoke, the chain of buckets broke up, and almost before the water had stopped hissing on the charred woodwork, a stream of people flowed into the house. Mrs. Meg was among them.

"There's your chance, little 'uns," said the man. "Run off now, and hide somewhere until Mr. Fane comes. You little Goddens ought to get home."

Hardly daring to breathe, we fought our way through the crowd, until we came safely to the deserted pebble ridge beyond Sea Walk. Two or three striped red and blue bathing-boxes were drawn up on the shore, and we climbed into one of them for temporary shelter. Madgy Dutton had disappeared, being separated from us in the throng about Candle Corner.

We were silent for a little while. Lady Moonshine spoke.

"All that we can do," she said, "is to run away."

"Run away!" faltered William and I.

"Yes, run away!" said Lady Moonshine, stamping her foot. "You and Will need not come unless you like, but Oliver and I must run away. If Mr. Ned is ruined, he will have no money to spare for feeding us. And as we have ruined him, it is only just that we should go away at once and take care of ourselves in future. Besides, if we go away, we may be able to earn some money to pay Mr. Ned for the fans. I have a good plan. There's a big seaport only twenty miles off along the sands. We will walk on till we come to it, and then we will hire ourselves out as cabin boys. There's a little tiny cabin boy in my papa's yacht who earns plenty of money. We could earn money, too, in other yachts and save it up and give it to Mr. Ned."

"But you and Elizabeth are girls," objected William.

"A cabin girl is every bit as good as a cabin boy," insisted Lady Moonshine; "that needn't bother us. Now, are you two coming? Oliver and I must start this minute."

We hesitated.

"I think that you ought to come back and face the row first," said William in a plain and stolid way. "You know that if you and Oliver go off, Elizabeth and I will get into the scrape all alone which is very unfair. You could go off afterwards, when the rowing had been properly shared out."

201

"Mr. Ned does not row people," said Lady Moonshine.

"No, but my papa does," said William, with warmth.

Lady Moonshine sat still and silent, her fair eyebrows drawn into a hard frown of thought.

"I can't come back," she said at last.

"You're a mean girl!" snapped William. "Come, Elizabeth."

"Oh, Will, not without Oliver and Moonshine!" I sobbed. "They were the worst, and we shall get into such terrible disgrace if they are not there!"

"You had better come with Oliver and me," said Lady Moonshine. "We will earn more money that way."

All this time Oliver had not spoken once; he was leaning against the door of the bathing-box in dumb, awful terror. But when Lady Moonshine took his hand to pull him down the steps, he obeyed without resistance.

I think that at the back of our minds we knew quite well that we ought not to go. If Oliver was past thought, William and Moonshine and I were in full possession of our wits. But it seemed daring and romantic to run away to earn money instead of going tamely home to face deserved punishment. And besides, William and I were honestly afraid to face our papa and the whole of our little world without the two chief culprits. William thought for a short time; and then, with a very sour look on his face, he climbed down the steps of the bathing-box and signed to me to follow Lady Moonshine.

So we set out on our journey into the world.

It was not a pleasant journey. We were miserable and fearful, dreading to be captured and brought back, ignorant of how we might fare in the seaport town where we meant to seek our fortunes. William walked with his face bent and his mouth tight. Lady Moonshine marched with her oat-colored head held high and her lips pressed together. She was holding Oliver firmly by the hand. As we stumbled along, I looked at him and wondered whether any one could be more wretched than he. His cheeks were bleached like white parchment; his lips were moving and quivering. When I saw him, I wanted to cry.

It grew darker and darker. We were far from the town, now, walking silently by the sea, which splashed in a gentle, monotonous way on our left side. The moon lighted us faintly; we could see our way, not without stumbling. Behind us, red and yellow stars, shone the windows of St. Barnabas Green. We were alone in a lonely place, where the sea wind rustled among the marsh reeds and sighed over the long low cliffs.

And I began to think of my dear mamma who had gone away so trustingly, not knowing that her Elizabeth would first help to arrange a wicked Fan Exhibition and would then be seen among Romping Mollies at a Gypsy fair. To think that I should never see dear Mamma again, never sit on the stool worked in red and blue cross-stitch, working at my sampler while she lay on the sofa and read aloud to me from "The Young Misses' Book," held so elegantly between her fingers! My mamma had a pretty way of holding a book, and her rings were pretty, too—garnets, rubies, and diamonds.

At these sad thoughts the tears rolled faster and faster down my cheeks until I was in an agony of silent crying. But even then I did not suggest that we should retrace our steps. I knew that we must go on and on to the end of the world.

At last we came to a part of the shore where the sea ran sharply inward, so that we had to leave the sand and the pebble ridge and climb over some large boulders. This was hard to do in the dim light.

"I've caught my foot," Oliver cried out sharply. "I can't get free!"

We scrambled to him. His foot had slipped between two masses of rock; it was tightly wedged. All his struggles, all our help, all Lady Moonshine's commands and heated scoldings, were in vain.

Tired out, we stood gazing at the weeping Oliver.

"We shall have to wait here till the morning," said Lady Moonshine. "We can't leave him alone."

"It's my opinion," said William in surly tones, "that one of us ought to stop here with Oliver while the other two go home and—and—tell Mr. Ned. The coach must have reached St.

203

Barnabas Green by this time. If Oliver stays here for the night, he will freeze and die. You know he isn't strong."

"Nobody cares for your opinion!" said Lady Moonshine.

"If you won't fetch Mr. Ned, I will!" said William. "Just you look at Oliver."

Lady Moonshine looked and looked again. Her little face was white and stern in the moonlight, but as she looked at Oliver it softened and became for the first time full of pity.

"But Mr. Ned wouldn't let Oliver come home now!" she said. "We have ruined him, Oliver and I."

And that was what we all felt. Our wild deed had cut us off forever from our old life in Candle Corner; and in spite of the care and kindness lavished on us by Papa and Mamma and Mr. Ned, it seemed to us quite a natural thing that they should cast us off completely and for always. We had been wicked, so wicked that nobody would or could ever speak to us again.

"Well, I think that we ought to try," said William in a dismal voice that sounded as though it came out of his boots. "Which of us shall go home to tell him—you or I?"

Lady Moonshine straightened herself. Her fingers shut and clenched over the palms of her hands.

"I will," she said.

"Suppose I ought to go with you," said William. "Girls can't run about alone. Elizabeth, you stay here and take care of Oliver."

I would much rather have gone in company with Lady Moonshine and William, but I knew that Oliver could not be left. So I climbed onto a flat piece of rock near Oliver and took his clammy hand into mine and tried to comfort him. Oliver did not understand where the others had gone, and he cried dreadfully for fear they might bring back sister Meg or our papa. Nor did he seem to be comforted when I told him that Mr. Ned would send somebody to set him free.

"I burnt up all the fans," he said again and again. And he crouched shivering in his light summer blouse against the rock.

The moon was blotted out behind black clouds. Soon the wind shrilled with such strange noises among the rocks and

sea grass that we clung to each other, afraid; and we said our prayers together, asking for forgiveness through the grace, mercy, and tenderness of God's only Son. I remember how sweet and solemn the words were, whispered there in the cold of night, with dark shapes and shadows about us. "Amen" had barely been said when a star of light pierced the blackness.

"Look, Olly," I said; "there's a lantern. It might be Jonas Dardle sent to look for us." Jonas Dardle was the odd-job man of the town.

"It might be a wicked robber," returned Oliver, through chattering teeth. "They come out at night; Cherry says so."

The lantern came nearer and nearer; it was swung high in air and flashed on the rocks; and we saw Mr. Ned looking at us.

I do not know what manner of look we had expected to see; but I know that what we did see banished the horrible vision of Mrs. Meg Meggotty's red, furious face. Mr. Ned was paler than usual, and his eyes were tired as from long hours of work at his fans; but there was no sign of anger or indignation to be seen. He smiled at us.

"Here is your cloak, Elizabeth," he said; and I saw that he was carrying my cloak and Oliver's coat. "Fasten it close— the night dews are falling. Now will you hold the lantern while I see what is the matter here?"

I held the lantern aslant at first; the light fell on Oliver's face instead of his trapped foot. He shrank back.

Mr. Ned laid his hand on the prisoner's shoulder.

"Come, Noll, don't wriggle," he said in an everyday voice. "Keep still while I try to move the rock, and draw your foot up quickly when I say, 'Now!' "

"I burnt up all the fans," said Oliver, speaking dreamily. "I forgot to put them in the press and blow out the paper lanterns. I burnt up all the fans."

"You must help to make some more, then," returned Mr. Ned in a composed and matter-of-fact way.

If Mr. Ned had brought anything to serve as a lever, it would have been easy to set Oliver free. Without such help, some minutes passed before he uttered a quick "Now!" that sent Oliver sprawling into safety. The rock fell back, and Mr. Ned set Oliver down on the flat boulder and examined the numbed and swollen foot.

"No bones broken; you'll be well tomorrow," he said, as Oliver clung to him, sobbing. He put his arm lightly round the boy, waited till poor Oliver's passion of tears had spent itself, and then helped him into his overcoat, buttoning it carefully under the chin with a gentleness that a woman could not have surpassed.

"Now we'll have some supper before we go home," he said, and he took from his pocket a flask and a parcel untidily rolled in brown paper. And instead of being dragged home hungry and tired and cold in our deep disgrace, Oliver and I sat on the rock with the horn lantern between us, eating our supper, which was what Cherry called "pieces of butter," roughly cut from the loaf and thickly smeared over, as if Mr. Ned had been in too great haste to consider appearances. No bread and butter ever tasted more delicious than that rock-supper bread, and the hot cocoa from the metal top of the flask.

When we had licked the butter from our fingers and had drained the last satisfying drop from the flask, Mr. Ned lifted Oliver into his arms, bidding me take the lantern.

"Now we shall soon be at home," he said cheerfully; but it was a long time before we came to Candle Street that night. Although Oliver was small and slight, he was eight years old; and Mr. Ned could not carry him so far without resting more than once on the journey. As for me, my feet and arms and legs ached so sharply that I would have given much to be able to change places with Oliver. I could barely contrive to stumble along with the lantern wobbling and wavering in my hand; and it was hard to make answer when Mr. Ned's kind young voice asked how I was getting on.

The lights of the town flickered and danced nearer and nearer; and at long, long last we left the sand strip by the sea, toiled over the pebble ridge, and came out at the junction of Sea Walk and Candle Street.

How sadly the wind moaned round the broken panes of Mr. Ned's workroom! The street was still wet and dirty from the trampling of many feet and the spilling of many pails; and thick black soot lay on the flags. Oliver buried his face in his brother's coat, and I did not know which way to look.

We had not once asked after the welfare of William and Lady Moonshine, but we were not surprised to find them sitting in rigid silence, one on each side of the parlor fire. The corners of William's mouth were buttery, so it was easy to guess that Mr. Ned had met them on their homeward journey and had paused to hear their story and given them food and drink.

Mr. Ned laid Oliver down on the wooden settle by the fireplace and straightened himself with a sigh. Before he had time to speak, Cherry bounced into the room, followed by our nurse, who was wringing her hands and looking angrier than we had ever seen her look.

"Well, sir, so you've got them back safe, the naughty, troublesome, wicked little things!"

"Quite safe," said Mr. Ned. "It is too late for any scolding tonight. They must go to bed."

"Come you with me, Master William and Miss Elizabeth," said Nurse in the coldest and iciest voice we had heard in our lives. "I'm sure I'm much obliged to you, sir, for fetching of them home, which is more than they deserved. What their papa will think of this here Esky Pad is more than I can tell!"

It was more than we could tell either, and our hearts sank low. Mr. Ned answered,

"Perhaps you had better leave me to tell Mr. Godden, Nurse." Nurse's face cleared. She curtsied politely.

"Thank you kindly, sir, I'm sure," she said.

We knew that Mr. Ned meant to make the telling as easy as he could. We bade him good night with many grateful tears.

As Nurse opened the door, a dismal yelling and howling was heard in the kitchen premises.

"That's Madgy Dutton, that is," said Nurse, with grim satisfaction. "Mrs. Throwhawke has locked her up in the coal-cellar for the night, which is where you did ought to be, too, all four of you. She come crying and booing home just before Mr. Fane set out to find you."

In her pleasure that one of us was getting her deserts, Nurse spoke a little too loud. Mr. Ned said, "I can't have that, Cherry. Let Madge out."

"I'll do nawthing of the kind!" snapped poor Cherry, goaded beyond bearing. "I nivver h'ard such nonsense. Let her bide where she be."

Mr. Ned then took a candle and went himself to the kitchen. While Nurse lingered, overcome by curiosity, we heard him open the door and summon Madge. She came out crying and trembling.

"Oh, maaster, I nivver meant to do nawthing wrong. That was Lady Cynthy that made me do that, so that was. She nip

208

me cruel with her fingers time I doan't obey ivery word she speak. Oh, maaster, that were Lady Cynthy's blame."

"Hush; no tales," said Mr. Ned. "Lady Cynthia will tell me the whole story herself. Go into the larder and take some supper from the shelves, and then go to bed. No, I won't send you away."

He must have remembered that she was only a small girl, not much older than Lady Moonshine; for he took the trouble to lift the great black kettle from the hob and pour some hot water into a basin that she might wash her grimy face, all streaked and smeared with crying. Mr. Ned's love of order and cleanliness ever gave him a fastidious distaste for that which was dusty and unkempt.

Cherry, still fuming, had pulled Oliver to his feet. With shakes, lamentations, and caresses she drew him to the door, where they met Mr. Ned returning from the kitchen.

"Perhaps, sir, you'll be so good as to keep an eye on Lady Cynthy time I put Maaster Oliver to bed first, that's just worn out, the naughty, precious lamb. But Lady Cynthy's for all the world as dodgy as one of them there Walberswick eels; and so an' somebody doesn't keep with her the whole time, she'll run off again and bring fresh trouble."

"Very good, Cherry," said Mr. Ned, bending down to kiss Oliver's white cheek. "I'll stay here until you are ready."

He went back to the parlor and dropped wearily into a chair.

Lady Moonshine had not yet stirred or spoken; she had shaken her pale hair round her face, and her silver-gray eyes burned like live coals behind the veil. Her small lips and chin were iron hard. I think that she was indeed planning to "run off again."

Mr. Ned looked at her.

"Well, Cynthia, aren't you going to tell me that you are sorry?" he asked.

And at that Lady Moonshine darted from her chair and flung herself into his arms.

"Oh, I am sorry, I am, I am!" she cried out passionately. "I will never be naughty again."

In the morning Mrs. Trusty met her pupils with a solemn face and a black cap on her head, so shocked and horrified was she by the news that had run like wildfire through the town on the previous night. There was not a soul in St. Barnabas Green who had not heard the full tale of what Nurse called the Esky Pad. And a very bad Esky Pad it was, too!

I think that Mrs. Trusty had prepared a lecture for the school in general, but she did not deliver it. Perhaps the note in a fine hand lying on her table came from Mr. Ned with a request that she would spare us; or perhaps she was touched by the listless looks and subdued speech of Lady Moonshine and Oliver. However that may be, no word of reproof was spoken. She only wore the high black turban from morn till eve in the gravest way.

And three days later we had the lecture after Master Henry Oldham had played a sad trick with two spiders and an inkwell. The lecture was divided into three heads, which were written on the blackboard. They were:

Perfect Obedience to Parents and Guardians.

Avoidance of Worldly Places of Amusement.

Perverse and Wayward Children a Plague to Society.

Master Henry was distressed to receive so severe a rebuke in public, in addition to being much perplexed by the second head of it. "I cannot understand," said he, "why Mrs. Trusty should speak of an inkwell as 'a worldly place of amusement.'"

Lady Moonshine said to us on the way home, "It was our scolding, of course; that's why it did not quite fit Henry. But pray do not tell him so!"

Apart from a lecture at second hand, William and I escaped lightly. Our papa and mamma returned home during school hours on the morning after the fire; and before we came back for the dinner-hour, Mr. Ned had explained to them about our visit to the Gypsy fair in the company of Lady Moonshine, Oliver, and Madgy Dutton. And although Mamma and Papa were naturally shocked and grieved to hear how ill we had behaved and how little we could be trusted, they yet kindly consented to forgive us at Mr. Ned's intercession.

210

I am afraid that Mr. Ned must have omitted to mention the part we had played in preparing the great Fan Exhibition; for on my mentioning it to my mamma some years later, she said in dismay, "Oh, Elizabeth, Elizabeth, we did not know that! How extremely shocking!"

But we children knew nothing of what he had said and what he had left unsaid; we were told that he had begged us off punishment, and we loved him heartily for that. When we heard our papa coming that day, we ran under our beds, but our fears, thanks to Mr. Ned, were unnecessary. Papa merely warned us never again to be led into mischief by that ill-behaved Cynthia Delphine.

His warning was not needed. After the night of the Fan Exhibition, Lady Moonshine was a different child. Something hard and cold had died out of her nature, and the tricksy sprite had become almost loving and human. She took pains with her lessons and her needlework; she led no more wild pranks; and she had learned to copy Mr. Ned's wise tenderness to Oliver. For Oliver was slow in recovering from the shock of seeing his home in flames and from the terror of our flight. He was quieter and more timid than of old, content to sit for hours alone.

But Mr. Ned had other troubles. His stock in trade was gone, and gone too were the rosy hopes of orders and commissions from the people who were visiting the Fan Exhibition. He had Oliver, Fanny, and the old cousins to care for—and Mr. and Mrs. Meggotty's debts to pay.

He toiled unceasingly. Far into the night, hour after weary hour, he made fans. They were not the fans of old days, rich in silk and lace, tiffany and brocade. His new fans were cheap, fragile fans made of paper, but nothing flawed or crumpled was ever permitted to pass muster.

He kept his troubles gallantly to himself. We should never have known of them had it not been for the ominous whispers and rumors that flew over the town. When Papa and Mamma talked French at the table we knew that they were speaking of Mr. Ned.

We children longed to be able to help him in the grim losing battle that he fought with poverty and despair. But we could do nothing. Papa did offer to lend him money, but Mr. Ned refused to take it. Both Papa and Mamma thought that he had done wisely.

"For if those Meggottys got wind of a loan, they would launch out into further extravagances," said they.

We wondered what Mrs. Hoddesdon thought. She passed him in the street without sign of recognition, save once, when she said to him loudly in the presence of several bystanders that he had not yet sent in any of his bills. Mr. Ned answered by a bow.

"I did not know that Mrs. Hoddesdon owed you any money, brother Ned," said Oliver.

"Mrs. Hoddesdon owes me nothing," said Mr. Ned. "I once cleaned some discolored miniatures for her—but it was not a matter of business. Now that she is vexed with me, she perhaps does not wish to remember that she once accepted such a small service at my hands."

Oliver did not quite understand, but Lady Moonshine stamped her slender foot.

"Godmother is unkind and discourteous," she said. "Yes, prodigiously so!"

"We first gave her reason to be displeased with us, Cynthia," said Mr. Ned.

Lady Moonshine shrugged one shoulder petulantly and said no more. From that morning she tried harder than ever to be good. Her lessons were learned with still greater care and diligence, Oliver was kept happy, and she herself would sit patiently for hours in the workroom, sewing or reading. "It is company for Mr. Ned," she told us.

But her gray eyes saw more than he guessed. He kept his troubles to himself, as I have stated, but he could not keep her from noticing sundry changes in the house. At last in distress she drew William and me aside.

"Mr. Ned is selling things out of the house," she whispered. "All his work is not hard enough, though it is often three o'clock in the morning before he puts out the light in the workroom. So things have begun to disappear. His oak bookcase from the parlor went first, then some big books in leather covers, then a beautiful chair, then his seal-ring—and now some of his father's pictures. Cherry Throwhawke will not tell us what has become of them, but Oliver and I know."

"It is most dreadful," said William and I.

"But he needs materials for his fans," said Lady Moonshine. "Godmother has a great trunk full of the loveliest things imaginable that she had when she was young; but she does not use them now because she says that a vain old woman is an insufferable creature. There's lace—point de fee, foamy and cobwebby as if fairies had made it; point rosaline, with rosebuds in it; lace of Mechlin, Cluny, Valenciennes, and all the other laces. There's silk from China, thick creamy silk with figures and leaves and flowers woven on it. There's satin and brocade and tiffany and wonderful feathers and glittering stones and shells. I peeped into it once. And before she had a quarrel with my papa she told him that she had left it in her will to young Ned Fane! I expect she has scratched those words out of her will now, but she did put them in once!"

"What a pity!" said I.

"And I can't do anything," said poor Lady Moonshine, sighing deeply. "I did so much want to help Mr. Ned. But at least I'm helping him by staying at Candle Corner—that's a very good thing. I have been here for nine months. How much is nine times four times seven times seven shillings, Elizabeth?"

We worked the sum out on paper and found that it came to over eighty-eighty pounds. This seemed much wealth to me and I was puzzled to understand why Mr. Ned should be poor when he had so much money.

Lady Moonshine was puzzled too.

We were playing with Oliver in the warm sunshine of his little garden when Mrs. Meg Meggotty came striding into our circle in her riding-gown.

"Hey, Noll, where's Ned?" she asked.

"I don't know," answered Oliver feebly.

214

Mrs. Meg's face was nearly as red as it had been on the day of the Fan Exhibition. She gave Oliver a shake.

"I'll drive a little sense into you, my boy, when you come to live with me. Ned's too soft with you by half!"

Oliver shrank back. Lady Moonshine sprang to his rescue at once.

"Who said Oliver was ever going to live with you, Mrs. Meggotty?" she said. "Mr. Ned wouldn't allow it. You're not kind enough to him."

"Highty-tighty, but beggars can't be choosers!" jeered Mrs. Meggotty. "Don't you pretend that you don't know Ned is done for, out and out. He will have to sell this house, leave Oliver with me, pack you off to your relations, and go to seek his fortune in London. There's a bill coming in that he can't meet from a creditor who is egged on, I do believe, by an old woman that has a spite against Ned."

"Whom does Mr. Ned owe money to?" said Lady Moonshine, still with her arm round Oliver. Her voice was haughty.

"General Hoddesdon, Mrs. Hoddesdon's brother-in-law!" said Mrs. Meg. "She's put him up to it, I cast no doubt, just to pay Mr. Ned out for harboring you, spoilt minx that you are. And he won't wait a day longer, not a day."

"Mr. Ned never owes money to people," said Lady Moonshine. "I know that it is you who owe the money. You got him to put his name to one of your bills. I know it; for I heard your servant telling Cherry so. It's your house that ought to be sold."

"You impudent baggage!" cried Mrs. Meg. "How dare you stand there lording it over me? You're no better than a beggar-wench for all your up-and-mighty ways! First you burn the shop down and your papa don't offer to pay for your freaks! And Ned's daft enough not to ask him for a penny; said he couldn't ask for money from your father when his own brother was about as much to blame as you were. Trumpery, folly and pride, I call that! And to make matters worse, your papa never offers Ned a stiver for all these nine months of feeding you and clothing you and paying all your school bills! Don't talk

215

to me of letters gone astray and all that! I know better! And I don't know how you have the face to speak to me, I really don't! The sooner you're packed bag and baggage out of this, the better!"

Mrs. Meg turned and flung back to the house, perhaps remembering that she had told Lady Moonshine something that Mr. Ned would not wish her to know. We were glad to see the door shut on the green gown.

Lady Moonshine sat down at the foot of the pear tree. She did not cry, though her face was more cloud-pale than her hair. After a few moments she said,

"That horrible General Hoddesdon must be made to stop. I cannot make him, but Godmother could. I will go to her this minute. She will be glad to have me inside her claws, and if I am living in her house she will write to my papa ordering him to pay Mr. Ned at once for me and for the fans. I did write to Mother about the fans, but I suppose she did not understand. I could not write very well then, you remember. But Godmother will know how to remind Papa to pay Mr. Ned. And she will make General Hoddesdon wait till the money comes. She will do that because she is pleased to have me."

"Shouldn't care to be in your shoes, going back," said William.

"I don't care to be in them myself," owned Lady Moonshine. "But it is the only single solitary thing that I can do to help Mr. Ned, and I must do it. I must! And I will!"

"Oh, dear!" said Oliver.

"I shall not see her at once," said Lady Moonshine. "I have thought out what to do. I shall take nothing with me except— my nightgown. I shall slip into the house by a side door and put myself to bed in the room I had last year. And when I am safely in bed I shall ring the bell for a maid, and I shall send the maid downstairs to say to Mrs. Hoddesdon, 'Lady Cynthia Delphine has arrived and *has gone to bed.*' That will soften her heart if anything will; she will be so delighted to think of me in bed in the daytime that she won't turn me out of the house, which she might otherwise feel inclined to do."

We did not plead with Lady Moonshine; for we saw that her mind was made up. After she had sent me to fetch her nightgown, she kissed each of us, even William; and then we went with her to the gate.

"I should like to say good-bye to Mr. Ned," she said sadly, "but I mustn't. I don't want him to be troubled about me. I shall go quite alone."

With her chin held high, Lady Moonshine stepped bravely down the street.

Lady Moonshine was not missed till bedtime, when Cherry came to our house in quest of "that mishtiful child." William and I were obliged to explain what had happened.

"Well, I nivver!" said Cherry. "The spirit the little lady has, to be sure! But I'm wholly glad on't, though I don't fancy the poor maid will soften Madam Hoddesdon's heart. She and her brother will fight to have that money paid, though they take all a young man has."

"Will it happen as Mrs. Meggotty said it would?" we whispered. Cherry nodded mournfully.

"Saving that I should take Master Oliver home to my father's farm," she said. "Mr. Ned wouldn't trust him to Mrs. Meg's care."

Mr. Ned strolled up and down the shore with Papa that evening. No Lady Moonshine danced beside him; and William, Oliver, and I walked sedately behind. Papa did most of the talking; for Mr. Ned had little to say, although his few words were brave and hopeful. On their return they stood over against the entrance to Candle Street, at the far end of which twinkled the lights of the Great House.

"Poor Lady Cynthia!" said Papa.

"I am glad that she has gone back to Mrs. Hoddesdon," said Mr. Ned. "It is an unexpectedly easy solution to one of my perplexities. But I am ashamed, bitterly ashamed that—"

He broke off, not wishing to blame Mrs. Meg for the unkind words that had put Lady Moonshine to flight.

"Mrs. Hoddesdon has kept the child," said Papa. "That speaks well for her frame of mind. She may forgive you yet!"

"I fear not, sir," said Mr. Ned.

But in the morning old Mrs. Hoddesdon took her black fan and silver-headed ebony cane and came tap-tapping down Candle Street to Candle Corner, where Mr. Ned was busy with the paper fans. Birds of the air carried the story of their meeting to every house in St. Barnabas Green; and this is what the birds told:

Mr. Ned rose to await her pleasure.

"What may I do for you, madam?" he asked, with the grave, formal courtesy that he used to strangers.

Mrs. Hoddesdon's cane rapped the floor.

"I came to ask for your sister Fanny's address. If her education is completed, she might serve as governess to the child out of school hours. I intend to allow Cynthia to remain at Mrs. Trusty's establishment, but I wish her to have some young life about her in the evenings. Your sister Fanny might suit me. Is she at liberty?"

"Thank you, madam; she is seeking a post," answered Mr. Ned, still distantly.

"This is her address, if you wish it."

218

He wrote the words on the ivory tablets which she set before him.

"You don't trust me," said Mrs. Hoddesdon, beetling her thick eyebrows at him.

"You dare not refuse a good offer; you wish to have her settled here. And yet you would give all you have for the power to refuse—you are afraid that I shall be unkind to the pretty young thing. Yes, Mr. Ned Fane, you and that precious god-daughter of mine are a pair!"

"I beg your pardon, madam," said Mr. Ned, taken aback at this shrewd reading of his thoughts.

"Well, let that pass," said Mrs. Hoddesdon. "I came on a double errand. I wish to apologize for certain words spoken to you in anger some months ago."

"There is no need for an apology, madam," said Mr. Ned. "You spoke the truth when you called me a tradesman. I am not ashamed of my calling."

Mrs. Hoddesdon laid her hand on his arm.

"You know what I mean, lad. Will you forgive an old woman who had been made sour and crabbed by many disappointments in her time? I was hurt and angry that the child had flouted me, for I loved that willful puss. So I would not hear your explanation; I insulted you; and I vowed that I would break your pride. I would not yield until you had first humbled yourself by coming to my house—and you would not humble yourself by coming. If I made no allowances for you, Ned, you made none for a cross old woman whom you had known from your childhood. You have suffered sadly because you could not bring yourself to come to me for payment; you ought to have known that I did not mean what I said in hot anger.

"But indeed, Ned, I did not know that you were in such desperate straits. I never listen to the gossip of the town, so I knew nothing about your troubles over and above the loss of your fans. Cynthia tells me that the charitable world thinks that I have been in league with my brother-in-law against you. That is false. I had not as much as heard that the Meggottys were in fresh trouble. As for you, General Hoddesdon took uncommonly good care that I should know nothing about the bill he held against you—he knew that I would defend you! But what trouble you would have saved, had you once stooped your proud head! Do you mean to tell me that you would have let the house be sold over you sooner than come to me to receive your lawful dues? How could you be so foolish?"

"I do not understand," said Mr. Ned. "You are strangely mistaken, madam. You owe me nothing."

"Tut, tut, boy; don't argue," said Mrs. Hoddesdon. "The payments for Cynthia's board and lodging that you never deigned to claim! Lord Delphine left money with me to be handed over to you as occasion required—money that will pay for that fan affair as well as her normal expenses. Surely he made you understand that!"

"I did not, madam," said Mr. Ned. "His lordship came to me in great haste and confusion—and I fear that I mistook—misunderstood—it was not clear—"

"Just like him!" said Mrs. Hoddesdon. "Well, after the child's revelations last night, I resolved that if you would not pocket your pride, I would. So you did not know? Oh, Ned, Ned, you foolish fellow not to have guessed!"

She laid a strip of paper on the table, marked with three figures. Mr. Ned gave a queer, shaky laugh that had tears in it, so great had been the strain, so overwhelming the relief.

"I must settle with you later for Cynthia's share in the burning of the fans," said Mrs. Hoddesdon. "I did not know the precise amount of your loss. But what you have here is enough to ease your mind, I fancy! Pay my brother-in-law part of it. He will wait for the rest; I'll see that he does. And with strict economy, young man, you ought to be able to live on what's left for some time to come."

There was little that Mr. Ned and Cherry Throwhawke did not know about strict economy; but Mrs. Hoddesdon always enjoyed giving advice.

"And let me warn you against backing other folk's bills," she added. "It is the rankest folly. You have burned your fingers sharply this time; let the smart keep you away from the flame in the future. Make Meg and Sam Meggotty fight their own battles!"

"I think they will, when once we are out of this scrape," said Mr. Ned. "Sam promises—"

"Hm! A gambler's promises!" said Mrs. Hoddesdon doubtfully. "Come, Ned, sit down and tell me how they came into such a plight. I must know all if I am to soften my brother-in-law's heart, for late last night he was hot against them. He said that they were no better than a pack of hornets that should be smoked out of the county! 'I've no grudge against young Fane,' he said, 'but 'twill be for the general good that those rapscallions should be driven off. And if he chooses to succor them in their need why, then he must share their fate!' Dear, how vexed he was to find that Cynthia had told me all!"

They sat together for an hour, and when Mrs. Hoddesdon rose, Mr. Ned was years younger. The drawn, tired lines had left his face, and he was a boy again.

"Now about Cynthia," said Mrs. Hoddesdon. "I'm not going to send her back to you at Candle Corner. It is not good for her to have her own way undisputed; neither will I make her sacrifice into a mockery. Also, the proper place for her is in my house. But before we leave that subject, let me tell you that she is improved almost beyond recognition. I should not have known her for the wild little creature of nine months ago. You have done well by her, better than I."

It was perhaps the first time Madam Hoddesdon had made so frank and open an acknowledgment that any other person could be her superior in any respect whatever. Silencing Mr. Ned's hurried attempt at contradiction, she went on.

"And now, Ned, what do you say to going yourself to fetch Miss Fanny home? If it is convenient to you, I should like you to take the journey tomorrow at my charges; for I do not think it seemly for a young lady to travel so far alone, nor do I wish to wait while letters are exchanged. Leave your fans and make holiday for once."

The thought of the three or four days' rest from work brought a look of eager delight to Mr. Ned's face. The arrangements

221

being concluded, Mrs. Hoddesdon said, "There is one more request, Ned. It is long since you visited my house. Will you do me the favor of dining with me tonight, to show that you have forgiven a cross and insolent old woman? Will you come?"

"By the back door, madam?" said Mr. Ned, very demurely, and for answer she tapped his arm smartly with her fan.

So Mr. Ned dined that night with Mrs. Hoddesdon. He had nothing to wear save the old Court suit that his father had worn when appointed drawing-master to some Royal Princesses; it was a dark green suit with yellowed lace ruffles and ancient silver knee-buckles. But we thought that he had never looked finer.

And Mrs. Hoddesdon, in black satin, with the frog-husband's miniature in the middle of her chest, was in her most benign mood. After dinner she and Mr. Ned played chess and backgammon in the drawing room under the shadow of the family portraits, while Lady Moonshine sat discreetly by, busied with needlework. As Mr. Ned rose to take his leave, Mrs. Hoddesdon lifted from a drawer a long piece of rolled paper, written very thickly in stiff handwriting. She pointed to three lines.

"This will was made six years ago, Ned," she told him. "The box would be yours in any case at my death; but I think that it might prove more useful to you now. My man shall take it to your house tomorrow."

"But, madam," stammered Mr. Ned, in great astonishment. "I cannot—there must be others with far better claim—pray consider—these are mementos of your past; surely you do not wish to part with them."

"Vanity of vanities," said Mrs. Hoddesdon sadly. "No, Ned, take them. That chapter in my life was closed long ago, and it better befits an old woman to think of the life which is to come. Cynthia, this conversation is not for you. Attend to your work."

But Lady Moonshine jumped up and pirouetted till her gown spread out like a whirling fan, so glad was she to know that the fairy treasure-box belonged to Mr. Ned after all, and that his name had not been scratched out of the will.

Three days later Miss Fanny came, prettier than ever with her sunny curls under her wide straw bonnet and her dress of lilac muslin. The Great House was no longer dark and dull when she was there; for as our papa observed (he being well read in the older poets and particularly in the works of Mr. Spenser:) "She made a sunshine in a shadie place." Candle Street was the gayer for her presence, and Candle Corner was more delightful than ever now that Miss Fanny was so often to be found in it, warbling like a bird as she tripped hither and thither, filling the house with flowers, helping Mr. Ned at his work, and playing with Oliver, who followed her about in speechless admiration.

Lady Moonshine did not at first share in the universal welcome given to Miss Fanny. She was inclined to look with jealous eyes on Miss Fanny's love for Mr. Ned; and I fear that she was ill-pleased to see Mr. Ned lose some of his staid, elderly gravity in his new happiness and relief from anxiety. But after a few weeks she said abruptly, "Since I can't live in Candle Corner, I don't mind having Miss Fanny. She is not so nice as Mr. Ned, but then nobody could be that; and if I hadn't met him first, I should have thought her very nice indeed."

And between games and merry-makings with Miss Fanny (who played battledore and shuttlecock to perfection), days spent at Mrs. Trusty's school and tea-drinkings at Candle Corner, Lady Moonshine managed to enjoy life tolerably well until Lord and Lady Delphine came back from India to carry her home to her castle in the north.

How well I remember the night when she left us! The formal good-byes had been said earlier in the day; but at the last moment Lady Moonshine escaped from the carriage where her papa and mamma were already seated, fled past Mrs. Hoddesdon and Miss Fanny as they stood on the steps (for Mrs. Hoddesdon had declined to part with Miss Fanny on the ground that she needed a young companion for her declining years), and ran headlong up the street to Candle Corner. William and I were there, in no pleasant temper, for our papa had just forbidden us to run down the street to look at the

prancing horses and the carriage with the "crested crownet."
"Prying is not permissible to properly constituted characters,"
he had said; and William and I went at once to see whether
Mr. Ned had allowed Oliver to pry.

We found them at family prayer, so we stayed to listen.
In our own home this custom was unknown.

We had knelt down when Lady Moonshine flashed into the
room, paused with the swiftness of a humming-bird stayed
in flight, and knelt down, too. Mr. Ned was praying a prayer
that he often used, a prayer made by a saint many hundreds of
years since. And as often as he used it, I thought of the old
man from the Holy House who had blessed us and bidden us
each one seek the peace of God.

"Look upon us, Lord, and let all the darkness of our souls
vanish before the beams of Thy brightness. Fill us with holy
love and open to us the treasures of Thy wisdom. All our
desire is in Thee, therefore perfect what Thou hast begun,
and what Thy Spirit hath awakened us to ask in prayer. We
seek Thy face, turn Thy face unto us and show us Thy glory.

Then shall our longing be satisfied, and our peace be perfect. Amen."

The moonlight shone over the waters, making them a radiant sea, an image of that other glory. Lady Moonshine raised her eyes to look at it, and her face was grave and earnest.

"I had to come again," she said. "I did not say good-bye properly when the others were there. Good-bye, good-bye."

She kissed us all, and turned to Mr. Ned with that sea-shell pink rising faintly in her cheeks.

"Good-bye, Mr. Ned. I made you this with my love."

It was a square mat covered with cross-stitch patterns in every color of the rainbow, probably intended to serve as a lamp stand. Mr. Ned thanked her and promised to keep it forever.

"I had a gift for you," he said, "but unfortunately I could not finish it in time to ask Lady Delphine whether she would permit you to accept it."

"What was it?" cried Lady Moonshine.

He showed her a delicate silver-gray fan with a miniature of herself exquisitely painted on ivory in the mount, protected by a crystal film.

"Oh, how beautiful!" said Lady Moonshine. "Was it really for me? Mr. Ned, I must have it—Mamma will certainly give me permission; you need not write to ask. Oh, it is the most beautiful fan you have ever, ever made!"

Her delight was Mr. Ned's reward for the hours spent on the fashioning of his gift. But he could not let her linger in the workroom once the farewells had been said. He guided her gently to the door, bidding her remember that the horses waited.

"Come with me down Candle Street, all of you," she pleaded.

"No, not this time," said Mr. Ned, who doubtless thought of Papa's good maxim. "We will watch from the doorway to make sure that you arrive safely at the other end of the street."

She looked up at him then, forgetting us.

"Dear Mr. Ned, good-bye," she said.

"Good-bye, Lady Cynthia," said Mr. Ned.

Part II: FOR OLDER READERS

Howard Pyle

ROBIN HOOD
AND THE SHOOTING MATCH

ILLUSTRATED BY *John Dukes McKee*

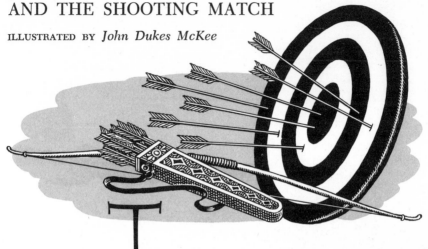

THE SHERIFF was very wroth because of his failure to take jolly Robin, for it came to his ears, as ill news always does, that the people laughed at him and made a jest of his thinking to serve a warrant upon such a one as the bold outlaw; and a man hates nothing so much as being made a jest of; so he said, "Our gracious Lord and Sovereign King himself shall know of this, and how his laws are perverted and despised by this band of rebel outlaws. As for yon traitor Tinker, him will I hang, if I catch him, upon the very highest gallows tree in all Nottinghamshire."

Then he bade all his servants and retainers to make ready to go to London Town, to see and speak with the King.

At this there was bustling at the Sheriff's castle, and men ran hither and thither upon this business and upon that, while the forge fires of Nottingham glowed red far into the night like twinkling stars, for all the smiths of the town were busy making or mending armor for the Sheriff's troop of escort. For two days this labor lasted, then, on the third, all was ready for the journey. So forth they started in the bright sunlight, from Nottingham Town to Fosse Way and thence to Watling Street; and so they journeyed for two days, until they saw at last the spires and towers of great London Town; and many folks stopped, as they journeyed along, and gazed at the show they made riding along the highways with their flashing armor, and gay plumes and trappings.

In London King Henry and his fair Queen Eleanor held their court, gay with ladies in silks and satins and velvets and cloth of gold, and also brave knights and gallant courtiers.

Thither came the Sheriff and was shown into the King's presence.

"A boon, a boon," quoth he, as he knelt upon the ground.

"Now what wouldst thou have?" said the King. "Let us hear what may be thy desires."

"O good my Lord and Sovereign," spake the Sheriff, "in Sherwood Forest in our own good shire of Nottingham, liveth a bold outlaw whose name is Robin Hood."

"In good sooth," said the King, "his doings have reached even our own royal ears. He is a saucy, rebellious varlet, yet, I am fain to own, a right merry soul withal."

"But hearken, O my most gracious Sovereign," said the Sheriff. "I sent a warrant to him with thine own royal seal attached, by a right lusty knave, but he beat the messenger and stole the warrant. And he killeth thy deer and robbeth thine own liege subjects even upon the great highways."

"Why, how now," quoth the King, wrathfully. "What wouldst thou have me do? Comest thou not to me with a great array of men-at-arms and retainers, and yet art not able to take a single band of lusty knaves without armor on breast, in thine own county! What wouldst thou have me do? Art thou not my Sheriff? Are not my laws in force in Nottinghamshire? Canst thou not take thine own course against those that break the laws or do any injury to thee or thine? Go, get thee gone, and think well; devise some plan of thine own but trouble me no further. But look well to it, master Sheriff, for I will have my laws obeyed by all men within my kingdom, and if thou

art not able to enforce them thou art no sheriff for me. So look
well to thyself, I say, or ill may befall thee as well as all the
thieving knaves in Nottinghamshire. When the flood cometh it
sweepeth away grain as well as chaff."

Then the Sheriff turned away with a sore and troubled heart,
and sadly he rued his fine show of retainers, for he saw that the
King was angry because he had so many men about him and
yet could not enforce the laws. So, as they all rode slowly
back to Nottingham, the Sheriff was thoughtful and full of
care. Not a word did he speak to anyone, and no one of his
men spoke to him, but all the time he was busy devising some
plan to take Robin Hood.

"Aha!" cried he suddenly, smiting his hand upon his thigh,
"I have it now! Ride on, my merry men all, and let us get
back to Nottingham Town as speedily as we may. And mark
well my words: before a fortnight is passed, that evil knave,
Robin Hood, will be safely clapped into Nottingham gaol."

But what was the Sheriff's plan?

As a trader takes each one of a bag of silver angels, feeling
each coin to find whether it be clipped or not, so the Sheriff,
as all rode slowly and sadly back toward Nottingham, took up

thought after thought in turn, feeling around the edges of each but finding in every one some flaw. At last he thought of the daring soul of jolly Robin and how, as he the Sheriff knew, he often came even within the walls of Nottingham.

"Now," thought the Sheriff, "could I but persuade Robin nigh to Nottingham Town so that I could find him, I warrant I would lay hands upon him so stoutly that he would never get away again." Then of a sudden it came to him like a flash that were he to proclaim a great shooting-match and offer some grand prize, Robin Hood might be over-persuaded by his spirit to come to the butts; and it was this thought which caused him to cry "Aha!" and smite his palm upon his thigh.

So, as soon as he had returned safely to Nottingham, he sent messengers north and south, and east and west, to proclaim through town, hamlet, and countryside, this grand shooting-match, and everyone was bidden that could draw a long bow, and the prize was to be an arrow of pure beaten gold.

When Robin Hood first heard the news of this he was in Lincoln Town, and hastening back to Sherwood Forest he soon called all his merry men about him and spoke to them thus,—

"Now hearken, my merry men all, to the news that I have brought from Lincoln Town today. Our friend the Sheriff of Nottingham hath proclaimed a shooting-match and hath sent messengers to tell of it through all the countryside, and the prize is to be a bright golden arrow. Now I fain would have one of us win it, both because of the fairness of the prize and because our sweet friend the Sheriff hath offered it. So we will take our bows and shafts and go there to shoot, for I know right well that merriment will be a-going. What say ye, lads?"

Then young David of Doncaster spoke up and said, "Now listen, I pray thee, good master, unto what I say. I have come straight from our friend Eadom o' the Blue Boar, and there I heard the full news of this same match. But, master, I know from him, and he got it from the Sheriff's man Ralph o' the Scar, that this same knavish Sheriff hath but laid a trap for thee in this shooting-match and wishes nothing so much as to see thee there. So go not, good master, for I know right well he

230

Robin Hood and his Merry Men in Sherwood Forest

doth seek to beguile thee, but stay within the greenwood lest we all meet dole and woe."

"Now," quoth Robin, "thou art a wise lad and keepest thine ears open and thy mouth shut, as becometh a wise and crafty woodsman. But shall we let it be said that the Sheriff of Nottingham did cow bold Robin Hood and sevenscore as fair archers as are in all merry England? Nay, good David, what thou tellest me maketh me to desire the prize even more than I else should do. But what sayeth our good gossip Swanthold? Is it not 'A hasty man burneth his mouth, and the fool that keepeth his eyes shut falleth into the pit'? Thus he says, truly, therefore we must meet guile with guile. Now some of you clothe yourselves as curtal friars, and some as rustic peasants, and some as tinkers, or as beggars, but see that each man taketh a good bow or broadsword, in case need should arise. As for myself, I will shoot for this same golden arrow, and should I win it, we will hang it to the branches of our good greenwood tree for the joy of all the band. How like you the plan, my merry men all?"

Then "good, good!" cried all the band right heartily.

A fair sight was Nottingham Town on the day of the shooting-match. All along upon the green meadow beneath the town wall stretched a row of benches, one above the other, which were for knight and lady, squire and dame, and rich burghers and their wives; for none but those of rank and quality were to sit there. At the end of the range, near the target, was a raised seat bedecked with ribbons and scarfs and garlands of flowers, for the Sheriff of Nottingham and his dame. The range was twoscore paces broad. At one end stood the target, at the other a tent of striped canvas, from the pole of which fluttered many-colored flags and streamers. In this booth were casks of ale, free to be broached by any of the archers who might wish to quench their thirst.

Across the range from where the seats for the better folk were raised was a railing to keep the poorer people from crowding in front of the target. Already, while it was early, the benches were beginning to fill with people of quality, who

231

kept constantly arriving in little carts, or upon palfreys that curveted gayly to the merry tinkle of silver bells at bridle reins; with these came also the poorer folk, who sat or lay upon the green grass near the railing that kept them from off the range. In the great tent the archers were gathering by twos and threes; some talking loudly of the fair shots each man had made in his day; some looking well to their bows, drawing a string betwixt the fingers to see that there was no fray upon it, or inspecting arrows, shutting one eye and peering down a shaft to see that it was not warped, but straight and true, for neither bow nor shaft should fail at such a time and for such a prize. And never were such a company of yeomen as were gathered at Nottingham Town that day, for the very best archers of merry England had come to this shooting-match. There was Gill o' the Red Cap, the Sheriff's own head archer, and Diccon Cruikshank of Lincoln Town, and Adam o' the Dell, a man of Tamworth, of threescore years and more, yet hale and lusty still, who in his time had shot in the famous match at Woodstock and had there beaten that renowned archer, Clym o' the Clough. And many more famous men of the long bow were there, whose names have been handed down to us in goodly ballads of the olden time.

But now all the benches were filled with guests, lord and lady, burgher and dame, when at last the Sheriff himself came with his lady, he riding with stately mien upon his milk-white horse and she upon her brown filly. Upon his head he wore a purple velvet cap, and purple velvet was his robe, all trimmed about with rich ermine; his jerkin and hose were of sea-green silk, and his shoes of black velvet, the pointed toes fastened to his garters with golden chains. A golden chain hung about his neck, and at his collar was a great carbuncle set in red gold. His lady was dressed in blue velvet, all trimmed with swan's down. So they made a gallant sight as they rode along side by side, and all the people shouted from where they crowded across the space from the gentlefolk; so the Sheriff and his lady came to their place, where men-at-arms, with hauberk and spear, stood about, waiting for them.

Then when the Sheriff and his dame had sat down, he bade his herald wind upon his silver horn; who thereupon sounded three blasts that came echoing cheerily back from the gray walls of Nottingham. Then the archers stepped forth to their places, while all the folks shouted with a mighty voice, each man calling upon his favorite yeoman. "Red Cap!" cried some; "Cruikshank!" cried others; "Hey for William o' Leslie!" shouted others yet again; while ladies waved silken scarfs to urge each yeoman to do his best.

Then the herald stood forth and loudly proclaimed the rules of the game as follows:—

"Shoot each man from yon mark, which is sevenscore yards and ten from the target. One arrow shooteth each man first, and from all the archers shall the ten that shooteth the fairest shafts be chosen for to shoot again. Two arrows shooteth each man of these ten, then shall the three that shoot the fairest shafts be chosen for to shoot again. Three arrows shooteth each man of those three, and to him that shooteth the fairest shafts shall the prize be given."

Then the Sheriff leaned forward, looking keenly among the press of archers to find whether Robin Hood was amongst them; but no one was there clad in Lincoln green, such as was worn by Robin and his band. "Nevertheless," said the Sheriff to himself, "he may still be there, and I miss him among the crowd of other men. But let me see when but ten men shoot, for I wot he will be among the ten, or I know him not."

And now the archers shot, each man in turn, and the good folk never saw such archery as was done that day. Six arrows were within the clout, four within the black, and only two smote the outer ring; so that when the last arrow sped and struck the target, all the people shouted aloud, for it was noble shooting.

And now but ten men were left of all those that had shot before, and of these ten, six were famous throughout the land, and most of the folk gathered there knew them. These six men were Gilbert o' the Red Cap, Adam o' the Dell, Diccon Cruikshank, William o' Leslie, Hubert o' Cloud, and Swithin o'

Hertford. Two others were yeomen of merry Yorkshire, another was a tall stranger in blue, who said he came from London Town, and the last was a tattered stranger in scarlet, who wore a patch over one eye.

"Now," quoth the Sheriff to a man-at-arms who stood near him, "seest thou Robin Hood amongst those ten?"

"Nay, that do I not, your worship," answered the man. "Six of them I know right well. Of those Yorkshire yeoman, one is too tall and the other too short for that bold knave. Robin's beard is as yellow as gold, while yon tattered beggar in scarlet hath a beard of brown, besides being blind of one eye. As for the stranger in blue, Robin's shoulders, I ween, are three inches broader than his."

"Then," quoth the Sheriff, smiting his thigh angrily, "yon knave is a coward, as well as a rogue, and dares not show his face among good men and true."

Then, after they had rested a short time, those ten stout men stepped forth to shoot again. Each man shot two arrows, and as they shot, not a word was spoken, but all the crowd watched with scarce a breath of sound; but when the last had shot his arrow another great shout arose, while many cast their caps aloft for joy of such marvellous shooting.

"Now by our gracious Lady fair," quoth old Sir Amyas o' the Dell, who, bowed with fourscore years and more, sat near the Sheriff, "ne'er saw I such archery in all my life before, yet have I seen the best hands at the long bow for threescore years and more."

And now but three men were left of all those that had shot before. One was Gill o' the Red Cap, one the tattered stranger in scarlet, and one Adam o' the Dell of Tamworth Town. Then all the people called aloud, some crying, "Ho for Gilbert o' the Red Cap!" and some, "Hey for stout Adam o' Tamworth!" but not a single man called upon the stranger in scarlet.

"Now, shoot thou well, Gilbert," cried the Sheriff, "and if thine be the best shaft, fivescore broad silver pennies will I give to thee beside the prize."

"Truly I will do my best," quoth Gilbert, right sturdily.

234

"A man cannot do aught but his best, but that I will strive to do this day." So saying, he drew forth a fair smooth arrow with a broad feather and fitted it deftly to the string, then drawing his bow with care he sped the shaft. Straight flew the arrow and lit fairly in the clout, a finger breadth from the center. "A Gilbert, a Gilbert!" shouted all the crowd; and, "Now, by my faith," cried the Sheriff, smiting his hands together, "that is a shrewd shot."

Then the tattered stranger stepped forth, and all the people laughed as they saw a yellow patch that showed beneath his arm when he raised his elbow to shoot, and also to see him aim with but one eye. He drew the good yew bow quickly, and quickly loosed a shaft; so short was the time that no man could draw a breath betwixt the drawing and the shooting; yet his arrow lodged nearer the center than the other by twice the length of a barleycorn.

"Now by all the saints in Paradise!" cried the Sheriff, "that is a lovely shaft in very truth!"

Then Adam o' the Dell shot, carefully and cautiously, and his arrow lodged close beside the stranger's. Then after a short space they all three shot again, and once more each arrow lodged within the clout, but this time Adam o' the Dell's was farthest from the center, and again the tattered stranger's shot was the best. Then, after another time of rest, they all shot for the third time. This time Gilbert took great heed to his aim, keenly measuring the distance and shooting with shrewdest care. Straight flew the arrow, and all shouted till the very flags that waved in the breeze shook with the sound, and the rooks and daws flew clamoring about the roofs of the old gray tower, for the shaft had lodged close beside the spot that marked the very center.

"Well done, Gilbert!" cried the Sheriff, right joyously. "Fain am I to believe the prize is thine, and right fairly won. Now, knave, let me see thee shoot a better shaft than that."

Naught spake the stranger but took his place, while all was hushed, and no one spoke or even seemed to breathe, so great was the silence for wonder what he would do. Meanwhile,

235

also, quite still stood the stranger holding his bow in his hand, while one could count five; then he drew his trusty yew, holding it drawn but a moment, then loosed the string. Straight flew the arrow, and so true that it smote a gray goose feather from off Gilbert's shaft, which fell fluttering through the sunlit air as the stranger's arrow lodged close beside his of the Red Cap, and in the very center. No one spoke and no one shouted, but each man looked into his neighbor's face amazedly.

"Nay," quoth old Adam o' the Dell presently, drawing a long breath and shaking his head as he spoke; "twoscore years and more have I shot shaft, and maybe not all times bad, but I shoot no more this day, for no man can match with yon stranger, whosoe'er he may be." Then he thrust his shaft into his quiver, rattling, and unstrung his bow without another word.

Then the Sheriff came down from his dais and drew near, in all his silks and velvets, to where the tattered stranger stood leaning upon his stout bow, whilst the good folk crowded around to see the man who shot so wondrously well. "Here, good fellow," quoth the Sheriff, "take thou the prize, and well and fairly hast thou won it, I trow. What may be thy name, and whence comest thou?"

"Men do call me Jock o' Teviotdale, and thence am I come," said the stranger.

"Then, by Our Lady, Jock, thou art the fairest archer that e'er mine eyes beheld, and if thou wilt join my service I will clothe thee with a better coat than that thou hast upon thy back; thou shalt eat and drink of the best, and at every Christmastide fourscore marks shall be thy wage. I trow thou drawest better bow than that same coward knave, Robin Hood, that dared not show his face here this day. Say, good fellow, wilt thou join my service?"

"Nay, that will I not," quoth the stranger, roughly. "I will be mine own, and no man in all merry England shall be my master."

"Then get thee gone, and a murrain seize thee!" cried the Sheriff, and his voice trembled with anger. "And by my faith and troth I have a good part of a mind to have thee beaten

for thine insolence!" Then he turned quickly and strode away.

It was a right motley company that gathered about the noble greenwood tree in Sherwood's depths that same day. A score and more of barefoot friars were there, and some that looked like tinkers, and some that seemed to be sturdy beggars and rustic hinds; and seated upon a mossy couch was one all clad in tattered scarlet, with a patch over one eye; and in his hand he held the golden arrow that was the prize of the great shooting-match. Then, amidst a noise of talking and laughter, he took the patch from off his eye and stripped away the scarlet rags from off his body and showed himself all clothed in fair Lincoln green, and quoth he: "Easy come these things away, but walnut stain cometh not so speedily from yellow hair." Then all laughed louder than before, for it was Robin Hood himself that had won the prize from the Sheriff's very hands.

Then all sat down to the woodland feast and talked amongst themselves of the merry jest that had been played upon the Sheriff, and of the adventures that had befallen each member of the band in his disguise. But when the feast was done, Robin Hood took Little John apart and said, "Truly am I vexed in my blood, for I heard the Sheriff say today, 'Thou shootest better than that coward knave, Robin Hood, that dared not show his face here this day.' I would fain let him know who it was who won the golden arrow from out his hand, and also that I am no coward such as he takes me to be."

Then Little John said, "Good master, take thou me and Will Stutely, and we will send yon fat Sheriff news of all this by a messenger such as he doth not expect."

That day the Sheriff sat at meat in the great hall of his house at Nottingham Town. Long tables stood down the hall, at which sat men-at-arms and household servants and good stout villains, in all fourscore and more. There they talked of the day's shooting as they ate their meat and quaffed their ale. The Sheriff sat at the head of the table upon a raised seat under a canopy, and beside him sat his dame.

"By my troth," said he, "I did reckon full roundly that that knave, Robin Hood, would be at the game today. I did not

think that he was such a coward. But who could that saucy knave be who answered me to my beard so bravely? I wonder that I did not have him beaten; but there was something about him that spoke of other things than rags and tatters."

Then, even as he finished speaking, something fell rattling among the dishes on the table, while those that sat near started up wondering what it might be. After a while one of the men-at-arms gathered courage enough to pick it up and bring it to the Sheriff. Then every one saw that it was a blunted gray goose shaft, with a fine scroll, about the thickness of a goose quill, tied near to its head. The Sheriff opened the scroll and glanced at it, while the veins upon his forhead swelled and his cheeks grew ruddy with rage as he read, for this was what he saw:—

> "Now Heaven bless thy grace this day,
>   Say all in sweet Sherwood,
> For thou didst give the prize away
>   To merry Robin Hood."

"Whence came this?" cried the Sheriff in a mighty voice.

"Even through the window, your worship," quoth the man who had handed the shaft to him.

ADAM QUARTERMAYNE lived at the end of the thirteenth century in England. His father, Roger, was a famous minstrel and with Adam, who also sang and played the harp, traveled from court to court. One day Adam got separated from his father when he set out to search for his lost spaniel, Nick, who he suspects was stolen by Jankin. This is the absorbing adventure that befell him before he found his father again.

Elizabeth Janet Gray

ADAM TO THE RESCUE

ILLUSTRATED BY *Robert Lawson*

ADAM climbed the steep hill through the woods and came out on what seemed to be the very top of the world. On one side miles of purple heather stretched away to the green lowlands beside the Thames, where the towers and spires of London itself showed like a fairy city in the misty distance; on the other side the deep forest marched to the blue line of the South Downs and the silver sea. Where he stood, bees were busy in the thyme and the blue milkwort; the fragrant breeze blew cloud shadows over his head.

After a while, as he followed the white chalk tracks southwestward toward Farnham, the road sloped downward, and the distances were hidden by trees and the shoulders of hills. More people were on the road now; he scarcely knew where they came from. He asked all he met if they had seen a minstrel with a red spaniel, or a minstrel alone hunting for a boy, but none of them had.

When he came into Farnham, where three roads met, he found the little town full of people on their way to the Fair at Winchester.

Now for the first time Adam began to be really worried. Where was Roger, and how was he to find him again among so many folk, all intent on their own affairs? The road, Roger had said, was home to a minstrel, but, thought Adam, *which* road?

In and out among the people he went all afternoon, asking everywhere his well-worn question. Three he found who had seen Jankin and Nick and thought they had gone to Winchester to the Fair, but none among them all had news of Roger.

When he got hungry, he went to the inn, and there he found one of the merchants whom he had seen at Burford Bridge. The other one had been taken ill at Guildford, and this one, who was called William of Dover, had come on alone with both their servants and their packhorses, so as to have their booths set up at Winchester when the Fair began. The sick man would follow as soon as he could.

"Loss of goods may be recovered, as the old proverb says," remarked Daun William, "but loss of time ruins us. If I am not at the Fair when it opens, I have lost half my trouble."

He made room for Adam beside him at the table, and listened to his story. "Hmm," he said musingly at last, "they told you at Guildford Castle that Roger had heard you were gone to Farnham and had set forth after you?"

"That's how the squire said it was," repeated Adam.

"Meanwhile, you had gone back to Guildford. Probably you were crossing the ferry while he was striding over the bridge! Very well, now, let's figure it out. He comes to Farnham. That would be yesterday. He finds out that Jankin has gone on to Winchester with the dog. He thinks you are close on their heels, and so he doesn't stay in Farnham, he keeps right on toward Winchester. Isn't that it?"

That sounded reasonable, Adam admitted, although it was just as likely that when Roger had not found Adam at Farnham he might have gone back to Guildford by the other road, the one past John Ferryman's house. But Daun William seemed so positive, so satisfied with his picture of what had happened

241

that Adam did not like to question it. After all, he was only a little boy, and the merchant was grown-up and rich and wise.

Daun William had another cup of hot spiced wine while Adam scraped his bowl of pottage. He was hungry still, for he had had only an apple and a piece of bread for dinner.

"Now I have a boy at home," said the merchant, washing his hands daintily in the bowl of water that his servant held for him. "Six years old he is, and a chip off the old block. His mother tries to make a baby of him, but he will have none of it."

A boy of six *was* a baby, thought Adam. Why, when *he* was six! He could remember the little stone house away in the north, and the music coming from the Minster, and his gentle mother, who taught him to read and to sing before she died. When he was six, he used to sit on her lap sometimes, and rest his head on her shoulder, and look into the fire while she told him in her soft clear voice how he would one day be a minstrel and go on the road with his father. He had been very young when he was six.

"I wouldn't like to see him drifting about alone," the merchant was saying. "Now your father's as good a minstrel as ever I met, and he had a fine letter from Sir Edmund de Lisle. I know how he'd feel about you wandering about by yourself. I tell you what! You don't weigh much. You can ride behind my man Oswald on his horse, and no doubt we'll overtake your father before we know it."

Last night at Guildford Castle, the night before at the Ferryman's house, tonight at Farnham inn under the merchant's care! Adam thought he knew now why Roger said the road was home to the minstrel. It was because people were kind.

He was a long time getting to sleep, because he kept thinking of Roger and wondering where he was and how soon they would find each other. He was missing Nick too. If only he could have that warm silky little dog to snuggle up against, he could sleep, he thought. Was Jankin being good to Nick and giving him plenty to eat?

In the morning Adam paid a penny out of the five still in his purse for his supper and half a penny out for his half of the bed, and he told the innkeeper what his name was and where he was going in case Roger came looking for him.

They took the road out of Farnham that went through the king's forest of Holt beside a branch of the river Wey. They rode along close together, Daun William first, then the other merchant's servant leading a packhorse with bulging saddlebags, then Daun William's man Oswald, with Adam perched behind him and a laden packhorse following them. It was not a swift progress, but it was pleasant to be riding again, though Oswald's tired and skinny horse was very different from Bayard.

It was a little mysterious to ride through the king's forest, where the trees, oak and ash and elm and beech, grew so tall, and the undergrowth was thick with fern and briar. Now and then they saw the river shining in the sunshine; now and then

243

they saw one of the king's fallow deer standing motionless and startled in the sun-splotched shade. The birds kept their late August silence, but sometimes there was a bit of yellow and gray flitting among the leaves or a flash of wings across the road. Most of the time Adam saw only the trees that came up close to the road's edge—not cut back two hundred feet on each side as the law decreed—and heard only the steady plop-plop of their own horses' hoofs. It made him drowsy after a while.

Suddenly there was a shout, and an arrow came zinging in front of them to bury its head in a tree not three feet away from Daun William. The next moment an arrow zinged behind Adam and stuck quivering in the tree nearest him. Daun William's horse, the most spirited of the five, promptly reared up on his hind legs, while the others plunged and backed against each other in fright and confusion. Amid a great crashing in the undergrowth, four men rode shouting out of the woods.

"Robbers!" thought Adam. "Robbers. This is happening to me."

One, the leader, wore full armor. From head to toe he was encased in chain mail that caught the sun and gave it back in a hundred winking bits. He was a knight—that Adam knew from his spurs and the crest on his helm—but he had gone to some pains to conceal his armorial bearings. His horse had no trappings; his own surcoat was plain black; even his shield had been painted over with black. Only his crest betrayed him: a gilded leopard that reared itself from the top of his steel helm. He had a sword with a jeweled pommel that caught the sunshine, and he carried a lance leveled menacingly at the surprised and shocked merchant.

One of the others with him was a squire, with sword and buckler and a dagger in his belt. The other two were yeomen in green with a long bow and a quiverful of peacock-tipped arrows apiece. The knight's visor was closed and nothing of his face was to be seen, but these three others had hard, leathery faces with small mean eyes.

Daun William had a sword, but he was too busy persuading

244

his horse to return its forefeet to the ground even to un-
sheathe it. Each of his servants had a long knife at his belt,
but what were two slightly dull knives against such an assort-
ment of lances, swords, daggers, and arrows, all very sharp
and plainly intended for use?

Adam peeped cautiously over Oswald's shoulder and wondered what was going to happen next.

"This is an outrage!" burst out the merchant angrily. "Sir
knight, whoever you are, call off your men and let us go on
our way."

The knight made no answer. The eyes of everybody almost
unwillingly turned to the two packhorses and their very large,
very bulging, very heavy saddlebags crammed with goods to
be sold at Giles's Fair in Winchester.

The knight nodded, and the squire without a word yanked

off the merchant's sword and threw it clattering to the ground, tied his hands behind him, and handed the reins of his horse to one of the yeomen to hold.

"Help!" bellowed the merchant with a burst of noise that amazed Adam. "Help! Ho! Robbers! Ho!"

The servants took it up, and for a moment the woods echoed with their clamor. They made so much noise that Adam more than half expected a troop of horsemen to come galloping to their rescue. Nothing of the kind happened. The robber knight and his men silenced the other three speedily and none too gently by stuffing their mouths with their own hoods. Adam, just before they reached him, steadied himself with his hand on Oswald's shoulder, and stretching out his neck like a rooster, screeched a final, "Help! Robbers! Ho!"

In that instant it occurred to Adam that he was still free. He slid down from the horse, bent low, and ran under his belly. A man lunged at him and grabbed his harp. With a quick twist Adam slid the thong off his shoulder. He stuck out his foot, hooked it around the man's ankle and jerked. When he felt the man topple and heard him fall, Adam turned and plunged headlong into the underbrush. Briars tore at his clothes, and bushes scraped his cap off. Shielding his face with his arm, he bent over and ran close to the ground as fast as he could put one foot before the other, plowing through the thick leafy growth and dodging around trees.

He heard shouts behind him. An arrow sang over his head. He doubled back, tripped over a root, and saw as he fell a beech tree arching its branches like a green tent above his head. The next second he was up again, thinking with his feet and hands, with his knees and elbows. Before his mind had caught up, he was climbing into that beech tree, swiftly, silently, like a cat, up into the sun-mottled tangle of leaves and branches. Just as he stretched himself out flat on a big limb, he saw a piece of dead wood that had lodged in a cleft. He seized it, and flung it out into the air to fall with a snap and a rustle into the bushes twenty feet away. In that moment, one of the yeomen, following close on Adam's trail, stopped short, and without looking up, turned in the direction of the noise he had heard and the ferns he saw stirring suspiciously.

Adam lay on his branch with his hot cheek against the smooth warm wood and panted softly. An ant, its pathway blocked, ran over his face and he blew it off, but silently. The loudest sound in the world just then, he thought, was the noise of his own beating heart.

The leaves, which were thick enough to hide him, also kept him from seeing what was happening. He heard footsteps as the two yeomen hunted for him, footsteps crashing nearer, then going away again, then returning right to his tree. He thought he was surely lost now, but the man had only come to get his arrow. "The boy must have gone to earth like a fox," Adam heard him call.

Presently Adam heard the sound of horses' hoofs. He raised his head and strained his ears to listen. They were departing at a walk, all of them, the riders and the lead horses.

Now there was silence in the wood again, except for a squirrel chattering. Adam sat up astride his limb. His face was red and throbbing, and streaming with perspiration. He wiped it with his sleeve, pushed his hair off his hot, wet forehead, and slowly swung himself down from the tree. Now that the danger was over, he discovered what that scramble had cost him, where his clothes were torn and where his flesh, how his shoulder ached and his knee bled.

The road, when he limped out onto it again, bore record of the struggle in a mass of hoofprints and scattered leaves and twigs. Daun William's sword, badly rusted, lay broken on the ground. The scabbard, which had been a pretty thing, was gone.

On the other side of the road a path went into a forest. Here were more footprints. This must be the way he had taken them, that black robber knight. Adam stood and looked up that path to where it curved and vanished. Determination rose slowly like a tide within him and set his wide mouth in a straight line.

Robbers. Stopping a good merchant who was going about his business without harming anybody! A knight, who had

247

vowed to be chivalrous and protect the weak! Somebody ought to go after him. The sheriff or the bailiff or somebody. Besides, they had *his* harp.

With a wag of his head Adam set off resolutely down the road to find the sheriff.

The sound of horses' hoofs behind him made him scramble off the road again to hide behind a big clump of ferns in the ditch. When he saw that it was only a couple of chapmen with their small trunks fastened behind their saddles, he jumped out and called to them:

"Hi! Stop! There's been a robbery and I want to find the sheriff!"

At the word robbery they turned pale, whipped up their horses, and galloped away, leaving Adam standing in the road looking indignantly after them.

After that Adam saw nobody till he left the wood behind. Then the first person whom he came on was a young shepherd, who was eating his dinner under a hedge with his dog sitting up watchfully beside him and his flock grazing in the field before him. Because Adam spoke the northern dialect and the shepherd an extreme southern one, they had trouble at first in understanding each other. The shepherd thought that Adam wanted something to eat and offered him some bread and salt herring.

Adam sat down crosslegged on the ground beside the strong young man with the kindly brown eyes and had first a drink of clear cold water from the stone jug, then, a little hesitantly, some of the fish and bread. There seemed to be plenty of it, and he was very hungry. Between mouthfuls, gesticulating with his hands and going back to find other expressions for words the shepherd did not understand, he told his story.

"I want to find the sheriff," he finished. "If we go back quickly enough, maybe we can catch the robber knight and rescue poor Daun William so he can take his things to the Fair after all."

"I don't know where the sheriff is," answered the shepherd. "But Sir Adam Gurdon is bailiff. He'll be your man. He's hot against robbers. His father was an outlaw knight himself—

almost thirty years ago it were, my grandam told me—and he frighted all the countryside from Farnham to Alresford. Then the king—but he was the Lord Prince then—challenged him to single combat, and they fought each other to a standstill. Prince Edward had a band of men with him, but he wouldn't let them help. So he and old Sir Adam shook hands and Prince Edward became king and made old Sir Adam bailiff of Alton. And now his son, young Sir Adam, is bailiff after him, and keeps the country clear of robbers."

"My name is Adam too."

The shepherd made a joke. His eyes crinkled first, and then his mouth twisted at the corners. "Look out for apples!" he said, and burst out laughing.

Adam smiled politely, though the joke was no new one to him. "Adam father of us all" the boys used to call him at St. Alban's, and it was considered endlessly funny to offer him an apple.

"It's the forest that gives them a chance to get away," said the shepherd, returning to the robbers. "You say he was a knight. Did you notice his bearings?"

"He'd hid them all, except his crest. That was a leopard."

The shepherd shook his head. "Sir Adam will know. He's lord of the manor here. This is his demesne land and his flock, and I'm his shepherd. The village over yonder belongs to him. You'll see the manor house beyond the church. Go tell him what you saw, and don't let the steward put you off. It's harvest time, and he'll be in a tizzy over it."

Adam thanked the shepherd for his dinner and got up to go. "Have you seen a minstrel pass this way?" he asked.

"There's many a minstrel passes this way. I don't pay much heed to them. A lass in the village told me there was one by with a dog that could walk on his hind legs like a little man—"

"When was that?" Adam interrupted eagerly.

"I don't remember. Two-three days ago."

"Was it a red spaniel?"

"Bless you, lad, I didn't see him. The lass said she wished

249

she had one like him, but I gave her a kitten instead—pure white it were, with blue eyes and one black paw. Eh, she was pleased. Liked it better than a dog, she said."

Just like a girl, thought Adam coldly. Two-three days ago Jankin and Nick had passed this way, and some girl would rather have a kitten than Nick!

The wind blew softly over the field and stirred the bracken around a rock. A bird perched on a sheep's back to look for ticks, and the sheep went on cropping the short grass without noticing it. Adam felt drowsy after his dinner, and this would have been a good place to lie down and sleep for a while, but he had tarried too long already. He set off at a brisk pace in the direction the shepherd showed to him.

He passed the fields that were being harvested and saw what must have been the whole village, men, women, and children, out working in the sun. Some cut the grain with long scythes; some followed behind and bound it into sheaves; some piled the sheaves into great wagons. Franklins with rods in their hands walked among them seeing that they were doing the job thoroughly and that all of the grain went into the wagons. It was the lord's fields they were harvesting now, putting in the days of "boon work" that each villein was required to give to his lord. Across the road Adam saw the fields that belonged to the villeins waiting to be harvested. They were laid out in strips, with unplowed land between them to separate one man's holdings from another's. The breeze sweeping over the golden grain made paths and swirls in it.

The village itself was deserted, except for a few mothers and babies and lame folk. The houses and the cottages, each in its garden, clustered together along both sides of the road, while the fields and the meadows and the pasture land and woodland spread out all around them as far as the eye could see. Beyond the church, as the shepherd said, was the lord's gateway, and beyond that, sitting on a bit of a hill where it could overlook the village and the land that belonged to it, was the manor house.

It was not easy for a boy with torn clothes and no cap to convince the lord's servants, in the height of the busy harvest season, that he had important business with the lord of the manor. Without his harp Adam could not even claim a minstrel's right of entrance.

Determinedly, he stood his ground with each one he met, with porter and with usher and with steward, and he found that if he repeated the words "robber knight" often enough and clearly enough he did eventually get passed on from one man to the next in order.

251

It was mid-afternoon and the church bells were ringing for evensong before he finally won through to Sir Adam, who was in his counting room conferring with his reeve about the harvest. The reeve had a notched tally-stick, on which he was figuring this year's yield, and the knight had a parchment roll on which was written last year's score, and between the two they were growing each minute more mixed up and cross.

"Well, what is it, boy?" snapped Sir Adam. He was a powerfully built young man, much less handsome than his own shepherd, but with the habit of authority.

"Please, Sir Knight, are you the bailiff?" said Adam respectfully.

"Yes," answered the knight. "I am. What then?"

"Can you catch robbers and put them in a dungeon?"

"Yes," Sir Adam smiled, as if he had not quite meant to, "I can. Have you got some robbers?"

"Yes," said Adam, copying the knight's style, which he admired, "I have. At least, we can get them if you hurry. They're up the Farnham Road in the forest. They took Daun William of Dover and his packhorses and his servants, but I got away. There were five of them, and the leader is a knight. He has painted over the charge on his shield, but his crest is a leopard."

Sir Adam and his reeve exchanged looks. Both stiffened to attention.

"What did I tell you?" said Sir Adam to the reeve. "That's de Rideware without a doubt. I've suspected him this long time. You're sure of the crest, boy?"

"A leopard rampant," repeated Adam firmly.

Sir Adam began to snap out orders. "Call Walter. Tell him to bring my hauberk and sword. Have Gerald get horses. You go yourself and collect me men with crossbows. We ride at once."

The manor house, which had been sleepy in the afternoon sunshine, began to ring with the sound of running feet, of quick commands, and clattering metal. Sir Adam's squire of the body brought his coat of chain mail and helm, his shield and sword and spurs. His squire of the stable brought his horse, with

252

trappings on which were blazoned, as on his surcoat and shield, the Gurdon arms. No hiding of his bearings for Sir Adam! From all directions men came running, some with long bows and some with the more powerful crossbows.

In an amazingly short time a band of men was ready to ride out. At its head was Sir Adam, and beside him—oh, wonder and joy!—was Adam son of Roger, on a brown palfrey to show him the way. Behind them were several squires, and the reeve, and then the archers. As they rode through the village, the people, home from the fields, crowded to the roadside to watch them pass, and several of the young men ran for their bows and followed on foot.

Adam rode along in a state of high glory, wishing with all his heart that Roger could see him now. He watched for his friend the shepherd as they went by the pasture and made up for all the others who were not there by standing up in his stirrups and waving violently to the shepherd.

Into the forest they rode, and everyone whom they met stepped off the road into the ditch to let them pass. It took much less time to get back to the place where the robbers had jumped out of ambush than it had taken Adam to go from there to the village.

"We're almost there," said Adam. "Look, that's the tree where I hid—over there—and now you can see where the road is all cut up with hoofprints, and there's where they went into the wood."

Without pausing, Sir Adam turned into the path. "Fall back, boy," he ordered, "and ride in the midst of the men. You're too exposed here."

Adam regretfully fell back. Still, he comforted himself, he was lucky to be here at all. He told the squires about Roger and Jankin and Nick, and how he lost his harp.

"We'll get it back for you," said one, "and then you can show us what kind of minstrel you are."

The path led deeper and deeper into the forest. Sometimes they had to bend over to keep from being scraped off their horses by boughs of trees. They rode silently. Even Adam stopped chattering after a while and felt his heart beating faster. Any minute, he thought uncomfortably, an arrow might zing through the air before his nose, or nearer.

They came to a park where the trees were sparser and the ground beneath them was cleared of undergrowth. A whole herd of fallow deer moved calmly here, scarcely even troubling to look up when the silent band of men rode past. Then the path forked, and Sir Adam took the left-hand branch. The squires nodded to one another. "He knows," said one. "He's been looking for a chance to catch de Rideware."

Before long they came to Rideware Hall, a stout stone house protected by a wall and a moat. Adam hardly knew what he expected when he saw the moat: a siege possibly, certainly a fight, and perhaps even hot lead pouring down from the top of the wall. What happened was that they found an ordinary plank bridge—not a drawbridge at all—across a stagnant and scummy bit of water shallow enough to wade. Sir Adam rode over and pounded on the door in the wall with his mailed fist.

After some delay it was opened by an agitated-looking porter.

"Sir Robert is not at home," he declared over and over, but the bailiff only pushed him aside, and the others crowded after him.

When Squire Walter leaned forward and said something in a low voice, Sir Adam, turning in his saddle, commanded:

"Surround the house. There may be a postern door."

Adam heard some of the men behind him obediently wheel their horses, but his eyes and ears were all for what was going on in front of him. They were in a muddy courtyard now, where various wooden sheds were built against the thick outside wall. Some chickens fled squawking with spread wings before them, and from a pen in one corner came the excited barking of several dogs. A monkey tied to a post scrambled up it and chattered shrilly from the top. The hall itself was a stone building jutting out from the wall opposite the entrance, with narrow pointed windows, and a rather impressive flight of stone steps leading to a stout wooden door banded with iron hinges ending in a fleur-de-lis design. This door now opened, and a pale, thin lady in a green gown with wide sleeves stood at the top of the steps.

"Sir Robert is away," said she in a thin reedy voice. "If he were here, he would resent this intrusion."

Her words were disdainful, but she looked frightened and sad. Adam felt sorry for her, and so, evidently, did Sir Adam, for he answered her gently enough as he dismounted and strode up the steps, "I have reason to believe that he is here. I must ask you to stand aside and let me enter."

His squires followed him with their hands on their swords,

and after them, alternately craning his neck to look over shoulders and ducking his head to look under elbows, went Adam. Lady de Rideware gave way without further argument, and they all marched unchallenged into the hall.

It was dark inside, for the wooden shutters had been closed. The first thing was to get them open. In the light that came bit by bit, Adam saw a long room with rough stone walls. The hearth was in the center, heaped with cold ashes and half-burned logs. Down both sides ran rough board tables and benches, and at the sight of these Adam drew in his breath. They were strewn with heaps of beautiful brocades and velvets and silks, and with little bags and boxes of rare spices. In that gray, chilly, musty hall the brilliant scarlets and blues and golds of the merchant's wares made a rare show of color, and the rich fragrance of the spices rose above the dank smell of the dirty rushes on the floor. On the benches, bound and gagged, sat the merchant of Dover and his two servants, showing in their eyes and joyful squirmings their sudden relief from fright and anger.

Confusion followed. Sir Adam ran up the stairs at one end of the hall to the solar above, looking for the missing knight; others searched in the chamber below, and in the buttery and the cellar. In the excitement of the search, they forgot to free the prisoners, who beat on the floor with their feet and uttered muffled squeals to call attention to themselves. Adam took his own knife out of his wallet and with some difficulty managed to hack away the bonds first of the merchant and then of the two servants.

"He escaped through the postern when he heard you coming," cried Daun William. "Don't waste time looking for him here."

At the same moment a shout from outside drew everyone to the windows.

"They've found his trail," shouted Sir Adam. "Walter, you and Hubert stay here and see the merchant and his goods safely out on the road again. Keep Rauf and Harry with you, in case of trouble. Simon! Gerald! The rest of you! With me!"

Stamping and clanking, they were gone. The clatter of horses' hoofs in the courtyard was followed by shouts and the thudding of hoofs on the grass on the other side of the moat. Walter and Hubert, the squires, and Rauf and Harry, the yeomen, watched from the windows with disappointment the departure of the rest of the band without them.

"They'll get him this time," said Walter, turning away at last. "Caught red-handed. He'd better run if he wants to keep his head on his shoulders."

Lady de Rideware had vanished. Daun William and his men were folding up the goods and repacking the saddlebags, groaning over the silks mussed and the spices spilt. It would be at best a lengthy process to get all those things back again into the proper bags in the proper order, and Daun William's nerves were in no condition to make short work of it. He fussed over the folding and refolding of each piece; he changed his mind three times about the particular box of spice and length of velvet that he would give to Sir Adam as a thank-offering. The squires tried to hurry him up, but soon, seeing that they only made him more nervous and therefore slower than ever, they gave it up and amused themselves by practicing with Rauf's crossbow, using the shabby canopy over the knight's seat at the high table as a target.

Adam prowled about looking for his harp which he found at last among the rushes under a table. Except for a piece chipped off one corner, it was unharmed. He tuned it lovingly and plucked the strings.

"It's a lucky thing there's a moon tonight," said Squire Hubert, casting a resentful glance at the merchant who, standing in a long ray of late sunshine, still folded and unfolded and refolded lengths of material, "or we'd never get home. I wonder if they've caught de Rideware yet."

"They'll come back this way when they do, surely," said Walter. "Since we aren't with them we may as well be here as anywhere. What songs do you know, boy?"

Adam perched on one end of the table, and swinging his legs in time to the music, he harped and sang:

257

> "Trolly, lolly, lolly, lo,
> Sing trolly, lolly, lo,
> My love is to the green wood gone,
> Now after will I go,
> Sing trolly, lolly, lolly, lo."

It was a catchy tune that Roger had taught him. They took it up, the two young squires and the yeomen. On the second round, Adam changed it:

> "The robber knight's to the green wood gone,
> Now after we will go."

To their surprise Daun William joined in with,

> "Sing trolly, lolly, lolly, lo."

The packing was finished.

"Sing trolly, lolly, lolly, lo," squeaked Oswald, three bars behind everyone else.

HUNTING SONG
Sir Walter Scott

Waken, lords and ladies gay,
On the mountain dawns the day;
    All the jolly chase is here,
    With hawk and horses and hunting-spear!
Hounds are in their couples yelling,
Hawks are whistling, horns are knelling,
    Merrily, merrily mingle they,
    "Waken, lords and ladies gay."

Waken, lords and ladies gay,
The mist has left the mountain gray,
    Springlets in the dawn are steaming,
    Diamonds on the brake are gleaming,
And foresters have busy been
To track the buck in thicket green;
    Now we come to chant our lay,
    "Waken, lords and ladies gay."

Eric P. Kelly

THE GOLDEN CUP
OF KASIMIR

ILLUSTRATED BY *Hardie Gramatky*

IN THE balcony of a high tower in the old Polish city of Bendzin, there stood, on a bright April afternoon, a boy and a girl. They wore the rich dress of the noble folk of that period. The boy had on a buttoned velvet coat, knickerbockers of the same material—dark and caught at the knees with silver clasps—silken hose, and soft leather sandals that curved up above the toes. The girl wore a simple tunic of white, held by a golden belt at the waist, and over it an unbuttoned short-coat, blue and silklike, with sleeves puffed at the wrists. She was bareheaded, her light yellow hair falling about her shoulders. She wore sandals of red leather on which were embroidered figures.

Below them, several hundred feet at least, the waves of a little lake lapped softly at the moss-covered stones, for the castle rose on this side sheer from the water. In the middle of the lake, fishing quietly, as if he had no care in the world, was Stanislaus, a half-witted servant, kindly, harmless. Stretched out full length in the flat-bottomed boat, he had pulled his leather headpiece over his eyes, and in his folded hands rested the tree branch which served him as a fishing pole.

"My dear cousin Elzbietka," exclaimed the boy, suddenly, "spring is really here at last!"

They had both been silent for some time as they stood there drinking in the beauty of the scene before them. He was a boy of perhaps fourteen years, but his voice had a ring and his words a meaning that indicated maturity, in mind if not in body. Looking up to him—she was below his height and perhaps two years younger—she said, "Stefan, I thought that it would never come."

Spring had come that year like the sweet lull after a storm. The tiny plants rose from the black earth, green and hopeful. White fleecy clouds floated up from the Black Sea and down from the Baltic; and the sun's soft rays fell in gentle benediction over the world.

But what a world! No more did the peasant sing as he went about his work. No more did the great folk in the castle turn the night into day with feasting. No more did the little flat-bottomed boats ply up and down the river with cargoes of good things to eat and wear. The church bells were silent; the criers were heard no more in the street. It was as if the hand of Death lay over a once happy and prosperous land.

For the Tartar horde of Genghis Khan had overrun their vast empire in Asia and had poured into Europe. Frightful they were, the Tartars: dark, lithe, quick to move, horseback riders of the most daring skill—terrible to look at, terrible to meet; for they were merciless with their curved swords and spared not man or beast.

It was the end of the world, said some. It was the downfall of civilization, declared many others.

"Two days it has been," spoke Stefan again, "since your father and mine rode away to the defense of Czestochowa. It is strange to be here alone. But you are not afraid, Elzbietka?"

She looked at him with blue eyes in which there was not a shade of fear. It was answer enough. He clutched at the hilt of the short sword that he wore in his girdle. "Let them come!" he said. "Let them come!"

For their fathers were among those deathless spirits of Poland who feared naught when their country was at stake. Bravely the Poles had fought at Liegnitz, just one year before, when Tartars felt the strength of Polish swords. Bravely the Poles had died there by the thousand—in vain, perhaps, the world had thought; for the Tartars were victorious, and it seemed as if Europe lay open for their taking.

But at this point of the invasion, instead of pushing on into Germany and France, the Tartars had turned south. During the rest of the summer and winter they had troubled the lands in the north very little; and in those cities where the Tartars had not been, life began to flow on as it had before. So quickly do men forget.

It was so at Bendzin. Although that ancient city lay but a few miles north of the line of invasion, it had not been touched. Stefan and Elzbietka had been together in the castle for several weeks. Their mothers had both perished in the great plague which swept the country a few years before the invasion. When Elzbietka's father had joined forces with the duke, Stefan's father, he had left the child in the castle, believing that there she would be safe.

"Are the Tartars near?" asked Elzbietka quietly.

"I do not know," Stefan said. "Perhaps we are too far to the north. Perhaps it is because we have not much gold—because there is not much to steal."

"But the Cup of Kasimir. Have they not heard of that?"

"Perhaps not," he answered. "But that reminds me that you must see it this very day. It has been hidden away lest the Tartars might come, and only yesterday was it returned again

to its place in the chapel. We will go down now and see it."

Hand in hand they went to gaze at that wondrous piece of craftsmanship famous in all Poland—a cup of gold set about with precious stones, a marvelous thing, the finest example of the goldsmith's art. It rested in a niche in the chapel. Noiselessly they sat there in an oaken pew, Elzbietka struck dumb with wonder, Stefan flushed with pride. Through the windows of stained glass streamed the colored rays, lighting the altar, lingering upon the silver eagle above it, and striking directly at this precious, gleaming chalice of finest, purest gold.

"The inscription is in Latin," whispered Stefan. "It says, 'Blest Be the Lips that Drink from Me.' It came here as a present from the first King Kasimir when my ancestor, the first Duke of Bendzin, built this castle. The king himself drank from it, and then the duke. So has it been through every generation, and none may rule these Bendzin lands unless he drink from this cup upon his accession."

They went out into the passage again, their eyes agleam with the glamour of the cup.

"Our fathers," asked Elzbietka, after a long silence, "must they not be even now at Czestochowa?"

"They are certainly there," Stefan answered.

Throughout the great castle a sense of security reigned. Down in the kitchen whole fowls roasted on the spits over the charcoal. There was much merrymaking, for when the master is away—well, the scullion boys will have their turn. At that very moment they were pelting each other with soot, pelting the cooks, plastering the walls, and covering each soldier of the guard with the sticky black stuff as he showed himself at the kitchen door.

"Stay!" shrieked Stas, the kitchen-master, holding his fat sides with laughter—the boys were careful not to pelt him. "Cease that nonsense and get about the kitchen business." Then, catching the nearest offender, he boxed his ears roundly. "Let that soot-box alone."

The soot-box—that was where the mischief started. It stood by the open ovens, high as a man's waist, and nearly full of

One blow Batu struck

the soot which was taken weekly from the chimneys. The urchins hung over the edge of the soot-box and, filling their mischievous fists, were making life miserable in the kitchen for all but Stas. He enjoyed the joke for some time, seeing that he alone was not a sufferer; but suddenly one boy, bolder than the rest, flicked a handful of the powder into his face.

Splutter, splutter, and Stas was on the warpath. He grabbed at a luckless youth near by and, pushing the boy aside, set the cooks and scullions to work preparing the meal.

The sun was low when the rough table was spread with smoking dishes, and the castle guards seated themselves on the long benches and began to pick out the best morsels with their short knives.

A choice meal in covered silver dishes was taken upstairs to Stefan, Elzbietka, their attendants, and the captain of the guard.

It grew dark. Torches were lighted in the narrow corridors; the high candles flamed in the great rooms. The musicians touched their lutes; while, from below, the wail of a bagpipe told of merriment in the kitchen.

But suddenly there came to the guards' ears the noise of horses galloping.

"So soon returned?" asked a guardsman, laying down his knife.

"They are riding hard," said another guard, rising quickly.

But a third soldier had risen with face white as snow in the red glare of the torches. "By heavens, that is not the tread of Polish horses! Those horses are light. The men ride light—" And at that, all were up in an instant, pale as their comrade, as a terrible scream rang out in the night.

"Tartars!" Surely that was the death cry of a watchman surprised at the drawbridge. "To arms!" and the soldiers thundered into the courtyard, seizing up their armor as they ran.

Oh, fatal day that saw Bendzin, which had never fallen before an enemy, stripped of its most valiant men! They had thought that it would never be molested. Oh, blind confidence! For did not all men know that in Bendzin was the most precious treasure in all Poland, the Cup of King Kasimir?

To make matters worse, the guards at the gate had fallen into the same error as those in the kitchen. Never dreaming of invasion, they had let down the drawbridge in the full expectation of admitting their master and his men. But when the first of that terrible company galloped into the light of the gate, the guards saw their mistake. Horror-stricken, they vainly tried to raise the draw. Before they could do so, the horses of the Tartars were upon the bridge.

In they dashed, like a pack of swift-riding demons, and darted through the undefended gate beyond and into the court, where they battled with a few desperate soldiers who struggled to hold them from the castle.

"To the tower!" shouted the captain of the guard, but there were few men left to retreat. He managed to slip inside the entrance of the central fortified tower just as a volley of thin, deadly spears crashed against the door. Outside in the court, one could hear the cries of dying men, Tartar and Pole; for although the Poles were but a handful, they had sold their lives dearly. The Tartars rushed at the tower door with gate beams for battering rams. In a few moments the door went down, and the whole castle lay at the mercy of the invaders.

This time, however, they did not rush in. They waited until the main body of their cavalry came up, and one grim, silent, threatening figure rode slowly through their midst.

He gave an order, and fifty men sprang into the castle corridor. He followed. They climbed the stairs unopposed, except where the guard captain and some attendants put up a vain fight on an upper landing, and entered the living quarters. Then the chief strode forward with but one man at his side.

Now when that first terrible cry of "Tartars!" came from outside, Stefan and Elzbietka were sitting at table, with the captain of the guard, himself a noble, near them. As the captain hastened away to join his men, Stefan sprang to the window on the side toward the drawbridge.

"It is true," he said, in as calm a tone as he could command; "the Tartars are already in the court and may be here at any moment. Elzbietka"—his heart was pounding like loud thunder in his ears—"Elzbietka, you can no longer stay here."

She looked up at him again, proud that she saw in him, in that moment of danger, that which made Poland great. "Stefan, I will remain with you."

He tried to think—failed; then came an inspiration. "Elzbietka, we must save the Cup of Kasimir. Run to the chapel and take it from its place; then go and tell Stas to hide you, for the Tartars will want food and so will spare the cooks." He drew her toward the door. "Go—go quickly!" he said.

The battle on the stairs was going on. Slight as the delay was, it allowed Elzbietka time to reach the chapel and hasten on to the kitchen.

Five minutes later the curtains at the entrance to the upper room were pushed aside, disclosing two men. Stefan, turning toward them, sword in hand, gazed in astonishment; for one was a Pole, unmistakable in dress, face, and manner. The other was a Tartar, tall, stately, muscular, clad in finely finished animal skins and decorated from head to foot with gold—earrings, neck chains, bracelets, belt, scabbard—the loot of pillaged cities. He returned the boy's steady gaze with small dark eyes, set close together, the nose between them small, and the mouth and chin hidden by a black beard, coarse, and braided into perhaps a dozen strands. Stefan went cold with fear, but hot with determination.

"Boy," spoke the Pole, "tell us where in this castle may be found the Cup of Kasimir, for we are in haste and would soon depart."

Stefan continued to gaze, but did not reply.

"Answer at once," demanded the Pole. The Tartar broke in with something. "He says your life depends upon it," continued the Pole.

Stefan drew himself up proudly. "I am a Pole," he said, "son of the Duke of Bendzin. Why should I answer this man whose name I know not?"

"His name," continued the interpreter, "is Batu, prince of the forces of the Emperor Ogdai, who is the son of the great Genghis Khan."

265

The Tartar spoke again.

"As there is but one sun in the heavens, so shall there be but one ruler on earth," translated the interpreter, "and he must be obeyed."

Batu! A name that was dreaded in every kingdom in Europe—a cruel, bloodthirsty Tartar, second only to the Khan himself in the doing of things terrible.

"Then tell Batu that I defy him, boy that I am. Tell him that I, a Pole, refuse to obey his command; that he shall not have the Cup of Kasimir while I live. Tell him that."

"I dare not," answered the interpreter.

"Then what manner of Pole are you? Have times come to this, that Poles are brothers to Tartars and help destroy their native land? Shame upon you, for you are no Pole!"

Bold words for a boy—or for a man, indeed—but they struck home.

"I am forced," the other answered. "Batu holds my wife and children. I dare not disobey him. I care not for myself."

Stefan was silent. He was thinking that by this time Elzbietka must be safe below stairs. The Tartar Batu stared at him as if not understanding his hesitation.

The boy looked up at him squarely. There was the distance of the room between them, but the candlelight fell full upon the Tartar chieftain's face. There was something in the man's eyes that held the boy's. They were cruel, determined eyes, but they held another look that Stefan could not understand. Batu should have had an air of triumph, of victory—but somehow that was not there. Then slowly the boy began to comprehend the truth—what else could mean this haste at which the interpreter had hinted? Could it be that the Tartars were beaten and were fleeing?

Stefan turned and glanced sternly at the interpreter. "Tell me the truth! Has some disaster overtaken the Tartars?"

The Pole spoke quickly. "Your wits are sharp, boy. You have guessed aright. My life is nothing if Batu learns what I'm saying. Yesterday we received word of the death of Ogdai, whose lieutenant Batu is. And since Ogdai is dead, there is

266

revolution at home, and the troops are eager to go back. The Tartars are discouraged. Batu is at this minute fleeing from Poland, but he turned aside to get the Cup of Kasimir. He has no time to lose, for the pursuers are hot upon his track."

At this moment the chief lost patience and resolved to take matters into his own hands. *"Dai—dai—dai!"* he said—using a Polish word that he had heard often and which means "Give"— advancing upon the boy threateningly. Then suddenly he drew his curved scimitar and strode across the room. There was a smile upon his lips, the sneering smile of one who crowds upon someone weaker than himself; but he had not counted upon the pride that stiffened Stefan's right hand. One blow Batu struck; it landed upon the boy's beloved sword. The blade snapped like a reed, and there remained in Stefan's hand only the jeweled hilt and a short piece of shattered steel.

Then in a flash another idea occurred to Stefan. With all his force he hurled the useless hilt and its bit of jagged blade directly into the Tartar's face. It struck fairly, laying open a swarthy cheek, and Batu staggered back. But only for a step, for, with the rage of a wild beast, he sprang at the boy. Stefan leaped back, and in an instant was upon the little balcony overlooking the lake, one foot upon the stone railing, and just as the enraged Tartar reached forward to grasp him, the boy flung himself off into space.

The loose stones rattled as he plunged. The Tartar, stretching his body over the parapet, his muscles taut, listened for the splash that would tell of the end of the brave leap. He waited— breathless. Then came the faint noise as of someone striking the water far below, so far that even the cruel Batu shuddered. Then he rushed from the room and plunged down the stairs, calling for his men to come up and plunder. He was satisfied that no man could fall that far, even into the lake, and live.

But he had not counted on two things: the first, that he had to deal with a boy of exceptional spirit; and the second, that old Stanislaus was at that very moment in his flat-bottomed boat not twenty yards from the place where Stefan struck the water. By the very violence of the plunge, for the lake was deep at that place, the upshoot of the lithe body took the boy to the surface beside the fisherman's boat.

Unconscious he was, and bleeding. But Stanislaus lifted him into the boat, loosened his clothing, and rubbed his limbs until he was satisfied that the boy was breathing. Then he swung about and rowed rapidly toward the farther end of the lake. Once there, he shoved the boat high among the rushes, lifted Stefan in his arms, and waded to solid ground.

Wrapping him in his own cloak, the fisherman left him in the shelter of a low-growing tree and hastened to a neighbor's cottage, where he procured coarse, homespun peasant breeches and a leather jerkin. This done, he was off for the sheltering tree.

With the return of consciousness to the boy's mind, he seemed to hear an imperative command—"To Czestochowa!" He murmured it to himself as the blood leaped out from his heart and warmed his cold limbs. "To Czestochowa!" he repeated as Stanislaus appeared with the rough garments. "Fetch us a cart and a horse, Stanislaus, for we must hasten to Czestochowa. The Tartars are in flight and will soon be gone."

By daybreak Stefan and Stanislaus were far away from Bendzin, jolting over the roads in a rough peasant cart. They drove on and on until, late in the afternoon, they saw a company of Polish cavalry coming toward them.

"See, Stanislaus!" Stefan rose from his seat and waved to the soldiers. "See! the White Eagle!—they are Poles! Perhaps we shall yet be in time."

They came alongside. The boy leaped from the cart. A tall stately rider in full armor, with a helmet surmounted by a red plume, leaned down from his horse, wondering what peasant boy might be rushing toward him, shouting and waving his hands in such fashion.

"Father! Father, the Tartars are at Bendzin! Stanislaus rescued me from the lake, but Elzbietka and the Cup of Kasimir are in the castle!" In a moment Stefan was raised to the saddle.

Then there went up a great cry through all that throng: "Tartars—the Tartars are at Bendzin! Forward for Poland!"

The hoofs beat the ground like flails upon wheat. And messengers, circling on steeds that foamed at the jaws, brought up behind them troop after troop of Poland's finest soldiers. For the threatened attack upon Czestochowa had been but idle rumor or perhaps a tale circulated by the Tartars themselves in order to empty Bendzin Castle, where lay the jewel that Batu desired—the golden Cup of Kasimir.

As they rode on, Stefan poured out his news: that Ogdai was dead, and that the Tartars were discouraged and in flight. Yet, no matter how much their spirits were lightened at that news, there was still a pressing fear among the Poles, and a terrible anxiety in the mind of Elzbietka's father, hastening along silently beside them.

Finally Bendzin came in sight, though dimly, for it was growing dark. With a shout, the horsemen dashed down upon the fortress. As Elzbietka's father led them on over the still-open drawbridge, there was no sign of life in the castle yard beyond. There was no smoke from the chimneys, and there was the silence of death.

They looked about in wonder. "The Tartars are gone!" shouted a noble.

True it was, they were gone, and in swift flight. They had barely had time to pillage the castle and kill the inhabitants and then dash again on their way.

These things were whispered from mouth to mouth as Stefan, his father, and Elzbietka's father darted into the kitchen. It was in darkness, but someone came with a torch. What a sight! There, heaped about with Tartar bodies, lay Stas, the valiant cook, his great kitchen knife clasped in his right hand. Everything has been rifled. The invaders had evidently been hunting desperately for something. And that something Stefan knew to be the golden Cup of Kasimir. The Tartars had not found it in the chapel, then.

Elzbietka's father, at the sight of the loyal Stas lying slain, abandoned his last, lingering hope. He fell upon his knees beside the faithful servant. Then the duke, Stefan, and every man there did likewise, and from the eyes of all of them, tears

270

started and the tears ran unchecked down their rough cheeks.

More soldiers crowded in silently. Suddenly one of them made an exclamation which caused all to lay hands upon their swords as they looked in the direction he was pointing. The hair rose upon their heads at the strangeness of the apparition they saw.

For out of a huge box by the side of the ovens emerged a figure, hideously black in the light cast by the flaring torch. It was alive, struggling, gasping, trying to speak, but uttering only shrill cries. For a moment it hovered on the box edge, then pitched forward on the floor—an imp, something from the supernatural world. But as it fell, a mass of black dropped from its hands and made a clang like metal as it struck.

In an instant the nearest soldier had caught up the object, and as he brushed the black away, a light from the torch fell upon it and transformed it into a dazzling brilliancy.

"A miracle!" shouted the soldier; "a miracle!" And Stefan, plunging forward, caught it up. Of all the marvels since the beginning of time, of all wonders since the creation of earth— it was the Cup of Kasimir!

But Stefan held it only for an instant. He was down upon the floor brushing away the soot from the face of the imp. It spoke, *she* spoke; for it was Elzbietka, who had hidden the cup from the Tartars in the kitchen soot-box—the one place they did not think it worth while to search. She was grimy, half choked, not much harmed, though much frightened. She had seized the Cup the preceding night; she had reached the kitchen, where Stas, after concealing her, had died in her defense. She had spent nearly twenty hours in the cramped, stuffy space, raising her head now and again from the box for a breath of air.

Then her father had her in his arms, and in spite of the soot which fell from her clothing in great flakes, he carried her up the stairs amid the wildest shouting that ever rang through the castle of Bendzin—shouting that made every rafter ring with echoes, like the dome of the sky when thunder peals.

271

A LIFE ON THE OCEAN WAVE
Epes Sargent

A life on the ocean wave,
  A home on the rolling deep,
Where the scattered waters rave,
  And the winds their revels keep!
Like an eagle caged, I pine
  On this dull unchanging shore:
Oh! give me the flashing brine,
  The spray and the tempest's roar!

Once more on the deck I stand
  Of my own swift-gliding craft:
Set sail! farewell to the land!
  The gale follows fair abaft.
We shoot through the sparkling foam
  Like an ocean-bird set free;—
Like the ocean-bird, our home
  We'll find far out on the sea.

The land is no longer in view,
  The clouds have begun to frown;
But with a stout vessel and crew,
  We'll say, Let the storm come down!
And the song of our hearts shall be,
  While the winds and the waters rave,
A home on the rolling sea!
  A life on the ocean wave!

DAVID BALFOUR was a Scottish boy who lived during an age of great unrest, for in the eighteenth century a group of men called the Jacobites plotted to restore the Stuart line to the throne of England, and they were persecuted by the Whigs. But David had his own troubles. His miserly uncle, in an attempt to steal David's fortune, persuaded Captain Hoseason to kidnap the boy and take him away on his brig, the *Covenant*. This is one of David's many adventures aboard ship before he returned home to claim his fortune.

Robert Louis Stevenson

THE MAN
WITH THE BELT OF GOLD

ILLUSTRATED BY *Rafaello Busoni*

MORE than a week went by, in which the ill-luck that had hitherto pursued the *Covenant* upon this voyage grew yet more strongly marked. Some days she made a little way; others, she was driven actually back. At last we were beaten so far to the south that we tossed and tacked to and fro the whole of the ninth day, within sight of Cape Wrath and the wild, rocky coast on either hand of it. There followed on that a council of the officers, and some decision which I did not rightly understand, seeing only the result: that we had made a fair wind of a foul one and were running south.

The tenth afternoon, there was a falling swell and a thick, wet, white fog that hid one end of the brig from the other. All afternoon, when I went on deck, I saw men and officers listening hard over the bulwarks—"for breakers," they said; and though I did not so much as understand the word, I felt danger in the air and was excited.

Maybe about ten at night, I was serving Mr. Riach and the captain at their supper, when the ship struck something with a great sound, and we heard voices singing out. My two masters leaped to their feet.

"She's struck," said Mr. Riach.

"No, sir," said the captain. "We've only run a boat down."

And they hurried out.

The captain was in the right of it. We had run down a boat in the fog, and she had parted in the midst and gone to the bottom with all her crew, but one. This man (as I heard afterward) had been sitting in the stern as a passenger, while the rest were on the benches rowing. At the moment of the blow, the stern had been thrown into the air, and the man (having his hands free, and for all he was encumbered with a frieze overcoat that came below his knees) had leaped up and caught hold of the brig's bowsprit. It showed he had luck and much agility and unusual strength that he should have thus saved himself from such a pass. And yet, when the captain brought him into the roundhouse, and I set eyes on him for the first time, he looked as cool as I did.

He was smallish in stature, but well set and as nimble as a goat; his face was of a good open expression, but sunburnt very dark, and heavily freckled and pitted with the smallpox; his eyes were unusually light and had a kind of dancing madness in them, that was both engaging and alarming; and when he took off his greatcoat, he laid a pair of fine silver-mounted pistols on the table, and I saw that he was belted with a great sword. His manners, besides, were elegant, and he pledged the captain handsomely. Altogether, I thought of him, at the first sight, that here was a man I would rather call my friend than my enemy.

The captain, too, was taking his observations, but rather of the man's clothes than his person. And to be sure, as soon as he had taken off the greatcoat, he showed forth mighty

274

fine for the roundhouse of a merchant brig: having a hat with feathers, a red waistcoat, breeches of black plush, and a blue coat with silver buttons and handsome silver lace; costly clothes, though somewhat spoiled with the fog and being slept in.

"I'm vexed, sir, about the boat," says the captain.

"There are some pretty men gone to the bottom," said the stranger, "that I would rather see on the dry land again than half a score of boats."

"Friends of yours?" said Hoseason.

"You have none such friends in your country," was the reply. "They would have died for me like dogs."

"Well, sir," said the captain, still watching him, "there are more men in the world than boats to put them in."

"And that's true, too," cried the other with spirit, "and ye seem to be a gentleman of great penetration."

"I have been in France, sir," says the captain; so that it was plain he meant more by the words than showed upon the face of them.

"Well, sir," says the other; "and so has many a pretty man, for the matter of that."

"No doubt, sir," says the captain, "and fine coats."

"Oho!" says the stranger, "is that how the wind sets?" And he laid his hand quickly on his pistols.

"Don't be hasty," said the captain. "Don't do a mischief, before ye see the need for it. Ye've a French soldier's coat upon your back and a Scotch tongue in your head, to be sure; but so has many an honest fellow in these days, and I daresay none the worse of it."

"So?" said the gentleman in the fine coat: "are ye of the honest party?" (meaning, Was he a Jacobite? for each side, in these sort of civil broils, takes the name of honesty for its own).

"Why, sir," replied the captain, "I am a true-blue Protestant, and I thank God for it." (It was the first word of any religion I had ever heard from him, but I learnt afterward he was a great church-goer while on shore.) "But," says he, "I can be sorry to see another man with his back to the wall."

"Can ye so, indeed?" asks the Jacobite. "Well, sir, to be quite plain with ye, I am one of those honest gentlemen that were in trouble about the years forty-five and six; and (to be still quite plain with ye) if I get into the hands of any of the red-coated gentry, it's like it would go hard with me. Now, sir, I was for France; and there was a French ship cruising here to pick me up; but she gave us the go-by in the fog—as I wish from the heart that ye had done yoursel'! and the best I can say is this: If ye can set me ashore where I was going, I have that upon me will reward you highly for your trouble."

"In France?" says the captain. "No, sir; that I cannot do. But where ye come from—we might talk of that."

And then, unhappily, he observed me standing in my corner and packed me off to the galley to get supper for the gentleman. I lost no time, I promise you; and when I came back into the roundhouse, I found the gentleman had taken a money-belt from about his waist, and poured out a guinea or two upon the table. The captain was looking at the guineas, and then at the belt, and then at the gentleman's face; and I thought he seemed excited.

"Half of it," he cried, "and I'm your man!"

The other swept back the guineas into the belt and put it on again under his waistcoat. "I have told ye sir," said he, "that not one doit of it belongs to me. It belongs to my chieftain"—and here he touched his hat—"and while I would be but a silly messenger to grudge some of it that the rest might come safe, I should show myself a hound indeed if I bought my own carcass any too dear. Thirty guineas on the seaside, or sixty if ye set me on the Linnhe Loch. Take it, if ye will; if not, ye can do your worst."

"Ay," said Hoseason. "And if I give ye over to the soldiers?"

"Ye would make a fool's bargain," said the other. "My chief, let me tell you, sir, is forfeited, like every honest man in Scotland. His estate is in the hands of the man they call King George; and it is his officers that collect the rents, or try to collect them. But for the honor of Scotland, the poor tenant bodies take a thought upon their chief lying in exile; and this

276

money is a part of that very rent for which King George is looking. Now, sir, ye seem to me to be a man that understands things: bring this money within the reach of Government, and how much of it'll come to you?"

"Little enough, to be sure," said Hoseason; and then, "If they knew," he added dryly. "But I think, if I was to try, that I could hold my tongue about it."

"Ah, but I'll begowk ye there!" cried the gentleman. "Play me false, and I'll play you cunning. If a hand's laid upon me, they shall ken what money it is."

"Well," returned the captain, "what must be must. Sixty guineas, and done. Here's my hand upon it."

"And here's mine," said the other.

And thereupon the captain went out (rather hurriedly, I thought), and left me alone in the roundhouse with the stranger.

At that period (so soon after the forty-five) there were many exiled gentlemen coming back at the peril of their lives, either to see their friends or to collect a little money; and as for the Highland chiefs that had been forfeited, it was a common matter of talk how their tenants would stint themselves to send them money, and their clansmen outface the soldiery to get it in, and run the gauntlet of our great navy to carry it across. All this I had, of course, heard tell of; and now I had a man under my eyes whose life was forfeit on all these counts and upon one more; for he was not only a rebel and a smuggler of rents, but had taken service with King Louis of France. And as if all this were not enough, he had a belt full of golden guineas round his loins. Whatever my opinions, I could not look on such a man without lively interest.

"And so you're a Jacobite?" said I, as I set meat before him.

"Ay," said he, beginning to eat. "And you, by your long face, should be a Whig?"

"Betwixt and between," said I, not to annoy him; for indeed I was as good a Whig as Mr. Campbell could make me.

"And that's naething," said he. "But I'm saying, Mr. Betwixt-and-Between," he added, "this bottle of yours is dry; and

277

it's hard if I'm to pay sixty guineas and be grudged a dram upon the back of it."

"I'll go and ask for the key," said I, and stepped on deck.

The fog was as close as ever, but the swell almost down. They had laid the brig to, not knowing precisely where they were, and the wind (what little there was of it) not serving well for their true course. Some of the hands were still hearkening for breakers; but the captain and the two officers were in the waist with their heads together. It struck me, I don't know why, that they were after no good; and the first word I heard, as I drew softly near, more than confirmed me.

It was Mr. Riach, crying out as if upon a sudden thought: "Couldn't we wile him out of the roundhouse?"

"He's better where he is," returned Hoseason; "he hasn't room to use his sword."

"Well, that's true," said Riach; "but he's hard to come at."

"Hut!" said Hoseason. "We can get the man in talk, one upon each side, and pin him by the two arms; or if that'll not hold, sir, we can make a run by both the doors and get him under hand before he has the time to draw."

At this hearing, I was seized with both fear and anger at these treacherous, greedy, bloody men that I sailed with. My first mind was to run away; my second was bolder.

"Captain," said I, "the gentleman is seeking a dram, and the bottle's out. Will you give me the key?"

They all started and turned about.

"Why, here's our chance to get the firearms!" Riach cried; and then to me: "Hark ye, David," he said, "do ye ken where the pistols are?"

"Ay, ay," put in Hoseason. "David kens; David's a good lad. Ye see, David my man, yon wild Hielandman is a danger to the ship, besides being a rank foe to King George, God bless him!"

I had never been so be-Davided since I came on board; but I said yes, as if all I heard were quite natural.

"The trouble is," resumed the captain, "that all our firelocks, great and little, are in the roundhouse under this man's

nose; likewise the powder. Now, if I, or one of the officers, was to go in and take them, he would fall to thinking. But a lad like you, David, might snap up a horn and a pistol or two without remark. And if ye can do it cleverly, I'll bear it in mind when it'll be good for you to have friends; and that's when we come to Carolina."

Here Mr. Riach whispered him a little.

"Very right, sir," said the captain; and then to myself: "And see here, David, yon man has a beltful of gold, and I give you my word that you shall have your fingers in it."

I told him I would do as he wished, though indeed I had scarce breath to speak with; and upon that he gave me the key of the spirit locker, and I began to go slowly back to the roundhouse. What was I to do? They were dogs and thieves; they had stolen me from my own country; they had killed poor Ransome; and was I to hold the candle to another murder? But then, upon the other hand, there was the fear of death very plain before me; for what could a boy and a man, if they were as brave as lions, against a whole ship's company?

I was still arguing it back and forth, and getting no great clearness, when I came into the roundhouse and saw the Jacobite eating his supper under the lamp; and at that my mind was made up all in a moment. I have no credit by it; it was by no choice of mine, but as if by compulsion, that I walked right up to the table and put my hand on his shoulder.

"Do ye want to be killed?" said I.

He sprang to his feet, and looked a question at me as clear as if he had spoken.

"O!" cried I, "they're all murderers here; it's a ship full of them! They've murdered a boy already. Now it's you."

"Ay, ay," said he; "but they haven't got me yet."

And then looking at me curiously, "Will ye stand with me?"

"That will I!" said I. "I am no thief. I'll stand by you."

"Why, then," said he, "what's your name?"

"David Balfour," said I; and then thinking that a man with so fine a coat must like fine people, I added for the first time "of Shaws."

It never occurred to him to doubt me, for a Highlander is used to see great gentlefolk in great poverty; but as he had no estate of his own, my words nettled a very childish vanity he had.

"My name is Stewart," he said, drawing himself up. "Alan Breck, they call me. A king's name is good enough for me, though I bear it plain and have the name of no farm-midden to clap to the hind-end of it."

And having administered this rebuke, as though it were something of a chief importance, he turned to examine our defenses.

The roundhouse was built very strong, to support the breaching of the seas. Of its five apertures, only the skylight and the two doors were large enough for the passage of a man. The doors, besides, could be drawn close; they were of stout oak, and ran in grooves, and were fitted with hooks to keep them either shut or open, as the need arose. The one that was already shut, I secured in this fashion; but when I was proceeding to slide to the other, Alan stopped me.

"David," said he—"for I cannae bring to mind the name of your landed estate, and so will make so bold as call you David—that door, being open, is the best part of my defenses."

"It would be yet better shut," says I.

"Not so, David," says he. "Ye see, I have but one face; but so long as that door is open and my face to it, the best part of my enemies will be in front of me, where I would aye wish to find them."

Then he gave me from the rack a cutlass (of which there were a few besides the firearms), choosing it with great care, shaking his head and saying he had never in all his life seen poorer weapons; and next he set me down to the table with a powder-horn, a bag of bullets, and all the pistols, which he bade me charge.

"And that will be better work, let me tell you," said he, "for a gentleman of decent birth, than scraping plates and raxing drams to a wheen tarry sailors."

Thereupon he stood up in the midst with his face to the

door, and drawing his great sword, made trial of the room he had to wield it in.

"I must stick to the point," he said, shaking his head; "and that's a pity, too. It doesn't set my genius, which is all for the upper guard. And now," said he, "do you keep on charging the pistols and give heed to me."

I told him I would listen closely. My chest was tight, my mouth dry, the light dark to my eyes; the thought of the numbers that were soon to leap in upon us kept my heart in a flutter; and the sea, which I heard washing round the brig, and where I thought my dead body would be cast ere morning, ran in my mind strangely.

"First of all," said he, "how many are against us?"

I reckoned them up; and such was the hurry of my mind, I had to cast the numbers twice. "Fifteen," said I.

Alan whistled. "Well," said he, "that can't be cured. And now follow me. It is my part to keep this door, where I look for the main battle. In that, ye have no hand. And mind and dinnae fire to this side unless they get me down; for I would rather have ten foes in front of me than one friend like you cracking pistols at my back."

I told him indeed I was no great shot.

"And that's very bravely said," he cried, in a great admiration of my candor. "There's many a pretty gentleman that wouldnae dare to say it."

"But then, sir," said I, "there is the door behind you, which they may perhaps break in."

"Ay," said he, "and that is a part of your work. No sooner the pistols charged, than ye must climb up into yon bed where ye're handy at the window; and if they lift hand against the door, ye're to shoot. But that's not all. Let's make a bit of a soldier of ye, David. What else have ye to guard?"

"There's the skylight," said I. "But indeed, Mr. Stewart, I would need to have eyes upon both sides to keep the two of them; for when my face is at the one, my back is to the other."

"And that's very true," said Alan. "But have ye no ears to your head?"

"To be sure!" cried I. "I must hear the bursting of the glass!"

"Ye have some rudiments of sense," said Alan grimly.

But now our time of truce was come to an end. Those on deck had waited for my coming till they grew impatient; and scarce had Alan spoken, when the captain showed face in the open door.

"Stand!" cried Alan, and pointed his sword at him.

The captain stood, indeed; but he neither winced nor drew back a foot.

"A naked sword?" says he. "This is a strange return for hospitality."

"Do you see me?" said Alan. "I am come of kings; I bear

a king's name. My badge is the oak. Do ye see my sword? It has slashed the heads off mair Whigamores than you have toes upon your feet. Call up your vermin to your back, sir, and fall on! The sooner the clash begins, the sooner ye'll taste this steel throughout your vitals."

The captain said nothing to Alan, but he looked over at me with an ugly look. "David," said he, "I'll mind this;" and the sound of his voice went through me with a jar.

Next moment he was gone.

"And now," said Alan, "let your hand keep your head, for the grip is coming."

Alan drew a dirk, which he held in his left hand in case they should run in under his sword. I, on my part, clambered up into the berth with an armful of pistols and something of a heavy heart, and set open the window where I was to watch. It was a small part of the deck that I could overlook, but enough for our purpose. The sea had gone down, and the wind was steady and kept the sails quiet; so that there was a great stillness in the ship, in which I made sure I heard the sound of muttering voices. A little after, and there came a clash of steel upon the deck, by which I knew they were dealing out the cutlasses and one had been let fall; and after that silence again.

I do not know if I was what you call afraid; but my heart beat like a bird's, both quick and little; and there was a dimness came before my eyes which I continually rubbed away, and which continually returned. As for hope, I had none; but only a darkness of despair and a sort of anger against all the world that made me long to sell my life as dear as I was able. I tried to pray, I remember, but that same hurry of my mind, like a man running, would not suffer me to think upon the words; and my chief wish was to have the thing begin and be done with it.

It came all of a sudden when it did, with a rush of feet and a roar, and then a shout from Alan, and a sound of blows and some one crying out as if hurt. I looked back over my shoulder, and saw Mr. Shuan in the doorway, crossing blades with Alan.

"That's him that killed the boy!" I cried.

"Look to your window!" said Alan; and as I turned back to my place, I saw him pass his sword through the mate's body.

It was none too soon for me to look to my own part; for my head was scarce back at the window before five men, carrying a spare yard for a battering-ram, ran past me and took post to drive the door in. I had never fired with a pistol in my life, and not often with a gun; far less against a fellow-creature. But it was now or never; and just as they swung the yard, I cried out, "Take that!" and shot into their midst.

I must have hit one of them, for he sang out and gave back a step, and the rest stopped as if a little disconcerted. Before they had time to recover, I sent another ball over their heads; and at my third shot (which went as wide as the second) the whole party threw down the yard and ran for it.

Then I looked round again into the deck-house. The whole place was full of the smoke of my own firing, just as my ears seemed to be burst with the noise of the shots. But there was Alan, standing as before; only now his sword was running blood to the hilt, and himself so swelled with triumph and fallen into so fine an attitude, that he looked to be invincible. Right before him on the floor was Mr. Shuan, on his hands and knees; the blood was pouring from his mouth, and he was sinking slowly lower, with a terrible, white face; and just as I looked, some of those from behind caught hold of him by the heels and dragged him bodily out of the roundhouse. I believe he died as they were doing it.

"There's one of your Whigs for ye!" cried Alan; and then turning to me, he asked if I had done much execution.

I told him I had winged one, and thought it was the captain.

"And I've settled two," says he. "No, there's not enough blood yet; they'll be back again. To your watch, David. This was but a dram before meat."

I settled back to my place, recharging the three pistols I had fired, and keeping watch with both eye and ear.

Our enemies were disputing not far off upon the deck, and that so loudly that I could hear a word or two above the washing of the seas.

"It was Shuan bungled it," I heard one say.

And another answered him with a "Wheesht, man! He's paid the piper."

After that the voices fell again into the same muttering as before. Only now, one person spoke most of the time, as though laying down a plan, and first one and then another answered him briefly, like men taking orders. By this, I made sure they were coming on again, and told Alan.

"It's what we have to pray for," said he. "Unless we can give them a good distaste of us, and done with it, there'll be nae sleep for either you or me. But this time, mind, they'll be in earnest."

By this my pistols were ready, and there was nothing to do but listen and wait. While the brush lasted, I had not the time to think if I was frightened; but now, when all was still again, my mind ran upon nothing else. The thought of the sharp swords and the cold steel was strong in me; and presently, when I began to hear stealthy steps and a brushing of men's clothes against the roundhouse wall, and knew they were taking their places in the dark, I could have found it in my mind to cry out aloud.

All this was upon Alan's side; and I had begun to think my share of the fight was at an end, when I heard someone drop softly on the roof above me.

Then there came a single call on the sea-pipe, and that was the signal. A knot of them made one rush of it, cutlass in hand, against the door; and at the same moment, the glass of the skylight was dashed in a thousand pieces, and a man leaped through and landed on the floor. Before he got to his feet, I had clapped a pistol to his back, and might have shot him, too; only at the touch of him (and him alive) my whole flesh misgave me, and I could no more pull the trigger than I could have flown.

He had dropped his cutlass as he jumped, and when he felt the pistol, whipped straight round and laid hold of me, roaring out an oath; and at that my courage came back again, or I grew so much afraid as came to the same thing; for I gave a shriek and shot him in the midst of the body. He gave the most horrible, ugly groan and fell to the floor. The foot of a second fellow, whose legs were dangling through the skylight, struck me at the same time upon the head; and at that I snatched another pistol and shot this one through the thigh, so that he slipped through and tumbled in a lump on his companion's body. There was no talk of missing, any more than there was time to aim; I clapped the nuzzle to the very place and fired.

I might have stood and stared at them for long, but I heard Alan shout as if for help, and that brought me to my senses.

He had kept the door so long; but one of the seamen, while

he was engaged with others, had run in under his guard and caught him about the body. Alan was dirking him with his left hand, but the fellow clung like a leech. Another had broken in and had his cutlass raised. The door was thronged with their faces. I thought we were lost, and catching up my cutlass, fell on them in flank.

But I had not time to be of help. The wrestler dropped at last; and Alan, leaping back to get his distance, ran upon the others like a bull, roaring as he went. They broke before him like water, turning, and running, and falling one against another in their haste. The sword in his hands flashed like quicksilver into the huddle of our fleeing enemies; and at every flash there came the scream of a man hurt. I was still thinking we were lost, when lo! they were all gone, and Alan was driving them along the deck as a sheepdog chases sheep.

Yet he was no sooner out than he was back again, being as cautious as he was brave; and meanwhile the seamen continued running and crying out as if he was still behind them; and we heard them tumble one upon another into the forecastle, and clap-to the hatch upon the top.

The roundhouse was like a shambles; three were dead inside, another lay in his death agony across the threshold; and there were Alan and I victorious and unhurt.

He came up to me with open arms. "Come to my arms!" he cried, and embraced and kissed me hard upon both cheeks. "David," said he, "I love you like a brother. And O, man," he cried in a kind of ecstasy, "am I no a bonny fighter?"

Thereupon he turned to the four enemies, and tumbled them out of doors. As he did so, he kept humming and singing and whistling to himself, like a man trying to recall an air; only what he was trying, was to make one. All the while, the flush was in his face, and his eyes were as bright as a five-year-old child's with a new toy. And presently he sat down upon the table, sword in hand; the air that he was making all the time began to run a little clearer, and then clearer still; and then out he burst with a great voice into a Gaelic song.

I have translated it here, not in verse (of which I have no

skill) but at least in the king's English. He sang it often after-wards, and the thing became popular; so that I have heard it, and had it explained to me, many's the time:

> This is the song of the sword of Alan:
> The smith made it,
> The fire set it;
> Now it shines in the hand of Alan Breck.
>
> Their eyes were many and bright,
> Swift were they to behold,
> Many the hands they guided:
> The sword was alone.
>
> The dun deer troop over the hill,
> They are many, the hill is one;
> The dun deer vanish,
> The hill remains.
>
> Come to me from the hills of heather,
> Come from the isles of the sea.
> O far-beholding eagles,
> Here is your meat.

Now this song which he made (both words and music) in the hour of our victory, is something less than just to me, who stood beside him in the tussle. Mr. Shuan and five more were either killed outright or thoroughly disabled; but of these, two fell by my hand, the two that came by the skylight. Four more were hurt, and of that number, one (and he not the least important) got his hurt from me. So that, altogether, I did my fair share both of the killing and the wounding, and might have claimed a place in Alan's verses. But poets (as a very wise man once told me) have to think upon their rhymes; and in good prose talk, Alan always did me more than justice.

In the meanwhile, I was innocent of any wrong being done me. For not only I knew no word of the Gaelic; but what with the long suspense of the waiting, and the scurry and strain of our two spirits of fighting, and more than all, the horror I had

290

of some of my own share in it, the thing was no sooner over than I was glad to stagger to a seat. There was that tightness on my chest that I could hardly breathe; the thought of the two men I had shot sat upon me like a nightmare; and all upon a sudden, and before I had a guess of what was coming, I began to sob and cry like any child.

Alan clapped my shoulder, and said I was a brave lad and wanted nothing but a sleep.

"I'll take the first watch," said he. "Ye've done well by me, David, first and last; and I wouldn't lose you for all Appin—no, nor for Breadalbane."

So he made up my bed on the floor and took the first spell, pistol in hand and sword on knee; three hours by the captain's watch upon the wall. Then he roused me up, and I took my turn of three hours; before the end of which it was broad day, and a very quiet morning, with a smooth, rolling sea that tossed the ship, and a heavy rain that drummed upon the roof. All my watch there was nothing stirring; and by the banging of the helm, I knew they had even no one at the tiller. Indeed (as I learned afterward) they were so many of them hurt or dead, and the rest in so ill a temper that Mr. Riach and the captain had to take turn and turn (like Alan and me), or the brig might have gone ashore and nobody the wiser. It was a mercy the night had fallen so still, for the wind had gone down as soon as the rain began. Even as it was, I judged by the wailing of a great number of gulls that went crying and fishing round the ship, that she must have drifted pretty near the coast of one of the islands of the Hebrides; and at last, looking out of the door of the roundhouse, I saw the great stone hills of Skye on the right hand, and, a little more astern, the strange Isle of Rum.

SCROOGE was an old miser who wished no one happiness. But on Christmas day a spirit, The Ghost of Christmas Present, came to show him how even the family of his poorest clerk, the Cratchits, was happy when they gave happiness to each other. And this softened Scrooge's heart. Here is the story of what Scrooge saw.

Charles Dickens

THE CRATCHITS' CHRISTMAS DINNER

ILLUSTRATED BY *Matilda Breuer*

SCROOGE and the Ghost of Christmas Present stood in the city streets on Christmas morning, where (for the weather was severe) the people made a rough but brisk and not unpleasant kind of music in scraping the snow from the pavement in front of their dwellings and from the tops of their houses, whence it was mad delight to the boys to see it come plumping down into the road below, and splitting into artificial little snowstorms.

The house fronts looked black enough, and the windows blacker, contrasting with the smooth white sheet of snow upon the roofs, and with the dirtier snow upon the ground; which last deposit had been ploughed up in deep furrows by the heavy wheels of carts and wagons; furrows that crossed and recrossed each other hundreds of times where the great streets branched off; and made intricate channels, hard to trace, in the thick yellow mud and icy water. The sky was gloomy, and the shortest streets were choked up with dingy mist, half thawed, half frozen, whose heavier particles descended in a shower of sooty atoms, as if all the chimneys in Great Britain had, by one consent, caught fire, and were blazing away to their dear hearts' content. There was nothing very cheerful in the climate or the town, and yet was there an air of cheerfulness abroad that the clearest summer air and brightest summer sun might have endeavored to diffuse in vain.

For the people who were shoveling away on the housetops were jovial and full of glee, calling out to one another from the parapets, and now and then exchanging a facetious snowball,— better-natured missile far than many a wordy jest—laughing heartily if it went right, and not less heartily if it went wrong. The poulterers' shops were still half open, and the fruiterers' were radiant in their glory. There were great, round, pot-bellied baskets of chestnuts, shaped like the waistcoats of jolly old gentlemen, lolling at the doors, and tumbling out into the street in their apoplectic opulence. There were ruddy, brown-faced, broad-girthed Spanish onions, shining in the fatness of their growth like Spanish friars, and winking from their shelves in wanton slyness at the girls as they went by, and glanced demurely at the hung-up mistletoe. There were pears and apples, clustered high in blooming pyramids; there were bunches of grapes, made, in the shopkeepers' benevolence, to dangle from conspicuous hooks, that people's mouths might water gratis as they passed; there were piles of filberts, mossy and brown, recalling, in their fragrance, ancient walks among the woods and pleasant shufflings ankle deep through withered leaves; there were Norfolk biffins, squab and swarthy, setting off the yellow of the oranges and lemons, and, in the great compactness of their juicy persons, urgently entreating and beseeching to be carried home in paper bags and eaten after dinner. The very gold and silver fish, set forth among these choice fruits in a bowl, though members of a dull and stagnant-blooded race, appeared to know that there was something going on; and, to a fish, went gasping round and round their little world in slow and passionless excitement.

The grocers'! oh, the grocers'! nearly closed, with perhaps two shutters down, or one; but through thoses gaps such glimpses! It was not alone that the scales descending on the counter made a merry sound, or that the twine and roller parted company so briskly, or that the canisters were rattled up and down like juggling tricks, or even that the blended scents of tea and coffee were so grateful to the nose, or even that the raisins were so plentiful and rare, the almonds so extremely white, the sticks of cinnamon so long and straight, the other spices so delicious, the candied fruits so caked and spotted with molten sugar as to make the coldest lookers-on feel faint, and subsequently bilious. Nor was it that the figs were moist and pulpy, or that the French plums blushed in modest tartness from their highly decorated boxes, or that everything was good to eat and in its Christmas dress; but the customers were all so hurried and so eager in the hopeful promise of the day that they tumbled up against each other at the door, crashing their wicker baskets wildly, and left their purchases upon the counter, and came running back to fetch them, and committed hundreds of the like mistakes, in the best humor possible; while the grocer and his people were so frank and fresh that the polished hearts with which they fastened their aprons behind might have been their own, worn outside for general inspection, and for Christmas daws to peck at, if they chose.

But soon the steeples called good people all to church and chapel, and away they came, flocking through the streets in their best clothes, and with their gayest faces. And at the same time there emerged from scores of by-streets, lanes, and nameless turnings innumerable people, carrying their dinners to the bakers' shops. The sight of these poor revellers appeared to interest the Spirit very much, for he stood, with Scrooge beside him, in a baker's doorway, and, taking off the covers as their bearers passed, sprinkled incense on their dinners from his torch. And it was a very uncommon kind of torch, for once or twice when there were angry words between some dinner-carriers who had jostled each other, he shed a few drops of water on them from it, and their good humor was restored directly. For, they said, it was a shame to quarrel upon Christmas Day. And so it was! God love it, so it was!

Mrs. Cratchit entered—flushed, but smiling proudly.

In time the bells ceased, and the bakers were shut up; and yet there was a genial shadowing forth of all these dinners, and the progress of their cooking, in the thawed blotch of wet above each baker's oven, where the pavement smoked as if its stones were cooking too.

"Is there a peculiar flavor in what you sprinkle from your torch?" asked Scrooge.

"There is. My own."

"Would it apply to any kind of dinner on this day?" asked Scrooge.

"To any kindly given. To a poor one most."

"Why to a poor one most?" asked Scrooge.

"Because it needs it most."

"Spirit," said Scrooge, after a moment's thought, "I wonder you, of all the beings in the many worlds about us, should desire to cramp these people's opportunities of innocent enjoyment."

"I!" cried the Spirit.

"You would deprive them of their means of dining every seventh day, often the only day on which they can be said to dine at all," said Scrooge, "wouldn't you?"

"I!" cried the Spirit.

"You seek to close these places on the Seventh Day," said Scrooge. "And it comes to the same thing."

"*I* seek!" exclaimed the Spirit.

"Forgive me if I am wrong. It has been done in your name, or at least in that of your family," said Scrooge.

"There are some upon this earth of yours," returned the Spirit, "who lay claim to know us, and who do their deeds of passion, pride, ill-will, hatred, envy, bigotry, and selfishness in our name, who are as strange to us, and all our kith and kin, as if they had never lived. Remember that, and charge their doings on themselves, not us."

Scrooge promised that he would; and they went on, invisible, as they had been before, into the suburbs of the town. It was a remarkable quality of the Ghost (which Scrooge had observed at the baker's) that, notwithstanding his gigantic size, he could

295

accommodate himself to any place with ease; and that he stood beneath a low roof quite as gracefully, and like a supernatural creature, as it was possible he could have done in any lofty hall.

And perhaps it was the pleasure the good Spirit had in showing off this power of his, or else it was his own kind, generous, hearty nature, and his sympathy with all poor men, that led him straight to Scrooge's clerk's; for there he went, and took Scrooge with him, holding to his robe; and on the threshold of the door the Spirit smiled and stopped to bless Bob Cratchit's dwelling with the sprinklings of his torch. Think of that! Bob had but fifteen "bob" a week himself; he pocketed on Saturdays but fifteen copies of his Christian name; and yet the Ghost of Christmas Present blessed his four-roomed house!

Then up rose Mrs. Cratchit, Cratchit's wife, dressed out but poorly in a twice-turned gown, but brave in ribbons, which are cheap and make a goodly show for sixpence; and she laid the cloth, assisted by Belinda Cratchit, second of her daughters, also brave in ribbons; while Master Peter Cratchit plunged a fork into the saucepan of potatoes, and getting the corners of his monstrous shirt-collar (Bob's private property, conferred upon his son and heir in honor of the day) into his mouth, rejoiced to find himself so gallantly attired, and yearned to show his linen in the fashionable parks. And now two smaller Cratchits, boy and girl, came tearing in, screaming that outside the baker's they had smelt the goose, and known it for their own; and, basking in luxurious thoughts of sage and onion, these young Cratchits danced about the table, and exalted Master Peter Cratchit to the skies, while he blew the fire, until the slow potatoes, bubbling up, knocked loudly at the saucepan lid to be let out and peeled.

"What has ever got your precious father, then?" said Mrs. Cratchit. "And your brother, Tiny Tim? And Martha warn't as late last Christmas Day by half an hour!"

"Here's Martha, mother," said a girl, appearing as she spoke.

"Here's Martha, mother!" cried the two young Cratchits. "Hurrah! There's *such* a goose, Martha!"

"Why, bless your heart alive, my dear, how late you are!" said Mrs. Cratchit, kissing her a dozen times, and taking off her shawl and bonnet for her with officious zeal.

"We'd a deal of work to finish up last night," replied the girl, "and had to clear away this morning, mother!"

"Well! Never mind so long as you are come," said Mrs. Cratchit. "Sit ye down before the fire, my dear, and have a warm, Lord bless ye!"

"No, no! There's father coming," cried the two young Cratchits, who were everywhere at once. "Hide, Martha, hide!"

So Martha hid herself, and in came little Bob, the father, with at least three feet of comforter, exclusive of the fringe, hanging down before him; and his threadbare clothes, darned up and brushed, to look seasonable; and Tiny Tim upon his shoulder. Alas for Tiny Tim, he bore a little crutch and had his limbs supported by an iron frame!

"Why, where's our Martha?" cried Bob Cratchit, looking 'round.

"Not coming," said Mrs. Cratchit.

"Not coming!" said Bob, with a sudden declension in his high spirits; for he had been Tim's blood horse all the way from the church, and had come home rampant. "Not coming upon Christmas Day!"

Martha didn't like to see him disappointed, if it were only in joke; so she came out prematurely from behind the closet door, and ran into his arms, while the two young Cratchits hustled Tiny Tim, and bore him off into the wash-house, that he might hear the pudding singing in the copper.

"And how did little Tim behave?" asked Mrs. Cratchit, when she had rallied Bob on his credulity, and Bob had hugged his daughter to his heart's content.

"As good as gold," said Bob, "and better. Somehow he gets thoughtful, sitting by himself so much, and thinks the strangest things you ever heard. He told me, coming home, that he hoped the people saw him in the church, because he was a cripple, and it might be pleasant to them to remember, upon Christmas Day, Who made lame beggars walk and blind men see."

Bob's voice was tremulous when he told them this, and trembled more when he said that Tiny Tim was growing strong and hearty.

His active little crutch was heard upon the floor, and back came Tiny Tim before another word was spoken, escorted by his brother and sister to his stool beside the fire; and while Bob, turning up his cuffs,—as if, poor fellow, they were capable of being made more shabby,—compounded some hot mixture in a jug with gin and lemons, and stirred it round and round, and put it on the hob to simmer, Master Peter and the two ubiquitous young Cratchits went to fetch the goose, with which they soon returned in high procession.

Such a bustle ensued that you might have thought a goose the rarest of all birds; a feathered phenomenon, to which a black swan was a matter of course,—and in truth it was something very like it in that house. Mrs. Cratchit made the gravy (ready beforehand in a little saucepan) hissing hot; Master Peter mashed the potatoes with incredible vigor; Miss Belinda sweetened up the applesauce; Martha dusted the hot plates; Bob took Tiny Tim beside him in a tiny corner at the table; the two young Cratchits set chairs for everybody, not forgetting themselves, and, mounting guard upon their posts, crammed spoons into their mouths, lest they should shriek for goose before their turn came to be helped. At last the dishes were set on, and grace was said. It was succeeded by a breathless pause, as Mrs. Cratchit, looking slowly all along the carving-knife, prepared to plunge it in the breast; but when she did, and when the long-expected gush of stuffing issued forth, one murmur of delight arose all round the board, and even Tiny Tim, excited by the two young Cratchits, beat on the table with the handle of his knife, and feebly cried, "Hurrah!"

There never was such a goose. Bob said he didn't believe there ever was such a goose cooked. Its tenderness and flavor, size and cheapness, were the themes of universal admiration. Eked out by applesauce and mashed potatoes, it was a sufficient dinner for the whole family; indeed, as Mrs. Cratchit said with great delight (surveying one small atom of a bone

upon the dish), they hadn't ate it all at last! Yet everyone had had enough, and the youngest Cratchits in particular were steeped in sage and onion to the eyebrows! But now, the plates being changed by Miss Belinda, Mrs. Cratchit left the room alone—too nervous to bear witnesses—to take the pudding up, and bring it in.

Suppose it should not be done enough! Suppose it should break in turning out! Suppose somebody should have got over the wall of the backyard and stolen it, while they were merry with the goose,—a supposition at which the two young Cratchits became livid! All sorts of horrors were supposed.

Hallo! A great deal of steam! The pudding was out of the copper. A smell like a washing-day! That was the cloth. A smell like an eating-house and a pastry-cook's next door to each other, with a laundress's next door to that! That was the pudding! In half a minute Mrs. Cratchit entered—flushed, but smiling proudly—with the pudding, like a speckled cannon ball, so hard and firm, blazing in half of half-a-quartern of ignited brandy, and bedight with Christmas holly stuck into the top.

Oh, a wonderful pudding! Bob Cratchit said, and calmly, too, that he regarded it as the greatest success achieved by Mrs. Cratchit since their marriage. Mrs. Cratchit said that, now the weight was off her mind, she would confess she had her doubts about the quantity of flour. Everybody had something to say about it, but nobody said or thought it was at all a small pudding for a large family. It would have been flat heresy to do so. Any Cratchit would have blushed to hint at such a thing.

At last the dinner was all done, the cloth was cleared, the hearth swept, and the fire made up. The compound in the jug being tasted and considered perfect, apples and oranges were put upon the table, and a shovelful of chestnuts on the fire. Then all the Cratchit family drew round the hearth in what Bob Cratchit called a circle, meaning half a one; and at Bob Cratchit's elbow stood the family display of glass,—two tumblers and a custard-cup without a handle.

These held the hot stuff from the jug, however, as well as golden goblets would have done; and Bob served it out with beaming looks, while the chestnuts on the fire sputtered and cracked noisily. Then Bob proposed:—

"A Merry Christmas to us all, my dears. God bless us!"

Which all the family re-echoed.

"God bless us every one!" said Tiny Tim, the last of all.

Jennie Hall

AT THE FALL
OF POMPEII

ILLUSTRATED BY *Kay Lovelace*

ARISTON, the Greek slave, was busily painting. He stood in a little room with three smooth walls. The fourth side was open upon a court. A little fountain splashed there. Above stretched the brilliant sky of Italy. The August sun shone hotly down. It cut sharp shadows of the columns on the cement floor. This was the master's room. The artist was painting the walls. Two were already gay with pictures. They showed the mighty deeds of warlike Heracles. Here was Heracles strangling the lion, Heracles killing the hideous hydra, Heracles carrying the wild boar on his shoulders, Heracles training the mad horses. But now the boy was painting the best deed of all— Heracles saving Alcestis from death. He had made the hero big and beautiful. The strong muscles lay smooth in the great body. One hand trailed the club. On the other arm hung the famous lion skin. With that hand the god led Alcestis. He turned his head toward her and smiled. On the ground lay Death, bruised and bleeding. One batlike black wing hung broken. He scowled after the hero and the woman. In the sky above him stood Apollo, the lord of life, looking down. But the picture of the god was only half finished. The figure was sketched in outline, Ariston was rapidly laying on paint with his little brushes. His eyes glowed with Apollo's own fire. His lips were open, and his breath came through them pantingly.

301

"O god of beauty, god of Hellas, god of freedom, help me!" he half whispered while his brush worked.

For he had a great plan in his mind. Here he was, a slave in this rich Roman's house. Yet he was a free-born son of Athens, from a family of painters. Pirates had brought him here to Pompeii and had sold him as a slave. His artist's skill had helped him, even in this cruel land. For his master, Tetreius, loved beauty. The Roman had soon found that his young Greek slave was a painter. He had said to his steward:

"Let the boy work at the mill no longer. He shall paint the walls of my private room."

So he had talked to Ariston about what the pictures should be. The Greek had found that this solemn, frowning Roman was really a kind man. Then hope had sprung up in his breast and had sung of freedom.

"I will do my best to please him," he had thought. "When all the walls are beautiful, perhaps he will smile at my work. Then I will clasp his knees. I will tell him of my father, of Athens, of how I was stolen. Perhaps he will send me home."

Now the painting was almost done. As he worked, a thousand pictures were flashing through his mind. He saw his beloved old home in lovely Athens. He felt his father's hand on his, teaching him to paint. He gazed again at the Parthenon, more beautiful than a dream. Then he saw himself playing on the fishing boat on that terrible holiday. He saw the pirate ships sail swiftly from behind a rocky point and pounce upon them. He saw himself and his friends dragged aboard. He felt the tight rope on his wrists as they bound him and threw him under the deck. He saw himself standing here in the market place of Pompeii. He heard himself sold for a slave. At that thought he threw down his brush and groaned.

But soon he grew calmer. Perhaps the sweet drip of the fountain cooled his hot thoughts. Perhaps the soft touch of the sun soothed his heart. He took up his brushes again and set to work.

"The last figure shall be the most beautiful of all," he said to himself. "It is my own god, Apollo."

302

So he worked tenderly on the face. With a few little strokes he made the mouth smile kindly. He made the blue eyes deep and gentle. He lifted the golden curls with a little breeze from Olympus. The god's smile cheered him. The beautiful colors filled his mind. He forgot his sorrows. He forgot everything but his picture. Minute by minute it grew under his moving brush. He smiled into the god's eyes.

Meantime a great noise arose in the house. There were cries of fear. There was running of feet.

"A great cloud!" "Earthquake!" "Fire and hail!" "Smoke from hell!" "The end of the world!" "Run! Run!"

And men and women, all slaves, ran screaming through the house and out of the front door. But the painter only half heard the cries. His ears, his eyes, his thoughts were full of Apollo.

For a little the house was still. Only the fountain and the shadows and the artist's brush moved there. Then came a great noise as though the sky had split open. The low, sturdy house trembled. Ariston's brush was shaken, and blotted Apollo's eye. Then there was a clattering on the cement floor as of a million arrows. Ariston ran into the court. From the heavens showered a hail of gray, soft little pebbles like beans. They burned his upturned face. They stung his bare arms. He gave a cry and ran back under the porch roof. Then he heard a shrill call above all the clattering. It came from the far end of the house. Ariston ran back into the private court. There lay Caius, his master's little sick son. His couch was under the open sky, and the gray hail was pelting down upon him. He was covering his head with his arms and wailing.

"Little master!" called Ariston. "What is it? What has happened to us?"

"Oh, take me!" cried the little boy.

"Where are the others?" asked Ariston.

"They ran away," answered Caius. "They were afraid. Look! O-o-h!"

He pointed to the sky and screamed with terror.

Ariston looked. Behind the city lay a beautiful hill, green

303

with trees. But now from the flat top towered a huge, black cloud. It rose straight like a pine tree and then spread its black branches over the heavens. And from that cloud showered these hot, pelting pebbles of pumice stone.

"It is a volcano," cried Ariston.

He had seen one spouting fire as he had voyaged on the pirate ship.

"I want my father," wailed the little boy.

Then Ariston remembered that his master was away from home. He had gone in a ship to Rome to get a great physician for his sick boy. He had left Caius in the charge of his nurse, for the boy's mother was dead. But now every slave had turned coward and had run away and left the little master to die. Ariston pulled the couch into one of the rooms. Here the roof kept off the hail of stones.

"Your father is expected home today, master Caius," said the Greek. "He will come. He never breaks his word. We will wait for him here. This strange shower will soon be over."

So he sat on the edge of the couch, and the little Roman laid his head in his slave's lap and sobbed. Ariston watched the falling pebbles. They were light and full of little holes.

Every now and then black rocks of the size of his head whizzed through the air. Sometimes one fell into the open cistern and the water hissed at its heat. The pebbles lay piled a foot deep all over the courtyard floor. And still they fell thick and fast.

"Will it never stop?" thought Ariston.

Several times the ground swayed under him. It felt like the moving of a ship in a storm. Once there was thunder and a trembling of the house. Ariston was looking at a little bronze statue that stood on a tall, slender column. It tottered to and fro in the earthquake. Then it fell, crashing into the piled-up stones. In a few minutes the falling shower had covered it.

Ariston began to be more afraid. He thought of Death as he had painted him in his picture. He imagined that he saw him hiding behind a column. He thought he heard his cruel laugh. He tried to look up toward the mountain, but the stones pelted him down. He felt terribly alone. Was all the rest of the world dead? Or was everyone else in some safe place?

"Come, Caius, we must get away," he cried. "We shall be buried here."

He snatched up one of the blankets from the couch. He threw the ends over his shoulders and let a loop hang at his back. He stood the sick boy in this and wound the ends around them both. Caius was tied to his slave's back. His heavy little head hung on Ariston's shoulder. Then the Greek tied a pillow over his own head. He snatched up a staff and ran from the house. He looked at his picture as he passed. He thought he saw Death half rise from the ground. But Apollo seemed to smile at his artist.

At the front door Ariston stumbled. He found the street piled deep with the gray, soft pebbles. He had to scramble up on his hands and knees. From the house opposite ran a man. He looked wild with fear. He was clutching a little statue of gold. Ariston called to him, "Which way to the gate?"

But the man did not hear. He rushed madly on. Ariston followed him. It cheered the boy a little to see that somebody else was still alive in the world. But he had a hard task. He could not run. The soft pebbles crunched under his feet and made him stumble. He leaned far forward under his heavy burden. The falling shower scorched his bare arms and legs. Once a heavy stone struck him on his cushioned head, and he fell. But he was up in an instant. He looked around bewildered. His head was ringing. The air was hot and choking. The sun was gone. The shower was blinding. Whose house was this? The door stood open. The court was empty. Where was the city gate? Would he never get out? He did not know this street. Here on the corner was a wine shop with its open sides. But no men stood there drinking. Winecups were tipped over and broken on the marble counter. Ariston stood in a daze and watched the wine spilling into the street.

Then a crowd came rushing past him. It was evidently a family fleeing for their lives. Their mouths were open as though they were crying. But Ariston could not hear their voices. His ears shook with the roar of the mountain. An old man was hugging a chest. Gold coins were spilling out as he ran. Another man was dragging a fainting woman. A young girl ran ahead of them with white face and streaming hair. Ariston stumbled on after this company. A great black slave came swiftly around a corner and ran into him and knocked him over, but fled on without looking back. As the Greek boy fell forward, the rough little pebbles scoured his face. He lay there moaning. Then he began to forget his troubles. His aching body began to rest. He thought he would sleep. He saw Apollo smiling. Then Caius struggled and cried out. He pulled at the blanket and tried to free himself. This roused Ariston, and he sat up. He felt the hot pebbles again. He heard the mountain roar. He dragged himself to his feet and started on. Suddenly the street led him out into a broad space. Ariston looked around him. All about stretched wide porches with their columns. Temple roofs rose above them. Statues stood high on their pedestals. He was in the forum. The great open square was crowded with hurrying people. Under one of the porches Ariston saw the money-changers locking their boxes. From a wide doorway ran several men. They were carrying great bundles of woolen cloth, richly embroidered and dyed with precious purple. Down the great

steps of Jupiter's temple ran a priest. Under his arms he clutched two large platters of gold. Men were running across the forum dragging bags behind them.

Everyone seemed trying to save his most precious things. And everyone was hurrying to the gate at the far end. Then that was the way out! Ariston picked up his heavy feet and ran. Suddenly the earth swayed under him. He heard horrible thunder. He thought the mountain was falling upon him. He looked behind. He saw the columns of the porch tottering. A man was running out from one of the buildings. But as he ran, the walls crashed down. The galley above fell cracking. He was buried. Ariston saw it all and cried out in horror. Then he prayed:

"O Lord Poseidon, shaker of the earth, save me! I am a Greek!"

Then he came out of the forum. A steep street sloped down to a gate. A river of people was pouring out there. The air was full of cries. The great noise of the crowd made itself heard even in the noise of the volcano. The streets were full of lost treasures. Men pushed and fell and were trodden upon. But at last Ariston passed through the gateway and was out of the city. He looked about.

"It is no better," he sobbed to himself.

The air was thicker now. The shower had changed to hot dust as fine as ashes. It blurred his eyes. It stopped his nostrils. It choked his lungs. He tore his chiton from top to bottom and wrapped it about his mouth and nose. He looked back at Caius and pulled the blanket over his head. Behind him a huge cloud was reaching out long black arms from the mountain to catch him. Ahead, the sun was only a red wafer in the shower of ashes. Around him people were running off to hide under rocks or trees or in the country houses. Some were running, running anywhere to get away. Out of one courtyard dashed a chariot. The driver was lashing his horses. He pushed them ahead through the crowd. He knocked people over, but he did not stop to see what harm he had done. Curses flew after him. He drove on down the road.

Ariston remembered when he himself had been dragged up here two years ago from the pirate ship.

"This leads to the sea," he thought, "I will go there. Perhaps I shall meet my master, Tetreius. He will come by ship. Surely I shall find him. The gods will send him to me. O blessed gods!"

But what a sea! It roared and tossed and boiled. While Ariston looked, a ship was picked up and crushed and swallowed. The sea poured up the steep shore for hundreds of feet. Then it rushed back and left its strange fish gasping on the dry land. Great rocks fell from the sky, and steam rose up as they splashed into the water. The sun was growing fainter. The black cloud was coming on. Soon it would be dark. And then what? Ariston lay down where the last huge wave had cooled the ground.

"It is all over, Caius," he murmured. "I shall never see Athens again."

For a while there were no more earthquakes. The sea grew a little less wild. Then the half-fainting Ariston heard shouts. He lifted his head. A small boat had come ashore. The rowers had leaped out. They were dragging it up out of reach of the waves.

"How strange!" thought Ariston. "They are not running away. They must be brave. We are all cowards."

"Wait for me here!" cried a lordly voice to the rowers.

When he heard that voice Ariston struggled to his feet and called.

"Marcus Tetreius! Master!"

He saw the man turn and run toward him. Then the boy toppled over and lay face down in the ashes.

When he came to himself he felt a great shower of water in his face. The burden was gone from his back. He was lying in a rowboat, and the boat was falling to the bottom of the sea. Then it was flung up to the skies. Tetreius was shouting orders. The rowers were streaming with sweat and sea water.

In some way or other they all got up on the waiting ship. It always seemed to Ariston as though a wave had thrown him there. Or had Poseidon carried him? At any rate, the great oars of the galley were flying. He could hear every rower groan as he pulled at his oar. The sails, too, were spread. The master himself stood at the helm. His face was one great frown. The boat was flung up and down like a ball. Then fell darkness blacker than night.

"Who can steer without sun or stars?" thought the boy.

Then he remembered the look on his master's face as he stood at the tiller. Such a look Ariston had painted on Heracles's face as he strangled the lion.

"He will get us out," thought the slave.

For an hour the swift ship fought with the waves. The oarsmen were rowing for their lives. The master's arm was strong, and his heart was not for a minute afraid. The wind was helping. At last they reached calm waters.

"Thanks be to the gods!" cried Tetreius. "We are out of that boiling pot."

At his words fire shot out of the mountain. It glowed red in the dusty air. It flung great red arms across the sky after the ship. Every man and spar and oar on the vessel seemed burning in its light. Then the fire died, and thick darkness swallowed everything. Ariston's heart seemed smothered in his breast. He heard the slaves on the rowers' benches scream with fear. Then he heard their leader crying to them. He heard a whip whiz through the air and strike on bare shoulders. Then there was a crash as though the mountain had clapped its hands. A thicker shower of ashes filled the air. But the rowers were at their oars again. The ship was flying.

So for two hours or more Tetreius and his men fought for safety. Then they came out into fresher air and calmer water. Tetreius left the rudder. "Let the men rest and thank the gods," he said to his overseer. "We have come up out of the grave."

When Ariston heard that, he remembered the Death he had left painted on his master's wall. By that time the picture was surely buried under stones and ashes. The boy covered his face with his ragged chiton and wept. He hardly knew what he was crying for—the slavery, the picture, the buried city, the fear of that horrid night, the sorrows of the people left back there,

his father, his dear home in Athens. At last he fell asleep. The
night was horrible with dreams—fire, earthquake, strangling
ashes, cries, thunder, lightning. But his tired body held him
asleep for several hours. Finally he awoke. He was lying on a
soft mattress. A warm blanket covered him. Clean air filled
his nostrils. The gentle light of dawn lay upon his eyes. A
strange face bent over him. "It is only weariness," a kind voice
was saying. "He needs food and rest more than medicine."

Then Ariston saw Tetreius, also, bending over him. The slave
leaped to his feet. He was ashamed to be caught asleep in his
master's presence. He feared a frown for his laziness.

"My picture is finished, master," he cried, still half asleep.

"And so is your slavery," said Tetreius, and his eyes shone.
"It was not a slave who carried my son out of hell on his back.
It was a hero." He turned around and called, "Come hither,
my friends."

311

Three Roman gentlemen stepped up. They looked kindly upon Ariston. "This is the lad who saved my son," said Tetreius. "I call you to witness that he is no longer a slave. Ariston, I send you from my hand a free man."

He struck his hand lightly on the Greek's shoulder, as all Roman masters did when they freed a slave. Ariston cried aloud with joy. He sank to his knees weeping. But Tetreius went on.

"This kind physician says that Caius will live. But he needs good air and good nursing. He must go to some one of Aesculapius's holy places. He shall sleep in the temple, and sit in the shady porches, and walk in the sacred groves. The wise priests will give him medicines. The god will send healing dreams. Do you know of any such place, Ariston?"

The Greek thought of the temple and garden of Aesculapius on the sunny side of the Acropolis at home in Athens. But he could not speak. He gazed hungrily into Tetreius's eyes. The Roman smiled.

"Ariston, this ship is bound for Athens! All my life I have loved her—her statues, her poems, her great deeds. I have wished that my son might learn from her wise men. The volcano has buried my home, Ariston. But my wealth and my friends and my son are aboard this ship. What do you say, my friend? Will you be our guide in Athens?"

Ariston leaped up from his knees. A fire of joy burned in his eyes. He stretched his hand to the sky.

"O blessed Heracles," he cried, "again thou hast conquered Death. Thou didst snatch us from the grave of Pompeii. Give health to this Roman boy. O fairest Athena, shed new beauty upon our violet-crowned Athens. For there is coming to visit her the best of men, my master Tetreius."

VENICE was the most exciting city of Europe in the Middle Ages, and a boy born there could expect a full and exciting life. Marco Polo belonged to a family of merchants and travelers. When he was a very small child, his father Nicolo and uncle Maffeo visited China to trade, and after a lengthy absence they returned to their home full of wondrous tales of the unknown far east. When they returned to China for the second time nothing in the world could keep Marco from accompanying them. Together with Tonio, a young Venetian gondolier, and Pietro, a faithful Tartar boy, they arrived in Cathay after many dangerous adventures. There they were received at the court of Kublai Khan, the emperor, where they remained for seventeen years, serving him in various capacities. The following story tells of one of their adventures while in the Khan's service.

Louise Andrews Kent

ON KUBLAI KHAN'S SERVICE

ILLUSTRATED BY *Robert Sinnott*

KUBLAI KHAN took a great fancy to Marco. The Emperor liked the young Venetian's frank, honest way of talking. He liked to hear all the things Marco had to tell of the strange countries he had seen between Venice and Cathay.

"I send my Barons on business all through my Empire," Kublai Khan said, "but when they come back, all they can tell me is about the errand I sent them to do. That is stupid. I like to hear about the people: how they look; how they talk; how they live. I like to know how the country looks and what grows there. Tell me now about this province of mine called Zardandan, for I have never been there."

And Marco began: "The people of that country all have gold teeth. Or rather every man covers his teeth with a sort

313

of golden case made to fit them. Both the upper teeth and the under. The men also put bands pricked in black on their arms and legs. This is how they do it. They take five needles joined together and with these they prick the flesh till the blood comes, and then they rub in black coloring stuff. It is considered a piece of elegance to wear this black band. The men are all gentlemen—in their own style—and do nothing but go to the wars or go hunting and hawking. The ladies do all the business, aided by slaves taken in war."

Kublai Khan went on asking questions about far-off places and Marco went on answering them for a long time.

Suddenly the Khan said to Marco, "What is that I see on your chin?"

Marco blushed. "It's—it's my beard, Sire."

"Why, so it is!" said the Khan, smiling. "Now it seems to me that a man with a beard is old enough to do business for me. Few men in my Kingdom have traveled farther or seen more wonders than you. I know that your father and uncle are as honest as any men in the world and I think you are the same. Honest men don't grow on every bamboo tree. Now there is a city of mine where I think the Governor is cheating me about the taxes. I want you to go there and find out what the trade is in that city and what you think the people pay in customs duties and taxes. You are so young that no one will think you know anything, but you have a pair of good eyes in your head. Stay there a month. Learn what you can without asking too many questions. Then come back and tell me what you have seen."

So Marco set off on his journey and took Tonio with him. Both young men could speak several languages by this time and also read the different kinds of writing used in Kublai Khan's great country. But the great thing about Marco was what the Emperor had seen: Marco always remembered the first line of the Merchant's Rhyme, "Honesty is always best." Both he and Tonio had learned that lesson, not only in Venice, but all along the road to Cathay. Their first errand was done so well that the Khan was pleased with the results of the

314

business. As usual Marco told him about many strange things that he had seen. That pleased Kublai Khan too.

Messer Nicolo and Messer Maffeo were often sent on errands too. Sometimes Marco did not see his father and uncle for months at a time. Sometimes all three traveled together on trading journeys. No one remembered that they had promised Aunt Bella that they would come straight home from Cathay. Venice seemed so small and far away that at times they almost forgot there was such a place. They spoke in the Tartar language so much that even their own Venetian speech began to seem strange to their tongues and ears.

Everyone called Marco "Messer Marco" now, and spoke to him with great respect. He was made a Commissioner and ruled over a great city in the southern part of Cathay for three years. All this time the Polos were trading and growing rich. Mar Sarghis, too, was sent as a Governor to one of the Khan's cities. Hans stayed at the court working in gold and jewels for the Khan. There was no need for making mangonels now to throw stones against the walls of cities. Kublai Khan was through with wars. His father and grandfather had conquered cities from Kambalu to Constantinople. Their Tartars—or Mongols as people sometimes called them—had ridden on their tough little horses even as far as Russia and Poland, killing people, burning towns, and stealing. Kublai Khan was not fond of killing and robbing. When he was young he had attacked and conquered cities, but now he only wanted to govern his great Empire wisely. Because the Polos helped him to manage his business well, he trusted them and made them rich.

At the Khan's great feasts the Polos stood with the other Barons of the Empire dressed in the splendid robes that Kublai Khan gave them. Three times a year—sometimes oftener if there was some special reason for rejoicing—the Khan gave all the members of the court new clothes—robes of silk sewn with jewels, broad girdles of gold, boots of soft leather embroidered with silver and precious stones. The robes were of different colors at the different seasons, but always the same color as the Khan's own robe. At other times the Polos were dressed in crimson, which was the color worn by the Khan's Commissioners. Tonio no longer had to wear clothes too tight for him. The Khan gave him suits the same color as Marco's, only not quite so handsome. Even Hans had new red boots, finer than any he had ever worn.

The Polos and their followers did not win the favor of the Khan without making enemies. One was the magician whose trick with the rope Pietro and Marco had seen through. Kao-Hoshang had never forgiven Marco for telling people that the fat little boy had been under his master's black silk skirts all the time he was supposed to be in the clouds at the top of the rope.

Another man who wished the Polos had never left Venice was a Saracen called Achmath, who was the Khan's Chief Minister. This man did more stealing right under the Khan's nose at Kambalu than any of the Governors of the far-distant provinces where Marco traveled. Everyone in Kambalu who wanted anything had to bribe Achmath in order to get it. Achmath lied to the Khan about the customs duties he collected on the pepper and spices, the rice and silk, that came into Kambalu every day. And he was cruel to the Chinese people— the yellow, slant-eyed people whom the Tartars had conquered.

It was not Marco's business to tell tales about the Khan's Chief Minister. Kublai Khan had never given Marco any orders to take part in affairs at Kambalu, and Marco did not intend to interfere with them. Achmath, however, felt guilty, and he did not like the Venetian's honest gray eyes that seemed to look through his lying face and see what was going on in his cruel mind.

One summer when the court went to Xanadu, Marco stayed behind in Kambalu. He had some business there with merchants from India who were expected to bring pearls and other jewels. The Khan had first choice of all the jewels that came into the country. Marco had been given the task of choosing the finest for the Emperor. If there were more jewels than the Khan wanted, Marco was to have the next chance to buy them. The Polos turned their wealth into jewels whenever they had a chance to buy fine ones. Precious stones were easier to carry than gold, and Marco never really liked a lot of paper instead of money. Even with Kublai Khan's red seal on it, it never seemed quite like real money to him. Those first rubies that Marco had bought in Badakshan now had plenty of companions.

Pietro and Tonio stayed in Kambalu with Marco. It was Pietro who came to his master with a piece of news that he hardly dared to whisper.

Marco and Tonio were alone in a shady courtyard throwing a ball to each other when Pietro found them. He looked around to be sure there was no one hidden behind the trees and bushes.

"What's all this mystery for?" asked Marco, tossing the ball in the air.

"It's Kao-Hoshang, master."

"All right. Who's Kao-Hoshang? I don't remember him," Marco said cheerfully.

"Don't talk so loud, Messer Marco. Kao-Hoshang remembers you, even if you don't know him. But you do know—the man who did the rope trick."

"Oh, the yellow-faced man in the black nightgown with snakes on it. Well, what does he want with me?"

"Only to kill you, Messer Marco. He is angry because you laughed at him. This year the Khan did not take him to Xanadu. He thinks you showed the Khan his tricks. He is going to poison you."

"Oh, he is, is he?" said Marco, tossing the ball to Tonio. "How did you find out this thoughtful plan, Pietro?"

"You know the little boy, master, who hid under Kao-Hoshang's skirts that night?"

Marco nodded, and Pietro went on: "Well, you gave him money several times. His master beats him and will not let him go, although he is now almost a man. He likes you and he warned me. They plan to poison you and the merchants from India and steal the jewels."

"They must be crazy," said Marco. "The Khan's guards would catch them easily."

317

Pietro lowered his voice even more: "This isn't all, Messer Marco," he muttered. "It's only a small part of a bigger plot. There will be no guards. All through the city the Chinese are saying, 'Kill the men with beards.' They hate the Khan's foreign Minister. They are going to rise against Achmath and the others and take the city for their own. The boy told me. As soon as the men from India come. And just now, as I was coming through a dark street, I heard one Chinese say to another, 'There will be no men with beards here next month.'"

Marco dropped the ball on the ground. The summer night was hot. He had slipped off his thin silk coat. Now he thrust his arms into the sleeves and stood for a moment, thinking.

In a moment he said in a low voice, "I believe you are right, Pietro. I've noticed restlessness in the city these last weeks. Now this is what we'll do. You, Pietro, will ride to the Khan with a letter from me. You'll ride from the posthouse with the bells around your waist. Ride all the way yourself day and night, north to Xanadu. A fresh horse every twenty miles. Do your sleeping as you ride. The Khan will send his soldiers. The Chinese here will be waiting for the merchants to come from India. That's to be the sign for the uprising—is that right, Pietro?"

"Yes, master."

"Very well. Then Tonio shall ride south and meet the merchants on the way. I had news yesterday that they were already on the canal. They are less than fifty miles away. I'll give you a letter, Tonio, to tell them to go straight to Xanadu. To see the Khan himself and show him their jewels instead of coming here to Kambalu. The Chinese will be waiting for them. That will give more time for the soldiers to come. We must be quick and get you started, for the great bell will strike and the gates will be shut."

In the center of the city of Kambalu hung a big bronze bell. When a man beat upon it at night, the gates were shut, and no one was allowed to go through them or even to leave his house.

Marco wrote his letters quickly while Tonio and Pietro

dressed for their journey and packed up some food. Pietro took a skin bag with a little sour milk, some grain, and some honey. It was all he would need for the hundred-and-eighty-mile ride to Xanadu.

They hurried through the gates to the posthouse. At Marco's order both Pietro and Tonio were given horses and leather belts sewn all over with jingling bells.

"What will you do, master, while we are gone?" asked Pietro as the keeper of the horses went back into the posthouse, leaving Marco standing with his hands on the horses' bridles.

"Why," said Marco, smiling, "I'm going to warn Achmath."

Tonio groaned.

Pietro gasped: "Your enemy! He'd never warn you, Messer Marco, if you were in danger."

"No. Probably not. But he rules here for the Khan. If people kill the Khan's Ministers, that is only one step from killing him. Achmath has ruled badly. He has robbed these poor Chinese and sold their children for slaves. But if he falls, we all fall. Remember the cry was not 'Kill Achmath,' it was 'Kill the bearded men.' Even you Pietro, have a few hairs on your chin. Kublai Khan himself has a beard, though it is thin and getting white. The Chinese mean to kill Tartars as well as Venetians and Saracens when they talk in dark streets about 'bearded men.' Go now. I'll take care of myself. On the Khan's service! Ride!"

The two horsemen galloped off: one north; one south. The jingling of the bells died out in the hot summer air.

Marco hurried through the dark streets to Achmath's palace. There were shadows in the doorways. Once he heard a laugh and the words, "The man with the beard walks fast tonight." He hastened along, not quite running, feeling more sorry for the Chinese than for Achmath. It must be hard, Marco knew, for the little yellow-faced men with the smooth chins to be ruled by Saracens, Venetians, Tartars—never by men of their own race.

"But things will be better now," thought Marco, "because Kublai Khan will find out the reasons the Chinese hate the Governor. The Emperor will make everything right."

In Achmath's palace there had been feasting. The servants were just clearing away the sweetmeats. Achmath—a dark-faced man with a black beard that grew almost up to his cruel eyes and fell far down over his robe of cloth of gold—was playing dice with another Saracen.

The Minister received Marco curtly. He did not offer him refreshment, scarcely looked at him, and kept on rattling the ivory dice in a shaker of jade and silver.

"I should like to speak to you alone," said Marco, after he had stood for some minutes listening to the clicking of the dice.

Achmath only laughed harshly.

"You swagger in here with your sword in your belt and ask to see me alone! What a fool you must think me! Say what you have to say and get out."

Marco swallowed his rage and said quietly,—

320

"You have nothing to fear from me, Lord Achmath. The danger is somewhere else."

He told Achmath in a low voice the rumor he had heard. He said nothing about the merchants or about the errands on which he had sent Tonio and Pietro. There was no use telling what he knew to the whole city. The servants were still clearing the table. Marco was afraid they would overhear what he said. There might easily be some of them who did not love the tall Saracen with the jade box in his hand.

"If you warn Baron Kogatai, his foot soldiers will guard your palace," Marco said in a voice hardly louder than a whisper.

Achmath only shrugged his broad shoulders and went on with his play.

"Now that you've told us your old women's tales you have our permission to go," he said, with a foolish laugh. He threw the dice again. "Beat that, friend, and I'll give you the two slaves I got today," he said to the other Saracen. "Twin boys they are. Painters on silk—clever little imps."

Marco bowed and left the room.

The voice of the big bronze bell clanged loud over the city as he reached his own door. Everyone in Kambalu must sleep now by the Khan's orders. But Marco lay awake a long time, wondering what was going on below the peace and quiet of the sleeping city.

Tonio came back the next day with the news that the Indian merchants were safely turned aside from Kambalu and started on their way to Xanadu.

"Fine!" said Marco. "Now today I shall not be poisoned! If Pietro has done his errand as well as you, then the soldiers will come and the city will be safe."

They waited through one long hot day after another, but no soldiers came from the Khan.

"It is a long road," said Marco. He began to count the miles on his fingers. "They couldn't possibly get here before tonight. Yes, tonight would be the earliest, Tonio."

Towards evening a messenger came to the door.

"Lord Achmath orders you to the Khan's palace; Prince Chinkin is there and demands your presence."

Prince Chinkin was Kublai Khan's oldest son. "That means the soldiers have come," said Marco to Tonio. "The city is safe now."

He dressed himself in his crimson silk with its patterns of beaten gold and went to the Khan's palace. There was a crowd of people near the doorway. In the dim light Tonio saw many Chinese faces in the crowd, but not the troop of Tartar horsemen he had expected. There were only the usual guards, some of Baron Kogatai's troops who belonged to Kambalu.

"The Prince must have left his soldiers at the gate," thought Tonio.

"The threshold! Tread not on the threshold!" bellowed the guards in their ears. Marco had almost stepped on the sacred threshold of the great hall. The lights were dim in the hall.

Prince Chinkin was sitting at the far end of it. He was in riding clothes with his bow still at his side. The lower part of his face was muffled in a cloth-of-gold scarf. His jewelled helmet was still on his head. It cast a shadow over his eyes.

One of the servants was lighting some candles just in front of the Prince. They dazzled the eyes of everyone who looked towards the throne.

Tonio muttered in Marco's ear,—

"I thought the Prince was taller than that. See, this man's head comes only to the bottom of the gold panel. When Kublai Khan sits there, his head comes to the tail of the pheasant painted on the gold. And Prince Chinkin is even taller than his father. That is the Prince's helmet—or one like it—but it's on the head of a short man."

Marco looked. Tonio was right.

Marco said softly, "Slip out, Tonio, as quietly as you can. Go to Baron Kogatai. Tell him the Prince is here. Ask him if he expected him. Tell him what you said just now."

Tonio slipped quietly along the painted wall, strolled towards the door, and went slowly out. When he got outside the palace and away from the crowd, he ran as fast as he could go to

Baron Kogatai's house. Fortunately it was not far, and the Baron was just at the door.

"A message, Baron, from Messer Marco Polo. Do you know that Prince Chinkin is in the city? There is a man on the Khan's seat who looks like the Prince, but Messer Marco is not sure. He is dressed like Prince Chinkin, but he is much shorter."

"Why, how could he be here?" asked the Baron. "How could he enter the city without my knowing about it? No one has passed the gate."

He ordered out a company of soldiers and set off for the palace. Tonio ran back ahead of them. The man in the Prince's clothes was still sitting behind the flaring lights, men of the court were bowing before him. In the crowd Tonio saw the yellow face and black dragon-covered shoulders of Kao-Ho-shang. Beside Kao-Hoshang was another man in a magician's robes. He was Chen-Chu, another of the Khan's jugglers.

There was a stir at the door. Lord Achmath came through it. He was taller than any of the men around him. The crowd fell apart for him to go through. He walked towards the throne where the man in the helmet sat behind the bright lights with

323

the gold scarf around his chin. His eyes stared at Achmath from under the shadow of his helmet.

Achmath bowed to the ground, walked forward again; bowed and walked forward. The man on the throne did not speak, only watched the Minister's tall figure and cruel, handsome face. Achmath bowed for the third time. The man on the throne snapped his fingers. There was a rustle of silk. Two black figures stepped towards the kneeling man. Kao-Hoshang had a mace in his hand. He whirled it into the air. As it fell, a sword flashed out of the folds of Chen-Chu's robe, quivered a second above the neck of the Saracen. There was the dreadful noise of steel on flesh. Lord Achmath fell groaning to the floor.

The man on the throne stood up, grasping his bow.

"Kill the bearded men!" he called.

Baron Kogatai rushed into the hall.

"Treason, my Lords! Treason!" he gasped, and shot an arrow straight at the man behind the lights. The arrow pierced the bare throat under the gold scarf.

The man in the Prince's clothes fell forward, upsetting the lights. His helmet rolled across the floor with a hollow clang. The face under it was a Chinese face. There was no beard on the chin under the gold scarf.

"Wang-Chu!" muttered Baron Kogatai, looking down at the dead man. "Guard the door! Let no one leave the hall!" he called.

Marco and Tonio had already seized Chen-Chu and taken his sword. Kao-Hoshang was wrestling with half a dozen Tartars. His mace banged on the marble floor. Marco's fingers were bleeding from the edge of Chen-Chu's sword. Tonio had a cut on his ankle.

The guards came in and led the two magicians away.

There were Tartar shouts outside the palace and the sound of horses' feet trampling on the stone pavement.

"Pietro! The men from Xanadu!" said Marco.

It was not only the Khan's soldiers. Kublai Khan himself was there. His elephants waved their trunks in the torchlight as the Khan walked down the ladder from his house of gold. With his soldiers behind him, the Emperor walked through the blood-stained hall and sat down on the seat where the dead Wang-Chu had been sitting such a short time before. Kublai Khan looked around the hall at the prisoners, at the dead bodies, at the waiting Barons in their splendid robes. His face was stern as he looked at them all. For a long time he did not speak. At last he called for an account of what had happened.

And the man he called on to speak was not one of the great Tartar Barons, but the young Venetian, Marco Polo.

This is what is written in the old Chinese records:

"The Emperor desired Polo, Assessor of the Privy Council, to explain the reasons which led Wang-Chu to commit the murder. Polo spoke with boldness of the crimes and oppressions of Achmath which had made him hated throughout the Empire. The Emperor's eyes were opened. He complained that those around him had thought more of Achmath than of the interests of the State."

After the death of Achmath, Kambalu was better governed and Kublai Khan's Chinese subjects were kindly treated. Kao-Hoshang's boy became a magician in his master's place. He moved cups and tossed ropes as well as Achmath's slayer had

325

ever done. Marco was more than ever in the Khan's favor. Pietro and Tonio were both richly rewarded for their help in discovering the plot. Some of the finest of the jewels that the Indian merchants had brought were given to Marco. Kublai Khan would have made Tonio Governor of one of his cities, but Tonio said he would rather stay with Marco.

"He is the head, Sire," Tonio said. "I am only an extra pair of arms and legs for him."

"A fine strong pair!" said Kublai Khan, with a smile. "Well, stay with him if you like. And you," he added to Pietro— "you won't leave him and be a captain in my guard under Baron Kogatai?"

"I—I will do whatever my Emperor commands," stammered Pietro.

"But you'd rather be a servant to this foreigner?"

Pietro nodded.

"Well, I don't blame you. Stay with him, then, both of you. And don't forget, Messer Marco Polo, that I've left you something more precious than pearls—two loyal friends." He gave bags of gold to Pietro and Tonio, and to each a horse and a splendid saddle with gold on the stirrups. "When you ride for me again, you must be well mounted," he said. "And, Messer Marco, if there is anything you wish, ask it now."

Marco bowed before the Khan. They were in his most beautiful garden. The ground was flat here, but Kublai wanted a hill, so his gardeners had made one. He called it his Green Mount. It was covered with splendid trees. His elephants had dragged them there full grown.

The Khan sat on a marble bench in the green shadows. Marco knelt on the grass at his feet.

"There is only one thing, Sire!" Marco said. "My father and uncle are getting old. We are so happy here that a year comes, and before we know it, it's gone. Messer Nicolo and Messer Maffeo wish to see our city of Venice again before they die. If you could send us home, Sire, it would make us happy. I would come back, of course, as soon as I could."

All the kind expression left the Khan's face.

For a long time he did not speak. At last he called for an account

"You ask the one thing I cannot give," he said angrily. "That is a strange way to pay courtesy and favor—to turn your backs on my Kingdom. To leave any traitor that likes to run a sword into my ribs or crack my head with a mace."

Marco knelt down. His honest gray eyes looked straight into the Khan's face.

"Surely, Sire, with all the men in your Kingdom, you don't need me or my friends."

"Did I not need you last night?" asked Kublai Khan grimly. "And why is it that you want to go back all those weary miles to that city of yours? What is it pulls you back there? Tell me. Not you, Messer Marco. I know what you will say: 'Venice is the finest city in the world.' Your friend with the gold beard there, Tonio Tumba. I remember the name. Stand up, Tonio Tumba. Tell me why Venice is better than Cathay. Is it so much finer than our cities here?"

Tonio stood up. "No, Sire," he said. "You have twenty cities bigger than Venice. Your bridges are more beautiful. Your gardens are greener. Your roofs shine with gayer colors. No sovereign in all the world has such wealth and power as you. Venice is only a little town. But it's our place, Sire. The sea goes ringing through its streets all day. The breezes are the coolest there and the sun the warmest. The Doge goes out in his scarlet galley and drops a ring in the sea because the sea is the bride of Venice. And the sea is kind to her master. It keeps out our enemies, it washes our streets. It is our road to the rest of the world. And the city floats on it, like a pearl rising out of the water. Venetians go everywhere that the sea takes them, but they always come back to Venice. You see, it's home."

The Khan shook his head. "No, I don't see. My home is anywhere that Tartar horse has ever trod: wherever Tartar arrows fly. I could take my palace of cane—as any Tartar might his tent—and where I set it up, there would be my home. But I see this: You are bent on going, and when the right time comes, you shall go. But not now. Not now."

He looked kind again. The anger had gone from his face.

And for the first time Tonio saw that Kublai Khan was growing old.

"Will they be glad to see you in that city where the sea rings through the streets?" asked the Khan, looking at Tonio with a smile. "You were a boy when you came. Will they know you now, do you think?"

"Madonna Bella will know us. We promised her we'd come home in seven years. She'll know us, won't she, Messer Marco? Even though we are away more than twice as long."

"Ah! Some beautiful Venetian lady?" asked Kublai Khan.

Marco smiled. "A lady older than my father—his sister, in fact—who will stay alive just for the pleasure of scolding us when we come home."

"You found no Tartar ladies beautiful enough for you, I suppose?" said the Khan. "Would you stay here with a Tartar Princess for your bride, Messer Marco Polo?"

"You've kept us too busy for us to think about brides, Sire," said Marco, smiling. "No Princess would want a husband who was in India one day and Persia the next."

"True enough," the Khan agreed. "And I remember now— you have sailed lately through my country to the west. Tell me now of some of the wonders you have seen there."

So all that warm summer afternoon Marco told the Khan about the lands through which he had traveled.

Tonio sat by the seat on the ground. He was very sleepy. There had been little sleep for anyone in Marco's house those last few nights. Messer Marco's deep voice went on and on. Tonio dozed off. When he woke up, Marco was saying,—

"After twelve days' journey you come to a fortified place called Taican where there is a great corn market. It is a fine place and the mountains are made of salt, the best in the world; so hard it can be broken only with iron picks. The people near by are worshippers of Mahomet, and an evil and murderous people they are. The most evil in the world. They wear nothing on their heads but a cord some ten palms long twisted about. They are excellent huntsmen; in fact, they wear nothing but the skins of beasts, for they make of them both

328

coats and shoes. There are porcupines that huddle close, shooting their quills at dogs and wounding them. The people live in caves which make fine houses . . ."

Tonio heard a strange noise above his head. He looked up. Tonio was not the only one who was sleepy. Kublai Khan was snoring!

The breeze blew gently among the trees of the Green Mount. A tame deer wandered through the garden nibbling at the grass. She stopped in front of a marble seat in the shade with her nose quivering and her bright eyes moving over the three figures in the green shadows. An old man with a tired face above his jewelled robe of gold cloth sat on the bench. One of his thin hands was resting on the curly brown head that leaned against his knee. On his other side a man with hair like wire of stiff gold sat with his head on his knees. Neither the two men in crimson silk nor the one in the flashing gold paid any attention to the deer. She came quite close to the brown-haired one, put out a careful tongue and touched the shoulder in its bright silk. Perhaps that is why only the deer heard the man with the curly brown hair murmur in his sleep,—

"But after all, Venice *is* the finest city in the world."

From KUBLA KHAN
Samuel Taylor Coleridge

In Xanadu did Kubla Khan
   A stately pleasure-dome decree:
Where Alph, the sacred river, ran
Through caverns measureless to man
   Down to a sunless sea.
So twice five miles of fertile ground
With walls and towers were girdled round:
And there were gardens bright with sinuous rills,
Where blossomed many an incense-bearing tree;
And here were forests ancient as the hills,
Enfolding sunny spots of greenery.

Eloise Lownsbery

THE MIGHT OF A SONG

ILLUSTRATED BY *DeWitt Whistler Jayne*

R ICHARD is taken! Richard is *taken!* He is held in Leopold's dungeon keep."

The news began as a whisper, no louder than a light breeze. Tongue whispered to tongue, lips to lips. It traveled from peasant to burgher, from squire to knight, from page to lady, from village to town, from castle to keep, from land to land.

"Did you hear the news? Richard of the lion-heart, Richard the untamed, on his way home from the Crusade, Richard is captured, is in prison."

"Where?"

"Who knows?"

"In which dungeon?"

"Who can say?"

The whisper blew to a *windy* shout. For some it was a shout of joy; for John of England, Richard's brother who might now seize the throne; for Philip of France who planned now to seize Normandy; for Leopold of Austria who smarted for revenge of insult done by Richard at Acre, and so hid his royal prisoner well; for all Richard's enemies who rejoiced to hear of his discomfort.

But for others the shout ended in a groan: for Richard's knightly brothers-in-arms; for his queenly mother, Eleanor of Aquitaine; for the brotherhood of troubadours, wandering poets

331

and singers of songs; for Blondel of Nesle who dearly loved him; for Blondel's apprentice and jongleur, Raimon d'Auvergne, who loved both Blondel and the King.

In the castle of Hautbois they were spending a fortnight, Blondel and his five jongleurs. To the Lady Fleurande, whose Lord was off on a hunt, they were singing the Crusade. Already they had sung the story of Richard's mastery of Sicily; of the coming of the Princess Berengaria with Queen Eleanor and her suite; of the sailing of the fleet and the storming of Cyprus; and the siege at Acre; of the might of Richard's arm; and of his three-year peace with Saladin.

So on the castle ramparts they sang to the Lady Fleurande, when who should enter the courtyard but Jacques the tinkerman, with his trade on his back, and the news on his tongue! "Richard is in dungeon—somewhere in the Austrian realm."

"You jest!" Blondel and his lads with the folk of the castle swarmed about Jacques like bees to a comb. "Do you swear by the Rood?"

"My life upon it," cried tinker Jacques. "I had it of honest Robert, and Robert of honest Pierre, and Pierre of honest Guillaume—"

Then Blondel begged for his tale.

So Jacques told of how a storm blew the ship from its course—Richard's ship as he sailed home from the Crusade. How a great wind blew the galley from the Mediterranean into the Adriatic, how it beached him on the shores of the sea. Of how Richard and his page made their way disguised as merchants to the city of Vienna—to the very stronghold of his enemy, Leopold of Austria. Of how, in the market this page bragged of his master with too loose a tongue, so that the secret leaked out. How, when it reached the Duke's ears, he sent armed men to the Inn where Richard slept. They found under the coat of a merchant the heart of a lion.

Yet for all Richard's valiance of arm, for all the blows he struck out at the guard, they took him at last. They hid him away, no man may ever know where.

"Now by St. Julian le Pauvre," Blondel cried, and he struck

a loud chord on his lute. "That is the sorriest, saddest tale ever man told. Come," he called to his five jongleurs. "Come, let us away. We must see what is to be done."

And they all took fair and courteous leave of the Lady Fleurande. When she entreated Blondel to stay on, he said he must go, for with Richard in peril, he must away to help him.

So, though his jongleurs armed him at the palace gate, and helped him to mount his high horse, Valiant, they looked back wistfully at the castle towers. Only Raimon pressed closer to his master to ask, "Where shall we go to look for our King, my master? Let us be on our way."

"We go first to castle Autofort," Blondel replied. "Surely the bold Bertran de Born will know how to free him."

Now it chanced that in the castle Autofort, they were the first to carry the news. And once told in the great hall, the whole castle soon swarmed about them.

The old warrior troubadour Bertran de Born swore a great oath, and he spat in his hands. "Now *that* for Duke Leopold, and God's curse be upon him. Let me ride at him till his teeth fall from his head at the shock; till the secret be forced from his lips red with gore."

And knight Bertran, who loved nothing so much on this earth as a fight, stamped the length of the hall till you would think the earth quaked, or a herd of wild boars had passed by.

"I who have broken a thousand spears, once I have learned where Richard is held, I will ride my horse, Bayard, well armed. I will hurl my battle-ax over the wall. Let me but find that glutton of Austria, and he shall know the cut of my sword. A mixture of brain and splinters of iron he shall wear on his brow."

Blondel let him storm. He dropped his head in his hands as he sat by the fire. Words were fierce things, but easy to speak. To lay siege to a royal castle was not a child's play, no, nor the work of one man. And Blondel saw in his mind's eye the map of Europe. He looked at the lands between the seas, from the Adriatic to the North and the Baltic. In his mind he spread out the lands: the mountains and valleys, rivers and plains, with a castle on every crag, sewn as thick over the peaks as dragon's teeth, and as fierce. Blondel lifted his head from his hands. The old knight stormed on.

"Not by lying in dungeon will Richard vanquish his enemies and banish the traitor John and assume his rightful lordship of England and Aquitaine. By Our Lady, I must gather my men. We'll not wait to know where he lies. We must fight a glorious fight. Our enemies will fall thick and fast. The splinters will fly up to heaven; silk and samite will be torn all to shreds, and tents and castles destroyed. So then Richard shall go free."

"Gently, gently, my brother." Blondel smiled. Such a mad storming of castles would take money, money and men.

And as he knew only too well, Bertran's money was spent. Not a war in the land but he had fought these many long years. Not a quarrel between knights but Bertran had cooked. He had come home from the Crusade a poor man.

Besides, who now would help him fight for Richard, the Lion-Hearted? All rebel knights now would gloat over his doom.

But Blondel's own jongleurs shared Bertran's fierce threats. With his own men, they rallied to him, blowing their horns. They liked well to imagine themselves starting off to do battle. So now they marched behind Bertran up and down the long hall.

Blondel smiled. He was fond of his lads, Maurice and Marcel, Raoul and Jehan, and Raimon, youngest of them all. Raimon's head was thrown back, his fair hair awry, his blue eyes shining with light, and he went marching and strumming and singing a war song.

Yet no, it would take more than force to liberate the young king. Someone must find him first. Blondel could see that well enough, now he had come here for aid. But what then? He thought how the guild of troubadours were to meet in Paris this month. Who but the brotherhood could cook up a plan, and season it to the king's taste?

So off they went to Paris, Blondel and his train: Marcel and Maurice, Jehan and Raoul and Raimon, youngest of them all.

In and out of castles, in and out of inns, singing the prowess of Richard, singing the third Crusade. Listening to the buzzing of tongues, listening for the secret that somebody knew, the secret of where Richard lay, thrust in some dungeon keep.

So they came to the gates of Paris itself. No need here for entrance fee. By the troubadours' law, Blondel and his group sang and strummed, piped and blew, and so through the gate, fee-free. They made their way to St. Julian's lanes, to the quarter east of the Cathedral of Our Lady, Notre Dame de Paris.

Here they found themselves among friends. From north and south, from east and west, troubadours and jongleurs foregathered here, till the narrow lanes swarmed with strumming

vagabonds. Surely, here they would find happier news. For who had not heard the sorry tale? It rode on all men's tongues. It leaped forth from all men's songs. Where was Richard hid? In which of the countless Austrian dungeon keeps? Who could say? Who could tell?

"This be a matter for warrior knights," the northern troubadours said.

The troubadour knights shook their mailed heads.

"This is a matter for kings," they said.

The kings among them shook their crowned heads.

"This is a matter for the church," they said.

Yet the monks of their throng shook their tonsured heads.

"This is not ours alone, but the business of everybody here," cried the troubadour monks.

"Then if it be everybody's business, it be nobody's, but at least it shall be my business," said Blondel, and he beat upon his chest. He drew his fingers across his lute so the strings twanged and his words rang out like a challenge.

"Ho, my jongleurs," he blew on his horn, the call they well knew.

They came running to him. "What is it, Master?"

Blondel drew them apart from the throng, to the porch of St. Julian's church.

"Now by our patron saint, lads, I am minded to go forth alone in search of our King. Sure, a song is mightier than a sword to storm castle walls. But I must travel fast and hard. I can take but one of you with me. Which shall it be?"

"Take me, my Master." "Take me." "No, no, take me."

All five pleaded at once. They looked at Blondel with shining eager eyes.

"What now! Would you be willing to start on the eve of winter?" Blondel watched their faces fall. For winter was the blessed time for staying within their own castle of Nesle. When the north wind howled without, and the sleet blew into men's faces, when the roads were knee-deep in mud and slush, and the snow piled to the eaves, then jongleurs hugged their warm chimney settles. They learned the new songs which their masters

336

composed. They laughed at the wind. All day they strummed and they sang, they tossed balls and caught naked knives in their hands, and they snapped their fingers at the cold and dragged on a fresh log, and practiced fair manners, and balanced a chair and swallowed an egg, and teased the pretty maid and harried the cook.

Aye, the schools of jongleurs were the merriest halls in the land, till spring set their feet on the roads once more. And then they made merry wherever they went, carrying the news, whether it was good news or bad.

So as Blondel looked at his jongleurs now, he read their thoughts. "Tell me, lads, just what would you do now for your King? How spend the cold winter months?"

"I'd learn a new ballad as will touch all men's hearts in the spring," Maurice said.

"I'd practice jousting and the use of the broadsword in our own courtyard, Master," said Raoul, "and so be ready to fight."

"Aye, so would we all," assented Marcel and Jehan.

Blondel turned to Raimon. "And you, lad, and you?"

"I'd walk now, to land's end for him, Master Guillaume; through mud or through snow. I'd storm every castle of Austria not with sword, but with song." Thus spoke the young Raimon, youngest of them all.

And Blondel's eyes glowed as if a fire had been lighted within. He turned to the four. "Go now back to the Autofort, lads," he said. "Say to Sir Bertran that Blondel sent you to his school of the sword. When Richard be found, I'll return. For this difficult quest, I need take only Raimon with me."

So Marcel and Maurice and Raoul and Jehan, thinking their master as mad as a hare, went back to make merry in the thronging Paris streets. Blondel drew Raimon with him inside the church, where both widened their eyes to see, for the light came dimly.

While his master prayed, Raimon looked about him. The thick stone walls shut out every sound of the revelers without. Here all was still. Tiny candle flames flickered on the altar to Our Lady before which Blondel knelt. St. Julian was here, patron saint of the troubadours, looking down from the gay painted windows.

Raimon's eyes came back from the windows to his master. For Blondel rose now, lighted two candles, gave one to the boy, so that Raimon remembered his manners. Quickly he crossed himself and knelt to make his adoration. He heard Blondel say:

"Now, by Our Lady and her knight Julian, we two humble singers of songs do set forth our pilgrimage, to find our Lord King Richard. Go with us, blessed patron saint, and deliver us from all peril of robbers and weather alike, that we may speedily accomplish our mission."

"Amen," murmured Raimon, "and amen."

He saw Blondel lift from his shoulder the blue ribbon that held his favorite lute, the one Richard once gave him. Reverently, he stepped inside the marble rail and hung it over the lovely shoulder of the blue-robed Virgin Mary.

"Wear it for me, my Lady, for I vow never again to touch its strings till our Lord King Richard be found."

Raimon's eyes shone. "He means that I am to play for him while he sings." And he felt half suffocated with joy that the mission was part his. The church was so still he could hear the beating of his heart.

"Give us now a sign of thy grace," Blondel pleaded.

And suddenly, out of the stillness, they heard a low chord, as if gentle fingers wandered over the strings of Blondel's lute. Startled, they looked up, then stared into each other's eyes.

Surely it was she—that sweet blue-and-white Lady of Heaven smiling down at them both. Surely it was her white fingers that had struck that low chord on Blondel's lute.

Dazed with wonder and joy they stumbled to their feet and tiptoed out past the storied windows, out past the great round pillars, out of the heavy oaken door.

Once in the porch, Blondel took Raimon in his arms, and kissed the boy on either cheek.

"Let this be our secret, lad," he whispered. "Surely, it was a sign. Surely, our quest will not be in vain. Come, let us be off." Blondel mounted Valiant. Raimon trudged behind.

Yet it was not so simple, this quest. The rains came; "the bad time" was upon them. The windy cold blew on their backs, whistled down their necks. Slush, slosh, the roads were deep with mud. Often enough Raimon shivered to his very bones. He was put to it to keep the instruments dry, all slung over his shoulders in their leathern cases. The sleet blew, the north wind tore at him. The snow fell. Very pretty to see, very cold to feel. Clump, clump, slush, slush, he plodded steadily on behind the horse's hooves.

And along the way, so many adventures befell them as would fill a book, a very thick and big book, too. But of these there is no time to tell, as they crossed France from Paris to Mainz, and crossed Germany from Mainz to Prague, and crossed Bohemia from Prague on to Vienna, with still no tidings of their King.

For all that the castles seemed myriad here in Austria, the secret was as well guarded as in France.

"Do the roads wind uphill all the way?" Raimon wondered.

"Yea, to the very end," Blondel said. For what Austrian castle but sat on a crag, what dungeon but perched on the very crest of a hill? With the land infested with robbers, a man was never a king but within his own castle walls, well guarded by stout men-at-arms.

Yet ever and ever they pressed on, inquiring of the underlings in each castle and town, "Have you prisoners, perhaps, in the near-by dungeon keep?" But never by any means at all could they discover tidings of a royal prisoner, by name Richard, by rights, king of England, lord of Ireland, Scotland, and Wales; duke of Normandy; count of Aquitaine, Gascony, Maine, Anjou, and Poictou; superior lord of Brittany, Auvergne, and Toulouse; king of Arles; conqueror of Cyprus; and ruler overlord of the kingdom of Palestine.

So the months wore on. Christmas and New Year's and St. Patrick's day sped by, and now it was almost Easter. And still the two kept on. From Vienna they took to the old Bohemian "salt road" which crosses the Danube at Linz.

"Surely, surely, my Master," Raimon would say, "this must be the way he came."

And Blondel agreed. "Yes, lad, keep a stout heart. Surely he came this way."

At last they did not say anything, but merely looked up at each frowning battlement, with a silent swift prayer to St. Julian to open all hearts against their coming.

One glad spring day, Raimon stood craning his neck to see. The castle called *Durenstein* sat on a mountain of rock above the Danube.

"Only an eagle would have chosen such a perch, Master," he said.

Blondel nodded. He, too, was staring up at the pennon flying from the ramparts. It was a two-headed black eagle.

"These Austrian nobles put on the airs of their lords." He frowned and pulled up his horse's head.

For that morning, Valiant had gone lame. Though Raimon drew out the stone, still he limped. The truth was, the horse was as fagged as his master, as fagged as his master's jongleur, whose tunic was tattered and torn. Blondel's coat, too, was shabby and worn. They did not stay long enough in one castle to earn a new coat. Yet he turned to the lad with a smile as he leaned against the fast-barred gate across the path up the castle hill.

"Up, lad, and over the gate. Announce our coming, and pray the lord courteously for his good cheer. And keep sharp ears and a sharper wit in thy head."

Raimon squared his shoulders, where the straps of his instruments bit deep. He forced his lips to smile.

"Stay here in the shelter of this plane tree, Master, and let poor Valiant rest his foot. Doubtless the lord will send a fresh horse to bear thee upwards."

Blondel nodded. "Thou hast a brave heart and a sweet tongue, lad. I shall ask Richard one day to make thee his troubadour."

Neither would admit defeat, nor discouragement, nor hunger, nor poverty. So Blondel got stiffly down from his horse, and Raimon leaped over the fence to begin his long climb. The path was uncommonly steep. The stones cut his feet. The way was all unkept. Since the winter storms, the stones washed down

340

from above still lay where they fell. Now, between them grew fresh tufts of grass and weeds, and violets and primroses bloomed. Surely, the lord and his men were from home. Neither men nor beasts had trodden this way. Surely, then, the castle must be deserted. Perhaps it was only an ancient ruin for all its flying pennon of a two-headed black eagle.

"No need to climb more," said his legs.

"Stop and rest here," said his feet.

"Both you and Master are too hoarse now to sing," said his throat.

Raimon's mouth began to water. His stomach was long empty of food. His tongue got thick and clove to the roof of his mouth. So now his tongue joined his shoulders, and his shoulders his back, and his back his legs, and legs his feet. All cried out together as with one voice:

"Come, stop, Master, let us rest. Use your head. What's it for? Reason it out. Without a lord there are no men, and without men there could be no prisoners, certainly, no such prisoner as Richard. He *couldn't* be hiding here."

Raimon stared up at the tower. He listened. Not a sound of man or beast above the chirping of birds.

"Well, then, have it your way," he said crossly, and he caught up two blades of grass, a short and a long, and shut them into his fist so that only the tops might show. "Which shall it be? Shall I press on to the very end or shall I go back down?

"That's the boy! Let the short blade say 'stay' and the long blade say 'go.' "

Raimon pulled. He made a wry face. It was the short blade he drew. "You see for yourself," he said to his aches and pains, "now we've *got* to keep on. If we drop in our tracks, the King *must* be found. Besides, we're happier climbing the hills than we'd be in a dungeon keep."

So he set off up the hill, and as he went he whistled a tune, panted and whistled and strummed as he went. And around the next curve he came to a halt. In a cleared space sat a girl and her geese.

The girl started up and her cheeks flushed bright and pink.

The geese fluttered their wings and scolded him in loud honks. From above he heard the sudden barking of dogs. He looked at the girl and bowed low as if to a princess, a long sweeping bow with his hand on his heart. He doffed his green hat with its long peacock feather. It was not hard to remember his manners. For the girl was very fair with eyes the blue of her long kirtle gown. And on her hair was a chaplet she had woven of violets and bluebells and primroses yellow and pink.

So as Raimon stared at her, he wished his tunic was not tattered nor his hair uncombed. Then he remembered his errand.

"Tell me, fair maid, who dwells in this castle? And is thy lord at home?" He spoke in the Austrian tongue.

She made him a curtsy as she shook her fair head. "The castle is his, Duke Leopold's, but my lord is from home this year-long."

"Just as I thought," said Raimon. "I might better have saved both my legs and my breath."

"Saved them? For what? For whom?"

Raimon laughed. "For castles whose dukes stay at home to guard prisoners that lodge in their dungeon keeps—" he nodded across to the next hill, "like that one over there, perhaps? Surely there are prisoners there."

"I doubt it, Sir. The Lady Marguerite is far too kindhearted for that."

Raimon sighed. She was smiling at him, looking hard at his lute. She came a step closer.

"Tell me, sweet sir, if you be a Minnesinger, would you sing me one song?"

"In my own land I'm a jongleur, which is nearly as good; but I've no songs left in my heart, and my throat is as hoarse as a frog in a dry pond."

At their sudden laughter together, the geese honked, and the dogs above barked ferociously. Raimon looked up in some alarm.

"Don't mind them," the girl said. "They are only our stout men-at-arms, lest a stranger prowl about the castle in the night."

"Oh, I see," said Raimon a little breathlessly. "Then tell me

343

what is your name? Violet, Rose, Carnation, Lily, Bluebell?"

She laughed. "Nothing so romantic, kind Sir, only Marie—plain Marie."

"Oh, you were named for our Lady."

"And I do so love music. If only you would sing!" She reached out her hand to the lute, and touched the string, a lingering touch that made a light chord.

Raimon looked at her with startled eyes. "That is the sign—Her sign, and you are Marie!"

Her blue eyes widened. Her chaplet shook till the bluebells nodded. Almost Raimon thought he heard them ring.

"Then listen to me, little *Marie des Anges,* and I shall sing you a song."

He closed his eyes and swept his fingers across the strings. He sang in French:

> "Your eyes are blue as waving flax,
> And your cheeks are as pink as a rose."

The tune was that of a little French song, but the words he made up as he sang.

Marie clapped her hands. "But that is the same tune the prisoner sings!"

"The prisoner! You mean, you, too, have prisoners up there in your dungeon?"

"Only one," she protested. "And often I hear him singing French songs." She clapped her hand over her mouth, and gathered up her long blue kirtle, and ran from him, up the hill path, calling her geese to follow.

With three strides, Raimon had caught hold of her kirtle. He barred her path.

"Listen to me, Marie, Marie of the Angels, go up there and tell your mother that for love of you, she shall have the honor of sheltering this night a famous troubadour, Guillaume Blondel—that's my master, and his jongleur Raimon—that's me. And you shall have songs and more songs, all the songs you most wish to hear. My heart is full of them. And tell her to chain up the dogs, and ask the hens to lay us an egg."

344

So as Marie started up the path driving her geese before her, Raimon was off down the hill. His feet had grown wings. His heart was light as new-risen bread. Surely, the sign could not fail. The one prisoner must be—

An hour later Raimon and his master strolled about the courtyard, in a corner of which abutted the great round thick-walled keep. Its windows, narrow slits, were barred with iron. Within, it was black as night.

Marie's mother bustled about getting supper. The castle was a lonely place with the lord and court all from home. She was delighted to hear the gossip of the wide world. So Raimon strummed his lute, and Blondel sang of the crusades, of Alex-

ander and the siege of Troy, of Berengaria in Rome, and Eleanor in Aquitaine. And at first, out of courtesy to their hosts,
they sang in the Austrian tongue.

They strolled then, close to the keep, while Raimon strummed,
and Blondel sang the first stanza of a *Sirventes,* which he and
King Richard had composed together.

The two listened. Hark! From within the shadows of the don-
jon came a voice, a voice singing the second verse of the self-
same song!

"Now praise be unto God and Our Lady," Blondel chanted
in the Latin tongue, "for that the quest is done, and the pil-
grims, Blondel and Raimon, may wend their way home."

And out of the dungeon came a hearty "Amen, and Amen.
And the humble shall be exalted, and the proud brought low.
The mighty shall fall from their thrones, but the little ones
shall be lifted to the stars."

Then Raimon could not help composing a stanza of his own,
about how the blessed Virgin had sent them a sign, a chord of
a lute, and about a bird carrying glad news on the wings of
song, a song that was mightier than a sword.

So they made merry at supper, and ate their fill of the fruit
of the hens, and drank their fill of the fruit of the vines. Blondel
sang wonderful songs, and Raimon played merry tunes till the
family's feet fell a-dancing of carols and a-singing of rounds.

And that night while they slept, Raimon hung up his lute on
a jutting stone of the dungeon wall, that the night wind might
play a tune of Provence for his King.

So with the dawn, the two bade a courteous but singing farewell to the little maid Marie, and sped them away, down the
steep hill. As fast as they could travel along the spring roads,
they hurried to tell the Plantagenet Court. Richard was found.
Now his friends could gather ransom for his release.

As for Bertran de Born, he wrote a *Sirventes* of joy, "because
now again we shall see walls destroyed and towns overthrown
and our enemies in chains," when Richard be free.

THE GLOVE AND THE LIONS
Leigh Hunt

King Francis was a hearty king, and loved a royal sport,
And one day, as his lions fought, sat looking on the court.
The nobles filled the benches, with the ladies in their pride,
And 'mongst them sat the Count de Lorge, with one for whom
    he sighed:
And truly 'twas a gallant thing to see that crowning show,
Valor and love, and a king above, and the royal beasts below.
Ramped and roared the lions, with horrid laughing jaws;
They bit, they glared, gave blows like beams, a wind went with
    their paws;
With wallowing might and stifled roar they rolled on one
    another;
Till all the pit with sand and mane was in a thunderous smother;
The bloody foam above the bars came whisking through the air;
Said Francis then, "Faith, gentlemen, we're better here than
    there."
De Lorge's love o'erheard the King, a beauteous likely dame,
With smiling lips and sharp bright eyes, which always seemed
    the same;
She thought, The Count my lover is brave as brave can be;
He surely would do wondrous things to show his love of me;
King, ladies, lovers, all look on; the occasion is divine;
I'll drop my glove, to prove his love; great glory will be mine.
She dropped her glove, to prove his love, then looked at him
    and smiled;
He bowed, and in a moment leaped among the lions wild;
The leap was quick, return was quick, he has regained his place,
He threw the glove, but not with love, right in the lady's face.
"By Heaven," said Francis, "rightly done!" and he rose from
    where he sat;
"No love," quoth he, "but vanity, sets love a task like that."

Margaret Leighton

FISHERMAN'S LUCK

ILLUSTRATED BY *Marilou Wise*

A FAINT wind stirred ripples on the sur-
face of the little stream, setting a thousand tiny mirrors dancing, sending a thousand flashes of sunlight into the face of the
boy. He was perched on a broad branch of a willow tree that
overhung the water, his back against its massive trunk. The
pointed, silvery leaves formed a cool green tent, but the light
dazzled up from the brook into his eyes. He shut them for
a moment—

Was it a dream, or did he hear someone shouting there
behind him? Struggling with sleep, he felt the fishing pole
in his hands jerked wildly away. He clutched at it, he slipped—
an instant later he was gasping in the shallow water. The
sound of loud laughter brought him scrambling to his feet,
blue eyes ablaze, a small furious figure in dripping doublet
and hose. A man stood on the bank, laughing at his plight,
hands on hips, head thrown back. The sight of the boy's angry
face stopped his mirth abruptly.

"Give me your hand." He stretched his out over the water.
"I'll give you a lift out of that." The boy took it, and thin,
strong fingers closed about his own. He was on the bank
again, surveying the stranger sheepishly, still hostile.

"It was a fish well worth the trouble that pulled you in,
my young friend," said the man. "I saw your line tugging and
tried to warn you. Sorry you had such a ducking." The stranger's

348

face was thin and very dark, but his smile gleamed pleasantly. The boy smiled, too, a boyish grin.

"Thank you, sir, for pulling me out," he said.

"That's better. I feared for a moment I had made an enemy, judging from the thunderous look you sent me from the water." He turned and pointed downstream. "Your pole has lodged itself between those rocks yonder. From the motion of it I'd say that your fish is still hooked."

The boy needed no second word. He was after it eagerly, and soon a fine shining perch lay on the bank under the willow tree.

"A noble fish, on my word!" said the stranger, bending over it. "And toothsome, too, I'll warrant. What do you say to cooking it here and now, and sharing it with a hungry traveler? The fire will help to dry out your wet clothes, moreover, before your mother sees them!"

"If you can kindle the fire, sir, I'll clean the fish!" assented the boy with delight. He drew the knife from his belt and carried the fish to where the stream washed against the pebbles of a tiny beach. When he returned, a spark from the dark man's tinder box had already ignited a little pile of leaves and dry twigs. Small bits of stick and bark carefully added—soon a clear little fire blazed merrily near the gnarled willow trunk. Seated on the twisted roots, they waited for the coals to form for broiling, and the warmth from the fire began to dry the boy's wet garments.

Across the flames he looked again at his companion. The stranger's dress was an odd mixture of elegance and poverty, fashion and rags. Over patched woolen hose he wore doublet and trunks of fine Genoa velvet, now much stained and worn. His boots were of russet leather, once the last word in Spanish workmanship, but now mended in a dozen places. A long velvet cloak lay on the ground beside him. His hat bore a ragged feather held in place by a handsome jewelled buckle. Small gold rings glittered in his ears. His eyes were bright and piercing.

"Well, my lad, you have looked me over thoroughly. Tell

349

me what you think of me," the stranger said smilingly.

"You are not English, are you? You do not look English, though your speech sounds English enough."

"I am English born," answered the stranger. "But though my mother (rest her soul) was a yeoman's daughter, my father came of the wandering folk. I lived within these borders when I was a boy, but since then my gypsy blood has led me to wander in many lands."

"What lands?" The boy's eyes brightened.

"Why, the Low Countries, and France, and Italy, and even Greece, far away beside the blue Aegean Sea."

The boy's face glowed. "I have never before had speech with anyone who has been so far! Will you tell me something of what you saw? Were you truly in Greece? And did you see the burned walls of Troy?"

The brown face turned on the boy with new interest. "Troy's walls lie buried under the sand these many years, no man knows where. But what does a country lad like you know of Troy, and its burning?"

"I go to school here in the town. In Latin class we have read the Roman poet, Virgil, and lately I have been learning a little Greek under Master Hunt."

"Ah! A fellow scholar! I myself hold a degree from the great University in Paris. And do you like these studies of yours?"

"Well—" the boy hesitated—"mostly not. In truth, I like roaming these fields and woods vastly better. But sometimes in my Latin book we come to a part where the words march and seem to sing themselves. Then I get a feeling—a great wish to do the like myself." He stopped abruptly, blushing.

"A young poet, perchance, in the making?" The man's voice, though mocking, was kindly. "Come, the fire has burnt down and the coals are ready. While the fish is over them I'll recite for you my own translation of a poem to fit this occasion. It was writ long ago by one who was, like myself, a Bachelor of the Arts at the University of Paris, and also, like myself, a reckless fellow enough, though his verses have lived this long time—a 'Ballade of Roast Fish,' by Master Francois Villon."

As he recited, the man's voice had a rich and sonorous quality. At the end both joined in laughter over the magnificent absurdity of the lines. An appetizing odor rose from the broiling fish, mingling with the wood smoke and the rising mist from the river. The sun set in a final crimson flare. Under the willow tree shadows thickened. They ate their meal with hungry relish, while, urged on by the boy's eager questioning, the dark wanderer unfolded his tales of distant lands and cities. At the end he wiped his mouth on his velvet sleeve and leaned back against the tree. The little ripples made pleasant chuckling noises about the roots of the willow. From the depths of the wood, faint and very far away, came the first sweet, hesitant notes of a nightingale.

"Hark!" said the man. They listened together, hardly drawing breath. A new brightness began to mellow the shadows about them as, from high in the sky, the moon thrust pale fingers down through the willow leaves.

At last something quieted the nightingale and the spell broke. The stranger let out a long sigh and got stiffly to his feet. "Well, my lad," he said, his brilliant eyes on the rapt young face below him, "there sang a poet who need learn neither Latin nor Greek." He wrapped his cloak about him. "Here am I, back in England where I started from, and all my travel and all my learning have brought me neither gear nor gold. Tomorrow I must take the road to Coventry Town, where I hope, by grace of my diction and my voice, to win me a place in the company of the Earl's players who are stopping there. So I may earn my bread for a few months."

"Are you a play actor?" The boy, too, got reluctantly to his feet. He picked up his pole and wound the fishing line carefully about it. "I have never yet seen a play, though in truth I should like nothing better."

"Yes, I am a player—an indifferent poor one—as well as a scholar and a gypsy."

The boy's face lighted. "If you are truly a gypsy, please tell me my fortune, good sir." He thrust a hard little palm into a patch of moonlight.

For a long moment the brown face bent over it. "Why; here's an odd hand—a hand that contradicts itself!" He frowned, then glanced sharply up into the blue eyes. "You have a world of travel written plain, yet here, by this sign, never shall you cross salt water! And here in the place where you were born shall you end your days! A puzzling hand, and beyond my

poor skill. Perhaps this moonlight deceives me, or—" he dropped the hand with a short, uneasy laugh—"or perchance your travels are to be astride Pegasus—the poet's winged horse! Strange— strange—" He drew his cloak about him again. "The air from Parnassus strikes cold! Can you guide me to an inn? And what, by the way, is the name of this town of yours?"

"Why, this is Stratford, on the River Avon. There be inns aplenty. The Swan, the Bear, the Angel, the Peacock—which- ever suits you, sir."

"The nearest one, then. This mist chills me."

Together they treaded the narrow path beside the brook, dappled with shadow and moonlight, to emerge where the main road wound dustily between rose-burdened hedges and low, thatched dwellings. In front of the largest of these, rec- tangles of orange light lay on the road, cast from unshuttered windows, and a signboard creaked above the door.

"If I can I shall make my way somehow to Coventry, to see a play, whilst you are there. This is the Angel, sir," said the boy. "Good night, sir, and thanks for your company and your tales!"

"Thanks to you for the fine meal of roast fish!" And the stranger waved his hand. "Good luck to you on your travels, sir poet," he said.

With a sudden impulse, he swept his hat from his head and bowed low—a courtly gesture, no trace of mockery in the thin, dark face.

The inn door closed behind him; the boy went on his way. Around the next turn moths danced in a long ray of light that stretched across the lane from the cottage window where Mistress Shakespeare had set the candle to guide her son, Will, home. Whistling softly, thoughtfully, barely above his breath, the boy turned in at the gate, and his fishing pole brushed dew from the roses as he passed.

Josephine Preston Peabody

THE WOODEN HORSE
AND THE FALL OF TROY

ILLUSTRATED BY *Helen Prickett*

NINE years the Greeks laid siege to Troy, and Troy held out against every device. On both sides the lives of many heroes were spent, and they were forced to acknowledge each other enemies of great valor.

Sometimes the chief warriors fought in single combat, while the armies looked on, and the old men of Troy, with the women, came out to watch afar off from the city walls. King Priam and Queen Hecuba would come, and Cassandra, sad with foreknowledge of their doom, and Andromache, the lovely young wife of Hector, with her little son, whom the people called the city's king. Sometimes fair Helen came to look across the plain to the fellow-countrymen whom she had forsaken; and although she was the cause of all this war, the Trojans half forgave her when she passed by, because her beauty was like a spell, and warmed hard hearts as the sunshine mellows apples. So for nine years the Greeks plundered the neighboring towns, but the city Troy stood fast, and the Grecian ships waited with folded wings.

In the tenth year of the war the Greeks, who could not take the city by force, pondered how they might take it by craft. At length, with the aid of Ulysses, they devised a plan.

A portion of the Grecian host broke up camp and set sail as if they were homeward bound; but, once out of sight, they anchored their ships behind a neighboring island. The rest of the army then fell to work upon a great image of a horse. They built it of wood, fitted and carved, and with a door so cunningly concealed that none might notice it. When it was finished

355

the horse looked like a prodigious idol; but it was hollow, skillfully pierced here and there, and so spacious that a band of men could lie hidden within and take no harm. Into this hiding-place went Ulysses, Menelaus, and the other chiefs, fully armed, and when the door was shut upon them, the rest of the Grecian army broke camp and went away.

Meanwhile, in Troy, the people had seen the departure of the ships, and the news had spread like wildfire. The great enemy had lost heart,—after ten years of war! Part of the army had gone,—the rest were going. The last of the ships had set sail, and the camp was deserted. The tents that had whitened the plain were gone like a frost before the sun. The war was over!

The whole city went wild with joy. Like one who has been a prisoner for many years, it flung off all restraint, and the people rose as a single man to test the truth of new liberty. The gates were thrown wide, and the Trojans—men, women, and children—thronged over the plain and into the empty camp of the enemy. There stood the Wooden Horse.

No one knew what it could be. Fearful at first, they gathered around it, as children gather around a live horse; they marveled at its wondrous height and girth and were for moving it into the city as a trophy of war.

At this, one man interposed,—Laocoön, a priest of Neptune. "Take heed, citizens," said he. "Beware of all that comes from the Greeks. Have you fought them for ten years without learning their devices? This is some piece of treachery."

But there was another outcry in the crowd, and at that moment certain of the Trojans dragged forward a wretched man who wore the garments of a Greek. He seemed the sole remnant of the Grecian army, and as such they consented to spare his life, if he would tell them the truth.

Sinon, for this was the spy's name, said that he had been left behind by the malice of Ulysses, and he told them that the Greeks had built the Wooden Horse as an offering to Athene, and that they had made it so huge in order to keep it from being moved out of the camp, since it was destined to bring triumph to its possessors.

At this the joy of the Trojans was redoubled, and they set
their wits to find out how they might soonest drag the great
horse across the plain and into the city to insure victory. While
they stood talking, two immense serpents rose out of the sea
and made towards the camp. Some of the people took flight,
others were transfixed with terror; but all, near and far, watched
this new omen. Rearing their crests, the sea-serpents crossed the
shore, swift, shining, terrible as a risen water-flood that descends
upon a helpless little town. Straight through the crowd they
swept, and seized the priest Laocoön where he stood, with his
two sons, and wrapped them all round and round in fearful
coils. There was no chance of escape. Father and sons perished
together; and when the monsters had devoured the three men,
into the sea they slipped again, leaving no trace of the horror.

The terrified Trojans saw an omen in this. To their minds
punishment had come upon Laocoön for his words against the
Wooden Horse. Surely, it was sacred to the Gods; he had spoken
blasphemy and had perished before their eyes. They flung his
warning to the winds. They wreathed the horse with garlands,
amid great acclaim; and then, all lending a hand, they dragged
it, little by little, out of the camp and into the city of Troy. With

357

the close of that victorious day, they gave up every memory of danger and made merry after ten years of privation.

That very night Sinon the spy opened the hidden door of the Wooden Horse, and in the darkness, Ulysses, Menelaus, and the other chiefs who had lain hidden there crept out and gave the signal to the Grecian army. For, under cover of night, those ships that had been moored behind the island had sailed back again, and the Greeks were come upon Troy.

Not a Trojan was on guard. The whole city was at feast when the enemy rose in its midst, and the warning of Laocoön was fulfilled.

Priam and his warriors fell by the sword, and their kingdom was plundered of all its fair possessions, women and children and treasure. Last of all, the city itself was burned to its very foundations.

Homeward sailed the Greeks, taking as royal captives poor Cassandra and Andromache and many another Trojan. And home at last went fair Helen, the cause of all this sorrow, eager to be forgiven by her husband, King Menelaus. For she had awakened from the enchantment of Venus, and even before the death of Paris she had secretly longed for her home and kindred. Home to Sparta she came with the king after a long and stormy voyage, and there she lived and died the fairest of women.

But the kingdom of Troy was fallen. Nothing remained of all its glory but the glory of its dead heroes and fair women, and the ruins of its citadel by the river Scamander. There even now, beneath the foundations of later homes that were built and burned, built and burned, in the wars of a thousand years after, the ruins of ancient Troy lie hidden, like moldered leaves deep under the new grass. And there, to this very day, men who love the story are delving after the dead city as you might search for a buried treasure.

They consented to spare his life if he would tell them the truth.

Constance Lindsay Skinner

OUT OF DEFEAT

ILLUSTRATED BY *Alexander Key*

THE villain! Scoundrel! Imposter! I'll have him out of there! Fetch me George!" His Excellency, Governor Dinwiddie of Virginia, pounded on the table, sending the letter, which was the cause of his rage, across the floor. It was caught by a tall, lean, dark youth in deerskin jerkin and leggings, who stood in the center of the room leaning on his long rifle. His snapping little brown eyes had been taking in the scene with delight. He came forward now and returned the letter to its place on the table.

"The French will seize an English trading post, will they?" demanded Dinwiddie. "French in the Ohio! But, I tell ye, I'll have them out!"

"Aye," the boy in frontier garb drawled, grinning broadly. "Chase the French. But I'm warnin' ye, they'll not move out of the Ohio because ye're roarin' and poundin' tables in Virginny."

Foster, the Governor's aide, waited speechless for the lightning to strike. The Governor stared, one clenched hand arrested in mid-air, his mouth open.

"But if ye'll go out and back yer shoutin' with powder," the lad went on easily, "then we—that's me and Willy Penn McNab here—" he slapped his rifle affectionately—"we'll help ye."

"What's your name?" Dinwiddie demanded.

"Will Findlay. Younger brother to John Findlay, that's the boldest young trader in Pennsylvany. It's him that spied on the French, turning our old trading house into a fort. And that's partly why I was sent to ye with yon letter."

"Well, now!" Dinwiddie's eyes glinted at him eagerly. "Ye're

Scotch, eh?" The boy nodded. "So am I, lad. Now, who is this McNab ye mentioned?"

Young Findlay grinned again. " 'Tis my rifle. McNab's the name of a great hunter who taught me to shoot. And once there was a verra clever good man—William Penn—that lived in Pennsylvany and had the same first name as me. So that's how I named my rifle."

"Ho, ho!" Dinwiddie laughed. "Ho, ho! Will Findlay and Will Penn McNab! Ho, ho!" He wiped tears of mirth from his eyes, and then looked at his aide with mild dignity. "I wonder what is detaining Lieutenant Washington," he said.

"I don't know, Your Excellency," Foster answered. "Doubtless I can speed matters by going in search of Lieutenant Washington myself." He bowed and walked quickly into the corridor.

"Well, lad, so ye're with me in driving out the usurping French," said Dinwiddie.

"Aye. Ye little know down here—tucked in snug with red curtains—what murderin's they're up to."

"George will tell the rascals what I think of them! There's a lad you can be friends with. George is little more than your age. Twenty-one, six feet three, and finely built and strong. I love him like a son. Ah! Here's George."

Washington was in the doorway. He came on in.

"George! You know the news?"

"There can be only one outcome, Your Excellency. The French must remove themselves."

"That's it, George! I knew you were my man in this affair. I'll write the French impostor a letter telling him to vacate the King's land—the usurper, the insolent—! There, there, I mustn't lose my temper. You shall carry the letter, George, and see to his removal. I'll send Colonel Trent to build an English fort at the forks of the Ohio to show all and sundry that the Ohio country is ours!"

The young lieutenant's fair, florid face colored deeply, and a troubled look came into his clear eyes. "Your Excellency, I—I deeply appreciate the honor—but—Sir—your personal good will

360

toward me leads you to overestimate my abilities. I haven't experience or wisdom for such a grave mission—on which may hang peace or war between England and France."

"Lieutenant Washington!" the Governor shouted wrathfully, "you're under orders from Virginia! You will go, with proper escort, and remove the French."

Washington bowed. "Sir, I am grateful—and proud." He stammered the words, evidently both moved and abashed.

"Then it's settled. You'll send the French packing! Now, George, here's a fine laddie from up there. Will Findlay. Take him out with you and see he has a bite of food. He'll give you information and arrange where to meet you a month hence. He's engaged by me now to act as your guide and scout in the Ohio."

"So we're to be comrades, Will Findlay." Washington smiled and shook hands with the frontier boy, to whom he had taken an instant liking. "Good night, Your Excellency."

It was several months later, after Washington had led an expedition from Virginia, that he met Will Findlay again. Washington's men, shivering in the winter cold, had reached a point only one day's march from the French fort when Will appeared. After a brief rest, the expedition set out once more.

"George, I've an idea," Will said as they plodded toward Fort Le Boeuf.

"Has it anything to do with the paint and feathers you're wearing?"

"Aye. I'm a dark, black-haired lad and grew up knowin' Injun ways and talk. I'm goin' to slip ahead of ye into Fort Le Boeuf and mix with French Injuns. I'll tell them I saw ye comin', and ran to warn them! I don't doubt I'll be hearin' things there ye'll be the wiser for knowin'."

His mouth stretched in his own innocent, happy grin. He gripped the hand which Washington gratefully held out to him, and then sped off alone—a dusky shadow in the dim dawn, lost presently in the cold mists among the hummocks and trees.

The expedition with its baggage and camp equipment followed after him more slowly. Washington's thoughts were heavy ones for so young a man. None knew what lay westward of the

Ohio territory, or how broad was the continent spreading to the Pacific. Virginia claimed it under her "sea to sea" chartered rights. The French claimed the Ohio country by right of discovery. The Ohio's value in furs was an untold wealth. Holding it, the French would block the English colonies from westward expansion; and then they could turn on those colonies, one day, and blot them out. The very life of English civilization in America depended on removing the French from the Ohio. Would they yield an empire because of a Virginia Governor's letter borne by Lieutenant George Washington, aged twenty-one?

The gates of Fort Le Boeuf swung open. Washington entered with his escort. Near the center of the courtyard Indians squatted round a huge fire, watching a deer turn on the roasting spit. The French Commandant advanced to meet him. An Indian dressed as a chieftain came out of the fort and stood almost at the Commandant's elbow. The Indian was a lean man, with a long neck and a narrow face. He wore a war bonnet, and a scalp of long reddish hair hung from his belt. The air of insolent pride with which he carried himself put the Commandant rather in the shade. His darting fiery glance, from eyes set close to his thin, curved nose, passed over the tall, vigorous body of the young Virginian, over the grave face with its firm lips and chin, its generous brow and steadfast eyes.

At the moment Washington was hardly aware of the Indian chief's presence. He did not see the near-set eyes glaze and become fixed with hatred. He was wholly occupied with his mission.

"I have the honor, Sir," he said, in English, to the French Commandant, "to present to you this letter from His Excellency the Governor of Virginia, with the hope and assurance that I may convey to him, in return, your favorable reply." He waited until his interpreter had repeated the message in French, and then he produced the document.

There was one Indian in the group round the roasting deer—a lad—whose eyes were on the scene with an interest not shared by the others. He had come in, bringing the deer and the news of Englishmen on the road to Fort Le Boeuf. That "Indian"—Will Findlay—saw the hatred born in those insolent, savage eyes as they stared at Washington.

"Yon Feathers has a slitherin' look I don't admire," he said to himself. "He'll bear watchin' by both me and Willy Penn Mc-Nab."

Washington was in the act of presenting the letter when the Indian chief lurched against him and knocked it from his hand. The Commandant spoke sharply. With an insolent sneer the chief obediently went to recover the letter. He deliberately stumbled and set his foot on it, rubbing it in the trampled and melting muddy snow near the fire, before he stooped and picked it up.

To the Commandant's apologies Washington replied calmly. "Do not be disturbed, Sir. I understand this is only the act of an ignorant savage."

The feathered foe shot a glare of hatred at the young Virginian and threw himself down in a sullen fury by the fire. Will withdrew into the shadow and watched the chief. He heard the Commandant say that the French would not leave the Ohio. He heard Washington's voice expressing sorrow and surprise that he must convey so unwelcome an answer to Virginia. Though the Commandant had sternly rebuked the insolent chief, there was a trace of malice in his own manner as he bade Washington farewell.

Washington bowed and marched out with his escort.

"Beaujeu!" In answer to the Commandant's call, the feathered chieftain sprang up. The two entered the fort together, and Will followed unobtrusively.

"Aye," said Will to himself. "Beaujeu's verra clever at playin' Injun. But I knew him for a white man the minute I set eyes upon him. Aye, I've plenty to tell George when I catch up with him. Now to wait till they're sleepin' and then slide out noiseless as a wood tick."

He discovered, an hour later when the fort slept, that someone else had the same idea. His quick ears heard the gate open. His keen eyes saw a thin moving shade in the darkness. Beaujeu? He was sure of it. He lost no time in following. There, moving over the snow ahead of him on the trail his friend George had taken, was Beaujeu. Will slid silently after him. It would be quite easy for him to shoot Beaujeu; but he feared that wouldn't do. The man was a French officer. Disgrace might come on George for it. Anything might happen to George if one of his men killed a French officer in time of peace. "Time o' peace!" he thought scornfully. He ran on, not trying now to be silent.

Beaujeu, wheeling sharply, thought he saw one of the Indians of Fort Le Boeuf running to him, and waited by the trunk of a large oak. The place was about two hundred yards from the fort.

"What is it? Why do you come?" he whispered, never doubting that the man he spoke to was one of his comrades. Will panted heavily as if unable to speak—he feared Beaujeu would suspect him if he heard his voice. Then, with the swiftness of a panther pouncing, he struck a well-placed blow and knocked Beaujeu out. Rapidly he tied the unconscious man's hands behind his back, and his feet together, with the stout deerskin

thongs of his leggings; he gagged him with a strip of his belt.
Now he fastened his long pack strap under his captive's armpits
and set off to the fort, dragging Beaujeu after him. Not far from
the fort there was a tree, opposite the gate. Will tied Beaujeu
to the tree.

"If George were far away, I'd have settled yon beastie with
less trouble," he grumbled as he ran back to Washington's camp.
"Toilin' and moilin' to save such a piece of carrion!" He thought
that it might be better not to tell Washington about this affair
—George was "civilized"—but he would warn him about
Beaujeu. He went into Washington's tent.

"Give me a hot drink and a blanket, George," he said as
Washington grasped his hand.

"I've failed, Will." Washington sat down by the blanket
bundle Will had turned into, and watched him devour the food
and drink brought to him.

"Aye. Anybody would. The French aren't leavin' for letters.
What's letters from Virginny compared to furs in Ohio?" He
chuckled. "But ye did fine, George. I was proud of ye." The
sympathy, loyalty, and humor expressed in the boy's speech and
in his merry, admiring eyes pierced Washington's gloom, and
he laughed.

"You're a good friend," he said gratefully.

"The best. Now, don't interrupt me. Ye didn't notice the war-
bonnet fellow? He's a French officer and no Injun. Beaujeu. He
took a terrible dislike to ye. He's vicious. So we're goin' to travel
tonight and camp farther off. But here's the great news I heard.
Ye remember how Mr. Dinwiddie sent Colonel Trent to build
a fort at the forks of the Ohio? Well, he'd no more finished it
when these verra same French took it away from him! And
they've built their own fort there and garrisoned it the strongest
of any fort in the land! 'Tis called Fort Duquesne. I doubt not
there'll be fightin' now, George."

Washington's eyes blazed. "Yes, there'll be fighting. But first
I must report to Governor Dinwiddie."

An hour later they were trailing through the dark.

In a few days Will left to pursue his business as a trapper, after exacting a promise that Washington would send for him if there were more "argyments" with the French. "Me and Willy Penn McNab'll never forgive ye, George, if ye leave us out of it."

Washington found the Governor wholly prepared for his news and still determined to promote him. He was grateful for Dinwiddie's continued confidence in him, but begged His Excellency not to put him in command of the force that had been raised to oust the French.

"Don't be stubborn, George!" Dinwiddie thumped the table. "I'm convinced of your talents. Tut, George! D'you think you can go through life without defeats? Even Caesar didn't. Get your defeats young, George; and you'll not get them later. Why? Because—to a thoughtful, modest, firm man like young George Washington—out of defeat comes the secret of victory. Bear that in mind."

In the spring young Washington—now Lieutenant-Colonel Washington—was rejoined by Will Findlay, who taught him the lesson of using Indian tactics in fighting against the redmen and their allies. "Sleepin' by night and surroundin' the enemy at dawn, and shootin' from ambush, and never showin' your hide if you can help it; that's the secret," said Will.

This secret they successfully used in an encounter with the Indians at Great Meadows. The enemy, surprised by a sudden attack at sunrise, was completely routed. But the engagement might have proved fatal to Washington if Will Findlay's keen eyes had not detected Beaujeu creeping stealthily through the forest. As the hated Frenchman leaped toward Washington with uplifted tomahawk, Will, swinging Willy Penn McNab with all his force, struck Beaujeu on the head and knocked him to the ground. He did not see the Indians rescue their idol and flee to the woods, for Will had been struck down by a blow from an Indian tomahawk. It would be weeks before he could fight again, but just before he lost consciousness he whispered to Washington, "Ye got a victory today, George."

The victory at Great Meadows was the last one that Washington and his friend were to have that summer. At Fort Necessity, which they built near the Youghiogheny River in Pennsylvania,

the French and Indians attacked in great numbers. The fort with its little garrison was completely surrrounded.

"What'll ye do, George?" asked Will. Then he added practically, "Whatever ye do, they'll have our fort."

"Yes," said Washington. His brows were drawn together; his face was pale. Here again was defeat; and, added to it, was the humiliation of surrender. "We might fight till all of us were dead or captured. But a commander has no right to throw his men's lives away for nothing." He walked heavily; he seemed an older man as he went to parley with the French.

"We'll march out in the morning," was all he said when he came back through the dusk. And so, in the morning sunshine, Virginia, represented by Lieutenant-Colonel Washington, aged twenty-two, surrendered Fort Necessity. Virginia marched out, and France took possession. Will kept at the side of his friend in silent sympathy. A week later he announced that he would be off next day to join his brother, John.

"I don't doubt I'll be seein' ye here again next summer," he said confidently. The next day he slipped off through the forest, and Washington went on by the long trail to Virginia.

"Now, George, no talk of defeats and surrenders!" The Governor was emphatic, with voice and fist. "If the other colonies had joined with Virginia, seeing their danger and their duty, you'd have had an army, and success. But they're asleep to the peril. Drowsy with jealous suspicions of one another! No unity, George. *Unity—Unity*—remember that word. There's no security without it. Now, I've told you I've got the King to send a British force. You'll be on the staff of General Braddock. And you'll be his most valuable adviser, for he's ignorant of Indian warfare."

Thus on a hot July day of 1755, Will Findlay came upon a host of redcoats, as well as colonial militia in deerskin shirts, with wagons and cannon, toiling down the bank of the Monongahela. He brought news which caused Washington to hasten to General Braddock.

"Sir," Washington said, "you have thought me foolishly alarmed when I have told you how French and Indians fight in our forests, from ambush. And you have rejected all advice

368

about using frontier scouts. Here is one of the best scouts in the wilderness, Will Findlay. He has just reported seeing signs of numerous Frenchmen across the river. I beg of you to halt and send scouts!"

"You Colonials lack regular army training," Braddock answered stiffly. He turned his back on them and moved away.

"George!" Will gaped at him. "He and his men aren't goin' to fight in those red coats, are they? George, 'tis plain murder! They'll never see the French; but the French and Injuns will gather them like strawberries! They're hidin' behind that suspicious natural-lookin' brushwork in front, and when ye come up to it—" He paused.

"Will, perhaps you're to be with me in yet another defeat," Washington said. He rode off to give what warning he could to his own Virginians. Will found his brother, John Findlay, among the wagoners.

The wagons toiled on in the rear and crossed the river. The open space was filled with the troops. At the head of his regulars Braddock rode, and they plunged forward with him to crash through that too natural-looking underbrush. As they stumbled and fell, a thunder of rifle fire broke upon them from behind it, and from the woods on their flanks. Every tree and rock belched fire. Militia and regulars fell like dry leaves from a tree. Some British officers struggled back through the confusion, bearing their general, mortally wounded. Indians surrounded the wagons, yelling and waving their scalping knives.

"Cut the traces and jump on a horse," John Findlay cried to his brother. John fled on one of his own horses, but Will did not follow. He turned back into the brush, looking for a certain man.

In the meantime, George Washington ranged the whole field of battle, utterly reckless of dangers. Shots whistled about him, but none touched him. He could do nothing with the British regulars. They were bewildered by the loss of their commander, and their morale was shattered by the first victorious impact of savagery. They broke and fled; fled blindly in a strange land. In fleeing, they fell, for their bright coats drew the enemy's fire from every quarter. But Washington rallied his own Virginians,

369

gathered the scattered men into a unit, and kindled them with new courage from the unwavering flame of his own undaunted spirit.

The battle was a rout; the French were completely victorious. But the colonial troops, unified by their glorious enthusiasm for one brave man, turned and gave battle again and again, in such fashion that the foe did not pursue their retreat.

Will Findlay found, at last, the man he sought. In the thick, leafy branches of an elm on the river's brink, Beaujeu crouched, waiting his chance at Washington. He could see the Virginians firing as they retreated toward the creek. He was too intent on his own business to see or hear Will, who climbed another tree, speedy as a squirrel. Holding Willy Penn McNab firmly in his left armpit, Will Findlay leaped to the bough above Beaujeu. The Frenchman was aiming down at Washington, who was almost beneath him, when his tree shook over him. He turned involuntarily to look up. Will swung his rifle butt against the half-turned head. Beaujeu crumpled and went hurtling into the river.

"With the compliments of Willy Penn McNab!" Will shouted after him. He slid down and, dodging and fighting, worked his way to Washington's side. A horse plunged by, riderless. Will sprang into the saddle.

Fighting furiously, foot by foot, inch by inch, the defeated army cut its way out of that blind alley of slaughter. The men reached Great Meadows, the scene of Washington's first victory and only surrender. Here they halted and buried the body of General Braddock.

"Well, George," said Will. "Ye and me, we know this spot! I've no love for it!"

"Nor I, Will. You'll leave me soon, I suppose, as usual?" His smile was a grave one.

"Oh, aye. I'll have to help John at tradin'—"

"What's that?" Washington rose hastily, and Will was quickly after him. The men, forming by companies, each from a colony, swept by his tent.

"Hurrah! Hurrah!" they shouted and called his name. He saluted and turned crimson, because so much was made of him for so little! These men were young—many of his own age and less—ardent and brave, loving high courage. They had seen a shining valor and honor before which their petty sectional jealousies fled away like wraiths. They carried the name of George Washington home with them to every quarter. In their splendid enthusiasm for him was the seed of American unity, which would flower about him a score of years later when all the colonies would accept his leadership.

Out of defeat comes the secret of victory.

Index